DREAMS
OF
BROKEN
KINGS

THE DREAMS OF BROKEN KINGS

LANA PECHERCZYK

Copyright © 2021 Lana Pecherczyk
All rights reserved.

The Dreams of Broken Kings Ebook ASIN: B0876S1N64
Illustrated Print Edition ISBN: 978-1-922989-08-6

This is a work of fiction. Names, characters, businesses, places, events and incidents are either the products of the author's imagination or used in a fictitious manner. Any resemblance to actual persons, living or dead, or actual events is purely coincidental.

Text copyright © Lana Pecherczyk 2021
Cover design © Lana Pecherczyk 2021
Title Page Artwork © Dominique Wesson 2021
All other Artwork © Lana Pecherczyk 2023

www.lanapecherczyk.com

THE ORDER OF THE WELL

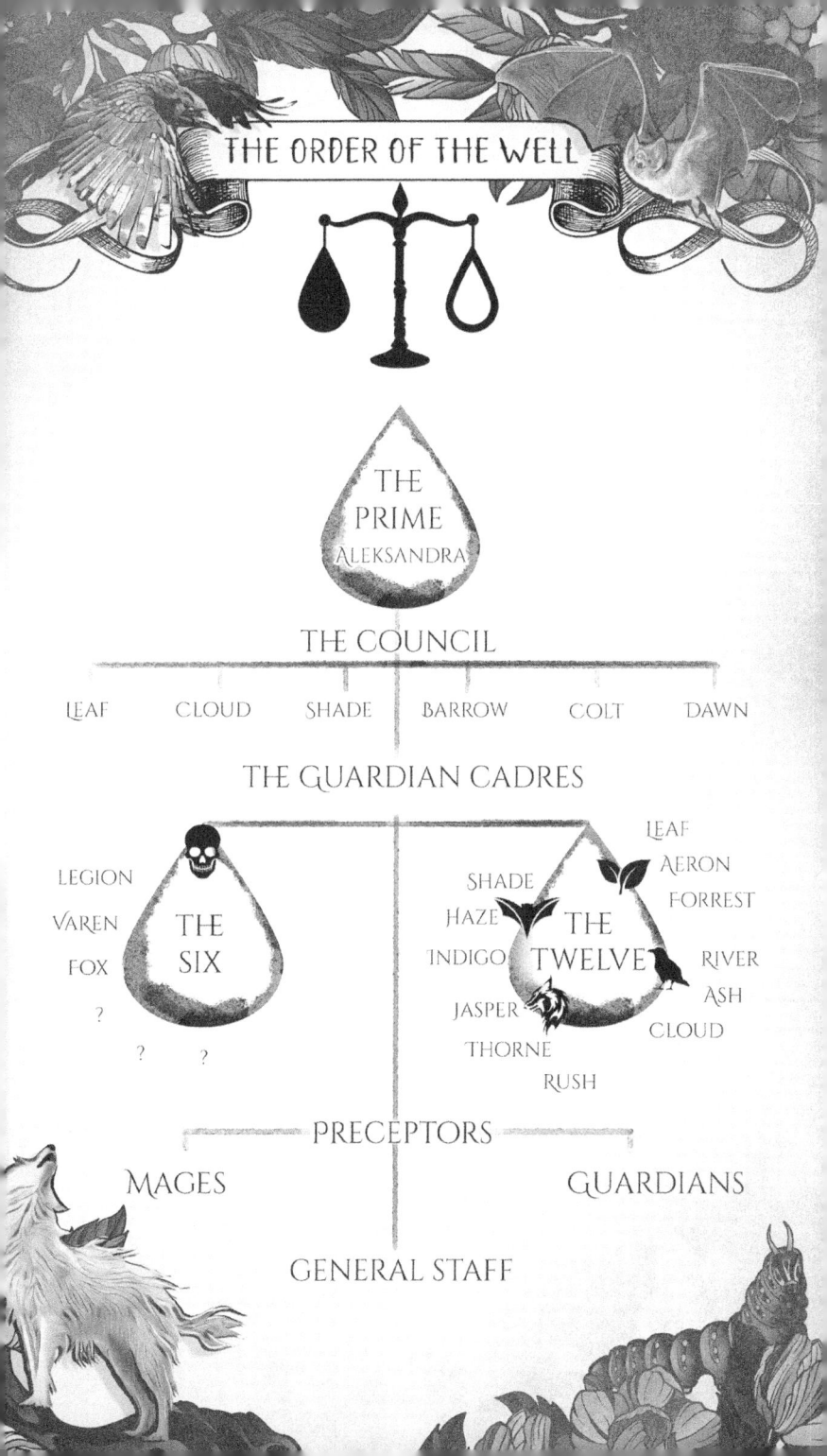

THE PRIME
ALEKSANDRA

THE COUNCIL

LEAF | CLOUD | SHADE | BARROW | COLT | DAWN

THE GUARDIAN CADRES

THE SIX
LEGION
VAREN
FOX
?
? ?

THE TWELVE
LEAF
AERON
FORREST
SHADE
HAZE
INDIGO
RIVER
ASH
JASPER
CLOUD
THORNE
RUSH

PRECEPTORS

MAGES | GUARDIANS

GENERAL STAFF

EL

WINTER COU
ACONITE CIT

ACONITE SEA

ICE WITCH

THE ICE FOREST

HUMAN TERRITORY

UNSEELIE KINGDOM
SEELIE KINGDOM

CRYSTAL CITY

RUSH'S CABIN

MEANDE WOO

WHISPERING WOODS

CRESCENT HOLLOW

OBSIDIAN MINE

CLAW BASIN

AUTUMN COURT
RUBRUM CITY

CORNUCOPIA
TRADE CITY

FENRYSFIELD

THE CEREMONIAL LAKE

THE ORDER OF THE WELL

DELPHINIUM CITY
SPRING COURT

HELIANTHUS CITY
SUMMER COURT

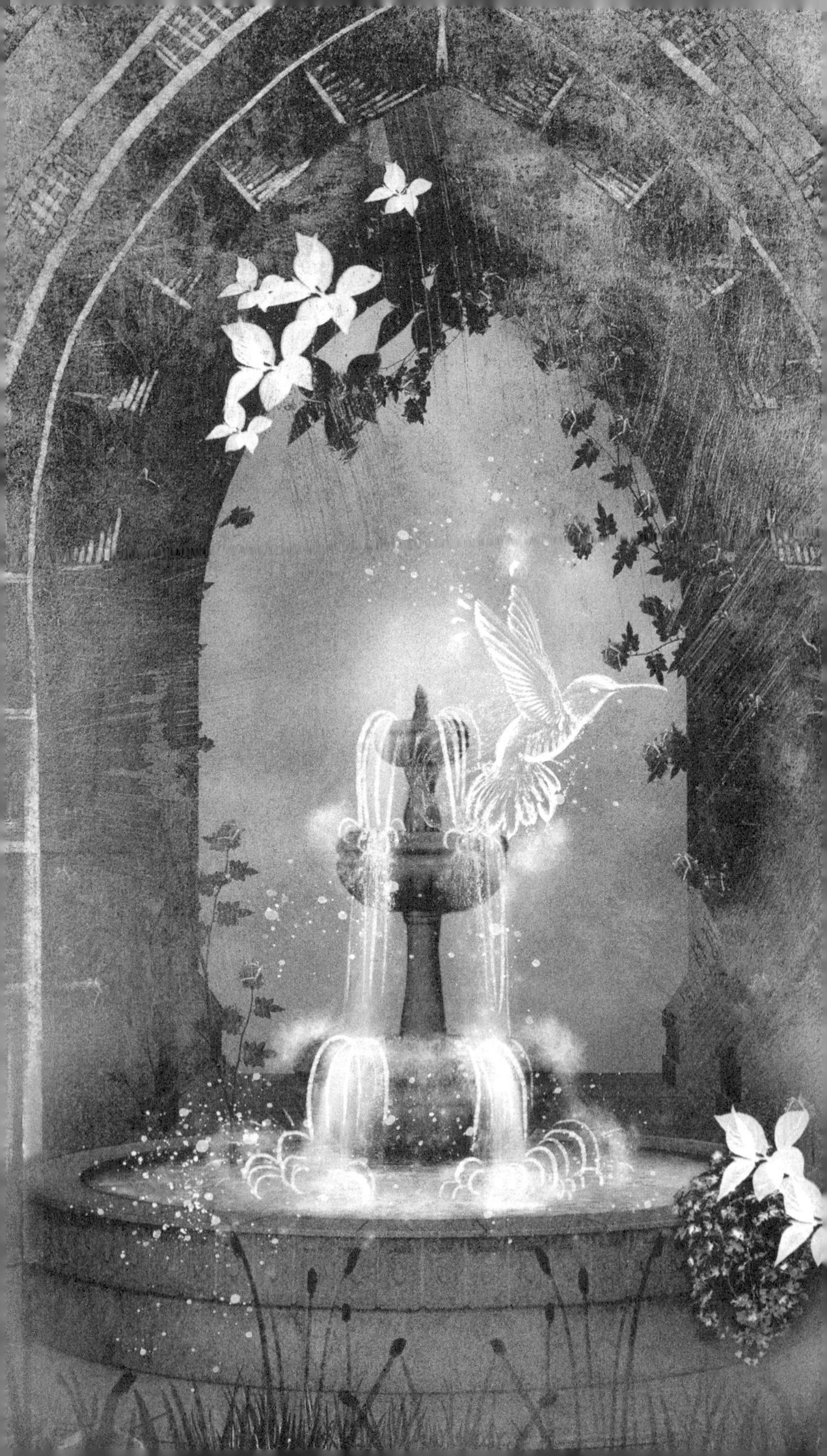

PROLOGUE

The boy watched with wondrous eyes as his mother coaxed water sprites from the fountain. A ripple of energy tingled his tongue as her invisible *mana*—her *magic*—left her body, entered the garden fountain, and formed shapes with the water. First, a seahorse bounced on the fountain's flow. Then, an explosion of fireworks churned the water. She added horses, hummingbirds, and flying kuturi. The small water sprites squeaked in joy and clapped their hands, spraying a fine mist everywhere.

The boy's mother turned to him with the same crooked smile many fae had pledged their life to see. They'd kneeled before her when she'd flicked her long, lustrous black and brown locks. They'd tried to kiss her red lips, but she'd always turned her cheek and walked away. She would return to him, her son.

His mother shifted her magic. The watery show skipped from the fountain and danced along the leaves of nearby plants. Her waterhorse galloped and neighed. Sprites followed the procession through their extensive garden, leaving behind their watery mist and coating every surface with droplets that glistened in the sun like jewels.

"Your turn, my love," she said. "Send your mana into the water and make a shape. But make it fun. Everyone works better when there is joy to be had."

He gathered control of his mana and steeled himself against the surge of energy in case it flitted about like water from a hose. Mana flowed eagerly from the stores of his internal Well, rising to meet his summons like the tide during a full moon. Always sitting beneath the surface of his consciousness, his inner wolf came alive. It liked his thoughts of the moon. It wanted to shift from two to four-legged and run through the forest, roll around in the dirt, maybe even snap his teeth at the sprites along the way. They looked extra delicious as they danced and sparkled.

And he was hungry.

When his mother spoke, he realized a wolfish snarl had trembled from his teeth.

"Love," his mother crooned a warning as she ran a hand through his shaggy hair. "Kindness before killing."

"But, Mama," he said. "I want to play too."

Her crooked smile widened and warmed him more than any sun. "I know, and you will, but you must learn to control your animal urges. You *must* remember that the wolf is a part of you, and not the other way around. You are more than the sum of your ancestors. This is very important. Do you understand?"

He nodded sullenly. She always lectured him about controlling his wolf. He didn't see the problem. His wolf liked to play. His mother always talked about having fun. Why couldn't she see they were the same thing?

She took him by the shoulders and looked deeply into his eyes. Her smile dropped and her expression grew still.

"What is fun for some, isn't fun for others. Look at the sprites, darling, what are they doing?"

He threw his hands up, exasperated. "Playing."

She turned his jaw toward a plant where they jumped and pranced, showering the fronds with glistening rivulets.

"Look closer, my love."

Water dripped onto the soft peat beneath, showering it with sustenance.

"They're watering our garden!" he exclaimed.

She grinned. "And what would they have done if we simply used our strength to demand their obedience?"

"They'd have hidden in the fountain until we were gone." He knew. He'd waited once in wolf form, snarling and snapping at the water. He'd waited all night and day and, still, they hadn't come out.

A wolf's long, drawn out howl ripped through the air,

and his mother's smile died. He didn't think a howl was unusual. They lived nearby a wolf-shifter village, after all. But she turned to him, eyes wide and black with panic.

"Hide. Where we practiced."

"Mama?"

She bustled him out of the garden and toward the small cottage. "Hurry. Faster."

Tears stinging his eyes, he stumbled. "You're hurting me, Mama."

No reply.

She took him into their living room, shifted a rug, and lifted the hatch in the wooden planks, then urged him to get into the dark crawlspace filled with musty smells and dirt.

Thundering hooves grew louder as horses crested the laneway outside their home. Howls lifted every hair on the back of his neck. His instincts knew the call. It was the call of a hunt. For blood.

"Hurry."

"Who is it, Mama?"

She bundled him down and then kneeled, a sad resignation in her eyes as she brushed his jaw with the back of her knuckles. The heart-shaped pendant dangling from her neck scraped along the floor, leaving a claw-like scratch.

"Remember how we practiced?"

He nodded. "No sounds. Don't come out until my wolf scents no intruders."

"You are kind," she said emphatically, and then cast a spell that felt like cotton wool wrapping his body. "You are brave. And you are worth it. Do you understand?"

"Mama?" his throat constricted. "I'm afraid."

"No movements, my love, or the spell will break and he will scent you."

"*Who?*"

A cold bleakness entered her eyes. "Your father."

She shut the hatch, swaddling him in the cold finality of muffled darkness.

He barely registered the rustling of the rug being pushed back into place and the bursting of the front door, but when the screams started, they pierced the dampening spell. He forced the thundering of his heart to calm and listened.

"You can't hide from me." A loud, booming male voice. "I am King of all the Seelie now."

"You may color your hair gold, wear gaudy clothes, and live in a castle of glass, but you can't hide the stench of rot underneath. I will *always* remember."

The silence raised the boy's hackles.

Crack. Like flesh hitting flesh. *Thud.* Something landed on the floorboards. His mother.

She made no sound, no cry of pain despite the trembling of her breath.

The boy lifted his face to where a shaft of light filtered through at the edge. Mama must have failed to flatten the rug properly. Too fearful to move further, he stared through the gap and tried to halt the breath in his lungs. Surely the intruder would hear the pounding of his heart.

Blurred shapes and shadows moved as boots and paws trampled across the wooden floor, shaking dust and sand through the cracks with every step. Louder and louder until they came to a standstill above the boy's head. A whimper caught in his throat.

"Where is the boy?" the King asked, voice flat and cold.

His mother was silent.

Something shifted above. Wolves snarled. Claws scratched against the wooden floor.

"This is the last time I ask you, where is the boy?"

"He is ten times the fae you are, ten times the soul, and he will be ten times the king."

"Search the place. Leave no stone unturned," the King boomed. Then his voice got closer, quieter. "And you will still be ten times the whore."

The choking sound that followed broke the boy's heart. But he'd practiced this moment, stayed beneath these floorboards, remained still and silent no matter what. No matter the sounds of teeth tearing through flesh. No matter the feel of warm liquid dripping onto his face. He squeezed his eyes shut and imagined the feel of fresh rain. The wet bracken beneath his paws. The smell of the forest. The call of the wild. Tumbling with his cousins. Nipping at dragonflies. Today, he added the sprites playing. Their joy in the water. How it called to him too.

It wasn't until the last footfall died, the scent of wolf lessened, and the sound of dripping grew louder, that his mother's final words expelled on the hiss of her dying breath. *"... kind... brave... worth it."*

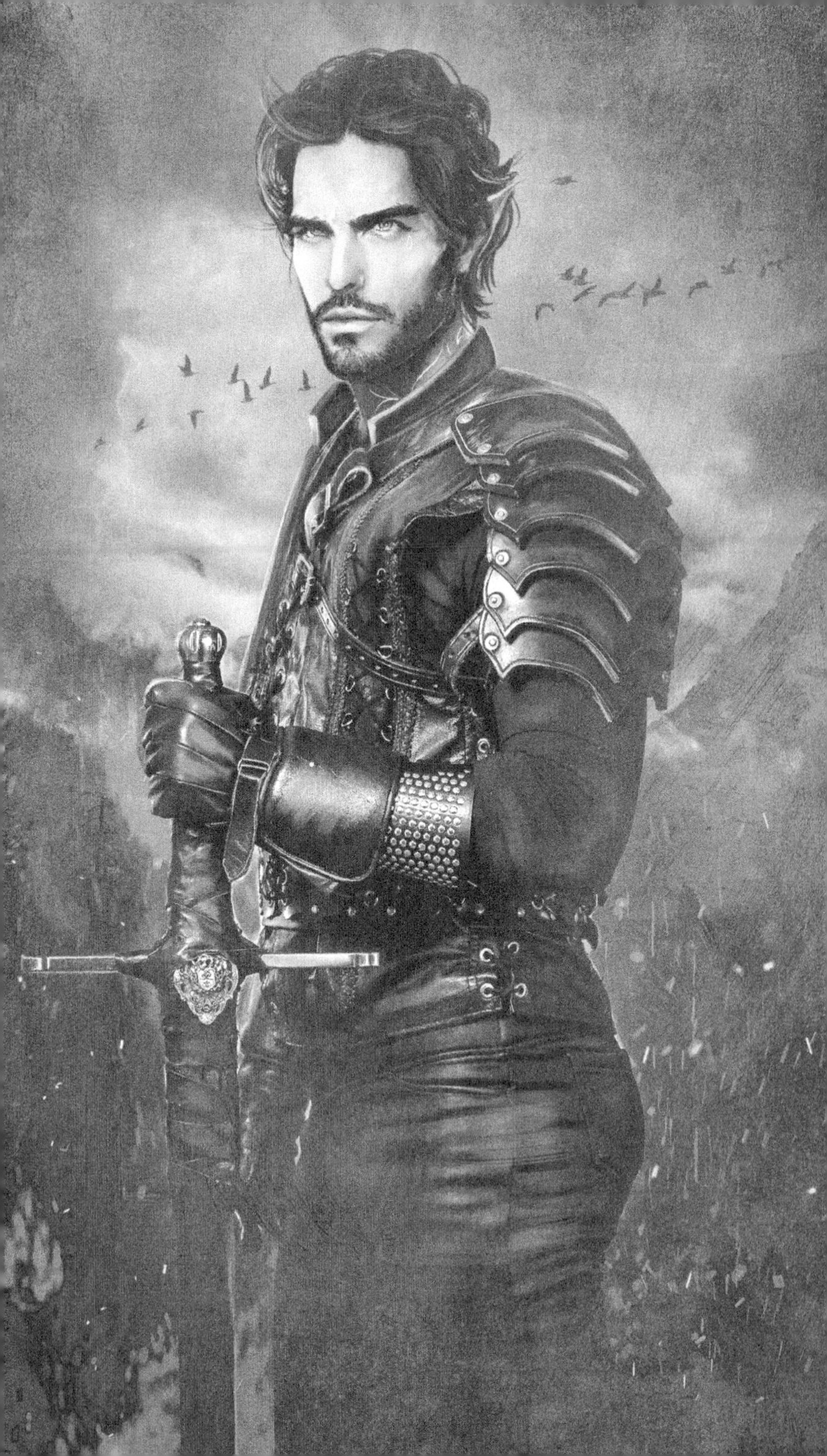

CHAPTER ONE

Amber eyes shrouded in thick lashes stared at Ada from across the cold, grimy bedroom. It shouldn't be possible for a man to look like both angel and devil at the same time, but there he was, caught in limbo somewhere between sin and a miracle. *Such striking features.* Tall and muscular with statuesque bone structure, yet soft, sensuous lips. Even his brown hair was extraordinary. Each tip of the medium length appeared to be dipped in black ink, like an artist's paintbrush. On the outside, he was a masterpiece. He should have been perfect. But the closer Ada looked, the more she noticed cracks in his canvas. All was not well with him.

It started with his unblinking eyes.

Work long enough with wounded, wild animals and the familiar signs of mistreatment were easy to recognize. The old pain. The soul crushing emptiness of surrender.

The fresh scars upon old scars at his neck. This man had suffered. He had been tortured. He had given up hope.

Whether his mind was still intact was another story.

He hadn't said a word, nor moved an inch, yet Ada sensed he was once as wild and carefree as the animals she'd rehabilitated. Now, he was at the end of his rope. She hoped she wasn't in the way when he snapped.

His blistering intent stayed locked solely on her, as it had done so for the past five minutes since her groggy awakening that ended with the vomit of something dark and viscous on the floor next to the old bed.

He didn't get up to help her. He never murmured a note of sympathy. He just kept staring.

He's cuckoo. Surely.

His linen clothing was as strange as hers which looked more suited to a cult that worshipped natural materials than her usual khakis and worn T-shirt. Someone must have dressed her because she hadn't been wearing the simple outfit when she'd... her brow puckered. What had she been doing before coming here? She couldn't remember a thing beyond going outside Clarke's apartment and lifting her awestruck face to the snow falling in Vegas.

The small miracle, or curse, depending on how you looked at it, had taken their minds off the bombs that had dropped around the world, devastating humankind. The cities that survived, like Vegas, were scrambling to find normalcy in the fallout, when the nuclear winter fell like a freezing blanket with a speed that baffled the TV weatherman. The drop in temperature had been so fast that the Bellagio fountains froze mid-flight. And then it had snowed... and then...

Ada struggled to grasp what had come next.

Had she been drugged? Panic sparked, tightening her chest, quickening her breath. Was that why she'd been sick? Where were her friends, Clarke and Laurel? They had been with her in the yard, looking at the snow.

The silent man stared at her as though she had a list of algebra equations written on her face.

"Are you going to stare at me all day, or will you tell me how we got here?" she asked.

Dark lashes blinked, and then he resumed staring as though he could see into her mind. She shivered.

Christ. This was insane.

She cringed, disgusted that her head had rested on the decayed bed. Thank goodness she'd moved and now sat in the corner, hands wrapped around her knees, bare feet on the dusty floor.

While she had been asleep, someone had tattooed glow-in-the-dark ink in a strange glowing blue pattern around her right arm—his too. She rubbed her marks for the tenth time. Definitely tattooed on there. Definitely twinkling, as though the undercurrent of the summer sea ran beneath it. If only it gave her the summer heat. A shiver wracked her body as cold air seeped into her bones.

"Right." She stood and rubbed herself briskly. "If you're not going to help, then I'll find my own way out of here."

Just like she always did. No use waiting for a hero to turn up. A familiar pang in her chest reminded her of the first time she'd learned this truth—the first time her mother failed to come home with food—but forced the memory aside before it took root. She had no time for that.

The instant she stood, he echoed by unfolding his long body, and straightening to a height that crowded her and sucked the air from the room.

Creepy.

She looked for a weapon, but... she cocked her head and studied him. She didn't *feel* animosity coming from him, strange as that sounded. Her instincts had never taken a wrong turn, and they were the only thing that had kept her alive on more than one occasion. Whether it was hiking in the wilderness, hunting for food, or navigating unfamiliar terrain, she'd learned to trust her intuition. And right now, it was telling her this man wasn't a threat.

But he also wasn't helping.

"I'm Ada," she ventured.

His brow furrowed, but he said nothing.

"Can you speak?"

A slow nod.

"What's your name?"

Amber eyes darted around the room. He flinched and scratched blue arcane markings around the thick column of his neck. Red welts meant he'd been itching for a while.

Whatever those blue markings were, they didn't agree with him. Not like the ones down their arms.

"Your name?" she prompted again.

"I don't know."

His voice was deep and smooth like honey. It matched his gorgeous face and perfect body. If he ever lost this creepy hesitancy, she imagined no woman would be safe from his charms.

"How can you not know?"

"Because I don't," he snapped, a faint snarl deepening his tone.

Ada startled.

Injured animal. Proceed with caution.

She held up her palms. "Was just asking."

He looked away. Not that there was much to look at in this room. Just a high, small window too tiny to climb through. She could break through the thin, stained ceiling, though. Debris littered the ground, but nothing she could use. Broken bits of wood, a few branches and some feathers as though a bird had nested inside. Damp puddles collected from leaking rain.

"Maybe this is one of those locked room scenarios," she murmured to herself. "I've seen *Saw*. Some Mad Max sicko has put us in here, drugged me, taken your memories, and painted weird cultist shit on us." She shot him a side-eye. "If you try to saw off my leg, I will kill you. Fair warning."

Perhaps the tall man was drugged too, because he just stared at her in confusion. Part of her didn't believe herself either. A locked room? No way. And she didn't feel drugged. But then again, she didn't believe the nuclear holocaust would actually happen. She didn't believe her precious wilderness would either be destroyed or covered in snow.

Maybe Vegas was gone too, and this dingy room was all that was left.

Maybe they were the last two people on earth and this was some rare pocket that had survived the fallout.

A new sense of urgency skated up her spine. This room was too small. She had to get out. She made an awkward face when he didn't move, so sidestepped and went to the door where she rattled the porcelain lock. It didn't budge. She peeked through the old keyhole. The lock probably worked from both sides. Light shone through, but all she could see was a wall.

"We need to get out of here," she mumbled. "I'm starving. And thirsty. And..."

And forget about sawing her leg off. The man in the room with her might try to eat her from the way he kept staring.

He moved. She flinched. A tiny twitch lifted one side of his lips, and she could have sworn she caught amusement dancing in his eyes before he shouldered her to the side and took hold of the doorknob. One wrench and it came off in his powerful grip. Ada's lips parted.

He uncurled his fingers, and the knob teetered in the dip of his palm. She reached for it, but he snapped his fingers around the knob and evaded her. Frowning, she looked up, expecting anger, but amusement flickered in his eyes again.

"You think this is a game?" she said.

Her irritation only made his lips purse as though he tried to hide a smile and then picked out the rest of the half-crumbled knob from the hole in the door. In moments, the entire contraption was gone. He jammed his fingers into the gap and yanked.

"Are you telling me you could have done that five minutes ago?"

Big shoulders bunched and lowered.

Joking one minute, brooding the next. Maybe he wasn't all there in the head—a few bricks short of a load. Maybe that tragedy in his eyes had taken more of a toll than she realized. Nobody deserved to lose their mind. She stepped into the hallway, but a big hand landed on her shoulder and tugged her back.

"I go first," he grunted and placed her behind his large frame.

"Oh-kay."

His bulk refused argument.

The corridor was as decrepit as the bedroom. Water trickled down the stone walls, peeling wallpaper and creating mold deposits in the hardwood floor that gifted her nostrils with tingling pungency. Ivy trailed down the wall, invading from holes in the terracotta tiled roof. Glimpses of cloudy sky flashed as she walked by. Small cameo oil paintings lined the wall, but the decay had eroded much of the canvas. Glimpses of faces watched Ada and her companion as they walked cautiously through the hallway. He snuffled, as though trying to get the scent out of his nose.

The next room was more jungle than living room. Plants and flowers climbed over old wooden furniture padded with patchy blue velvet. Arched windows let in light, but a flourish of thorny brambles blocked escape through the window.

The blue markings on their arms glowed and glanced off their surroundings as they passed. A flash drew her eye to a table toppled with a collection of junk. She strolled over and inspected the goods. They looked like something you'd see at a junkyard, or a hoarder's house. Perhaps the state of Vegas was more dire than it had been when she'd... she frowned again, frustrated that she couldn't remember how she got here.

Maybe she had amnesia too.

Rusted copper pennies lined the bottom of a shallow bowl overflowing with rain water still dripping from the ceiling in sporadic plops. Ada flicked a box-like rectangle that may have once been a cell phone. She touched a round smooth surface that was probably a squash ball and then flicked a thin garland that might have been Christmas tinsel in another life. She picked up a jar of rusty ball-point pens and jiggled them.

"Stop." A hand knocked the jar from her fingers. It clattered loudly to the floor.

"Why did you do that?"

He scowled. "Metals and plastics are forbidden by the Well."

She raised her brows and muttered under her breath, "Definitely a few screws loose."

I'm done with this. Shaking her head, she left the weird shrine and searched for an exit. She just wanted to find her friends. They had been with her in Vegas. Chances were, they'd be around somewhere. She hoped.

Dripping water echoed as it landed in puddles. Leaves rustled and a whisper of sound flittered behind her, but when she looked, she found nothing except the plant life.

Searching beneath vines on the wall, she asked, "How do you know metal is banned, but you don't know your name?"

When he gave no answer, she sent him a sidelong look. He seemed as perplexed as she was.

A beam of light filtered through a crack in the ceiling and landed on some ivy with a dark door shape behind it. *Bingo.*

"Help me get this off." She hauled great curtains of vines and tried to pull it off.

No help came. Ada turned and found the man staring at his feet, a deep crease between his brow as he studied a tattered, patterned rug.

"What is it?" she asked.

"I know this." He crouched and ran a finger over the pattern. His trail left a wake in the sodden rug. "I've been here before."

Here, as in this cottage, or here as in the city woven into the tapestry of the rug? Either way, he was more familiar than she was.

"You have? Well, that's great. You should know how to get out of here."

He shook his head. "I don't..."

The man was troubled. A stab of sympathy pushed Ada to meet him on the floor. Amber eyes clashed with hers. They were almost luminous in the dark. Coupled with his thick, dark lashes, she could get lost in his eyes. And that wasn't a sentiment she was familiar with. It unnerved her more than the small blue teardrop tattoo twinkling beneath his right eye. She hadn't noticed it before.

Fear stabbed through her. Was this her future? Would some nut job come and paint her and then take her memories too?

"We'll figure it out," she murmured, eyes darting to his sparkling blue tattoo collar. Welts scored his skin from all the scratching he'd been doing. Unable to help herself, she touched one of the blue lines on his neck. He hissed. A wave of *hurt* washed through her, as though she'd felt the pain herself. She lowered her hand. "Hurts, huh?"

He looked affronted, and a little defensive, but nodded.

"We'll figure that out too," she announced.

Drop Ada in the desert, and she'd survive. In high

school, they voted her most likely to succeed in a zombie apocalypse. None of them knew she'd only attended school for the first time from her junior year. They were cruel enough without knowing she'd spent most of her childhood surviving on her own in the woods... well, there was Harold, the old-timer she would visit in exchange for hunting and reading lessons. But the point was, she would get through this.

Dusting off her hands, she straightened and went to the door. She lifted the last of the ivy, turned the doorknob, and used her foot to push the wooden length. It shifted an inch. Elation lifted her spirits. She turned to share her excitement, but almost bowled into a broad chest.

"Personal space, dude," she mumbled.

He'd better not be the type to imprint on her after a few moments of compassion. The last thing she needed was a sad puppy following her around. After she'd assimilated into society and graduated high school, Ada had taken a job rehabilitating animals. There had been a rescued cougar kitten that refused to return to the wild. She'd almost considered moving to live in the forest with it, or bringing it home, but by that stage, she'd made friends in the city and knew she would miss them too much. The city and her friends had tethered Ada to reality. Without them, she would have returned to the lonely life of a hermit like Harold.

Once again, he shifted Ada to the side and used brute force to open the door. It might have taken all her energy to move it a simple inch, but he'd barely twitched a muscle to shift the entire frame.

"What do you bench?" she asked. "Seriously, like, two hundred pounds?"

No answer, so she followed him outside and into a courtyard overrun by nature, much as the inside had been. But out here...

"I can't believe it," she murmured, eyes lifting to the sky. "Blue."

She'd assumed the gray through the gaps in the ceiling was the dull nuclear blanket of their scorched sky, but... *blue* interspersed with regular storm clouds. Could this be a surviving pocket, unaffected by the fallout? But the scorched sky had covered the entire globe.

Twittering birds leaped in the sunshine, hopping from branches to a three-tiered stagnant fountain, washing their beaks, and then dancing back. She turned in a three-sixty-degree rotation. Lush vegetation filled the garden courtyard. Vine-covered limestone walls surrounded them, along with the occasional shrubs and small fruit tree.

Ada rushed to the trees and searched for fruit. Who knew when she'd eat again? She riffled through the leaves, but disappointment dropped in her stomach like a stone. Nothing.

Wrong time of year, perhaps.

"This is incredible," she breathed, and scrambled on top of a long stone table that may have been for outdoor entertaining. In her haste, her foot slipped on the slippery moss and she tumbled. Strong hands caught her around the waist. For a few moments, she held her rescuer's gaze as he lowered her gently to the ground.

He looked at her as though *she* were the marvel.

She gave an awkward laugh. "I slipped."

"You did." A small smile tugged his lips. The light glinting in his eyes had only been fleeting, but a rush of reward hit right in her chest. She wanted to chase that high... to get him to smile again. He held out his hand and, when she reached for it, he snatched it back with an eyebrow waggle. She giggled like a damned school girl. Perhaps he enjoyed seeing her smile too, because he played the same game until eventually she stopped smiling. He got the picture, and he helped her onto the table like a proper gentleman. Heat warmed her cheeks.

He might be a little mute, or dumb, or whatever, but the dude had understated magnetism. Everything about him disarmed her. The random games. His heart-stopping smile. His weird chivalry. Clearing her mind, she forced her attention to the cottage surroundings and gasped.

The land beyond was a punch in the chest.

"It's back," she croaked. "It's all back!"

The nuclear fallout had stolen the biodiversity of her adored wilderness. Everything had been dying. But now... now there were rolling green hills damp with recent rain and luscious trees bursting with life. Some sort of farm animal grazed in a distant field. She couldn't see it clearly, but it had horns. Further afield, smoke curled from a cottage chimney. *People.*

Her temporary elation washed back with a wave of dread. Rotating, she surveyed the rest of the land surrounding the cottage. Land and forest stretched for miles... everywhere. While the abundance of natural life called to her carefree, nomadic spirit, the obvious and foreboding truth was too hard to ignore. No city scrapers. No lights. No hustle, bustle, and burnished party limos. They were nowhere near Vegas. Nowhere near home.

"Where are we?"

CHAPTER TWO

The shock of displacement felled Ada. Her knees thunked onto the stone table. Big hands encircled her tiny waist, dragged her to the floor, and held her while she trembled at the knees. She brushed him off to stand by herself.

At best, she'd thought perhaps she was in a small pocket of untouched land that had survived the holocaust. Or maybe some crazy apocalyptic bunker. Visions of Mad Max types playing a locked room game with them had been her *logical* assumption. Ha!

Logic wasn't a factor in this reality.

They'd said the scorched sky would take decades, perhaps centuries, to clear. They'd said the land would suffer immeasurably. They'd said flora and fauna would become extinct, and it was inevitable. Farming had turned from green pastures to hydroponic warehouses. Forests turned from luscious to barren. Their best hope had been to ride it out and weather the storm of their own doing. This couldn't be Ada's world. It just couldn't.

"You look lost."

Ada pressed her lips together. "I don't know where I am."

"At least you have a name." His brow puckered. "And memories."

She sent him a merciful glance.

"Are we in a dream?" Were her friends alive? Was she? She pinched her arm. "Ouch."

"Why did you do that?"

"For fun," she snarked. He failed to pick up her sarcasm, so she added, "I wasn't sure if this is reality."

For a few heartbeats, he shared her silence, and then a blue glow at the stagnant fountain drew his attention. He cocked his head, as though listening to something. Ada heard naught but the aria of birds and the scampering of some tiny animal within the weeds. Every line of his body tensed, from his broad shoulders to his balled fists, and then, like a predator catching a scent, he stepped closer to the fountain. Long legs prowled silently. Ada was reminded of a wolf in a field of grass, stalking its prey. So sleek. So quiet. So unnoticed. Until its lethal claws ripped through the flesh of its next meal.

All she saw was the old three-tiered fountain, its pools filled with recent rain water. Slugs crawled along the base and deadnettle weeds spilled into the basin, leaving purple debris that had turned rancid. But the water glittered blue, much like their arm markings, as though a foreign force existed in the shallows.

That light had to come from somewhere.

She bent and checked for power cords, or perhaps a spotlight plugged in. Nothing. Strange. But maybe she needed to get closer. Wiring could be hidden within the base.

"What is it?" she asked.

"Shh." He held a finger out, halting her approach.

Her jaw clicked shut. The hairs on her arms pricked up. She searched the courtyard for a weapon, and found a long, wooden pole that may have once been a broomstick.

His boots hit the fountain base and then he stared into the water for so long she thought it had bewitched him, if such a thing were possible.

Clutching her broomstick, she inched close enough to see inside the basin where a moving picture flickered beneath the water, much like a video on a screen. An ageless man with smooth tan skin, long golden hair, and pointed, fur-tipped ears tapped his finger on his lips. The glass coronet balanced on his head wobbled with every tap. A Scandinavian king, perhaps? Also weird, considering half of Europe had been bombed.

His shrewd eyes locked onto the man next to Ada, as though he could see him, which was ridiculous. Television screens weren't two-way, unless there was a camera somewhere.

She glanced around the garden, but found nothing technological. She supposed if the comment about metal and plastic being forbidden was to be trusted, then there would be none.

And this wasn't a television screen.

"It's time for you to return, Jasper." The Golden King's decree warbled and echoed as though he truly were underwater.

Jasper. That was his name.

Jasper frowned at the water. "Who are you?"

The Golden King stilled. Thoughts calculated behind shrewd eyes. First, he appeared startled, then he looked pensive, and then his expression darkened with excitement. He spoke to someone off screen—or puddle, or whatever this was.

The King's expression lifted in surprise and he raised his brows at his companion, not seeming to care that Jasper could overhear his next words. *"Seems like it's holding. How long will it last?"* A pause. *"Good. The last thing we need is for him to realize who he is before we can get to him."* The man nodded, then returned to Jasper. *"Tell me where you are, and I will send someone after you."*

Send someone *after* Jasper? Not for, or to help, but after him.

"He seems like a real delight," Ada drawled, trying to lighten the mood.

Jasper's scowl clashed with hers, but his lips twitched in an almost smile.

"Who's that with you?" the King snapped, trying to see to Jasper's side. Ada felt the need to step out of view, just to piss the bastard off, but it was unnecessary—Jasper dashed his hand through the water, dispelling the picture, effectively cutting communication as one would switch off a device.

All that remained in the fountain pool were pebbles, broken glass, and purple petals covered with furry mold. And the slugs she might have to eat if she couldn't find food soon.

"So what was that all about?" she asked.

Jasper's growl started as a low rumble that built into a snarl of hostility. Ada could virtually *feel* his emotion vibrate through her as though it were her own. His lip-curling attention locked onto the fountain as the blue light flashed again. Something small and slick launched out of the pond with a splash. She glimpsed tiny piranha teeth, a monstrous face, and slimy knobby limbs. Claws pierced Jasper's front. He caught it moments before vicious teeth collected his nose. One clench of his fist, and the creature's spine snapped, wilting its body. He threw it to the side and rubbed the spots on his chest, now oozing a slow release of blood through the black fabric.

Ada nudged the slimy, small carcass with the end of her pole. Its skin had a layer of jelly over it, as though it lived underwater. Whiskers on its nose reminded her of a catfish. The stain of Jasper's blood still coated its sharp claws.

And then something strange happened—by far the weirdest since she'd woken. Tiny balls of glowing light lifted from the creature's body and floated like fireflies into the sky before disappearing altogether.

She jolted and pointed at the sky. "What the hell was that?"

Jasper didn't answer. His pained gaze was locked on the water in the fountain where the King had returned, this time with a dark hooded figure loitering behind him. Both had the black gazes of a serial killer as they watched and waited.

What were they waiting for?

Jasper grunted. His hand went to his wounds, fingers flexing against his shirt as though he had a heart attack. He dropped to a knee. Ada's heart leaped into her throat. Her instinct was to run to him, but the men in the water would see her. Panicked, she stayed, her heart warring with her mind.

"That should do it," a snaky voice said from within the water. *"He won't survive a ponaturi bite."*

"He is strong," the King reminded him. *"He has survived worse. Much worse."*

"Not even a Guardian can survive the ponaturi."

A grunt of agreement, and then the communication cut off.

Goddamn. This was an assassination attempt.

Ada kneeled next to Jasper and put a palm to his clammy, scruff covered cheek. She lifted his shirt to inspect the wounds. They weren't deep but, if the shadowed figure in the water was to be believed, Jasper had been poisoned.

"Don't stress," she murmured, forcing herself to remain calm. "I know what to do."

She didn't. She did. Oh, God... did she?

"Take your shirt off," she said.

Jasper tried to lift his arms but winced in pain. He jolted forward and gagged. Oh shit. *He's going to vomit.* The wounds near his collar bone rapidly turned an angry purple. The toxin could already be working into his blood. She was probably too late.

Regardless, she had to do something, so she lifted the shirt, placed her lips on a wound and sucked. Bitter blood laced with something acrid filled her mouth. She spat it out and then repeated, trying to ignore the way Jasper's heavy body drooped as he used her for support.

"I got you." *I won't let you die.*

Because then she would have no one.

She moved to each of his four claw wounds and repeated. Suck, spit. Suck, spit. Each time she silently willed the poison to come out, to leave Jasper's body, and to end up on the floor. She envisioned it as black slime in clear water. Each suck removed the slime, leaving nothing but purity. On the final wound, Jasper's hold on his posture gave way. He collapsed onto Ada. They flopped to the floor. She maneuvered them sideways so she wouldn't be crushed, but jarred her shoulder painfully against the stone floor.

Frantically, she checked his wounds, thinking she might have to open the flesh to gain more access to the poison, but there was no festering around the site. It looked healthy and strangely, smaller. As though it were healing. Maybe she'd imagined it being worse. The King's dark companion had said something about no one surviving the bite of a ponaturi, but these were claw punctures.

"Hey, Jasper." She patted his cheek. "Wake up."

Long lashes fluttered, a deep groan rattled his ribs, but his lids stayed glued shut. Ada hovered her ear over his mouth and felt the warm push of even breath. Good. She pressed her ear to his bare chest, right over the blue glowing marks that gave him welts. Now that she'd pushed up his shirt, she could see the welts clearly. More marks and scars extended south over his torso.

She listened. Steady heartbeat. Good.

He was okay. At least for now. She needed to clean his wounds properly, but there was no clean water. Grimacing, she used the fountain water to rinse her mouth out. She wasn't sure she wanted to risk using the dirty water on his open wounds. Maybe she'd just given herself a disease, but it was that or the poison residue on her tongue. An overwhelming sense of helplessness filled her, and a burst of traitorous fear caused a small whimper to escape. She wiped her face with the back of her hand.

"Just stop it, Ada," she said. "This isn't like you. You can manage on your own, no problems. You've faced worse shit than this. You're the female version of MacGyver." But her pep talk did little to assuage her fear. She squeezed her eyes shut, felt the burn of tears, and squeezed tighter. Where were her friends? Where were Clarke and Laurel? The rest of her city? "I need help, damn it."

Even in the darkest days in Vegas, the city's first responders hadn't buckled under the nuclear crisis. They'd continued to take each drama as it unfolded with awe-inspiring, unwavering confidence. They just kept going.

So keep going.

Ada opened her eyes. Poking its head from beneath the purple flowers of a deadnettle weed was a tiny, winged person. Green and brown all over, it was no bigger than her thumb. Ada rubbed her eyes and checked again.

Nope. Still there.

"You're a fucking fairy," she gaped. The little thing tittered angrily at her. She held her palms up. "I'm sorry, so... not a fairy?"

Or was it because she'd cursed?

It shook its head, but its eyes lit up. It pointed at her, and then at the ponaturi carcass, and then at itself, squeaking in a language too tiny for her to understand. She had the weird feeling that she'd offended it, and she owed it something.

"You want the body?"

It nodded.

"Fine. Take it."

It might have been edible, but Ada had eaten her fair

share of poisonous plants, bugs, and animals. She'd made herself sick from them, too.

The little winged not-fairy jumped out, latched onto a leg of the tiny carcass, and then dragged it back into the weeds surrounding the fountain. The ponaturi's translucent skin wobbled and bobbed as it went over cobblestones.

Jasper started thrashing, twitching, and dreaming. He was afraid. And full of hate.

Why would she know that?

She lifted her blue tattooed arm and darted a look between her hand and his. Their marks were identical. Could it be they connected the two of them somehow?

"Hey," she whispered and placed a steady palm on his chest.

He released a slow breath and stilled almost immediately. She took her hand off and he frowned so quickly that she placed it back down.

"You like that, huh?" she murmured. She supposed if she couldn't find clean water, then comforting him was the next best thing.

Comfort and prayer to the higher entity she knew existed somewhere. In all her times lost in the woods, recovering from a snake bite, or hoping the berries she'd eaten wouldn't kill her, she'd prayed to this nameless being. She didn't believe in the Judea-Catholic God, or any other, for that matter, but she'd always believed in *something*.

Because each time she'd been close to death, fearful that no one would save her, she'd prayed and survived. She'd lived another day. Perhaps it was a guardian angel, except this benevolent presence had no wings. It was in every part of nature. It was the very lifeblood of the world. And it was thankful for the time she put into preserving its little furred residents.

She knew her romantic notion was dumb, but it was all she had for company on the many lonely nights growing up by herself. And it felt right.

Keeping her palm on Jasper's front, she let her thumb slowly graze the T-shirt fabric, bumping across the scars she'd glimpsed beneath. They'd looked like battle wounds. Maybe he was some kind of soldier.

He was hot, but not feverish. The shirt bunched at his abdomen, revealing tiny veins delineating the muscles and dipping into his pants along with a trail of dark hair.

Her heart beat faster. In repose, he was more stunning than awake. He smelled like unadulterated male but edged with something sweet like blackcurrant. Before she knew it, she'd shifted closer to inhale that intoxicating scent deep into her lungs.

"Don't be stupid," she mumbled to herself, then shifted back. "Pick something else to think about."

So she focused on the blue arcane marks peeking out from his shirt's collar. They were different than the pattern on their arms. Those marks were almost natural and flowed in a linear pattern that moved in harmony with the shape of their limb. It was almost like a fingerprint, or the contour lines of a map. She liked that idea. This man had a history as intriguing as a map. His body revealed untold stories. From the scars, to the slabs of honed muscle, to the callouses on his fingers, to the glowing tattoos.

He'd lived. He'd seen a lot. And that resonated with her. She had scars too, except hers were mainly on the inside.

The marks around his neck seemed cruel. Straight, angry slashes mixed with jagged curves. They didn't belong on his body. She swept her touch over them, and he murmured in protest, but soon fell back into the dream he seemed to be having. She hoped that was a good sign. He had no fever, no sweat on his upper lip or brow, and no discoloring of his wounds. They continued to close over cleanly.

"Remarkable," she murmured, and looked closer.

She tugged down the shirt collar and touched around a wound near where a claw puncture had hit the blue markings around his collarbone. The blue lifted under her thumbnail as she scraped, separating from skin, revealing a dark oil slick beneath. Gross. She wiped the dark residue away and glanced at the sleeping patient to see if it bothered him, but he made no move, so she kept peeling. She couldn't explain it, but it seemed like the right thing to do. Surely if they were creating angry welts, they should be gone. Another pick, another peel. And she kept talking to herself. The habit probably stemmed from a lonely childhood, or the years spent rehabilitating wounded animals, but she found her voice soothed both her and the animals she worked with.

"You should wake up soon, Jasper," she said, picking at more of his collar tattoo. "We've only just met, but so far, you're okay. I mean, you're kinda the *only* person I've met here, so I suppose that's not saying much. Unless you count the King and his buddy, but I think anyone would look okay next to them, if you know what I mean." She snorted, but then took a breath to force her usual sarcasm to disappear and started again. "I don't really know where *here* is, but it's definitely not home. There are weird things. Little fairy things that squeak at me for calling them a fairy. There are fountains that let you speak to someone through the water. There are fanged, slimy creatures that conjure out of said water when they hadn't been there before. And there are men with pointy, fur-tipped ears—" She cut herself off and glanced warily to Jasper's ears, partly hidden behind his tousled hair. Her heart stopped, and she resisted the urge to check beneath the dark locks. What if his ears were pointed too? *Only one way to find out.* She reached over, brushed some hair aside, and then snatched her hand back with a startled gasp. "You're one of them."

Whatever *they* were. Not human, that was for sure.

His ears were the same as the King's. Pointed with a furred tip that matched the color of his hair. Ada drew her studious gaze back to her patient's face.

"You're one of them, but the King wasn't your friend.

He sent that *thing* to hurt you. Which means he knows you, and he's afraid of you."

Thoughtful, she went back to picking at the blue mark.

"To be honest, if you hadn't helped me, I'd probably be afraid of you too. You're pretty imposing. You belong in this place, unlike me. If you get better, maybe you can help me find my friends. Maybe we can help each other. But you need to wake up, Jasper."

A piece an inch wide, and two inches long came clean off, bringing with it another few inches of tattoo. She wiped the black oozing oil residue clean. Its darkness resonated with a sinister echo. She shivered and flicked it to the side.

Jasper catapulted upright with a roar so deep and loud, it rattled the air.

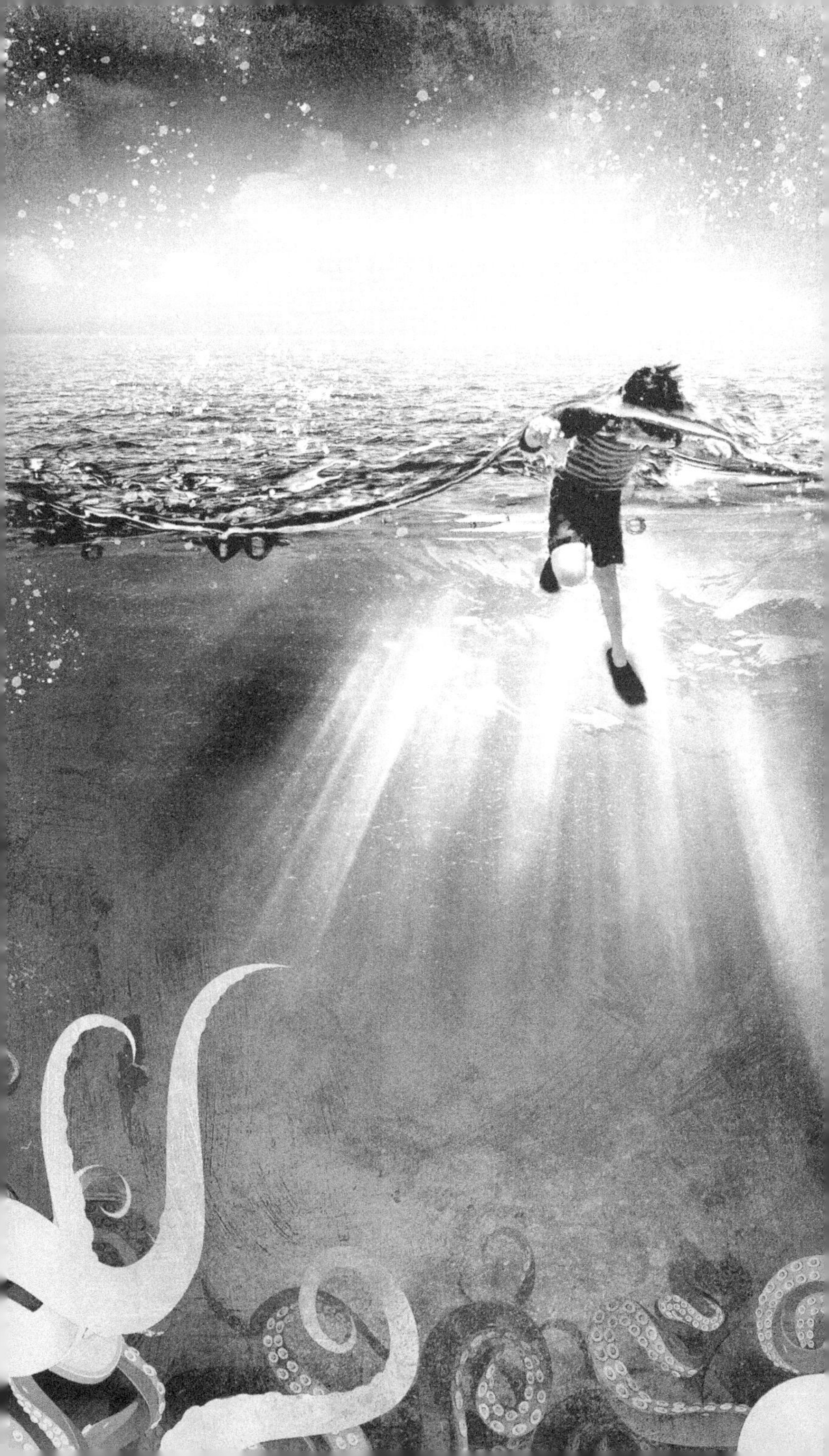

CHAPTER
THREE

J asper dreamed he swam in the warm waters of the ceremonial lake, painfully aware of Well Worms circling beneath. Still to outgrow the weak trappings of his youth, his limbs burned from keeping his head above water. Time was running out.

Snowflakes drifted onto his face. Despite the arctic winter, the lake was always warm, lit from beneath by some primal furnace. His gaze locked onto the luminescent aquatic life beneath him and the same vibrant color along the trees surrounding the shore, winding up the trunks like festive decorations. The glowing life signaled a source of mana from the Well—the very cosmic energy that birthed life for all Elphynians. If he were to die tonight, at least it was pretty.

Wolves howled in the distance, breaking the silent

night. His heart beat a little faster. His keen shifter ears picked up plants and underbrush, rustling as paws padded closer through the woods. Birds cawed and took to the sky as marauding sycophants and the King's fae invaded their peaceful home.

They're coming.

He tried not to sink too low and prayed he had the courage to survive what would happen next. The Well Worms would take him under. It was that or face a bastard's death by the King's hand.

He would rather face the worms.

He would rather let the Well judge his twelve-year-old heart.

His mother had bid him to be kind… to be brave. So he'd come to the place where the bravest go. The legendary Guardians came here as plain fae. They left as heroes. If deemed worthy, the Well blessed them with the gift of using magic-destroying metal weapons without having their own mana blocked. Fae had a limited supply of mana within their body from which to draw for magic casting, and no matter how many times they replenished from a power source, like this lake, there was a limit. But after completing the initiation, a Guardian's capacity to hold mana expanded. They could last longer in battle than even the Highest Fae, those like the King.

But this power came at a cost. Guardians dedicated their long lives to upholding the integrity of the Well. They slayed mana-warped monsters; they policed possession of forbidden metals and plastics—because these blocked the flow of mana—and they protected fae-kind from the human enemy which sought to return the world to its old, greedy and barren ways.

Two-thirds who entered the lake were deemed unworthy and failed to emerge alive. Instead of sinking and being imbued with the essence of the Well of life itself, their bloated carcasses floated to the surface, their shame for all to see and a warning against those who dared contemplate taking power when it was not deserved.

Could a cowardly boy be worthy?

His sins came back to taunt him. When he should have screamed, he had stayed quiet. When he should have fought, he'd hid. He should have done something instead of tremble in fear as his mother's warm blood dripped onto his face as he lay in the dugout beneath the floorboards.

The last thing he saw before dipping beneath the lake surface was his father's cruel smile from the shore, his hunting wolves snarling at his side. He didn't believe Jasper was worthy either. He assumed Jasper would float.

Slimy, thick worms wrapped around Jasper's ankles, and he plummeted.

Down, down, down into the murky cold inky water, to the fathoms no one dared venture. Only the bravest sank. Only the worthiest survived. Around his body, long worms coiled, tightening and constricting until his arms pinned to his sides. His lungs burned. His heart hammered.

Fear turned his blood to ice. The worms slid across his closed lips, begging for him to open and let them in.

No movements, my love, or the spell will break, and he will scent you.

If he survived this, he would become a Guardian. He could save the fae his father murdered in the name of secrets and power. He could protect them. All of them.

He had to be brave so the next time his father tried to silence a female, a mother, or a daughter, he would be there.

He stopped struggling. He submitted. The worms slid around his neck and invaded his mouth. They swam down his throat and judged him from the inside. They swallowed his screams.

The dream twisted. This time, the experience was unique. Initially, he had been judged on a mere twelve years of life. This time, he was no longer a child. His years numbered in the hundreds. Somewhere in the back of his mind, he knew he shouldn't be back here. That it must be a dream. No one submitted twice to the judgment of the Well. No one wanted to. But here he was. The worms choked. They invaded. They wreathed. They feasted on the ink in his soul. They surrounded his heart and squeezed.

Had he done what he'd promised? Had he protected the innocents—made sure those like his mother had been helped?

Tearing into flesh of the enemy for the applause of a fickle crowd.

Wasting his mind on hallucinogens.

Spending his coin on Rosebud Courtesans and welcoming the empty pleasures they offered.

Fae spitting at his feet as he walked through their villages to collect the tax the Order of the Well demanded, or their tributes of initiates—children.

Watching his best friend's female executed after giving birth... by decree of the King.

He could have done something. He could have protected her.

"You are brave," Mama's memory sneered at him. *"You are kind."*

The worms choked. They stole his breath. Darkness closed in.

Another voice warbled from a distance, a life raft for his heavy soul.

Her tone was gentle and carried a dry, husky sweetness that warmed him like spiced wine.

"We've only just met, but so far, you're okay..."

He tethered himself to her voice as she drifted in and out of earshot.

"You belong in this place, unlike me. If you get better, maybe you can help me find my friends. Maybe we can help each other. But you need to wake up, Jasper."

Pain sliced through him and he roared awake, heaving in great lungfuls of air.

A blond woman blinked at him, startled. Pain at his chest. *Her fault!*

Catapulting himself off the ground, he lurched at her, taking her down and pinning her by the shoulders. His inner wolf battered against the confines of Jasper's body. It wanted out. It wanted vengeance.

"You hurt me!" He snapped his teeth an inch from her face.

She flinched, shut her eyes and stilled.

She's not fighting.

She's breathing quietly. She's not afraid.

She was... concerned. He felt the emotion come to him through the blue marks on his right arm. She had the same on hers. He should know what they mean, but... his neck itched. It burned.

He eased a fraction and studied her. Blond long hair twisted into a messy braid splayed on the cobblestones. Pretty flushed face. Pink lips. Freckles. Fragile woman. His eyes tracked to the side. He snarled at her round ears.

"Human."

His wolf was so close to taking over. His eyes stung from the power of it. It wanted to do the protecting, the investigating, the surviving. But there was something about the human... *Different.*

He sniffed her. She reeked of mana, of power. His nose buried into her hair, then down the vein in her neck to her front. Lower. He took in the sweet-spicy scent of her womanhood, and a low rumble caught in his throat. A surge of carnal want slammed into him.

Need. Mine. Take.

The wolf demanded Jasper take his due. It took every ounce of restraint to hold his primal instincts at bay. He shut his eyes and breathed through his emotions.

"The wolf is a part of me, not the other way around," he mumbled to himself. Then repeated it, again and again, until the demanding urge to shift abated.

When he opened his eyes, she avoided his gaze. Prying his fingers from her shoulders, he eased back. Her alluring scent affected him in a way his logic couldn't comprehend. He needed her as though she was his mate—his one true match—the female he would spend the rest of his immortal life with. Yet she was human.

Enemy.

He clutched his head and pulled his hair. His mind was a fog.

"What did you do to me?" he rasped.

His hand went to the pain still radiating from his chest.

Finally, she met his gaze. He found caution, intelligence, and something he recognized every time he met his reflection's gaze—the will to survive. Well... he used to have it.

She wouldn't go down without a fight, this one. It sent another thrilling spark of the hunt jogging through his senses. So why had she submitted to him?

"I pulled this from your neck." A blue, gelatinous strip dangled from her fingers.

He looked down at his chest. From what he could see,

more blue marks covered his upper torso. He poked his finger through a hole in his shirt and saw more blue beneath. When he touched his neck, he felt it slightly raised and irritated. The markings at his arm were different. Smooth, shaped in curved lines like the contour lines on a map, they felt like they belonged.

He rubbed his neck. Those marks were responsible for his foggy mind. They had to be.

"Take more off," he demanded and pointed to his neck.

"Um." She bit her lip and slowly lifted herself to a sitting position. "Okay. A please would be nice."

"Please."

She raised her hand, hesitated, then met his eyes. "It might hurt."

"I was unprepared last time. This time, I am ready."

He balled his hands into fists and sat back on his haunches. He nodded.

She stroked the skin of his collarbone. A shiver prickled through him at her touch. He shifted to get comfortable and then noticed four small healing puncture wounds on his torso. He touched them but had no memory of the injury.

"You know," she said. "I also sucked the poison out of your wounds. You're welcome."

"You're welcome," he murmured.

She laughed. His gaze clashed with hers and for a moment, he was lost in the flecks of gold dancing in their rich brown depths. Then something she said connected with primal satisfaction. A smile curved his lips.

"Your mouth was on me?" he asked slowly. "Sucking?"

"Yeah, well, I had to. I wasn't exactly going to let you die, now, was I?"

She'd protected him?

The profound notion tugged at his heart. On the outside, he stilled. On the inside, he became a raging torrent of sensation, desire, and possessive instinct.

Her brow puckered as she tried to pick a neck mark, but couldn't grasp it. "It's not working this time."

He barely listened. His mind was still on the hunger burning in his veins, urging him to draw her closer. Just an inch. Maybe more. It became an incomprehensible maelstrom of sensation. His eyes watered. If he didn't taste her soon, he would...

"I would advise you to step away, human."

"Why?"

He growled low, voice rattling with gravel. "Because my wolf wants me to claim you."

She startled and shuffled back.

Desire simmered in a volatile cocktail within his body.

Take her, claim her.

He would never take a female against her will, even a human. The act was despicable. So he stood, turned, and swiped at the first thing he could reach—a vase sitting on a stone table. It flew, then crashed against the stone wall, shattering into tiny pieces and crumbling to the ground.

Next, he flipped the stone table itself. An almighty howl of defiance released.

Heaving great breaths through a clenched jaw, he lifted his chin and howled at the sky. When the last note died, he found himself on all fours and caged inside the body of a wolf. *No!* Without his consent, it had drawn on his mana and shifted. It had broken through.

The wolf was everything he wasn't. It was brave. It was ruthless. It was vicious.

It did what it needed to survive.

And it was hungry.

Nose tipped, it caught a scent. Female. *Mine. Mate.*

He stalked her, found her crouched by a fountain. She avoided his gaze and lowered herself further, as though she sensed not to provoke him.

But she wasn't a wolf, she wasn't even fae. How could she be his mate? Curiously, he paced before her. And then she started talking.

"I'm not your enemy," she mumbled, still not engaging in eye contact. "I'm Ada. You're Jasper. At least I think you are. You seem to have forgotten yourself. To be honest, it didn't really seem like you remembered much. But whatever we call ourselves, the same thing remains. We are in this together. We arrived at this place, neither of us with any clue to how we got here. I'm from somewhere called Las Vegas. It's in the United States..."

She continued to talk softly and in calming tones. It was the same voice that called him out of his dream. He cocked his head and sat back on his haunches and then listened to her story about how they both came to be in this place. It resonated. It felt right.

Slowly, with every word out of her mouth, his anger and fire washed away until eventually she stopped speaking. He whined softly.

She faced him and met his eyes. "Jasper?"

Jasper wrested control of his mana from the wolf. He changed back into fae form, panting from the strain. Lifting his sullen gaze to hers, he used his fist to trace a circular motion around his heart. Shame washed through him and he hung his head.

"I don't know what that means," she said. "The hand sign."

Crimson.

He scanned the moss-covered ground until he found his breeches and then shook them out to inspect. Still in one piece, thank the Well. He must have stepped out of them, however, his shirt hadn't survived the sudden shift. It lay in tatters. Clenching his jaw, he gave her his back and stepped into his pants, only facing her as he buttoned them.

"It means I have apologized," he explained.

"Why don't you just say sorry?"

"Because then I would owe you a boon. You would be well within your rights to use your mana to enforce a bargain with me." He raised his brow, feeling a little more like himself—whoever that was. "I'm not that sorry."

"Mana?" Her hands fretted.

The human probably had no idea what mana was. She'd saved his life, so he felt he owed her an explanation at least. So he explained the laws of the Well to her—that it refused to flow through metal and plastic, that it was the life force of the earth itself—and then pointed at her arm.

"Somehow, by some miracle, you've been blessed by the Well. I can smell it on you."

She raised a brow. "I can shift into a wolf, too?"

He regarded her round ears shrewdly. "Unlikely. But what you can do is a mystery to me. Perhaps it is linked to how you remove the markings on my neck."

She shook her head. "But this time I couldn't get it."

"Learning to harness your mana takes time and training." He frowned. "I'm not the right person to help you. I don't..." His neck flared again, halting his train of thought. He gave a frustrated growl and flexed his fists.

"So... what happened? Before?" she asked.

"You tell me."

"One minute you were staring into the water of that fountain, talking to that golden-haired man, and then this thing jumps out and claws you. It was poisoned. I leeched some poison out, but you passed out." She shrugged. "While you were out, you seemed in pain, but when I put my hand on you... I don't know. It's dumb." She raised her eyes to the sky. "This whole situation is insane."

"Tell me anyway," he urged.

"You calmed when I put my hand on you."

Mate, his wolf snarled. *Mine.*

He gave her an assessing once over. From blond top to dainty bared feet, she was attractive. Very. And she had the same blue markings on her arm. He frowned as an explanation tried to come to him, but a sudden burn and itch at his neck pilfered it away.

He scratched.

"Stop," she admonished.

"I can't help it."

"Whatever that is on your neck, it's not the same as what's on our arms. And I think it's connected to your lack of memory."

He had the same inkling. He couldn't escape the feeling that he should be somewhere else, that he had responsibilities. His memories were blocked, and she'd cracked them open... just a little, just enough to clear some fog.

"Do you remember who you are?" she asked with a quick glance at the fountain.

"No," he replied. The name Jasper sounded foreign.

"How did we get here?"

"I don't know."

"Do you even know that you turned into a big black wolf?"

His brow arched.

"Right. Stupid question, okay, so, what *do* you know?"

That question stupefied him more than anything else. His mind hurt to reach far back. His neck burned. He only knew what had come to pass since he'd awoken with vague feelings he should be somewhere.

"I know that you did something that seemed to help. I know that I should be somewhere else... that I have responsibilities. I know that my wolf wants me to claim you, that these arm markings connect us in a way I should respect." He looked down at his hand, mumbling, "Blessed by the Well."

It was inconceivable. She was human. It went beyond everything he felt to be right. "I know you're mine, human. But I don't have to like it."

She folded her arms and cocked a hip. "Yeah, and I'm just over here having the time of my life." Her brows slammed down. "And, hang on a minute, I am most certainly not yours. I belong to no one, thank you very much... whatever you are."

"Fae," he replied.

"Bless you."

His lip twitched. "What?"

"You sneezed."

"No, I said I'm fae. That's what I am. You're human, and I'm fire-fae, to be precise. I shift forms, unlike other fae races."

"Fae? As in the Fair-Folk from ancient fairy tales?" She looked at the sky. "What's next, flying pigs?"

He shrugged. "It's possible they existed in the old world."

"Old world?" Her brow puckered. "Oh, you're serious."

Another shrug.

"Right. You can't remember." She sighed. "We need to find someone who can help us. Neither of us is capable of much at the moment, and I really need to eat." She glanced toward the gate leading to the fields outside. "I've seen a few things around the place I can use to fashion a trap. I'm starving, and we need to get moving before the sun goes down or make camp here for the night. I'm guessing it gets cold in this place."

Jasper wasn't afraid of the cold. He could walk in the snow for miles and feel fine. His neck itched as though a memory tried to surface, and he grunted with annoyance. The human was right. Food first, and then they could find help. But he would be the one to provide.

"Stay here," he said, and walked to the gate.

"Where are you going?"

"To hunt."

Ada chased after him as they emerged outside. A forest lay to their left, and hills of grass to their right. Somewhere down in the valley, smoke curled from a cottage chimney. He sniffed but caught a whiff of enemy.

Ada pointed at the cottage. "Look."

He shook his head. "Don't go there."

"But they could help us."

His hackles raised. "Trust me. It's best we stay away, and you stay here."

"Why?"

"Whatever is down there will be no friend to us.

Elphyne is a dangerous place, human. Dangerous things come in pretty packages."

And he was one of them. He slid his pants off and shifted to wolf form before trotting to the tree line without a backward glance.

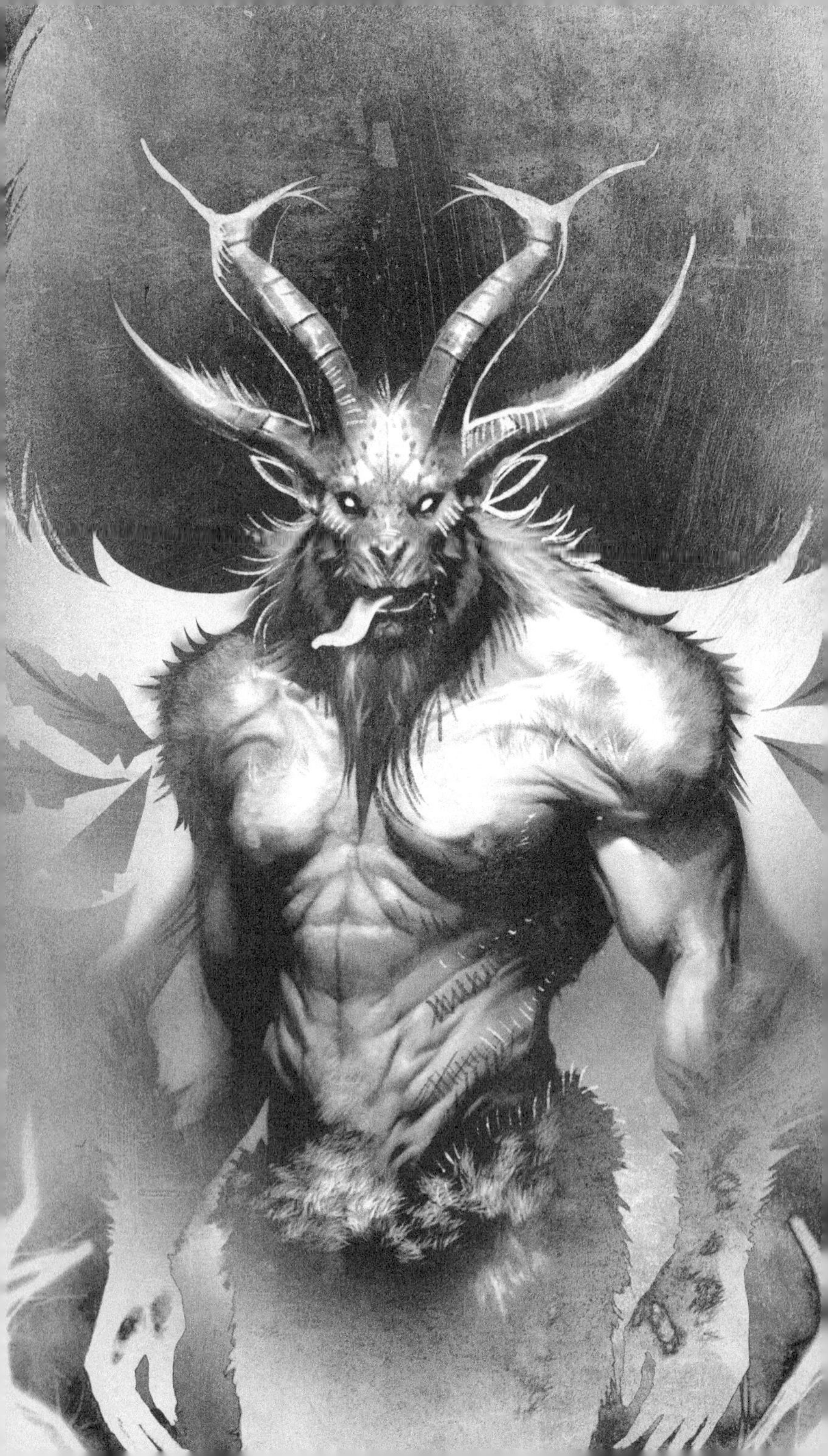

CHAPTER
FOUR

The moment the fae shifted to wolf form and disappeared into the thick of the forest, Ada set about collecting items from within the junkyard cottage to build herself a snare trap. While he'd been assessing her, and perhaps arrogantly accepting her—for now—she'd been silently screaming in her mind.

This was insane.

He'd changed into a wolf before her eyes.

His ears were pointed. He'd said he was part of a mythical, magical race.

And the asshole seemed to think she belonged to him.

She *did not* belong to anyone.

They might be stuck together until they could find help, but she certainly would not let him think he could boss her around. She could take care of herself.

I know you're mine, human. But I don't have to like it.

Her nose scrunched up. *Whatever, jerk.* She didn't have to like it either.

She forced her mind to the task of setting traps. If she didn't set something soon, then she'd have to forage in the forest at night, or worse, eat the slugs.

First, she went to the hearth and picked out some old charcoal to rub against her hands. That way when she touched the trap items, her scent wouldn't transfer. Then she rummaged about the cottage, searching for things she could use. The best she came up with was an old curtain cord, a basket, and pens she could use as lever sticks for the snare. The stinky slugs were bait. Not as good as peanut butter or sardines. Hopefully she wouldn't need any of it if Jasper came back with food.

Feeling proud of herself, she gathered sticks from trees, and then set up stick-snares near the forest's edge, and the basket one closer to the field leading to the farm in the distance. If only Jasper let her go down and investigate the animal she'd seen grazing. It could be a cow.

Her environment looked innocent enough, but then again, she knew nothing about this Elphyne place. A goblin-like creature had jumped out of the fountain and almost killed Jasper—a man who seemed pretty hard to kill.

And that brought her mind to the most boggling thing of all. Magic was real, and he believed she had it. She shook her head, unable to let the overwhelming truth in. For now, she needed to focus on survival.

Tomorrow, she would ponder the wonder of her displacement.

Once the traps were set, she ventured back into the cottage and found a bowl to collect rainwater. Thunder still rumbled occasionally, and the dark rain clouds hadn't left. Hopefully that meant a fresh supply of water.

Keeping warm was the next item on her list. The low overnight temperature could kill them quicker than any lack of food or hydration. While waiting for the traps to spring, she collected kindling for the fireplace, but without a flint or matches, she wasn't looking forward to setting it alight.

Finally, she settled against the outside garden wall, picked up the long cord length ending on the basket trap and waited for a poor unsuspecting animal to venture beneath it. With each passing moment, the golden sun set over the green rolling hills. She tried to stay positive. Snare traps were a numbers game. The more she had, the better chance of catching food, but she would be lucky to catch something tonight. Slugs might be crap bait.

For now, it was nice to take a moment to appreciate the sight of nature restored. Always a visceral reaction, tension unwound in her body, but the moment it went, a heavy sadness sliced through her. She dashed burgeoning tears away from her eyes, hating that the fae might come back and see her weakness.

Every thought she'd held at bay since waking crashed to the surface.

Her joy at seeing the world born again.

Her sadness at missing her friends.

Her warring fear and attraction with her new companion.

Her confusion at this world's rules.

Every emotion washed about inside until her throat closed and she coughed to clear the tension, shaking herself out of her melancholy. Falling into despair would only get herself killed. A shuffling sound snapped her head up.

A small fluffy animal hopped about beneath the cane basket cage. She yanked on the cord. The basket fell, trap sprung. Elation fizzed through her and she wanted to shout her triumph. Rabbit for dinner. Her mouth watered. Getting to her feet, she cast a worried glance to the forest. It had been hours and Jasper hadn't returned. Just as well she'd decided not to wait for him. He might never return.

Dangerous things come in pretty packages.

She snorted.

Jasper certainly was pretty. And she believed he *was* dangerous. That first time he attacked her by the fountain, she'd almost peed her pants, and she'd faced down a black bear once. Well, faced a bear and escaped by playing dead. Same thing. An ache in her marked arm flared, and she tried not to think about getting attached to him already. She was a loner. Always had been, always would be. With the exception of her two friends.

She was not the kind of girl to be owned or claimed by

a man, let alone a damaged, wolf-man who just happened to have an incredible body. And face. And smile. Those lips...

Stop it.

As she drew close to the trap, the small animal came into clear view. It wasn't a rabbit like she'd first thought, but rabbit-like. It had the same body and face, but chicken wings sprouted from its back, and tiny antlers protruded from its forehead. Big eyes glistened as she approached. Her heart tugged. It was cute.

And another sign that this world was not as she'd left it, but perhaps had grown out of the ashes of hers. Jasper had said something about the old world, so maybe she'd somehow—*nah*. Time travel was impossible.

As impossible as no sign of an extinction level nuclear holocaust?

Wherever she was, there were similarities and differences. Maybe she could learn to live here. She could learn to love it... if she could get over missing her friends.

But she wouldn't be getting over anything if she didn't eat. She was so hungry.

"I'm so sorry, buddy, but a girl's gotta eat."

Readying the glass shard she'd taken from within the house, she crouched low and put her hand on the basket, ready to lift. She bit her lip, took a deep breath and then—

Air shimmered around the animal. A slice of recognition warned her moments before the creature exploded into a larger form with a roar. Hurtling backward, Ada landed hard. Her vision blurred. She bit her tongue and tasted blood. *What the hell?*

The tiny, winged bunny had become something else. No longer on all fours, the creature—*monster*—stood on two furred and clawed feet. Its grotesquely shaped body was humanoid, yet covered in patches of matted fur. Only the pectorals were bare pink skin. Long wings draped from his broad shoulders. His nose was part bunny. His mouth had buck teeth. His eyes were red, and long sharp antlers angled from his forehead—no longer tiny and cute. A long pink tongue whipped out to lick a strand of dangling drool from his leering mouth. She gulped as her eyes traveled south to where a very large and laden erection jutted out from the white fuzz of his groin.

Ada was never the kind of woman to scream. Perhaps it was her long-instilled survivalist instinct. Fear would only signal she was prey. Yet, as the monster leered and stroked himself with a very human hand, she screamed.

It grinned salaciously.

"You *owe* me, human," it declared. "You apologized, now you owe me."

She had?

Idiot, Ada. You just did what you weren't supposed to do. Regret pulsed through her. Damn it. She should have waited for Jasper. She forced her heart to slow, her breath to steady, and to assess the situation with a level head.

Jaws snapped at her.

Can't.

She shut her eyes and averted her face. Hot, putrid breath tickled her face, signaling he'd come closer. Vomit rose. She forced it down. Flaring her nostrils, she steeled herself and gripped the glass shard tighter, barely mindful of it stinging her own skin.

Come on. Do this. Toughen up. Destroy it before it destroys you.

It was the voice of Harold, the old crotchety hunter she'd met when wandering the woods as a child. Instead of calling the authorities and putting her in foster care, he'd grumpily taught her how to survive. She opened her eyes and glared.

Survive.

"Get away from me," she demanded. "Or I'll slice your dick clean off."

The rabbit-eared monster cocked its head and studied her with curiosity. A moment, that's all it gave her, but it was enough for her to go on the offensive. She lurched forward and embedded her shard somewhere into its front. Hot sticky blood spilled over her hand.

Strike the belly. Rip up, gut it. Hesitation means suffering for both sides.

She pulled her hand out and stabbed again. Its furious roar cut mid cry when a dark blur hit side-on. Ada's arm yanked, still stuck in the creature's gut. She let go of her weapon just in time to escape two snarling bodies as they grappled and rolled away down the hill. It was Jasper.

Dark hair, tanned and muscled body flashed against pink, furry and feathered. They moved too fast.

Who's winning?

Alarmed, she searched for another weapon, but found none. Didn't matter. The fight was swiftly over. Little balls of light floated out of the monster. Jasper levered off the body, blood coating his naked chest, hands, and dripping from his chin. Amber eyes glowed with adrenaline as he locked onto her with feral intensity.

Heart leaping into her throat, Ada backed up at the sight of an angry, virile, and naked fae stalking toward her as though he wanted to spank her. Worse... eat her.

"I told you to stay inside," he growled.

Her eyes dipped down to what hung from the nestle of dark hair at *his* groin. It wasn't erect, but long. Big. Thick. She resisted patting her too-hot cheeks.

"I was hungry," she murmured.

"I was handling it."

"Um. Do you want me to get your clothes?"

He grunted in frustration, searched the area and found where he'd left his pants. He shoved them on, then returned to her, still fuming.

"Happy?" he asked.

"Over the moon," she replied, a snipe to her tone. "I've already had one unwelcome dick wagging in my face tonight. I don't need another."

He jerked back and his expression turned thoughtful. "What?"

"That thing had a goddamn erection. And it was... you know. Pumping the ol' pipe. Spanking the monkey. Going to town with his hand."

His brows lifted in recognition. Amusement crinkled his eyes. "A wolpertinger has no females of its own kind to mate with, so it tricks females from other fae races into bargains. They lure you in with their cuteness and then kidnap and mate with you. You're lucky I sensed your fear and dropped the berries to come running. A mana-infused bargain is hard to break." He rubbed his stubbled jaw. "You know, if there are more around, my scent on you will deter them."

"You want to rub yourself on me?"

"No, pretty human. I want to mate with you. I want to mark you."

Her jaw dropped. She wasn't sure which part to comprehend first. The fact the beast had wanted to impregnate her, or that Jasper had found berries and dropped them, or that he'd basically just asked to have sex in a casual "It will save your life" sort of way.

"This is absurd," she murmured with a blush. "I'm not *mating* with you. And I will not end up as some horny bunny's sex slave. I need to wash this blood off."

Three things she never thought she'd say.

"I won't hurt you," he promised, and that made her gape even more.

"You don't even like me." Heat flared in her cheeks at

the blistering attention. She swallowed and stepped back. "What's in the water here?"

"Fine," he said with a pout. "I will skin the wolpertinger. At least your stupidity has gifted us with a hearty meal."

She spun on her heel, furious at her body's reaction to the rich sound of his laughter following her.

***

Two hours later, they'd cleaned up as best they could. Jasper had returned with his berries, and skinned a fleshy portion of the beast, and then lit the fire with his mana. Like magic, the flames sprung to life on the hearth and they cooked their stew over the fire in a cracked ceramic pot.

It made her stomach curdle to eat the stew, but she'd had worse. And it tasted like chicken, so she just closed her eyes and pretended it was exactly that. As long as she replenished her energy, she could try to make it to some sort of city or town. Surely there must be a village nearby. She hadn't given up on the idea of finding her friends, although it was sounding less likely that they were also alive. She made a mental note to ask Jasper more about how much time had passed since her time.

With the food gone and their stomachs full, they settled on the floor by the fire. Jasper reclined against an old torn armchair and watched her with an intensity that made her shift and squirm. She hadn't forgotten his offhanded proposal, or his earlier comment about her belonging to him. The way he looked at her was proprietary and almost Machiavellian, as though he hatched devious plans to get what he wanted, and he was prepared to wait.

He chewed on a piece of straw Ada had scattered before the fireplace. If she didn't still sense a strange bond of trust between them, she would have run by now. As it stood, he'd said some things, but his actions were respectful.

He'd helped her down from the table earlier and then let go. He'd tried to keep her from harm, whether that had been by going through a door first, or by trying to keep her here while he went out to hunt.

"All right, fun time is over," she said, a little sleepy from the heat of the flames. "Time for you to explain some shit."

His lips quirked. "Fun time is just beginning."

He pulled out a handful of berries from his pocket. They were different than the ones they'd added to flavor the stew. He handed her one. "Try it."

She arched her brow. "Why do I have the feeling you're not telling me something?"

He shrugged. "You may feel a little relaxed from eating them, that's all."

"Those are relaxing berries, like a drug? Are you kidding me right now?"

He frowned. "They're no big deal. Just something to loosen up with."

He made a face she'd expect on a teenage boy when his mother confiscated his first beer.

"We're both lost, Jasper. You have no memories. We might not survive the night because it's going to be pretty cold. For all you know, I'm a serial killer. And you want to take some sort of drug?"

He dared her with his eyes, popped a berry into his mouth, and chewed.

She huffed. "Fine. Be an ass."

"We're not lost," he said, voice already turning a little slurred. The berries must work quick. "I used to live here. There's a village nearby. We can go there tomorrow."

"Have you remembered things?"

"Nope."

"Then how do you know?"

"Gut feeling. Just like the feeling that said not to go near that cottage. And look what happened. A wolpertinger lived there." He grinned smugly.

Damn him. It was cute. Puffy-eyed, grinning frat boy, cute.

"How can you be so nonchalant about this?"

But no answer came. He'd already started snoring softly.

Ada didn't get it.

He was important enough for a king to assassinate and for someone to block his memories. He was strong enough to kill a monster with his bare hands. He had scars all over him. He seemed like someone who should act a little more responsible.

"You've definitely changed," she murmured. Since taking the blue mark from his neck, more of a playful personality had shone through. If she could get more of the blue off, surely he'd recall some of their situation. If his gut feelings were right, then actual knowledge would be better.

Perhaps he had to be asleep for her to peel the marks off.

Shuffling closer, she checked to see if he noticed her. Once satisfied he was well and truly under, she went to work at the neck marks, picking at the edges with her fingernails. This time, she tried to channel some of this internal mana he had talked about but had no idea what she was doing. Perhaps she felt a tingle down her arm, perhaps not. In the end, she settled into a routine of how she'd approached it before—visualizing the bad stuff gone.

Maybe it was the lack of performance anxiety without his watchful eyes on her, or how she hummed quietly, but her nail caught on some blue. She picked and peeled until a strip came free.

His fingers wrapped around her wrist and held her immobile.

His eyes defocused, his brow puckered, and he tugged them to the ground.

"Tomorrow," he whined. "Sleep now."

She tried to remove her arm so she could shift back to her side, but he held tight.

"I'll keep you warm," he muttered.

"I'm not comfortable with that," she shot back.

He grunted. "I'll shift."

The air shimmered, and fur sprouted from his skin. Within moments, a stunning black wolf crawled out of a pair of pants and then curled around her lazily. He was big enough to shelter her. His fur was thick and, as she looked closer, she found it was like his hair—brown with black tips. He would be warm to sleep up against. The wolf cast a reproachful glance her way and then huffed in annoyance at her reticence.

"Fine," she muttered and curled into his side.

While she wasn't ready to sleep with a pointed-ear fae, she was completely at home next to an animal.

Unable to help herself, she reached out and scratched him under the chin. "You're gorgeous," she muttered.

The moment her head hit the floor, her eyelids grew heavy. She sighed. The wolf sighed. And it was... nice. It took her some time to let her tension go, but she didn't want to live her life destroying everything before it destroyed her. That may have been the way she had survived growing up, but it wasn't how she ended up living. Meeting Harold had taught her how to hunt and read, but after knowing he died alone in his cabin, she knew she never wanted that for herself.

The fire crackled, and Ada drifted, remembering the

faces of her friends. Clarke's red, unruly hair. The way she drank soda like it was going out of fashion. Laurel's inevitable rebuke about Clarke looking after her health and how much sugar was in said soda.

Ada drifted to sleep, smiling at imagined conversations in her head.

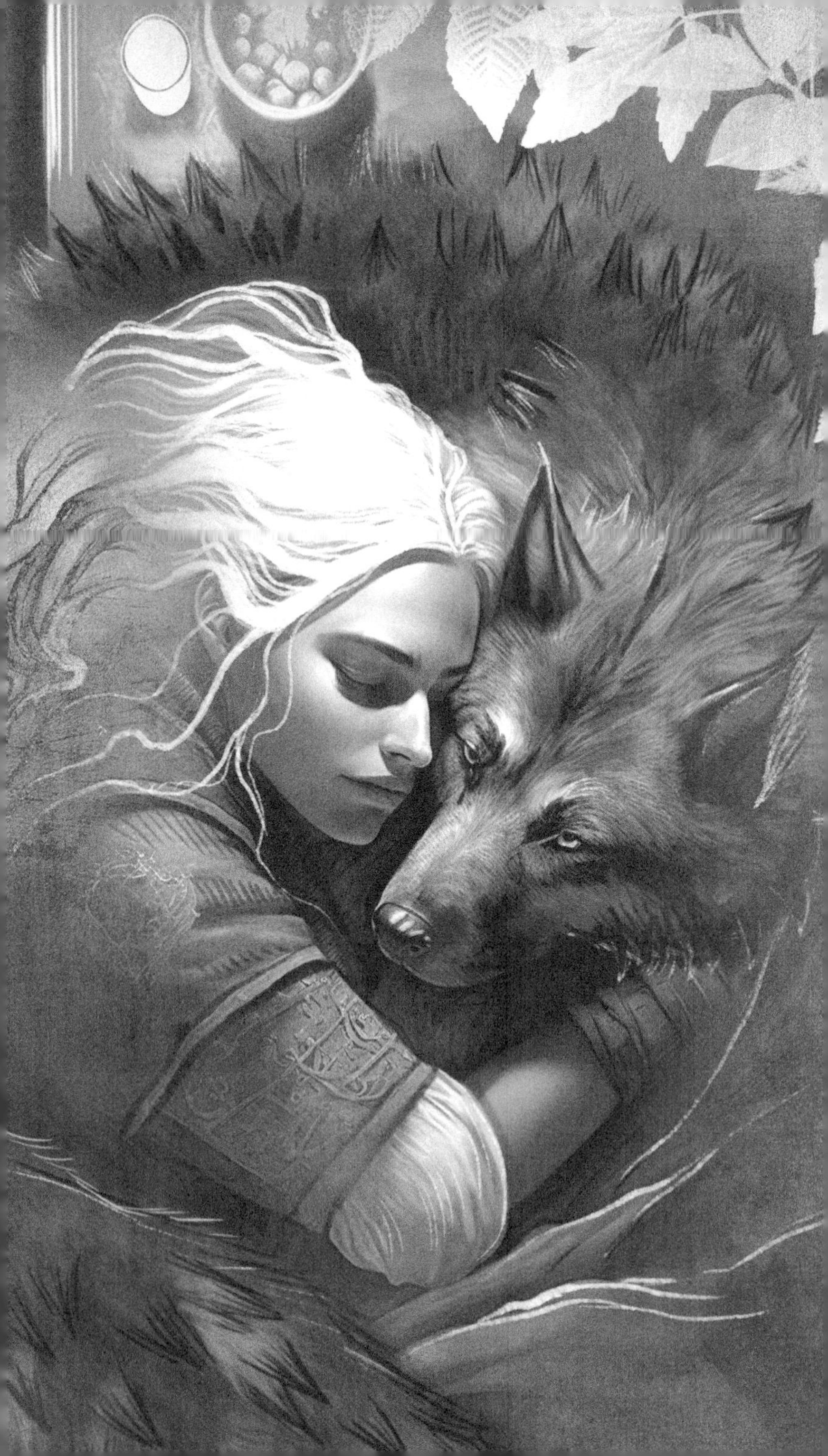

CHAPTER
FIVE

J asper continued to chew mana-weed berries for the duration of their walk from the cottage to the nearby village. Fenrysfield, he thought it was called. Maybe. It took them half a day of walking through rain-soaked mud. He hated every minute, and it had nothing to do with the water falling from the sky, but with the manner with which he'd awoken.

He may have fallen asleep in wolf form, but during the night, his wolf had conceded control of his body. It knew the woman was theirs, that she was human, that she was Jasper's to claim. When he woke, his fae form was wrapped around her alluring body, hugging her within the shelter of his arms, his arousal hard and stiff between the nestle of her bottom. The situation had confounded him, and he couldn't place why.

Had he never awoken with a female in his arms?

Had he not embraced?

Surely he'd been with a female before. Plenty. He may not remember, but he knew it with a solid certainty. Why else would his blood sing at the thought of taking her, of licking her all over, and burying his face between her legs? He enjoyed sex. That was not why he'd been out of sorts when he'd awoken.

Perhaps it was because she was human. Although, he found he cared less upon waking because she was unlike any human he knew... he thought. Perhaps. She certainly held mana within her body. That in itself was highly unusual for one of the forsaken Untouched. The very name fae called humans—Untouched—meant the Well had failed to touch them.

She'd also helped him on more than one occasion and claimed to know nothing about the humans of Crystal City. She claimed to be from a place called Las Vegas. How could he place her in the same category?

All he knew for sure was that her feminine scent drove him to distraction. His skin had buzzed every time she'd moved in sleep, or her hair tickled his skin, or she made a little whimper-sigh that hardened him to the point of pain. He couldn't think, couldn't move, couldn't breathe because he feared the seduction of her scent clawing at him.

With great effort, he'd disentangled without waking her, and then dressed in his breeches.

He'd only popped the first berry to calm his nerves, but then the next berry went in, and the next. Before he staggered out of the cottage, she'd tried again to peel more of the markings from his body but had no luck. He should have let her continue last night. It was a sorely accepted concession on his behalf. One he kept to himself.

The mana-berry effect had worn off by the time they approached the village nestled between the Ceremonial Woods and the Seelie River. Buildings with mosaic tiled walls and thatched roofs crowded together in clusters. Smoke curled from chimneys into the overcast sky. Voices shouted as daily activity carried on—a market was being packed away or set up. Fishermen dragged their catches in great baskets from the river docks. Goats bleated as they scattered and roamed freely. A note of something familiar caught on the breeze, and he lifted his nose for a stronger scent. Wolves. Lots of them. This was a shifter village.

Ada stopped. "This is it?"

He squinted at it, then down at her pillowy lips, still taunting him, and shrugged. "I guess."

It made sense that his instincts would lead them to a shifter village.

"Any idea of where we go first?" she asked. "Or who we speak to?"

He gave another lift of his shoulder.

"Some enthusiasm would be good," she said wryly and then sighed. "I suppose we could just head in."

Slowly they approached the village entrance. There were no gates, just a path that wound past the small market and entered the cluster of buildings to become the main street. On second glance, there had been gates once, but they were recently damaged. Perhaps forced down under attack. Wariness licked down his spine. As he surveyed the buildings, more signs of battle were evident. The glass and gem mosaic walls were cracked. Wooden doors were split. Plants had been trampled and destroyed. The sound of construction rang as they drew close.

But the villagers were rallying. They repaired and washed clothing and hung them on lines strung up from building to building. There were groups of repotted plants. Decorations hung from house to house, eave to eave. Strings of paper flowers, red ribbons, and dangling glass wind chimes, shifted and swayed in a gentle breeze. There must be a festival soon.

This town was resilient. Whatever hardship had befallen them, it hadn't broken them.

Wolves were good like that.

They were scrappy. They survived. And they knew how to have fun.

As Jasper and Ada passed the first house, the smell of baked goods made his stomach rumble. Bread and berries. He moistened his lips and glanced at Ada. She'd be hungry too. Hungry, wet, and cold.

He was painfully aware he had no coin with which to procure food and lodgings. He'd have to come up with something, perhaps he could work off their board.

The first fae they walked up to was a tall female with long black hair, making half-face masks entwined with crafted flowers and red ribbon she sold on her cart. Glass beads tinkled in her hair and on her ankle jewelry. She smiled, but then her gaze snagged on Jasper's face, more precisely to the mark on his right cheekbone. Her eyes widened in fear, and she ran into her nearby house, long skirts billowing behind her, before she shut her wooden door with a loud bang.

"That was weird," Ada said. "Not a friend of yours?"

"Guess not."

A male fae further up, who was in the middle of speaking to a cluster of children, jolted upright at seeing Jasper, and hurried them away.

"You don't smell that bad," Ada joked.

"I would have thought they'd run from you, not me."

"Why's that?"

He gave her ears a look.

"Oh." She touched her hair and tugged bits over her ears. "Is this better?"

"They'll find out, eventually. Not to worry. I will keep you safe."

She snorted. "Okay, Rambo."

He stopped her and scowled. "Do you think I cannot protect you?"

"No. It's just that, like I said before, I'm fine on my own. I mean, how bad can it be? As soon as we..." Her voice trailed off as her attention caught on the growing cluster of villagers brandishing dark looks and the occasional snarl. Some held weapons in their hands—broomsticks, serrated bone swords, and glass daggers reinforced with stone.

Two black wolves trotted out from behind a mosaic building and snarled a soft warning.

Jasper's hackles rose and he tensed, gaze tracking warily around the group, waiting for the first poor buffoon to take a stab at him... or Ada. He let his claws distend from his fingertips.

A fae wearing a wide-brimmed hat pointed his finger at Jasper. "You're unwelcome here, Guardian."

Guardian? Something he'd dreamed tried to climb through the fog of his mind, but failed. He folded his arms and planted his feet.

"There are no monsters here," another said. "So you cannot claim a tax for something we've not requested assistance for."

Ada's brows lifted as she met Jasper's gaze. "Are you some kind of bounty hunter? You don't seem to be very welcome. Maybe we should go elsewhere."

She shivered against a gust of wind. They needed food, shelter, and a place to dry their clothes. His upper lip curled. "They will not run us out of town."

"You heard her, Guardian. Leave," said the fae with the hat. His dagger glinted in the light as he pointed it Jasper's way.

Ada stepped to the side, probably intending to go around, but a large male holding an ax blocked her way. He shook his head and tsked softly. "Turn back, little female."

Defeat flashed in her eyes, and she turned. The large fae pushed her between the shoulder blades. It was the last mistake he made.

Cold fury rocked through Jasper. He used his mana to throw a solid wall of air outward, not even realizing what he'd done until it was over and the fae flew backward into a row of others. Shocked shouts rose, tempers riled, and he drew more mana in preparation, letting it rise and bubble to the surface, ready for release in whichever spell he crafted. Fangs pierced his bottom lip as he partially shifted and growled, low and gravelly.

Violence and murder coursed through his veins, comforting him into believing the well-worn routine meant he'd fought before, and he'd excelled at it.

A wicked grin curved his lips. He blasted more air at the wolves daring to stalk closer. They yipped when hit and staggered back.

Well-damn, it felt good to release his mana.

He would drain his supply dry and not care because he had access to another supply—Ada's. None of these villagers were strong enough to take him. Their own personal Wells were finite, poor, and subpar. Most standard fae only had enough within them to shift, or to cast small magics. Even if there was a source of power nearby for them to replenish, he could melt them where they stood before they had the chance.

How *dare* they think to order him around?

If he had his sword, he would be invincible—his neck

burned, blocking his memory before it arrived, wiping it clean from his consciousness. It annoyed him further.

"What's the matter with you people, you don't recognize one of your own?" someone shouted over the crowd. "Let me through."

Murmurs and dissent passed around, but the crowd reluctantly shifted. No, not reluctantly. He caught the relief in more than one gaze. They understood a fight picked with him could not be won.

Bodies made way for a female shifter with short brown hair. The long, loose gown she wore was a classic style in pure shifter communities such as these. It made for easy removal if the need to shift became urgent. While she appeared the same age as Jasper, that wasn't a signal of age. In fact, the older fae became, the more ageless they appeared. It was the eyes that held their secrets, and within hers, he saw fathomless experience. She smiled at him knowingly.

"The Well preserve us," she murmured, taking him in as though he were a ghost. "As I live and breathe, if it isn't Reed Darkfoot, only living heir to the Seelie Mithras throne, finally coming home to visit his roots."

"My name is Jasper." Wasn't it?

"D'arn Jasper"—she spat on the floor—"is the Guardian name forced on you by the Order of the Well when you emerged from the ceremonial lake some two hundred years ago. *Reed* is the name your Darkfoot mother gave you. It is the *only* name we will call you in Fenrysfield.

Well, perhaps—" She gave him a wry smile. "Perhaps we may call you princeling, seeing as the King legitimized you a week ago."

Hushed murmurs broke out among the crowd. They spoke the word *prince* on more than one occasion. Somewhere in the middle, he also caught the word *bastard*.

Anxiety crawled up his spine, causing his heart to race. He looked for an escape, but his eyes clashed with Ada's.

The King. As in... the golden fae who'd tried to assassinate him.

"Your own father wants you dead?" she gasped.

"Bah," said the female alpha. "It's not the first time. So, you've come home to seek refuge, is that it? The Order can't do that job anymore?"

His lips parted, but he had no reply.

"He's lost his memories," Ada filled in for him and pointed to the marks around his neck. "That's doing something to him."

The alpha's gaze snapped to his marks, and then trailed down to the ones on his arms. She darted a glance to Ada, frowned, and then she clapped her hands in the air loudly. "Enough. Everyone disperse."

Reluctantly, the villagers, once keen to pry his eyes out with their pitchforks, filtered away.

"Come with me," the alpha beckoned.

Jasper surveyed the village and the way out of town. They had no choice. This woman knew him. She could help. So he strode after her.

The alpha took them to a two-story stone building plastered with a mural of mosaics. Black wolves danced and played, half-wolves battled, and naked fae—he squinted. What were they doing? Ada squinted too, with a hitched intake of breath.

"Good Lord, they're *doing it*," she whispered with a hint of humor.

He shot a sideways glance at her. Her cheeks were flushed. He sensed bashfulness coming from their bond-marks. Was his little mate a shy lover? His stomach dipped with the thrilling thought that he'd get to find out.

The alpha had seen them halt and returned. She, too, gave Ada a thoughtful look.

"You're not a wolf," she clipped. Her chin lifted as she scented. "But I can't place what you are."

"Keen nose," Jasper remarked, but he didn't feel the need to enlighten her.

"Live as long as I have, and there's not much I miss." Her gaze dipped to their matching blue arm markings. "Like the fact you're both locked into a Well-blessed union."

"A what?" Ada choked.

Jasper folded his arms. "I told you."

"We should talk inside." The alpha continued into the building, dipping to avoid the strings of glass wind chimes tinkling in the wind. They hung from the building eaves. In fact, he checked over his shoulder, the wind chimes were on most buildings, gifting his ears with a pleasant melody hard to hear beyond.

For privacy, he realized. So other shifters couldn't hear what went on in their neighbor's house. He smirked. If the mosaic murals were to be believed, plenty of battles, fun, and procreation.

Maybe he would like it here after all.

He shifted the wind chimes and followed the females inside to a large empty hall with a long table surrounded by chairs. It was either for meals or business. Perhaps both. Windows showed the village main street on one side, and a garden with a bubbling fountain on the other.

"Please, take a seat," the alpha said. "I suppose since your curse prevents you from remembering, I must take it easy on you. Not that you deserve it, Reed. Your mother would turn in her grave to know how long it's been since you've come back to us." She raised her eyes to the ceiling and made the apology hand sign against her breast. "I suppose since we're in the middle of Lupercalia preparations, perhaps she is looking after us."

He scowled at her, but took a seat. *Lupercalia*... vague recollections came to mind. Plenty of celebrations and carousing. Sounded good to him.

"I've sent for refreshments," she said.

Ada smiled and nodded. Beneath the table, she fidgeted.

"You really don't remember, do you?" The alpha asked, staring intently at him.

His only reply was a flare of his nostrils.

She sighed. "Very well. My name is Clara Darkfoot. I'm the pack matriarch. And your mother's sister."

When he kept his silence, her eyes dipped to his neck marks, then across to Ada. "How long has he been cursed?"

"Cursed?" she repeated.

A nod.

"I'm not sure," Ada continued. "We both woke up in an abandoned cottage not too far away. Neither of us knows how we got there. For me, I'm a world away from my home. And my friends. I was hoping maybe you could shed some light on my situation, too."

"I'll do my best." She shot Jasper a disapproving stare. "If only for the memory of my sister, and the hopes of her heart."

A knock came at the door, and Clara beckoned in two female fae with a pitcher of water, and a platter of cheese, and dried fruit with crackers. After filling glasses, they left. Ada made quick work of digging into her food.

"Out there they called me a Guardian," Jasper said. "What is that?"

"Guardians work for the Order of the Well," Clara explained, still with a disbelieving look in her eye. "When your mother was murdered, you went to the ceremonial lake and offered yourself as tribute." She sighed. "I suppose the Order was good for one thing, keeping you out of your father's way. They operate above the laws of Elphyne. Becoming a Guardian stripped you of any claim to the

Seelie throne. That's why it surprised us all when only a week ago you were announced as the High King's heir. The abolishment of the unsanctioned breeding law also surprised us. We all assumed it was your doing considering how it came into being in the first place." She gave him a studious, long look. "Yet here you are, cursed, without your memories, and with a Well-blessed mate."

Ada patted the table. "Yeah, about that. What exactly is this Well-blessed mating thing? I feel like I should know."

Clara jerked. "There was no mating ceremony?"

Ada shook her head. "Not that we're aware of. We just woke up, and it was there."

"That cannot do. A Well-blessed mating is rare. In all of Elphyne, only two have been announced in the past few centuries."

"How do I find out who cursed me?" Jasper asked. "And how do I get it removed?"

"Casting a curse is forbidden, and irreversible. Even if it was the Order who placed that block on you, they wouldn't be able to remove it. It's simply not done. Either there is a timed deadline linked to the curse, or some unknown event has to take place, if any. It could simply hold forever."

"That's not true," Ada remarked. "I've peeled pieces from his body."

Clara stilled. Her gaze bore into Ada. "Where did you say you hailed from again?"

"I didn't."

Jasper mulled it over. If this matriarch was truly his kin, then she would be the best person to reveal Ada's heritage. Loyalty between kin ran deeper than any other bond. They might not come across help like this again. He could travel to the Order, since he seemed to have worked for them, but as Clara mentioned—it might have been the Order who'd cursed him. It was more likely the King's fault, but Jasper had to be sure.

He would rather control this information getting out than have Clara discover by surprise that she had the enemy in her midst. At least this way, it came from family.

"She's human," Jasper explained.

Clara jumped out of her seat. Blue flame licked at her hand and she glared at Ada. Jasper slowly rose. He raised his blue-marked, Well-blessed palm, reminding her of the connection.

"She's not our enemy," he intoned.

Clara's eyes dipped to his hand, then back to his eyes. She growled, "You don't understand. We barely survived the last raid. And you've invited one of them into our homes?"

"Raid?" he asked. "Please, Clara. Sit. Use your senses."

Ada made no move through it all.

Clara's flame extinguished. She took a hesitant step toward Ada and then lifted her nose. She took another step, and another, before finally meeting Jasper's eyes. Her brows lifted. "She's filled to the brim with mana. It's impossible."

"Evidently not."

"Who *are* you?" Clara asked Ada, a note of awe in her voice.

"I'm just a girl from Vegas," she murmured. "The last thing I remember is that it snowed in the city, and then—"

"Crystal City?"

"No. Las Vegas. Have you truly not heard of it?"

Clara shook her head. "There are no other human settlements but Crystal City in the wasteland."

"Then I have no idea how I got here." She bit her lip.

"No, you have some idea," Jasper prompted. "I can sense your hesitation."

"How?" She gaped at him. "How are we sensing each other's feelings?"

"It's the bond," Clara confirmed. "It links your mana with the other. You can borrow his, and he can borrow yours. You strengthen each other. That the Well paired someone so bountiful in mana as you with a Guardian seems right." She frowned. "In fact, if rumors are true, I've heard gossip that the other two Well-blessed matings happened to other Guardians."

Ada sat back and slumped. "Where I came from, there was no Well. There were no fae except in storybooks. We lived in tall skyscrapers, we had electricity and computers and cars and planes that flew in the sky. It was nothing like this. I feel like I've stepped back in time."

"No," Clara mused. "Perhaps you've stepped forward. What you describe sounds like the old world. What we call the Age of Man. The one destroyed by the greed and warring of humans."

Shock, then relief washed through the bond to Jasper.

Ada's brows puckered. "You have no idea how it feels to finally know. To be grounded. I mean, I had an inkling. I saw the remnants of my world at the cottage, and all this life bursting in nature was definitely not around when I left. At least I know now. Or some of it. I still need to figure out how I got here."

"Will you go back?" Jasper asked. *Can she go back?*

"Like you said, my time was dying."

She's from another time? How was that possible? The woman was full of surprises. Jasper didn't need his memories to see that. She could use mana. She'd bonded to him—been chosen for him. She'd somehow skipped thousands of years of history to be here. It also meant she didn't belong to the humans in the wasteland... at least, so far as she said.

Jasper looked at his hands. They were warrior's hands. If what Clara had said was true, and he was a Guardian, then he must have seen his fair share of battles.

Blood on his hands.

He blinked and shook his head. He could have sworn his hands were covered in blood when they were not.

Hot, crimson blood running down his clawed hands and furred forearms to drip on the sand below.

A crowd roared. Buzzing in his ears pierced his brain. He winced. So loud. So violent. They wanted more. Violence ripped through him. He stretched his arms wide and snarled his frustration.

They cheered more.

He would eat them. He would jump the barricade and tear into their flesh and feast on their entrails.

Pain and fire stabbed him in the lower back. He snarled through the iron mask, tried to snap and bite but the metal blocked his teeth. He whirled around, heaving lungfuls of air, ready to strike, but a small infidel shoved something electric into his side.

"Move," someone shouted. "Back to your pen. Show's over, champion."

More fire. More lightning.

A shameful whimper squeaked out of his lungs as he staggered out of the arena and toward a dark tunnel.

"That's it, nice and slow." The raspy voice—a male—held a note of sympathy.

He collapsed just inside the long, dark corridor.

Bloodthirsty thunder exploded around him. They wanted more blood. They called his name—Champion.

Small hands went to his neck, unclipped something, and released the iron mask. He cried out in agony as they pulled bolts from inside his flesh, but when the last of the metal was removed, he shifted forms, back to fae. The wolf was exhausted. It was ashamed. Why?

He lifted his lashes and craned his neck to peer over his shoulder.

"I wouldn't do that if I were you," came the small raspy voice.

But he had to see.

He glimpsed scattered fae bodies in a circle—a ring—as though they'd gone to their dying breath to protect something inside. Females, males, winged fae, horned fae. All with gores through their bodies, entrails stringing from their guts, and limbs torn off and thrown to the side.

"Shut the gates!" shouted the attendant. "For Crimson's sake."

But he got to his feet, one at a time. He used the stone wall to heave his body up in time to see the small childlike form at the center of corpses before the closing gates blocked the carnage from view.

"Nooo!" Jasper roared and lurched off his chair. He landed on the tiled floor. And then he vomited the water he'd drunk.

"Jasper!" Ada's chair scraped.

Footsteps came running.

A cold hand met his sweaty forehead, but he shoved her away.

"I did it," he murmured, eyes burning.

"Did what?" she asked. "Whatever it is, it's okay."

It wasn't. Flashes of what he saw hit his mind, and he retched. He couldn't breathe, couldn't hold himself upright.

"This is your doing," he growled at her.

"What?" she gasped.

"You tried to heal me. You"—he gagged—"you set memories loose."

Outside, a loud piercing howl rent the air, cutting down to his bones. His wolf sat up, alert. Another howl joined the first, and then another. It was their warning system.

Danger.

Coming in fast.

Clara jogged to the window. Screams filtered through the tinkling of wind chimes.

Clara snarled at Ada. "You lied! You brought them back."

"Who?" Jasper asked.

"The humans."

He dragged himself to the window. Panicked villagers ran through the street, rushing into homes and locking doors. Those who didn't hide brandished weapons. Some shifted to wolf form right there, tearing through clothes or stepping out of them.

"I need a weapon," he barked.

No one answered. When he turned around, Clara advanced on Ada.

"Stop." Jasper grabbed Clara as she passed him. "You don't touch her."

Clara's wild amber gaze snapped to his. "You said this was her doing."

"I was talking about my memories." He lifted Clara by

the collar and narrowed his eyes. "Let me make this very clear. You hurt her, I kill you."

"Jasper," Ada admonished. "She's confused. I'm sure—"

"I'm not confused," Clara hurled back. "You turn up on the day of a second raid? It's not a coincidence."

Ada lifted her chin. "I also brought with me someone you seem to want here."

Clara's eyes slid back to Jasper.

"She may look like them, but she is not your enemy," he said.

"Why would they be back?" Clara gaped.

"What did they take last time?" Ada asked. "Maybe they want more."

Clara's eyes widened. "They came for the—" she turned to Jasper with a guilty look.

"What?"

"Please don't tell the Order."

"Tell them what?"

"We should have handed over the metal, but..." A disgusted expression flitted over her face. "The Order are no friends of ours, and the King asked... well, more like demanded we stockpile. Since the Order has taxed us until we've got nothing left, we needed the coin. We can take care of our own protection. We can rid the woods of mana-warped creatures ourselves. We don't *need* the Order."

He tried to make sense of her scramble. "The humans want metal?"

"They use it to create weapons that work against fae. We thought if we simply sell the King what we scavenge from the river, then no one will know. At the very least, we thought he would protect us. But..."

"The humans found out."

She nodded.

"There must be more," he said. "Show me."

"You're going to tell the Prime, aren't you? We'll be punished."

He gritted his teeth. "I'm going to find a weapon I can use."

Clara stared at him for a long moment, then a scream and a loud crash jolted them. "Fine. Follow me."

Jasper followed her out of the room, but when Ada jogged after him, he forced her back. "Stay here. Stay safe."

"There must be something I can do," she said.

"Are you a fighter? A warrior in your time?"

She shook her head. "I guess I'm more of a carer."

"Then stay and help care for the wounded. There will be many."

CHAPTER
SIX

Ada was reeling. Hit after hit of information swam through her mind while she waited for Jasper and Clara to return.

She was from another time, long before everyone here. All her friends were probably dead. She now lived in a world where the residents had drastically changed. They could access magic—and she could, too. Except she looked like their enemy, who couldn't access magic.

And they were attacking.

The small piece of world she'd come to understand grew inexplicably tighter, like a band constricting around her chest.

Ada had magic, yet she couldn't help.

Filled to the brim with mana. That's what Clara had said.

Ada must be able to do something. When they'd arrived, Jasper had magicked a strong wind to push back a villager. He could shift into a wolf. Clara had conjured blue fire. There was so much Ada didn't understand about this world. Maybe if she tried something, she could help. She went for the door, but it opened suddenly.

Her heart leapt into her throat.

But it was only Jasper and Clara. He looked fierce with a long, metal sword dangling from his hand. Livid amber eyes scanned the room, landed on her, and frowned before darting back to Clara.

"Keep her safe," he ordered. "If I sense she is in danger, I will drop everything and come here. Do you understand?"

Clara's lips flattened, her eyes dipped to his Well-blessed arm marks, and she reluctantly tipped her chin. "As a fellow Darkfoot, you have my oath. I will keep her safe."

Jasper returned her curt nod and then left.

Ada watched through the window as he plowed through the street, barking for fae to get in their houses, and to leave the battle to him.

Just him?

Adrenaline surged, pushing blood through Ada's veins, causing her to break out into a cold sweat when a group of black clad humans encroached down the street. They wore fatigues like modern soldiers from her time. They looked so strangely familiar that a splice of doubt dipped in her stomach. Did she belong with *them*, or the wolf outside who seemed so very different from her? Then she saw the weapons the humans carried—swords, grenades, and—

"Gun," she gasped, pointing. "He's got a gun."

She slammed her palm against the window, trembling the glass. Jasper wore naught but breeches and blue glowing marks. A bullet would tear through his flesh like it was paper. A bullet would go straight through his heart.

Two fae came up behind Jasper with bone swords brandished in their fists. One had silver long hair, the other's was similar to Jasper's. These fae were ill prepared for modern warfare... or past warfare. Whatever it was, she had to warn them.

Heart galloping in her chest, she spun, intending to run out the front door, but ran straight into Clara. For a small woman, she was incredibly strong. She stopped Ada with a hand to her shoulders.

"I gave my oath to keep you safe," Clara growled, eyebrows down. "Don't make me break it."

"But you don't understand. They've got guns. I have to warn him."

"Your bond-mate is a Guardian," Clara returned, face hard. "He will endure, and he will protect. This is what he does. Now, help me prepare this room for wounded." She pointed at the long wooden table. "We can use that for operating. We need clean cloths and water. Come with me. And keep your ears hidden."

Ada gaped at her, then darted a glance back out the window.

Wind buffeted Jasper's dark hair, whipping the strands into his long-lashed, scowling eyes. Veins writhed down his hard muscles as each limb pumped full of tension. Tendons in his neck popped. Every ounce of his flesh said not to mess with him—except his face wore a wolfish grin and displayed a hint of sharp canines. Was he about to fight, or play a game?

Upon seeing his face, the humans hesitated.

Big mistake. Jasper threw his sword, point first, like a spear. It embedded in the middle of a man's head. Not waiting a second, he flicked out his hands. Sharp claws shot out from his fingertips. His guttural growl curdled Ada's stomach. She wanted to flee, just from the sound of it.

The humans balked, again.

Another mistake.

Then one with a sword lurched forward. Faster than her eye could see, Jasper ran forward, long legs gracefully eating up the street. He met the group, blocked the sword by taking the man's wrist. Ada should have been watching his other hand. It buried deep within the soldier's chest. When he pulled out, he dropped something sloppy and red on the floor.

Oh God. Ada covered her mouth and looked away. It was his heart.

Clara took her shoulder and yanked her away from the window.

"Snap out of it. I need your help."

The sounds of fighting filtered in—wet thuds, grunts, gurgles, cries—Ada wanted to look, to check on Jasper, but felt his fury vibrating down their bond like a plucked string. *He's fine. He's fine.* He's a mother-fucking, brutal warrior. Maybe *she* wasn't fine.

That wet slop as the heart landed on the ground.

She shuddered.

Jeez. She forced her attention to the back of Clara's pixie haircut and followed her into another part of the building to a kitchen and food storeroom.

Clara pointed to a pile of folded towels. "Take those."

Ada grabbed the towels, found sharp knives, and took them back into the hall. Back and forth she and Clara went, gathering supplies and bowls of water, ignoring the shouts and clashes from outside with determination. She refused to look, instead, focusing on the feeling in her arm—the sensation of energy, and the blind rage from Jasper. If he was angry, he was alive.

When the fight moved on from the front of their building, Clara went to the door and waved down a tall grayhaired fae carrying one of their wounded—a youth that couldn't have been more than fifteen years of age.

"In here!" Clara shouted.

They burst through the front and were spirited into the hall.

"Put Lake on the table, Percival," Clara ordered.

Percival put the youth down with a wince. A long, thin metal rod stuck out from the patient's stomach. His face had gone green.

"I thought maybe I could pull it out, but..." Percival's

eyes watered. "It's metal. I don't know if I should. Don't worry, son. We'll get you right." To Clara, "He just wanted to help."

"I know." Clara put her hand on Percival's shoulder. "Lake needs to shift to heal. We will have to remove it. Can you hold him down?"

"Wait!" Ada blurted. "You can't. What if its hit an artery, or pierced a vital organ? What if he bleeds out before he can shift?"

Clara looked at Ada as though she'd gone mad. "Shifting is how we heal."

"Doesn't metal block the flow of mana? I'm sure Jasper mentioned that to me. What if we pull it out and metal filings are stuck in there? Can he still shift?"

Silence stretched. It appeared as though no one knew the answer to that question.

"You healed Reed," Clara noted. "You said you also removed parts of his curse."

"I did, but... did he tell you that when you were gone? I don't know *how* I did it."

"Well, we're going to find out." Clara took Ada's hand and put it on Lake's chest. He winced. "Tell me what you feel."

Ada knew enough about healing animals and first aid that she understood never to let the patient see her worry, or her incompetence. If the patient thought Ada didn't know what she was doing, then panic would set in. They could go into shock. That was the last thing anyone needed. As her friend Laurel used to always say, fake it until you make it. She forced her breathing to calm and hoped to high hell that the boy didn't see the perspiration dotting her upper lip.

"Lake, is it?"

Shaggy gray hair dipped onto his forehead as he nodded.

"We're going to get this out of you, don't worry. I have a unique gift. Apparently I'm overflowing with *mana*." She held up her arm so he could see the blue glowing marks. "See this?"

He nodded.

"They said it means the Well has blessed me. It means I'm going to do everything I can to help you live. Okay? Will you let me try?"

A glimmer of awe entered his eyes as he took in her arm before nodding.

"Okay, let's see what I can do. While I'm doing that, why don't you see if you can count the lines on my markings." Half doubting, half hoping, Ada placed her palm on Lake's chest, careful not to disturb the foot-long rod coming out of his side. He flinched, but he zeroed in on her arm. Whether or not he was counting, she couldn't tell, but it seemed her distraction worked. She didn't want him looking at the wound.

She shifted her hands an inch to see if she could feel anything but felt ridiculous. His flesh was hot. That's all she felt. Nothing happened.

Ada flared her lashes at Clara. *What now?*

"What did you do when you helped Reed?"

She cast her mind back. When he was poisoned, she did what she always did. Sucked it out. But even as the thoughts flittered in her mind, she knew in her heart it went much deeper than snake bite first aid. Jasper's wounds had turned black and purple. The venom had worked into his bloodstream. The sucking should have come too late. Part of her knew it.

So what did she do that was different?

"I imagined it happening," she murmured. "I envisioned the poison coming out of his body."

She'd done the same thing again when peeling the curse marks off.

"Connecting with your mana comes on an intrinsic level. There are six elemental affinities fae can have with the well. Earth, air, water, fire, chaos and spirit. Healing is a mixture of everything. Place both hands on him. Close your eyes. Feel the water flow through his veins. Feel the energy of his spirit. The fire of his life force. Try to listen to his mana."

Sure. Easy peasy. It made perfect sense.

Her second palm joined the first. Ada's lashes lowered, and she slowed her breathing. She blocked the sounds of battle. She ignored the chimes tinkling. She focused on the beating of her heart, of Lake's heart beneath her touch. His breathing. The clamminess of his skin. She pushed her awareness into her hands, and then she went lower.

She trusted her intuition.

Clara's voice murmured softly, "Just do what you did with Reed. What comes naturally? What needs to be done?"

The heat of Lake's body grew hotter. It scorched her palms as her awareness spread outward, to the side, up, down, and then back again. It took her a moment, but she realized this confined heat map was his body. Where it went was his life force. Elation lifted her spirits, and she lost focus for a moment, shook her head and frowned in concentration.

"I feel the limits of his body," she said without opening her eyes.

"Good. What else?"

Ada continued to search the heated area with her mind's eye. Her awareness shifted with sluggish strokes at first, but the more she flexed the muscle, the easier it became. She swam around, getting to know the sensation, until she came to a cold spot where the heat wouldn't flow.

"There's a cold spot," she whispered with a shiver. "A dark area I can't see."

"That's the metal rod," Clara said. "Look closer. Are there any other cold spots?"

Ada searched, but came up with nothing. "I don't think so."

"Good."

The cold spot suddenly burned hot. Lake screamed in pain. Ada's lashes flipped open, and she jolted back just as

Lake jackknifed up, his hand to his now rod-free, wounded side. Blood flowed between his fingers and he glared at Clara with a mix of accusation and relief.

"Shift, my boy," Clara barked, the bloody rod dangling in her hand, dripping onto the floor.

Air shimmered around Lake, hair sprouted on his jaw, on the back of his hands, and his teeth elongated. He gave a long, strangled whimper. Sweat plastered his forehead, but he dropped back to the table, still in fae form, panting hard.

"I can't," he whined, thrashing his head. "I can't."

Clara's face paled. "There must still be metal in him. I thought you said there was only one cold spot."

"There was!" Ada flattened her lips, biting back a retort that she'd been right. "I didn't know you were going to just yank it out. Some must have broken off!"

She took the rod and inspected it. The metal was rusted.

"Search again," Clara said. "Find the shard."

Shit.

Ada put her palm on Lake's chest, but Clara guided her hand down to the wound. He squirmed, bottom lip and hand trembling as he made way for Ada by letting go of his wound.

"It's okay, son," Percival said, taking Lake's bloody hand.

Blood oozed from the hole. Ada slammed her palm over

it. Hot, wet mess flowed onto her hand. She slammed her eyes shut and concentrated.

Feel the cold spot.

Heat. Heat, everywhere.

Vaguely she heard Clara direct Percival out of the room with orders to send the wounded here. He was reluctant to go, but when Ada found the cold spot, she knew why he'd been sent away. No father should see his son screaming in agony. And that was going to happen next.

"I found it," she said grimly to Clara, swallowed, and glanced at the puncture wound. "It seems to be in one piece."

"Do it," Clara said. She gave Lake the rod to bite down on and then took his hand. "She's going to dig it out, love. Okay?"

He nodded, eyes wild and darting.

"Good boy. Brave boy."

Clara nodded at Ada. She dug her finger into the wound and used the lack of heat she sensed as a guide. The boy screamed through the bit. His back arched, and both Ada and Clara held him down.

They should have antiseptic. They should have *anesthetic*. But this was a species like no other. They healed when they shifted. Ada had to trust Clara knew what she was talking about. Ada gritted her teeth and dug around his wound with her finger until she found it. A small sharp prick. It felt *wrong*. Never had she simply touched an inanimate object and felt something, but she wanted to throw the metal splinter into the darkest depths of the ocean and forget about it. Better yet, launch it into space.

Like the rod, her awareness wouldn't extend through the splinter. It was simply an empty void of nothing. Was this the Well's aversion to metal she sensed? Was this why metals and plastics were forbidden? She gritted her teeth and inserted her second finger to clamp onto the splinter, then pulled it out.

"Got it," she gasped.

The boy spat out the rod, and then shifted so fast that Ada had trouble seeing anything but a blur of air and fur until a gray wolf with brown feet lay on the table, panting heavily, eyes bright.

Clara made short work of checking the fur around the wolf's abdomen and then nodded. "Skin is closed. You'll be fine, lad. Scarred, but you'll live. Go find somewhere to lie low until your mana is replenished."

The wolf gave a soft whine of annoyance, but heaved himself to his paws, and hopped down from the table. He snuffled Ada's leg briefly before trotting out the door.

Ada turned to Clara. "He's okay?"

She nodded grimly. "He's lucky he had enough mana to shift. Most of us can only do so once or twice a day. Unless, of course, you're a Guardian." Her eyes skated outside. "Some won't be so lucky."

Ada looked at her hands, still tingling with heat and sticky with blood. This time, the awareness she sensed felt alive inside her own body. As though it were a buzzing, living thing. This was her power, her gift. Her eyes shifted back to Clara.

"Can you teach me more?" she asked.

"We'll soon find out." Clara lifted her chin toward the door where Percival brought another fae limping in, blood dripping from a gouge in his thigh.

Behind them, two more wounded limped, using each other as a crutch. One was the fae who'd accosted them on arrival. His wide-brimmed hat no longer on top of his head but carrying something at his stomach. As they drew closer, she noticed dark rivulets of blood streaking from it. When Ada looked into it, her stomach dipped.

His intestines.

"How are you still alive?" she gasped. Alive *and* walking, let alone helping an injured fae walk.

His glazed eyes met hers and seemed to see right through her.

Clara took one look at him and then shook her head. "Why haven't you shifted?"

"Used the last of my mana to portal us all here from the docks."

"*Well-damn*, you're a tough wolf." Clara swallowed, then gave Ada an almost imperceptible shake of the head. *He's not going to make it.*

He must have known because he handed his companion to Clara and stepped aside. So they were just going to leave him?

Clara pointed at the first two who'd arrived and said to Ada, "You take them."

Hardly able to breathe, she forced herself to triage the first who'd arrived with Percival. He had a gash down his calf, and one over his eye. His arm hung limply at the side.

"In there," she said and pointed into the hall. "Find somewhere to sit. You're not on death's door yet. I'll be with you in a moment."

Then she went to the man with his guts in his hat. His face had turned a paler shade of green and he leaned heavily on the wall, barely holding onto his package.

"What's your name?" she asked.

From the way he'd accosted them upon arrival, she thought he might clam up. But he either didn't recognize her or didn't care. "Moon."

"Alright, Moon. Can you come with me to the table inside the hall?"

There was no way she'd be able to carry him. She placed her hand on the hat's cap, swallowed when she felt the contents through the fabric, and whispered, "I've got you. It's okay. Let's do this together."

"Ada," Clara warned as she helped her patient.

But Ada ignored her. She knew in her soul she could help this fae. She knew her gift went beyond finding cold spots and draining poison. It had to. Even if it didn't, she would not let him die without trying. Never in her life had she abandoned a wounded animal, no matter how fierce or stubborn, and she wasn't about to start now.

"Let's go, Moon," she said and fit herself under his big arm.

He fell heavily onto her shoulder. She staggered, gained her footing, and together they shuffled into the hall. With effort, they got him onto the table. He laid back and met her eyes.

"I'm the only one in town who can create a portal," he croaked.

She wasn't sure what that meant, probably exactly what it sounded like, but nodded. "You did good. They're safe."

He nodded. His lashes drooped.

"Stay with me, Moon. Your job's not done."

But his hands fell from the hat. She caught it before everything spilled. Time was running out.

"Moon?"

No response. Ada looked at the long abdomen gash with clinical distance. She wasn't a surgeon, not even a doctor or veterinarian, but she had *something*. It was the same thing that kept her alive all those years ago when her mother left her for days on end. It was the same thing that put her in Harold's path. The same thing that brought her here to this time, and it was the same thing that gave her this ability.

Call it fate. Call it the Well. Whatever it was, she wouldn't run from it.

This time, when she focused inward, the buzzing energy of her gift rose to her call and danced within her, as though it had been waiting. She knew a little about anatomy from what she'd studied during high school, and from dissecting frogs and rats. Even what she'd learned while rehabilitating wild animals and on the flip side, hunting to keep herself fed and alive. Occasionally, she had to skin her hunt herself.

Holding her breath, she peeled back the jagged flesh of the wound and checked around, both with her eyes and her senses. No cold spots. No metal blocking what she was hoping to do next. Exhaling, then inhaling, she held her breath and tried not to think about the punctured intestinal smell that she'd just inhaled. She started putting entrails back into his body, slowly and surely. With every yard she put in, she tested it with her awareness, searching for... she wasn't sure. Just anything not right. When the heat of her gift fluctuated, she focused intently. She envisioned his wounds healing, just how she had with Jasper's wounds back at the cottage. *Get better. Heal. Knit together.* Fire in her touch burned hotter, brighter, with more power. For a moment, she was afraid she'd either burn him alive, or herself. But she kept her mind focused on willing him to become what he was before the injury struck—whole.

When the last of her heat waned, she opened her eyes and inspected the flesh beneath her hands. She swiped her thumb over the red-orange sticky mess and found clean, puckered scars beneath. Ada dropped her ear to the fae's chest, listened, and heard his heartbeat. A smile tipped her lips. She did it. She hoped.

Lifting her head, she found not only Moon's eyes on her, but everyone else's in the room.

Clara finished wrapping the leg of the fae with white hair, and came over with wide, almost fearful eyes.

"You did what the shift does," she said to Ada.

"I healed him."

"Oh, you did more than that, love." She peeked at the scarred stomach. "He was on death's door."

Moon, still staring at Ada, rasped. "You're human."

A coldness entered the room. It was as though the very air froze. Ada's fingers fluttered to her ears and found her hair had been subconsciously tucked sometime while she'd worked.

"We don't know what she is," Clara clipped, eyes narrowing. "Because a human can't do what she just did. A human can't be in a Well-blessed union with a Guardian. But she is. For now, we carry on. She is on our side."

The tension relaxed. A word from their matriarch was all they needed.

Ada washed her hands in a bowl and rushed to the one she'd told to find a seat and began to triage. He said he had no reserve mana left to shift. She was about to treat the wound with her gift, but Clara cautioned against using all of her mana for non-life threatening wounds. She felt fine, not empty, if that was such a thing, but could see the logic in Clara's warning, so treated the wound the old school way—with water, stitches, and a cloth. Behind her, Moon rolled to his side and spoke to Clara.

"They came from the dock," he rumbled. "But not by boat."

"How is that possible? Crystal City is weeks away by foot."

"I fear they portaled in."

"But that's impossible. They carried metal weapons. And they're here to collect our hidden stash. Metal won't travel through a portal. Not unless a Guardian held it or created the portal."

Neither said anything beyond that. More wounded came in and Ada became lost in treating them for the next few hours. From one fae to another, she attended the injured. By the time the room became crowded with moaning and groaning shifters, her arms had turned to lead and her legs moved like rocks.

A loud roar filled the air, somewhere outside. The building shook, wind chimes fretted as though blasted with wind, and agony sliced down the bond from Jasper.

Ada's head snapped up.

"He's been hit," she said, eyes blurring.

Fireworks went off, but that was impossible. Who would shoot fireworks? Not fireworks. Gunfire.

A draining sensation pulled through her arm. Energy tugged from her body as though she'd been hit with a tranquilizer dart that kept drugging. She dropped to her knees, gasping and holding onto the chair of the patient she'd been treating.

"What's happening?" she gasped, chest heaving.

The patient shouted. Clara jogged over, blood smeared on her face, wariness on her expression.

"Ada?" she said, and bent low to check. "What's the matter?"

"My arm," she held up the blue marked arm, but couldn't move. *Too heavy.* "It's like I feel my life draining through there."

"He's borrowing your mana."

"What?" she croaked. But then she realized the truth in those words. "Jasper's injured. I felt his pain."

Ada used Clara to push to her feet. She staggered to the door. "I have to go to him."

"You can't!" Clara urged. "I gave an oath you'd be safe."

"I'll go," Moon offered.

He'd recovered since she'd mended his stomach. While still a little green in the face, he'd been walking around the room, helping as best he could.

Before Ada could protest, or even take another step, Moon left.

"Sit down," Clara ordered. "Have a drink."

She guided Ada to the side where her aching body collapsed on a velvet covered dining chair. Her arms barely lifted to take hold of the terracotta cup Clara handed her. When the water hit her lips, she found her throat parched and guzzled it down.

"I don't understand how your bond works," Clara said. "It's been a long time since we've seen a Well-blessed union—perhaps hundreds of years—so I can't tell you why this is happening. But I can tell you that there are rumors of other Guardians bonded like you. The wolves are whispering from pack to pack. When you're finished in this town, I suggest you find them. They will teach you more about your bond."

The front door burst open. Moon and another large fae —the same one who'd pushed her when they'd arrived— carried a big, heavy, bullet riddled fae between them, his dark head hanging low.

Ada's heart clenched. *Jasper*.

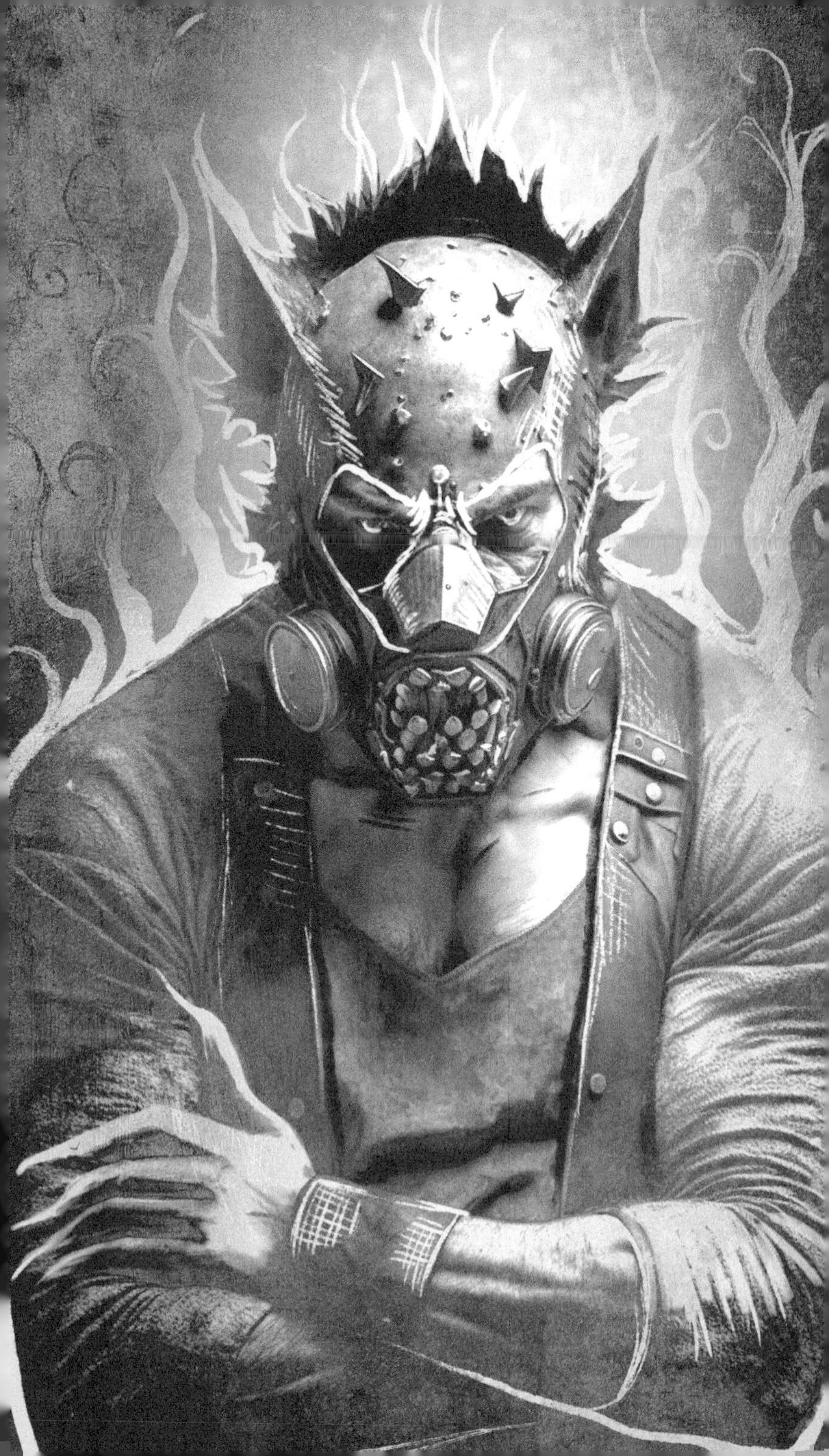

CHAPTER
SEVEN

Jasper dreamed of blood and fire. Crimson on his hands, in his mouth, and on his skin. Fire in his veins, arrowing toward his heart, burrowing closer with only one end in sight—and he welcomed it. He deserved it.

He was not brave. He was not kind. He was not worthy.

He'd taken so many lives... and the worst part was, he'd liked it. Or at least, his wolf had. Who could tell the difference these days? Flashes of the carnage at the Ring swam before his eyes, taunting him with his cowardice. The crowd cheering for it. All he'd needed to do was give in and let his opponents take his life instead of the other way around. His suffering would have been over. But on the day his mother had died, he'd promised to live.

So, while in the Ring, he'd submitted control of his

body to his wolf—that primordial part of him with the hunger for blood—every Well-damn time.

Tiny fingers curled and covered in blood.

"No!" he bellowed.

Tiny fingers touching his chest.

"Get off!" He shoved.

Chains held him back. He whipped his head to the side—not chains, a big hand. To the other side—a large hand, one of the guards. He *bellowed*. Another on his abdomen, moving with the rise and fall of his heaving breath, then sliding over to a bloody wound.

Tiny fingers tested the tiny wounds in his chest.

Tears burned his eyes, and he choked.

"*No!*" He thrashed his head, took gulping breaths until he had the power to shout. "*Leave it in.* I want the suffering to end."

"Jasper."

Her voice. His angel calling through the water.

"It's okay, Jasper."

"No," he grunted. "Leave it in."

The icy burn in his body arrowing toward his heart. He knew what it was. He'd felt it so many times. Usually it pierced into either side of his neck, halting his transformation, ensuring when he killed it wasn't all wolf, but part him, part the fae who was once worthy, who was once kind and fun and brave.

"I deserve it," he moaned through the agony swamping

his senses, slicing his veins open as the metal reached for his heart. "Just leave it in. Let it take me."

Finally.

He dropped his head back. It clunked on something hard.

"I'm getting it out."

She's stubborn, his wicked angel.

Scorching pain in his pectoral, under his rib. She followed the flight of the bullet deep inside him. He shouted, knocked her tiny fingers away and roared his fury with great trembling fangs and dripping saliva.

Large brown eyes glistened. Blond hair. Perfect plump lips opened into the shape of an O.

"Leave me," he begged.

His limbs felt heavy. His head lolled to the side. Fog curled into his mind and, he thought, at least he'd done something right before he died. He'd put his clawed fist through every single raiding human he could find until their blood had painted the street. They would never get the metal to make more killing pellets like the ones lodged in his chest.

He would never give them an advantage over fae land. He would never let them take control of the Well. It was his job. His duty. And he'd at least done some of it. At least he remembered that.

"Jasper, look at me." Cool fingers touched his stubbled jaw.

He squeezed his eyes shut.

Then... soft pressure at his lips. Movement. Kissing. She tasted like sugar and sin, like everything his body wanted, but his soul didn't deserve. She kept pressing her lips to his, and he felt... he felt—compassion, kindness and hidden yearning scorch down their bond. It struck him deeply. It stoked the fire inside until he felt the echo of her desire become a raging furnace of want. He opened to her kiss, welcomed her with a groan full of longing and need. His tongue delved inside her mouth, tasting her life-giving flavor that frenzied every cell of his body. She pulled back, and he chased her, nipping the air between them. Beautiful. She tasted like his. Like... mana-berries and cider and everything nice.

More.

Straining to reach her, he tried to capture her lips again, but almost fell from the table he lay on. Pain stabbed his middle as he settled into a sitting position.

Her small, teasing smile. "If I'd had known that's all it took to make you fall in line, I would have kissed you a while ago."

He growled in warning.

"You want it so bad, let me get the bullets out so you can heal. Then you can have another kiss."

He licked parched lips, bit back his hunger, glanced down at the bloody mess on his torso, and saw the room for the first time. It was filled with injured fae, two of which held him down by the shoulders, and Ada... his beautiful... what was she? His mate? A distraction? A reprieve until he finally caught the oblivion he didn't deserve?

If his memories were true, then he'd committed the most heinous atrocities known to Elphyne. He'd brutalized and killed for entertainment in the gladiator pit that served as a corporal punishment in Cornucopia, the border town between the Seelie and Unseelie kingdoms.

"Jasper." She patted his chest.

He met her gaze and could feel hope trickling down their connection. She wanted to help him, to keep him alive. He didn't have the heart to disappoint her.

He may as well add cowardice to his list of failures because, when his gaze dropped to her lips, all he wanted in that moment was another taste of her sugar. The idea consumed him.

Damn, he was so weak.

Swallowing hard, he set himself down on the table and looked hard at the ceiling. He clutched the table's edge with each hand and readied himself, then nodded. Bone deep agony filled his body as she hunted the cold, killing metal, but he didn't scream, didn't cry out. This was his penance, or the beginning of it. Maybe this never-ending wretched life of shame and regret was his worth.

The notion took root in his heart, and when she stripped the last metal pellet from his body, he knew it was true. Happiness was not reserved for someone broken like him.

Feeling the connection to the Well spring to life in his

blood, he siphoned Ada's mana down their bond and shifted into wolf form. A flash of guilt stabbed him at taking something she hadn't offered, at seeing her eyes flutter because he was draining her, but he was beyond shame now. What was one more act of cowardice?

The wolf took over—just like it had always managed the preservation of his life—and Jasper's consciousness faded. He lay on his side, panting heavily as his body repaired, and when tiny fingers stroked his face and scratched behind his ear, he turned away with a small whine. He retreated into the locked cage of his mind, knowing it didn't matter which part of him reigned. Whether it was the primal instincts of his wolf, or his fae logic, it was all him. There was no escaping what he'd done.

⚖

Jasper awoke to the sound of a crackling fire. Other strange sounds filtered in—the slow tinkling of wind chimes, the soft regular breathing of another, and the musky scent of female. The heat of a body pressed close. His lashes lifted to find a dim, softly furnished room flickering from firelight. Stone walls plastered with mosaics depicting scenes of black wolves chasing dark-haired maidens, catching them. He'd seen those images before, on the outside of the great hall... and... perhaps somewhere in his memory.

His gaze swept to the sleeping blond-haired angel

nestled within the curve of his body—his furred body. He was in wolf form. The awareness settled on him with the accompanying thought that she would only sleep with him in this form, so he should stay.

Resting his head back down, he pushed his awareness around his body. No longer did he feel the sting of injury, and no longer did he feel the emptiness of having spent his mana stores. Enough time must have passed that he'd been refilled by the Cosmic Well. Usually it took the passing of the moon to soak up mana from the earth. Finding a source of power could replenish him within minutes. Maybe he'd discovered a source and had soaked in it. Or maybe it was her.

How did he know that?

His memories were seeping back into him, that's how, and he wasn't sure he wanted them to.

His lids drooped again as he languished in the comfort of his position. She might wake soon. She might try to peel more of the curse away.

But she couldn't see it through the fur covering his body.

So he stayed wolf.

And he dreamed.

"Why is he after us, Mama?" he asked and plopped another picked berry into her wicker basket as they strode from manaberry bush to blackcurrant.

Her elegant fingers paused over an overripe berry, then she twisted it on the stem and added it to their growing collection.

"Because I did something I wasn't allowed to do," she replied.

"What?" he asked, this time, plopping the berry into his mouth, letting the tart juices explode on his tastebuds. He licked his lips. "Mmm."

Again, she held her tongue, but he wanted to know.

"Mama? Why?"

She placed her basket on the floor and crouched low to touch his cheek. She smiled warmly.

"Because, my love, I chose you over him. There's not a day that goes by that I'm not thankful for that decision. You are going to make many people very happy. You will save lives."

His skin suddenly felt tight, his body too big. "Me?"

"Yes, my love. You."

"How do you know?"

"Because the Well showed me."

"I don't want to make everyone happy, Mama. Just you."

He lifted his chin proudly and went to another bush to snap a berry off, but before it could enter his gaping mouth, she pushed it away.

"No!" she cried. "Not those berries."

Tears burned his eyes at the shock. What had he done? His bottom lip trembled as she took his hands in hers.

"I'm sorry, my love, but you must never eat those berries. They addle the mind."

"Sun said they were fun. Why is that so bad?"

"Sun's head is full of wool."

"But you said fun is good."

She sighed. "Yes, but it's a fine line between fun and wasting your life pretending it doesn't exist. Just... don't waste for too long."

CHAPTER EIGHT

"Not a nasty cut," Ada said, inspecting Primrose's finger wound.

Like the last two patients Ada had received today, she had the sense Primrose was there to inspect Ada, not the other way around. Two twitching, pointed, and lightly furred ears poked out from beneath long wavy blond hair tied at Primrose's nape. White baker's flour dusted her form fitting dress. She appeared in her late twenties but could be as old as Clara—somewhere in the hundreds of years. Somehow, that unsettled Ada more than knowing the female shifter had come to snoop.

"I honestly don't know how I did it. It's so silly of me," Primrose said.

Sure you don't.

It had been two days since the raid, and while most

injured fae had been treated, a trickle of snoops kept coming in. Ada couldn't blame them. She looked like the enemy, yet she had a gift reserved for the fae. But if they were snooping, they were curious, not angry. She could deal with that.

Ada smiled gently. "Don't worry. Accidents happen to the best of us."

"I was so busy with preparations for Lupercalia that I wasn't watching what I was doing. I'm the official baker, you know."

"Congratulations." Ada still wasn't clear about the festival, but knew the village had been preparing for weeks, and still had a few days to go before the big event.

Ada focused her awareness on the shallow finger cut, feeling it out with her sixth sense, seeing if she could coax the broken skin back together. Clara had kept up her tuition over the past few days and was keen to keep teaching all she knew about healing, which wasn't much, but it was better than nothing. Apparently Fenrysfield had no official healer. Since most of them shifted, one wasn't really needed.

"It looks pretty shallow to me. Is there a reason you're not shifting to heal it?" *Or putting up with it?*

Primrose's posture stiffened. Tension sliced through the air.

In the background, Clara's actions grew inexplicably louder as she cleaned and restocked the room. She must have heard Ada's question because she came over carrying her bowl of fresh water.

"You must be patient with Ada, Prim. She doesn't quite understand the intricacies of fae manners." To Ada, she added, "Prim is Lesser Fae, meaning she doesn't hold enough mana to shift or to harness. She was just born like that. There's nothing she can do about it, but it doesn't do to talk about it in front of her face. There are many other Lesser Fae in all races. If a fae can't shift or cast, then it's not up to us to pry." Clara looked back at Primrose's finger. "Ensure you keep going until every bit of flesh knits together. You've got time."

Ada bit back words about Clara doing exactly what she'd just told Ada not to do—talk about the Lesser Fae in front of her face.

But there was so much to learn. If no one talked about it, Ada would continue to be ignorant, and in the days since waking in this time, she'd accepted her new reality. She needed to blend in.

Ada's brain hurt. There were many new cultural idiosyncrasies she wasn't sure she'd ever learn. And this was just a shifter village. Apparently, there were different customs within different fae races all around Elphyne.

They ranged from horned and antlered fae, to pixies with dragonfly wings, to elves, vampires, and more. The list was never-ending.

Clara swapped Ada's dirty bowl with the clean one and then continued around the room, replenishing stock, as if she hadn't just dropped the most awkward bomb in the room, and then headed toward the exit.

Prim's pointed ears flattened as Clara passed. *Interesting*. Ada was fast learning that a particular pattern of ear behavior had either something to do with aggression or submission. It was much like the natural behavior of the wolves they shifted into.

Clara stopped at the door before leaving and turned to Ada. "We must be patient with you, but also remember to be patient with us too. Change takes time. For both sides."

Ada watched the empty space Clara left for a long moment, wondering if she'd said something to make Clara think Ada was impatient. But perhaps it was just a friendly warning.

"This might feel a bit warm," Ada said as she went back to the wound.

"Can you fix me?" Prim blurted. "I mean, give me the ability to shift?"

So that was why she came.

"I don't think so," Ada said slowly, thinking about it. "As far as I know, it's beyond the scope of my gift. But I'm only just learning. Clara said I should head toward the, um, Order of the Well, or one of the Elven Courts to train from the best. I don't really know what that means yet, but it's a start. Who knows what my gift could do after I receive more training."

Prim sighed. "That's okay. I thought it was worth a shot to ask. I didn't really want to ask around Clara. I know the Well is the only thing that can grant the capacity to hold mana within, and since I'm not as brave as your mate, I'll never enter the ceremonial lake. I'll just have to keep making do without it."

Ada frowned. "Did he not have mana before entering the lake? Or is that rude of me to ask too?"

"Unlike some others around here, I'm not as concerned with stuffy manners and tradition. I don't mind if you ask me. How else are you supposed to learn? You know, Reed would have been the new alpha if it wasn't for... well, it's best I don't talk about that part. That's only gossiping." Prim's eyes turned distant and dreamy, and Ada felt a brief twinge of something she couldn't decipher as Prim explained. "He's the son of the King, so he had a good amount of mana to start. We used to play together as children. He always had a bigger capacity for holding mana, but then he joined the Guardians. And now—" Her eyes snagged on Ada's Well-blessed markings. "Now I suppose he has you. I know my wound isn't big, but I wanted an excuse to meet you. If there's anything you want to know about, well, anything, I hope you ask me." She straightened. "Maybe come down to the bakery where we can talk more freely. I can show you around."

Ada finished healing the cut and stood back. Maybe Prim wasn't so uptight as she'd initially thought, and Ada needed a friend. Clara was the alpha and not exactly easy to approach. Primrose's big eyes blinked with such earnest regard that Ada couldn't help smiling.

"Sure, I'd like that. It's definitely hard being someone who looks like the enemy around here."

"I know what it feels like to be the outsider, don't worry, and I've lived here all my life." Her gaze dipped to Ada's neck, then back up to meet her eyes. "While we're being honest, if you don't mind me asking, why is it that your mate hasn't marked you?"

"Marked me?"

"Yes, well, shifters mark their mates. On the neck." She pointed to Ada's bare neck. "With their teeth."

Ada's hand fluttered to her neck. "Why would they do that?"

"It's a sign of possession. Don't humans do that?"

"No." Ada's brows lifted, derisively. "No, we don't maim each other to prove ownership."

Prim's nose crinkled. "Oh, I didn't say he owned you. Just that... well, yes, I suppose it is like ownership. But he also belongs to you. His scent and mark on you proves to all the other potential mates that you're both taken."

Ada snorted, about to make some female empowerment speech, but then realized the marking could be construed as something similar to an engagement or wedding ring. So this was some kind of arranged marriage. The very idea of having that choice taken away from her made her squirm.

"Jasper and I aren't in that kind of relationship," she explained with a tight smile.

"Oh."

Prim opened her mouth to say more, but movement at the door nabbed both their attentions. A tall shifter walked in. Messy brown hair brushed his collar. A black tattoo curled up his neck on one side. Just the hint of the hilt from his bone sword poked over a brown, leather clad shoulder. Ada remembered him as the other shifter who'd brought Jasper in to get treated during the raid.

"Sun," Prim said as she got to her feet and raised her brows, unimpressed. "I'm not done with the human. Your turn is coming."

The human?

Sun smirked and leaned his lithe body against the doorjamb. "I'll just wait here then, shall I?"

Prim made a frustrated sound and then rolled her eyes. "I suppose I am done here, then. The test cakes need to come out of the oven." She touched Ada's arm and her tone turned syrupy sweet. "Don't forget to come down to the bakery."

She left with a suspicious side-eye turned Sun's way, and an extra sway in her step. Ada got the impression those two enjoyed picking at each other's threads to see who would unravel first. There was a history there. Maybe they'd dated once. Sun pushed off the door and strode into the room. He glanced about, searching for someone, and then sat on the chair Prim had vacated.

Ada washed her hands in the bowl. "You're the last one waiting, right?"

He shrugged.

There was something so familiar about him, more so than the fact Ada had already met him a few nights ago.

"What can I help you with?" she asked, giving him a once over in case he was injured.

"I'm here because my mother is too stubborn to ask you something."

"Okay." She stood back. "Who's your mother?"

He arched his brow as if Ada should know. "Clara."

"Oh." Now it was making sense why he was so familiar. That dark hair. That devil-may-care expression. Clara was Jasper's aunt, which made Sun Jasper's cousin. And Moon. "My goodness. Moon is also Clara's son?"

Ada's mind went back to how Clara had been prepared to accept her son's initial prognosis, but Ada had saved his life.

"That's why she doesn't want to ask you this. She feels as though she's already in debt to you, and all you've asked for is a room and some training in return for the lives you saved."

"I don't want anything in return. Saving lives shouldn't come at a price."

Sun rubbed his jaw and scrutinized Ada. All fae seemed to want something in return for a good deed. Keeping track was getting tiresome, but maybe Ada could see how the cultural expectation had formed. In a ruthless post-apocalyptic world, when the economy had shut down, favors could be currency.

"So," Ada said. "She's sent you because if you ask me

for the favor, then it's you who will owe me the debt? If there even is one."

He smiled, slow and pleased. "Now you're catching on."

"Okay. So what is it?"

"Lupercalia is in a few nights' time. We want you and Reed be our guests of honor."

"That's it?" she asked. "No kidney? No blood transfusion?"

When Sun stared at her blankly, she elaborated. "I was expecting some sort of mammoth quest."

"Lupercalia is a time-honored tradition that we haven't been able to follow until a recent change in the law a few weeks ago. It's been a long time since our crops were plentiful. We've been plagued with mana-warped monsters, both in the river and in the woods surrounding our village. All our coin has been taxed by the Order for the culling of these monsters. And as you've seen firsthand, we're being targeted for raids, and the High King has failed to come to our aid. Our luck is running out. During Lupercalia, we make tribute to the Well and pray for our seed to be blessed for the coming harvest. Clara believes since you're Well-blessed, and your timely arrival saved so many lives, that the Well would look favorably on us this year if you and Reed honor us as Luperci."

After that speech, how could she say no?

"Sure. Well, I can't really speak for Jasper—I mean, Reed. But I can ask him."

"We would have a better outcome if the question came from you."

"Is there something else you're not telling me?"

"One of the last traditional Lupercalia festivals was when the King set his sights on Reed's mother. She had Reed after that and hid it from the King. We used to have a Seer in the village who'd prophesied one of the King's offspring would take over his throne and be the end of him. When Mithras found out about Reed, he came for them. Reed escaped. His mother didn't." He took a deep inhale, then let the air out slowly. "Clara pretends the reason there's bad blood between us and Reed is because he left to join the Guardians. But we all know it's because she feels guilty she couldn't keep him safe. For an alpha to admit that would be akin to acknowledging a debt."

"And Fae hate to be in debt."

"Exactly."

"So, if he participates at Lupercalia, it's a bridge mended. For both sides."

"An answer tonight would be great." Sun stood and gave Ada's shoulder a lingering touch. "And if my cousin doesn't grow some balls and show his face soon, I'll be happy to take his place as one of the Luperci with you."

He shot her a smirk, and then sauntered away, leaving her confused.

"Um." Ada lifted her finger to stop him, but he'd already gone. "What's a Luperci?"

Somehow, she had the sense she would not like it. Her

mind already traveled back to that cult that worshiped linen clothing.

Ugh. Come on, Ada. Get your head in the game.

She guessed she would find out on the night, or maybe Prim would tell her. The Luperci duties couldn't be too hard to fulfill, and they wouldn't put one of their own in danger. Jasper was a Darkfoot. He grew up in this town. If they wanted them as special guests, then it must be a good thing.

Maybe Jasper's memories had returned enough for him to know. With that thought, Ada packed up as best she could, and after waiting for Clara, who never showed, she decided she would head back to the inn. Night was falling and the tavern's meat stew called to her. It tasted so much like regular beef, and not wolpertinger meat, that she felt like it was a slice of home. A small smile played on her lips when she thought of what Laurel would say if Ada ordered the meal at a restaurant.

"Pretty Kitty, again? Really? You eat cow every time we get take out."

And then Clarke would pop her soda can in Laurel's face and the two of them would make extra yummy sounds as they enjoyed their "unhealthy" vices.

Ada was still smiling when she returned to the inn, a quaint two-story mosaicked stone and terracotta establishment. Before she went in, she emptied a piece of fish she'd had in her bag and put it in a small basket by the doorway. A meow and a growl later, and a cat-like creature she'd been told was a fee-lion meandered up and snatched the fish away. Apparently if Ada showed too much attention, the fee-lion wouldn't leave Ada alone, but she didn't care. The animal had looked a bit too skinny when she'd first arrived.

Once satisfied the animal had been fed, she pushed through the heavy front door, went upstairs and entered their room. After the raid, Clara had insisted she cover the cost of the room as a gesture of gratitude for their help against the humans. The assumption was that their Well-blessed marks kept Ada and Jasper together. Ada had felt awkward asking for a separate room and couldn't impose more on their hospitality, so had remained tight-lipped. As it turned out, it was a good thing she'd stayed with Jasper. He didn't seem mentally well and had remained in wolf form for much of the time.

"Honey, I'm home," she joked.

Unsurprisingly, Jasper's dark wolf form reclined by the fireplace. Since the fire had stayed alight all day, and there were no sprites—she'd politely declined when the innkeeper had offered some—to maintain the blaze, she knew he'd transformed into fae form during the day. How else would he have placed fresh wood on the hearth?

He may have kept the fire going during the day, but now it fizzled. Probably because he'd known she would return soon and stoke the flames back to life. Ada sighed and went over to a stacked pile of logs and threw one in.

Sparks flew from the embers and drifted like lazy fireflies before settling down.

She watched Jasper for a few minutes until she decided he would not shift into fae form and say hello. Just like the other nights she'd arrived home, he stayed in his wolf form and would most likely stay like that until she left the following morning. It wasn't right, but she was still learning about the customs of this world. Perhaps staying in wolf form was something they did after being injured, although, she hadn't seen Moon do the same and his injuries had been debatably worse than Jasper's.

Unless Ada wanted to reveal Jasper's condition to a town already afraid to owe her a debt, she had to keep this to herself. She didn't trust them, and after the conversation with Sun, they weren't quite ready to trust her either.

Ada cleaned up and then went back downstairs to the tavern for a meal. It was still early enough that patrons were yet to crowd the room, and the scent of that stew was fresh in the air. Ada's mouth watered as she walked up to the bar. The top of a shifter's head could be seen as he, or she, tended to something beneath the bar. Upon Ada's approach, the bartender stood. He had a mop of brown hair and was long and gangly. His ears flattened upon seeing Ada's round ears, but then his eyes tracked to the marks on her arms and the tension in his shoulders released.

"You must be Reed's lady."

"That's debatable," she replied wryly.

A confused look flitted over his expression, and Ada realized that associating herself with Reed wasn't a bad thing in this place. They felt more at ease knowing she belonged to him, whether it was true or not. And if they were at ease, then they weren't frightened or aggressive.

"I'm Ada," she said and gave a small wave.

"The name's Puck. The innkeeper's nephew."

"Nice to meet you."

"Can I help you with something?" he asked.

"I'd like some of that delicious smelling stew please. Two servings." Ada dug around in her pocket for some coin Clara had given her earlier in the day.

She placed all the glass coins onto the counter and dragged her bottom lip through her teeth. She had no idea how much each coin was worth. A few were clear, and one was blue. All had the etching of an M in the middle.

"You want anything to drink with the stew?" Puck asked.

"What do you recommend?"

Puck scratched his head and studied her. "Well, I don't know what you humans like to drink, but we don't carry no elixirs in this inn. Uncle doesn't like them. Says they cause mischief and ruckus and only attract the kind of clientele Rosebud Courtesans like to service. He don't want none of that here. We're a family establishment. If you know what I mean."

Yeah, sure. Ada knew exactly what he meant. At her

blank look, Puck elaborated and pointed at three terracotta jugs. "We have cider, ale, and lemon water."

"Right. I'll take two lemon waters, please."

He gave her a short smile, then pointed at the coins on the counter. "Two clear will suffice. The blue is worth ten of the clear, then the gold is worth ten of the blue. Red coin is the most. You ever get your hands on one of those beauties and you use it wisely."

With a blush of gratitude, she separated two and slid them across to him, then touched her fingers to her lips and pushed them down and out, signing her thanks.

"Don't mention it." He gave her another thoughtful look then said, "Anyone who saved Moon's life is welcome here."

The kind words made her blush further and she felt a little more closer to home. Clarke probably would have said something about there being no such thing as free advice, but then again, if Clarke were here, maybe she'd be different too. God knew Ada was becoming a different person. Someone who wanted to belong more than she wanted isolation, and that frightened her more than anything because the moment you made friends, there was the potential for them to be ripped away.

A loud burst of chattering voices boomed into the room as a group of fae entered the tavern. Two tall males and a short, rotund female. They all stopped short upon seeing Ada.

Her cheeks heated and she turned back to Puck. "Could you make that order to-go?"

Puck's lips pinched. "Like I said, you're welcome here."

She signed her thanks again, but then shrugged. "I need to take it back to the room. For Jasper, I mean Reed."

He gave a curt nod. "I won't be long."

Ada stood awkwardly to the side, both wanting to say hello to the newcomers at the same time as wanting to run upstairs to their room. Since no one approached, or even acknowledged her, she said nothing either. By the time Puck returned with her meal on a tray, she smiled briefly at him and then bid him goodnight.

When she got back to the room and found Jasper sleeping, her shoulders drooped. That longing for friends gnawed at her and she couldn't deny she felt it more around Jasper. After eating the meal, and waiting to see if he would wake, she went to the toilet and then curled up next to him with a pillow and blanket pulled from the unused double bed. He stirred as she laid down, but just snuffled into her neck, licked her, and then went back to sleep. A flitter of relief mixed with anguish filtered down their bond. He wanted her there, but still refused to talk to her, or anyone else. If she couldn't get him down to this Lupercalia festival in a few days, then everyone would know.

Jasper didn't seem the kind to be okay with his secrets splashed about town. It must be the curse keeping him like this. If she could only get beyond his fur to the curse marks, she might ease some of his pain. Something tragic had happened in his past that he didn't want to remember, but pretending it didn't happen would only make things worse.

"Oh, Jasper. What are we going to do with you?" she murmured as her lids grew heavy.

A little whimper-sigh was her reply.

CHAPTER
NINE

After a few long days at the clinic with Clara, Ada returned to their room at the inn, carrying a bundle of clothes they were to put on for the Lupercalia festival.

It was tonight. And with most of the villagers now healed, her time at the makeshift clinic was up. After tonight, her future hung in the balance. She could either stay here or move on and find someone else to teach her.

They'd been living in the inn for the past week, and while Ada's relationship had grown with the townspeople, she hadn't the courage to let Clara know Jasper was very likely not going to make it to their all-important festival unless he trotted over in wolf form.

She stopped inside the door and closed it gently behind her. Jasper wasn't by the fire as he'd normally slept.

Surprise curled through her. Maybe he'd emerged finally, after all. The fire had extinguished, and with no candles lit, it was hard to see through the dim room. The smell of wolf tickled her nose along with a hint of something sweet she couldn't place.

She went to the lone window, pulled back the drapes, and cracked the glass pane. Afternoon light and fresh air rushed in and pushed the staleness out. The wind chimes synonymous with the village tinkled outside the window. Ada glanced down at the street a level below. Fae milled about, putting the finishing touches on tonight's festival decorations, stringing garlands and bunting between buildings, and setting out bowls of floating glowing balls used as a light source. The same glowing balls would float inside glass lanterns dangling from the garlands once dusk fell.

The balls were manabeeze, the mana essence of all fae after they died. Ada had asked Clara whether they worried the manabeeze contained the fae's soul, and if they were disrespecting it by using the manabeeze as a source of energy. She'd just looked at her oddly. From what Ada had gathered, they believed mana was just part of the Well. It resided in their bodies for a while and then returned to the cosmic energy of the Well in death. There was no personal attachment to it.

Unless, of course, you ingested a manabee. Then you relived memories of the life form it came from.

After the raid, they'd postponed the festival for as long as they could, but being a celebration of the end of winter and the start of a new life, they had to do it soon. Apparently, this was the first time they'd celebrated the traditional Lupercalia for hundreds of years. There had been some kind of law that prohibited parts of it until recently, and they were excited to have the guests of honor—a prince and his Well-blessed mate.

Now that some light had been let in, Ada searched for Jasper and found him naked and twisted in the sheets of the double bed he'd not slept in until now. He must have forgotten to shift back into a wolf.

She paused and let that fact sink in. She'd suspected he shifted into fae form during the day, but over the past week hadn't seen it once. Why today?

Did he know about their roles at the festival, or was he always like this when she left the room? A dark thought teased her—maybe he was always in wolf form when she came back because it was his friendly way of telling her to leave. After all, she had given him the kiss she thought he wanted, teased him with another, and yet he'd failed to claim more.

He either didn't care for it, or there was something else going on and, to be honest, she was thinking he didn't even want her help. If that was the truth, then it was time for her to leave. Her traveling feet were calling. Being in one place for so long wasn't really her thing. Back in Vegas, she'd had an apartment in the city, but also one near a state park where she worked with injured animals. Her time was spent between the two. Unlike Laurel and Clarke, who'd loved living in the city, and partying on the strip, Ada's idea of a good time was under the blue sky, smelling the rain on the pines, and listening to the cicadas on a warm day. Moving kept her from thinking too hard about life.

One thing was for sure, she would not stick around if she wasn't needed or wanted.

She perched herself on the edge of the bed. Jasper's even breathing continued. The moment her palm landed on the hard slab of muscle on his scarred back, her tension fled and she felt a rush of compassion. This was a brutal world. She'd learned some of its history from Prim while visiting the bakery this morning. She'd told Ada of how after the bombs went off in Ada's time, life was cutthroat for the survivors. And then the primordial Well bubbled to life, reclaiming the land and its inhabitants. When humans realized some were merging with animal and plant life, becoming fae for the sake of surviving the harsh unfamiliar landscape, they quarantined themselves in fear behind the walls of what has now become Crystal City. Because the city was on desecrated land filled with metal and plastic, the Well couldn't flow there, and no one changed to fae. They remained human, untouched by the Well.

While humans had cloistered themselves in fear, the fae had become the custodians of the new land. Food was hard to find, at first. Survival in the cold extremes of the nuclear winter was even harder. Two thousand or so years had passed since Ada's friends had breathed their last breath. Perhaps more from her time had awoken in Elphyne, like Ada, but she wouldn't know anything unless she started searching for answers. And, unfortunately, she couldn't do that until she was sure Jasper was okay.

It had crossed her mind more than once to find the Order of the Well—the experts in all things magical—and these other rumored Well-blessed mated couples, but every time she'd convinced herself she owed no loyalty to this town or to Jasper, she found a reason to stay. Fae had opened up to her. They trusted her now. Clara wasn't the only one who'd taught her about the rules of the Well. Soon she'd feel confident to ask for more history on the humans of this time, and try to figure out how she fit into the grand scheme of things.

And Jasper was hurt. His injury might not be one of the body anymore, but his mind still healed. A person who wanted to die was someone who thought he had nothing to live for.

She couldn't leave him. At least not until she knew that he would not find another piece of metal and find a way to leave it in.

Inspecting the curse marks on his body, she felt the wrongness in them—the griminess. They extended from his front to the back where more scars puckered. Some scars were great slices. Others were slashes as though he'd been whipped.

"You know," she said to his sleeping form. "Moon's brother is called Sun. Did you also know that they're Clara's children and your cousins?" She gave a soft snort. She started picking at his markings, this time feeling out the curse with her sixth sense, probing it for weaknesses. She'd learned that the Well felt pure, warm and bright. Places where it didn't flow were cold, and then there was what lay beneath these blue curse marks—the dark, grimy ink.

"I wonder if Moon or Sun have children and if they're named after stars or planets. Do people even know about the planets now? Jeez. Never thought of that. How much knowledge has been lost since our time?" She took a deep breath and exhaled. "I also learned about the King, and what he did to your mother. I'm... at a loss for words at what to say. It must have been horrible for you at that age to have thought the only way you could survive was to jump in a dangerous lake that takes more lives than it saves. You know, I didn't have a great childhood either." She peeled off a curse piece and wiped the black ooze it left with her sleeve. He made no move, so she continued with a frown. "My mother didn't care enough to feed me. She preferred to go out partying with her boyfriends. I learned from a young age to look after myself."

She picked off another strip of blue, lifting it from his skin and adding it to a growing pile at her side.

"There was this old cantankerous man who'd stumbled across me when I got lost in the woods the first time. He was the scariest thing an eleven-year-old girl could see, but the weird thing was, he was so kind. He taught me a lot about surviving in the wild. I guess, maybe he'd been avoiding people too. Harold was his name. I used to call him Har-*old* when he used to give me shit about doing something wrong." She laughed softly, a pang of affection rising at his memory. "He had hair coming out of his nose, and wrinkles that made his eyes sloped. He knew how to chop the tail off a scorpion so you could eat the rest. He knew how to fish. And he knew how to hunt." Another blue strip came off. "And he taught me how to read, math basics, and about economics, of all things. I certainly learned never to judge a book by its cover with him."

Jasper remained still, so she kept going. She supposed she should take advantage of him sleeping through the process. The more she removed, the quicker he would regain his memories, and the sooner she could leave.

"You don't get many old people here. I mean, they're old. Clara told me she's a few hundred years of age—maybe close to five hundred, can you believe it? She also said you're a few hundred as well, but she's lost count over time. So you're all super geriatric, but none of you look it. It's so weird." More strips, more blue, more inky ooze. Her voice grew quiet. "A few days ago I saw some human corpses... what was left of them... and some of them were old and wrinkled. So, they definitely age. I asked Clara about it and she said it was the access to the Well that kept fae young. It was a reward for living in harmony with the planet. I like that idea. I can see why you're all more protective of the environment... you're actually around to see the changes bad choices cause."

A piece of blue resisted, but she gripped tight and yanked as though it was a wax strip on her leg. It ripped off.

Jasper flinched, and then went so still, his breathing stopped. Power rippled in the air and the sense of danger loomed. Her heart rate picked up speed. Suddenly, Jasper rolled from his back, captured the wrist of her hand holding the strip and bared his sharp teeth. Flushed and feverish eyes glared at her through dark lashes. Tousled hair draped over his forehead. A full dark beard covered his sharp jaw. Rose tinted his cheekbones. It was hard not to be attracted to him.

"I told you not to remove it," he growled. "I don't *want* to remember."

"Tough titties," she replied and wrested her hand from his iron grip. "You've wallowed for long enough."

"You have no idea what you're talking about."

She arched a brow. "Maybe I don't, but that's because you're not sharing with me. All I know is that wasting your life by pretending it doesn't exist is no way to survive."

All the signs pointed to him being healthy enough in body, so this was some kind of depression. Maybe this kick in the butt wouldn't be enough, but it was a start. It was all she knew how to do.

He blinked at her. Some sort of recognition ghosted in his eyes and then it went. He shoved her away, and she almost fell off the feather filled mattress. He stumbled to his feet, giving her a flash of well-muscled posterior before staggering to the bathroom door, flinging it wide open, and relieving himself in the toilet, one hand on his—*ahem*. The other hand braced on the wall.

"A hello would be nice!" she shouted, averting her gaze.

The sound of urine cascading into water made her blink, stupefied.

"Guess some things never change, no matter how much time has passed," she muttered, then huffed and straightened the bed, taking her anger out on the sheets. "Being a dickhead must be ingrained so deeply into the male psyche that it survived a holocaust and the mutation of DNA."

At least they had plumbed sewage in this town. Some places in Elphyne weren't so lucky, she'd been told.

When she moved the sheet, two berries tumbled out of a purple stained area. She picked them up and smelled them. Mana-berries? What were they doing there?

Jasper had staggered to the bathroom.

"Are you fucking kidding me?" She squished the berries. "No wonder you've been sleeping for days. You've been *high*."

His lazy-lidded glance over his shoulder made her think he was still high. Then he kicked the bathroom door closed, blocking her view.

She jumped to her feet, fuming.

"You know what?" she shouted at the door. "I don't even know why I'm sticking around. You don't want my help, fine. After this Lupercalia festival thing is over, I'm out of here."

"You're not going anywhere." His deep voice permeated the wooden door, rattling it.

The flush came, and the door flung open. He'd found a towel and had wrapped it around his waist, but the small thing barely came halfway down his thick thighs and split on one side from the lack of fabric. Still fever-eyed, he prowled toward her.

She folded her arms. "Ooh. I'm so afraid of you and your tiny towel."

He stopped before her and dipped his chin to meet her eyes. All humor dropped from his expression when he spoke. "You're not going anywhere because you belong to me, Ada."

Her fury was so sudden and strong that no logic could get through. When she finally moved her mouth, her words came out slow and steady through clenched teeth.

"I think maybe you're right. Removing those curse marks isn't a good idea because you're getting confused. I *belong* to myself."

What kind of arrogant asshole was he?

A prince. A king's son. That's who.

She was only now understanding what that meant. The Seelie High King of Elphyne. Half of the land was under his rule. He was the same king who'd instructed the town to hoard metal and then failed to protect them when humans came raiding. He'd also tried to assassinate his son. And Jasper was the guy who had been named as his heir. Maybe she'd been wrong, and there was another reason the King wanted Jasper dead. Maybe it was because he was a dickhead and the apple didn't fall far from the tree.

"Our union was chosen by the Well," Jasper declared, as though that excused everything.

"Yeah, about that," she said. "While you've been sleeping, I've been asking around, and no one has said that this union means we have to stick together. Prim said if I'm not marked on the neck by the bite of my mate's teeth, then I'm my own person."

"That's true for shifters." He blinked, shocked. "But a Well-blessed union is held in the highest regard. There is no other mating more revered. Marking you with my teeth is purely to satisfy my wolf. If I have to mark you that way, I will."

Her brows lifted. "You'll do no such thing. There's no rule that says I belong to you, and there's no rule that says we have to be together sexually, and there's no rule that says we have to stick together. Fae-kind mate in many ways, and I'm pretty sure, *any* kind of mating is consensual for both parties. This"—she held up her arm—"was *not* consensual."

"I didn't choose it either, but I'm willing to accept it."

"You shouldn't have to! It should be something we choose."

He went to the window and flicked the drapes aside to peer outside with a scowl darkening his handsome face.

Ada pinched the bridge of her nose. Honestly, this festival couldn't come sooner. It was definitely time for her to leave and find her own way.

Jasper wasn't the worst sort to be stuck with. He looked great. He was a scary warrior who could protect her in a world she was fast learning was far more ruthless than the one she left. But they weren't suited to each other. She could never be with a person who insisted he knew what was better for her than her own desires. What was next, telling her how to dress and what to eat? No, thank you.

The sooner she could get away from all of this, the better.

"We have an hour to get ready." She picked up the bundle of clothes she'd left on the bed. "Clara said that because we're the Luperci, we have to wear these. Something to do with ritual and tradition."

She shook the dress out. It was similar to what many female shifters wore—loose, bone-colored, and made of linen. She'd been instructed to wear her hair out, and to go barefoot.

Ugh. Catching herself in a spiraling mood, she rubbed her face.

"I'm having a bath," she announced, and left him brooding by the window. As she closed the bathroom door, the last thing she saw was a small, smug smile curving his lips as he watched the festive lanterns go up.

CHAPTER TEN

Pounding on the bathroom door woke Ada with a jerk. Warm water sloshed over the bath lip and she slipped, barely grappling the edge before she dipped beneath the surface and dunked her head.

"Time to go," Jasper grumbled through the door.

Shit.

"I'll be right out," she called.

She must have fallen asleep. The water was just so warm. Heated by special mana-infused stones, it kept the temperature constant.

She pulled the plug and climbed out of the rose-scented water. She toweled off, ran her fingers through her long wavy hair and dried the damp ends as best she could. A quick check in the black-glass mirror over the wooden vanity showed her cheeks flushed from the heat. She dragged the loose dress over her head and let it drop. The bottom pooled on the floor, leaving a small train behind her. It was made for someone much taller, but it would have to do. The straps were thin, and the neck was a V-shape that dipped below her bust line, revealing more flesh. The same V left most of her back uncovered. She supposed, if a fae was to shift into a wolf, the wide neck would be easy to climb out of. Unimpressed, she plucked the fabric from her chest where it revealed the outline of her pebbled nipples. Bras and formfitting clothes just weren't a thing here. With a sigh of capitulation and a last check in the mirror, she opened the door and walked into the main room.

Jasper wore loose, cream linen pants and *no* shirt. He came right up to her, dipped his chin and looked into her eyes before saying succinctly, "Hello."

For a moment, Ada's mind muddled at his closeness. *Why is he being so obvious?* Then she remembered her offhand comment after he'd awoken and stormed off to the bathroom. *"A hello would be nice."*

Her lip twitched, wanting to smile. Was this his apology for being a dickhead? Instead, she pursed her lips and folded her arms.

"Do you ever wear a shirt?" she asked. "Or are you allergic?"

"No male will wear a shirt tonight," he said, and when she gave a questioning eyebrow, he added, "It's easier to shift without one."

"Of course. Makes sense."

Why shifting was involved in the festivities was beyond her, but in a town where they all turned into a wolf, maybe they howled at the moon or something. She'd not gleaned a lot from the townspeople, except that they were extremely excited. There would be much feasting, and much celebration. Sounded like a good old party. She could handle that.

Jasper itched the remaining curse marks on his neck with an agitated frown. Only half of what he'd originally had still remained. He still had a slight feverish look about him, but had found somewhere to clean up and shave his beard. His usual messy hair had been brushed, and she had a rare view of pointed ears twitching in irritation.

Ada glanced about the room and found it tidied. A used bowl of rosewater sat near the fireplace. Perhaps he'd called for some from the innkeeper. Ada tried to stifle her next words, but found she was helpless to ask. Just because he was stubborn, didn't mean she would be too.

"Have there been any ill effects from the latest curse mark removal?"

His sideways glance said there was, but when he clenched his jaw and faced the door, she knew he would never willingly confide.

"Memories?" she prompted. "Headaches?"

His fingers twitched at his side and she sensed a sliver of something she could only describe as need, or yearning, filter through their bond. It was as though he wanted to tell her something. Then he somehow clamped it down because it cut off. She narrowed her eyes at him. He'd never before hidden his *feelings*. This was new, and perhaps something he'd only just remembered how to do.

"Sit down," she said and pointed to the bed.

The look he gave her could have wilted a lesser woman, but she honestly didn't give a fuck. She meant what she'd said about leaving, and she was stubborn enough to do it. There was no way she'd stick around when she was treated like that. She raised her brow and waited.

One fur-tipped ear flicked back, and then he moved with a stiff gait to the bed. He sat down, placed his fists on his thighs and stared blankly ahead.

"I'm trying to help you, Jasper," she said, her tone clipped. "Have you got a problem accepting help?"

He squirmed.

Oh, shit. Maybe he did.

She pushed tension from her shoulders to reset her mood and then stepped up to his knees. Placing a palm on each shoulder, she pushed her awareness into his body and tried not to think about the virile, carved body staring her in the face. Damn him for being so annoyingly attractive.

She cleared her throat. "You may not know this, but while you were lazing about getting stoned on berries, I was learning how to use my gift. Clara's been teaching me, but I'm getting to the limits of her knowledge. Apparently, healers are rare among Mages, and even rarer in shifter villagers."

"I know," he grunted.

"You do?" That healers were rare or that Clara had been teaching her?

Long lashes flicked up, honeyed eyes clashed with hers, then lowered again. "I heard your stories when I was in wolf form."

So he had been listening to her nightly ramblings after all. She let go. Nothing was amiss in his body except the griminess she associated with the curse marks. Maybe a sluggishness she knew was linked to headaches, but that was most likely because of his recent habit. The effects of withdrawal weren't kind after any vice.

"So you have been ignoring me," she said.

"No... I've been—" He clamped his lips hard.

"Jasper." She sighed and looked at the ceiling. "You can't profess that we're meant to be together and then hide your feelings from me. I felt you shut them off, and to me, that feels like lying. I'm not going to stick around someone who's dishonest."

"I belong to you. Isn't that enough?"

She tensed. "Actions speak louder than words, and for the past week you've not acted like we're together."

Her shoulder lifted half-heartedly at his lack of response, but when her eyes drifted back down, she found he wasn't staring into the distance anymore, but straight ahead—at her chest. More specifically, the rise and fall of her breasts. She folded her arms and cocked a hip.

"Seriously?" she said. "I'm asking you to pour your heart out and you're drooling over my tits."

"Tits?" His gaze lifted to hers, a quirk to his full lips.

"Breasts." She waved at her own. "Whatever you call them in this time."

"I call them mine," his voice was low and raspy, and damn her, it triggered a bolt of traitorous heat straight through her core.

The cocky bastard knew it too. His eyes only grew heated as he drank in the sight of her body.

Having enough, she turned away, but he tugged her back by the hand. Dark desire washed over his features.

"You want to know why I've kept myself in wolf form? Why I've dulled my senses with mana-berries?"

"Yes!" It would be a start.

He slowly stood until he towered over her, and the impressive arousal tenting his pants jutted out, almost hitting her stomach. Down their bond, lust so raw and thick lashed at her. She staggered back until her shoulders hit the wall and her arm knocked the table holding the rosewater bowl. Her hand flew down to steady it.

Jasper prowled closer, sex written over his expression and in every line of his body.

"Since I first caught your scent, I've wanted you, pretty little human. I want to eat you, to lick you, to be inside you. Something about you calls to me. It's inexplicable, and it consumes my every waking moment. I don't need all my memories to know I've never felt this way before. I've hidden myself and dulled my senses because you're not ready for this. I can see it in your eyes."

He stopped a few inches from her. The heat of his body licked her front, scorching her skin. All she could see was his defined torso, ridged abdominals, and broad shoulders. Flashes of blue twinkled at her. Her eyes locked straight ahead.

Looking down would mean to acknowledge—she blushed. Nope. Not looking down.

Up meant being caught in the snare of his rich eyes.

To the side would be straight at the bulging biceps now caging her against the wall.

She swallowed.

He was right. She wasn't ready for what he felt. It was too real. Too soon. Too reliant on one person. A slash of pain pinged in her chest. She couldn't put all her eggs in one basket, because if it broke, she would too. She needed to find her feet in this world first. Despite her brain telling her this, her body wanted something else. It didn't care about waiting. It only wanted what was right here before her eyes.

Jasper dipped so his lips whispered hotly against her ear. "You forget, human, I sense your desire. I know what your body wants, even if your mind is still fighting it. You belong to me, but I also belong to you. I will never leave you. Never."

Her lashes fluttered closed. The smell of his sweet, rosewater-laced skin made her mouth water.

His teeth trailed along her neck. "I will protect you, feed you, pleasure you, revere you."

"We should go," she said without opening her eyes. "They're waiting for us."

A pause. His teeth rested on the tendon between her neck and shoulder. Then a rasping at her sides as his hands left the wall.

She opened her eyes and found he'd pushed back to study her with his head cocked to the side, ears pricked forward eagerly, a dark lock of brushed hair hanging across his forehead. She thought their encounter was over, but the moment she moved to leave, he said, "I'll be honest with you when you're honest with me."

Their gazes clashed, and he gave her a rakish grin full of secrets and dares. Her breath caught. It was a smile that powered a thousand stars. And then it was gone.

A wash of regret dipped in her belly as he walked to the door. She'd forgotten how his smile affected her, but her body hadn't. It made her think... what if? What if she let go and shared herself with him? What if he did the same?

I will never leave you. Never.

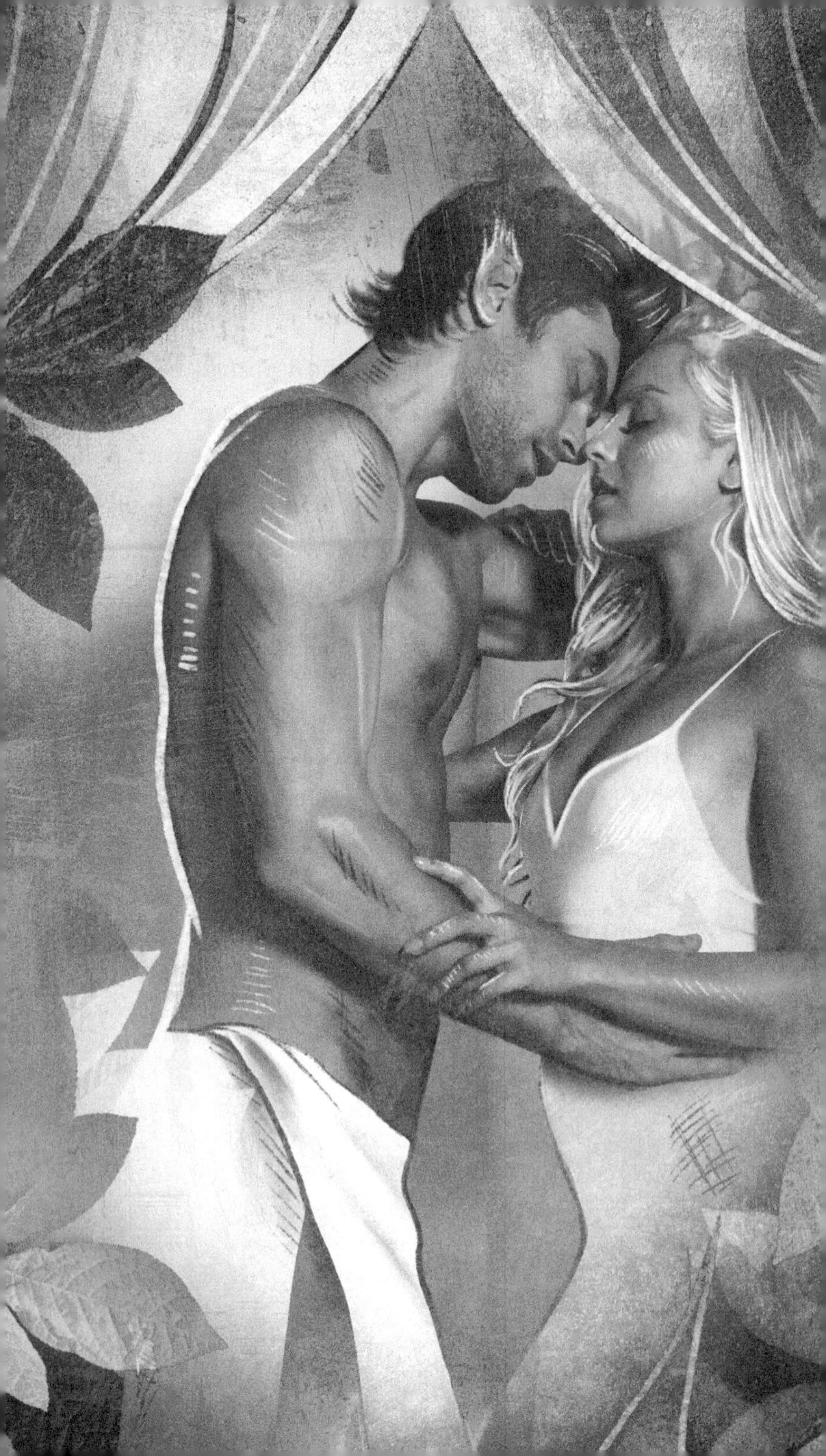

CHAPTER
ELEVEN

Jasper walked beside Ada down the lantern-lit main street. Trapped manabeeze buzzed and cast reflections on glass mosaic squares plastered to the sides of every building. The tinkling of chimes followed them, as did the footsteps of a small crowd of villagers that followed. It was as though the fae folk had been waiting in their homes to join them on the pilgrimage to the Luperci grotto.

He should be excited.

Lupercalia was something he'd always wanted to take part in, but as a child, had been prohibited because of his age. Then the unsanctioned breeding law came in—a fact he'd remembered recently, along with many other bombarding memories he tried not to focus on. But try as he might, he couldn't stop the flashes of his childhood self running through the village streets, holding a red ribbon high and watching it cascade behind him in the air. The sound of childish laughter as his cousins ran along beside him, holding their own streaming red ribbons. His aunt's voice shouting for them to not tangle the lengths before the big ceremony...

"Come on, Clara," said Jasper's mother as she walked beside her, carrying a basket. "They're having fun. Leave them be."

Clara turned to her sister with a scowl. "Are you going to detangle the lengths?"

"If I have to."

"Of course you are," Clara replied sourly. "The fun always outweighs the bad with you, doesn't it?"

Jasper's mother's lips flattened.

Clara gave her a contrite look. "I didn't mean that."

"Yes you did."

Jasper remembered their conversation ending after that. It took him years to know why. But the older he got, the wiser he was. What seemed like fun with the King—a matching at Lupercalia—had ended in a pregnancy. And then death.

That night they ran the street with streaming ribbons was the last traditional Lupercalia. It was the one where the King returned to participate again, but discovered Jasper's heritage. It was the last one where Jasper's mother was alive.

Not tonight.

He shook his head. Tomorrow, he would face his demons.

All he wanted now was to feast, to find something delicious to numb his past, and to indulge. If memory served correctly, the purification elixir they offered at the main meal would cause the body to tingle and sweat, preparing it for the Lupercalia rite. There would be much cider and ale.

Flashes of past indulgences swam before his eyes. He flinched and tried to shake them away, but unwanted visions of elixirs and meaningless sex crowded his mind. How could he be so ashamed of it now when back then he'd reveled in it? He'd loved it so much he'd bought himself an apartment in Cornucopia, the almost lawless border town between the Seelie and Unseelie kingdoms. It was the only place fae could mingle without the laws of their kingdoms getting in the way. It felt more of a prison than a sanctuary now. It was the place Jasper had gone to forget about his shortcomings.

And they were all coming back to him now—his failure at being a Guardian, a friend, a mentor. His failure at protecting his Guardian partner and friend, Rush, and the female who bore his child. Then, as if he couldn't sink any lower, Jasper had failed to protect Rush's son, Thorne, and it was unforgivable. Jasper knew exactly how harsh life was for someone without parents in Elphyne, yet he'd hid behind his duty to the Well.

The truth was, he was a coward hiding from his father. He had been all along. He should have floated.

The glow of his blue arm markings caught his attention.

Why?

Why, after everything he'd failed to do, had the Well given him this gift? It was a gift so strong that it saved the town from complete devastation during the raid. It gave him access to her untapped mana source. It had given him *her*.

Not that she accepted their partnership.

She was... he glanced at Ada's profile as she walked. Her blond wavy hair danced down her back. Freckles dusted a small, petite nose. She had a sun-kissed tan he'd only seen on the fish-tailed fae that liked to bake on the warm rocks of Helianthus City beach. He could smell summer on her. She was the promise of something all winter fae wanted. She was the promise of effervescent life.

His human was beautiful, inside and out. And she had stayed with him. She had slept by his side. She had dug the sacrilegious metal out of his body with her own fingers. She'd healed him and his kind without judgement. And she wanted him. He knew she did.

It was something else that made little sense. He'd been nothing but despicable to her, but she'd remained loyal. A rush of desire so strong and thick coursed through him, and he had to snap his gaze to the flower petals littering the dirt street ahead.

When she had threatened to leave him, he'd felt sick. He couldn't fathom being away from her.

In one of her nightly ramblings, she'd spoken of wanting extra training at the Order. Perhaps it was time to take her there, to the place he'd spent most his life.

A vague memory of his cadre itched at the edges of his mind. He knew they had been involved in his rescue from his father—and Jasper's captivity at the Ring—but couldn't quite uncover the truth of their identities. When he tried to remember more, blurry faces entered his mind. The rest was occupied with his feelings for Ada, rage, and thirst for vengeance against his father. Sometimes, that anger occupied more space than Ada. Sometimes it was the other way around. And, occasionally, after more curse marks were removed, other dark parts of him tried to edge in. If he gave those parts space to breathe, they would consume him.

Better to focus on the thrill of the chase he knew was coming. The fact that his mate kept denying what they meant to each other thrilled him further. He would enjoy watching her realize their union was inevitable.

The walk out of town took them down by the river and along a bubbling brook that fed into the woods. Sprites flittered in the trees, chasing fireflies and squeaking. Lanterns and glass chimes swayed gently from branches of oak trees, guiding the way. Soft murmurs of excitement and anticipation came from the villagers walking behind. Jasper felt no cold, but Ada's nose was pink from the crisp twilight air. When they arrived at the sacred grotto, he would insist she sit by a bonfire stationed around the pool.

Dirt turned to soft grass underfoot as they followed the winding brook through trees growing bigger and sheltering them from the dusk sky. Ada's face tipped up. Awe washed down their bond and he couldn't stop the smile playing on his lips. Being the Luperci during this walk was the pride and joy of the Darkfoot pack. He not only got to share it with her, but to experience it as someone the pack revered and respected.

His mother would be proud.

He is ten times the fae you are, ten times the soul, and he will be ten times the—

He shut his mother's voice out with a wince. Still, after so many years, her sound was as sharp as it was the day she spoke.

Ada's soft gaze slid over to him. She raised her brow in silent question. He must have let some of his emotion slip. She kept staring, and he knew he had to give her something.

"My mother would have liked to see this," he admitted, and looked out at the glowing lights filtering through the haze of the trees. "It was her favorite time of year."

They'd come to the top of the grotto. Moss-covered stone steps led down to a grassed landing, and a waterfall feeding the sacred pool. If his vague memories were to be trusted, the Lupercal cave was hidden behind the curtain of water. The smell of roasting meat watered his tastebuds, and his ears pricked up. Voices and the low breathy melody of pan pipes filtered up. They were almost there.

"The last leg of the pilgrimage is tricky," he said to Ada and held out his hand. "Watch your step on the descent."

Ada clutched his forearm, her eyes wide and earnest as she looked up at him. "You remember?"

"Some." Again, her gaze lingered on him. She wouldn't let it go. And, if he was being honest with himself, a part of him would feel offended if she did. She wasn't some stranger. She was the one the Well had chosen for him, made more special because of her journey through time. This, in itself, was so rare a fact that he should sit up and pay attention.

She had been right; pretending his life didn't exist, didn't make it so. His mother had said something similar, long ago, and it had struck a chord deep inside. There were things he'd never atone for, but if she wanted to learn those parts of him, then so be it. How much worse could his life get?

"I will share after," he conceded quietly.

It was enough. She nodded.

He put his hand over hers on his forearm and held her gaze. A moment of connection passed between them, and then she smiled and stepped forward. He wouldn't release her hand and pulled her back to him.

"Keep hold of me," he murmured and walked them down together.

Down in the grotto beside the pool were multiple dining tables laden with food and drink. Scattered bonfires blazed, casting heat into the otherwise cool evening air. A waterfall spilled over a small cliff to finish in the pool where it churned the water emitting tendrils of steam.

Villagers and guests already mingled at the tables, drinking and carousing. Most of the females wore blood red versions of Ada's dress, and the males wore red, drawstring pants. The cream, pure color had been reserved for Jasper and Ada—the two Luperci.

He noted representatives from other fae races had come to experience the festivities, which wasn't unheard of, but rare. Perhaps it was because this was the first authentic Lupercalia in centuries. The excitement was shared with everyone.

Satyrs with curved-horned heads and cloven feet shared a table and spoke quietly with Darkfoot shifters. Stag fae with forked antlers huddled at a table, talking with a few local shifters. On the outskirts, near the trees, two Oak Men chatted. One was tall and craggy with striations of wood over his wrinkled face. His beard and hair of orange and brown leaves signaled old age. Soon his leaves would fall, and he'd enter the last stage of his life—Winter. Next to him was a young spring Oak Man, barely a sprout of green leaves on his head.

Jasper searched the grotto for females of their kind, because surely if they were to participate in Lupercalia, they wouldn't be alone. Sure enough, a group of females sat at a round table with a string of lanterns dangling overhead from branches.

When the knowledge freely sprang into Jasper's mind,

he knew the cloud renting space in his head had almost cleared. With both equal parts sadness and acceptance, he understood his time for hiding from his responsibilities was almost over.

One last night of fun.

He glanced down at Ada and found her eyes like two big saucers as she took in the scene.

"I've never..." she gaped. "I mean... I've not seen..."

"This must be all very new for you." To come from a race where the major physical difference was the color of their skin, he imagined the diversity of fae would be something to behold.

Her eyes met his, and she nodded. "I don't know why, but I just didn't expect to see so many appearances."

"This is nothing," he said. "Wait until you visit Cornucopia, or the Unseelie lands."

"Will you tell me about them?" she asked. "I'd love to know more."

Her eagerness pervaded him and wrapped its way around his heart. She might not have realized it, but her question broached a future together.

"Of course." He squeezed her hand still clutching his forearm. "The night has only just begun."

His cousin, Sun, stood at the foot of the stone steps with his arms folded. He glanced warily at Jasper, but brightened his smile at Ada.

"Glad to see you made it," Sun said to her.

She returned his smile and Jasper felt that initial warmth around his heart dissipate.

"I'm honored," she said.

Their gazes held for too long.

With a repressed growl, Jasper's hackles raised. Even though no sound emitted, Ada glanced at him with a disapproving frown.

Sun tipped his chin at Jasper. "Good to finally see you out, Reed—"

"It's D'arn Jasper, now. Has been for centuries. You know that."

Both Ada and Sun gaped at him.

"What?" he scowled.

"Nothing, just... you remembered," Sun murmured.

Of course he remembered. He couldn't stand it when his cousins brushed off his commitment as a Guardian. Every time he had come back to Fenrysfield, they refused to believe he wasn't back for good. Sometimes Jasper believed this was the reason neither Sun nor Moon had stepped up to become the alpha. Both were clearly capable, and strong enough, but hadn't. Then again, perhaps it was because Clara was a force to be reckoned with.

Jasper scratched the curse marks as they flared.

Sun blanked for a moment, but then grinned. "You old dog. You do remember."

Then he launched at Jasper and punched him hard in the gut.

CHAPTER
TWELVE

Ada froze. Why on earth would Sun *hit* his cousin?

Jasper doubled over, wheezing... then he tensed, every muscle in his body going rigid. A spark of danger sizzled in the air.

Apprehension skipped over Ada's skin and she tensed, ready to break up the fight that would surely ruin the festival. She glanced around for a familiar face, for help, but found none. If this erupted, she was on her own.

Jasper straightened and glared at Sun, who stood with a stupid grin and a come-get-me expression. If he had a tail, Ada imagined it would be wagging.

"It's going to be like that, is it, Cousin?" Jasper took him by the shoulder and then planted his fist in Sun's gut. Soon, they were roughhousing on the grassy floor, tumbling and fighting like brothers. Fists flailed, knees became missiles, and ears were bitten.

"Yeah, they get like that."

Ada turned and found the youth she'd healed on her first day.

"It's a wolf thing," Lake explained with a grin. "We're a competitive lot."

"Right." She raised her brows at them. "So I should just leave them?"

Lake shrugged. "Guess so."

"So, you're participating in Lupercalia?" she asked him.

He laughed nervously, a blush hitting his cheeks. "No I'm a few years away from being allowed. But I'm here to play in the band." He lifted a wooden musical instrument that sounded like a maraca. "Yay me."

"Well, I'm glad you're all healed. You look good."

This time, red colored his arched ears. He touched fingers to his lips and pushed them down and out to her.

"Don't mention it," she smiled warmly.

They both jumped back when Sun and Jasper rolled over, but not far enough. Lake's maraca fell to the ground.

Clara jogged in, clapping her hands loudly. Moon trailed after her with an unimpressed expression.

"Enough!" Clara shouted. She took each of her recalcitrant relatives by the twitching ears and yanked them to their feet. "I swear to the Well, you two have learned nothing. *Crimson save me.* This is a sacred festival!"

"He started it." Jasper shrugged Clara off and pointed at Sun, who only waggled his brows at his mother.

"I don't care who started it—" Clara gasped at Jasper's

grass-stained pants. "What have you done? They're meant to symbolize purity, and you've soiled them!"

Jasper smirked, wiping a drop of blood from the corner of his lip with his thumb. "Let's be honest, Aunty, if you wanted someone pure as Luperci, you shouldn't have asked me."

Fury mottled Clara's expression, but it was with humor warring in her eyes. "I will skin you alive and wear your pelt as a coat. *Please* try to remain civil. We have Royal dignitaries and emissaries from other towns present." She lowered her voice so only they could hear. "If we want to gather allies so we're not beholden to the King, then we need to make an impression. Gah!" She threw up her hands and then walked back to the guests she'd been entertaining at the long table by the poolside.

Jasper mumbled something Ada couldn't hear. But Sun did. He burst out laughing. Ada tried not to join in, and she wasn't the only one. The rough, familiar play had dispelled a certain tension.

Not all were smiling. Moon still stood with his arms folded, and brows low at his brother and cousin. Long gray hair trailed over his broad, naked shoulders. Ada was glad to see his stomach wound was nothing but a faint scar.

The mood sobered. Jasper and Sun straightened themselves.

"Honestly," Prim said, arriving down the steps, carrying a tray of ceremonial sweet cakes. "You'd think the Darkfoot alpha heir apparent and the prince of, oh, I don't know, *half of Elphyne*, would be a little more responsible."

"Whatever gave you that idea?" Jasper joked.

Prim rolled her eyes and then gave Ada a curt smile before saying to Moon, "Where do you want these?"

"Give them to Halona at the banquet table."

Prim sashayed away, her red dress billowing behind her. Soft notes of the pan flute floated over the misting waterfall and echoed up the grotto rock walls and trees. The vibe was haunting... until shaking maracas joined in. Ada grinned, loving the rush of endorphins rising to greet her.

"What's so funny?" Jasper narrowed his eyes.

"Nothing. Private joke," she replied, looking at Lake doing his best to appear entertained.

Jasper's scowl deepened, but Ada only gave him a look that said, *I can hide things too.* It was stupid. It was teasing. But it gave her a small slice of satisfaction to know Jasper would understand what it felt like to be shut out.

"So..." Sun wiped his running nose and then pointed between Ada and Jasper. "What's the deal with you two?"

"*Sun*," Moon admonished.

"What? If you didn't have a mate, you'd ask too. Especially for tonight."

"Ada and I *are* mates," Jasper insisted.

"We're just friends," Ada said at the same time.

They both glanced at each other. Ada caught a flash of offense in Jasper's eyes, but she would not back down. If she let some notion of a cosmic power choose her love life for her, then what did she have left? Her friends were gone. Her world was gone. This was the last ounce of her control.

She explained, "We're not mated."

Jasper cocked his brow and raised his blue, glowing arm. "What do you call this?"

"A business relationship."

"Ooh," Sun goaded Jasper. "She has you there, Cousin."

Jasper's brows slammed together. "That's not a thing, Ada."

"It is now."

"So does that mean you're free game at the matching ceremony?" Sun's eyes lit up.

What?

"No," Jasper growled, his features twisting. He tensed and took a step toward Sun, who only smirked wider.

"Jasper, chill out." She touched him on the arm, but his eyes bored holes into his cousin. Everything in his posture said the next time he touched Sun, game time would be over. How Sun wasn't shitting his pants right now was beyond her. If Jasper ever turned that anger her way, she wasn't sure she'd be so brave. She tapped Jasper's arm for attention. "What's the matching ceremony?"

Since Jasper was consumed with violent thoughts about his cousin, Moon took his suicidal brother's shoulder and tugged him back before answering Ada. "It's when all the unmated pack members are paired up after we complete the Lupercalia rite."

Like The Bachelor, *or a romantic reality TV show? No thanks.*

"Oh, well, no, I won't be participating, but I appreciate the invitation."

"You just said you weren't mated to me."

Ada didn't like the mocking tone in Jasper's voice. "So by default, all single people must take part?"

"Well," Sun drawled. "Since the event is a symbol of health and fertility, both for our lands and ourselves, it would be disrespectful and a scandal not to. It's not like it's a lifelong commitment. Just a night of fun."

When Ada had heard they were asking for their seed to be blessed, she'd thought they meant *crop* seed. Now she realized there were two meanings.

"She is mine," Jasper said. "Whether or not I've marked her."

"Why don't we see what the Well thinks?" Sun asked Jasper. "I mean, if you're so certain that she's your true mate, you should have no problems, right?"

"This isn't a competition," Moon growled at them. "The Well has already paired them."

"It's always a competition," Sun returned.

"I'm standing right here." Not that they heard Ada anymore.

Jasper's luminous gaze narrowed on her. "You keep telling me you don't believe our matching is fated, so here's your chance. If we're not matched again, then..." His nostrils flared. "I'll back off."

"Why do I have to pair up with anyone?"

The idea of being forced into any kind of relationship was inconceivable.

Moon cleared his throat. "I regret to inform you, but when you accepted the role of one of the two honored Luperci, we assumed you would take part in the fertility rituals. Whether that's together, or with someone else, then we can't argue with that. For the record, no one will force you to mate. There are about fifty potential couples. When you match, it's up to you how you spend the night with your chosen one. But to deny it is to disrespect the rite and a sign of bad fortune for the coming harvest. We'd rather pick another Luperci to replace you." He glanced over at the banquet table. "I think Prim was interested. I could ask her."

Ada's stomach revolted at that idea, and it must have shown on her face because Jasper's eyes twinkled knowingly at her. He knew she liked him. And he knew her resistance was wearing thin. But Ada didn't do things by halves. If she entered any kind of relationship with Jasper, it was going to be deep. She feared being able to climb out of it if things got rough.

She had no support system in this world. She would be alone.

Ada opened her mouth to respond, but the music suddenly stopped. Clanging on glass silenced conversation. All they could hear for a moment was the rushing of the waterfall and the chirping of crickets. Ada was sure the beating of her heart picked up a few decibels.

Clara stepped on top of a table and addressed the hushed gathering.

"As alpha and matriarch of Fenrysfield, I officially declare Lupercalia open."

Cheering burst out. Drinks in hands chinked and sloshed. Smiles and grins were abound with infectious joy. Ada knew then that she couldn't rain on their parade any more than she already had. It was one thing to deny the bond between her and Jasper as romantic, but refusing to participate in their sacred traditions would be offensive. Moon had said no one would force her into any situation she wasn't comfortable with. She trusted that. These people had clothed, fed, and taught her their ways. It was the least she could do.

"Fine," she mumbled, knowing they'd all hear her above the noise. "I'll do the matching rite."

A grin broke out on Sun's face, but Jasper's expression remained much darker. It simmered with an intensity that brought a flush to her cheeks. A flicker of doubt tickled the edge of her mind... perhaps this rite wasn't as light-hearted as she imagined.

Another tinkling against glass, and the carousing quietened. When Ada looked over, Clara straightened regally and lifted her chin before sweeping her gaze across the crowd. In the space of a heartbeat, the mood turned serious. When Clara spoke, her clear voice traveled across the grotto, and lifted above the cascading waterfall.

"Lupercalia is a sacred, time-honored tradition—and for most wolf-shifter packs around Elphyne. Let us remember how it all began."

She dipped her head and closed her eyes.

Every fae around the grotto reverently did the same.

Ada followed suit and lowered her gaze, listening to Clara's cutting tale.

"When the humans and their insatiable greed wiped out the first world, the Well brought it back through harmonizing life and joining many forms as one. We celebrate Lupercalia to remember the birth of our race, of when the first fae changelings were born.

"When poisoned ice dropped across the world, and the Well was beaten back with a rain of fire, the human mother of the first stumbled into the Lupercal cave for refuge from a bitter snowstorm. Near death, she gave birth to twin babes but died shortly after, not knowing the cave was the den of a starving she-wolf.

"Coming in from the cold hunt, the she-wolf found the twins—one male and one female—and instead of eating them, she showed mercy and nursed them. Through this life-giving milk, the babes not only survived, but transformed into wolf. The first shifters grew to be strong. With their she-wolf mother, and from gaining sustenance from the sacred pool, they grew to hunt together. They survived together. But most importantly, they thrived together. Thank the Well."

"Thank the Well."

The chorus rippled over the gathering. Ada glanced down at the blue contour lines twining up her arm. They seemed to glow brighter tonight.

"We celebrate this first stage of Lupercalia to remember that the Well nourishes us. If we harmonize with nature, it makes us strong. Now, before we feast, it is time for the first Lupercalia rite." Clara returned her gaze to Jasper and Ada. "We are honored to have Luperci this year who reflect the first shifters. One wolf male. One human female. Both blessed by the Well."

A round of cheers echoed against the grotto wall. Fae clapped each other on the back, hugged and threw tiny glass beads into the air. They were so happy. They truly believed Ada and Jasper would bring them luck and a flourishing harvest. She met his fierce amber gaze shrouded in dark lashes. Her heart thundered against her ribcage, and a crack formed in her wall of denial. She averted her eyes, but the feeling remained, wedged between her ribs and the fluttering in her stomach.

How can this be real?

Clara lifted her arms into the sky. The crowd silenced, and then she spoke six words Ada would never forget.

"It is time for the sacrifice."

CHAPTER
THIRTEEN

Jasper had to hold his smile when Ada's face paled, and a bolt of fear came charging down their link.

He whispered at her ear, "It's not us they're sacrificing."

"Oh." Her shoulders dropped, then her eyes met his. "But... who?"

"Not who, what," he replied with a half-hearted shrug. "Just a goat for the feast."

"Oh." She nodded to herself.

"Don't worry, Pretty. I'll keep you safe."

This time when their eyes clashed, a flicker of confusion crossed her expression.

"Did I say something wrong?" he prompted.

"It's just that my friends used to call me Pretty Kitty. It was weird you said that." She grimaced. "And for the record, I hate it. Don't call me that again."

A memory pinged in his head. Not Pretty Kitty, but something else... a small voice. Little fingers grasping his own.

"Sleeping Pretty needs a kiss to wake."

"Reed?" A sigh. "Fine, *D'arn Jasper*, are you ready?"

He lifted his gaze to Clara waiting for him, holding the skull of a wolf with curved goat's horns protruding from the head.

She held it out to him. "Your mask."

"Mask?" he repeated vacantly. Ada already had hers on—a smaller bone-dry human skull. Her brown, subdued eyes watched him closely from beneath. She lifted the chin of the skull to rest the mask on top of her head, smiling gently at him.

If either of them had a right to be apprehensive about this, it was Ada. Not only was everything about this rite so different to what she'd be used to, but she had to wear the skull of her own kind. But it was she who gave him the courage to continue.

Clara's eyes narrowed. "You remember what to do, don't you?"

"Of course I do." He mentally shook himself. *Snap out of it.* But the memory of the little girl's voice and her words picked at his mind, begging him to pay attention. With a growl, he took the horned skull and placed it over his head, at the last minute, sliding it to the top of his head so Ada could see the smirk he tossed her way, before covering his face and becoming the wolf.

A band constricted around his chest. Air stifled under the heat of the mask. His smile dropped. Everything darkened, despite the eye sockets being wide. The sound of a crowd cheering entered his mind, banging on the stadium stands. He blinked and shook his head.

I'm not there. I'm here.

He clenched his bare toes in the soft grass. It wasn't the dirt of an arena.

I'm here.

"Let's go," he grunted and started for the Lupercal cave.

Pan flute notes lifted in decibel, climbing with the beat of a drum and the shake of maracas. It sounded too much like the beating against the stadium floor—boots as they stomped with bloodlust.

The crowd of fae parted to make way for their procession. Both Ada and Jasper moved down the grassed bank, to the sandy shore, and then along its edge until they arrived at the rocky wall next to the waterfall. Behind the veil of misty water, he could see a single flame flickering in the darkness.

The Lupercal cave.

The creation place of the first shifters. Two species coming together with a single goal—survival. Throughout his life, Jasper had been reminded of this fact. You could be furred, you could be pale skinned or dark, horned or winged, but one common goal united them all—the health of the land they lived off.

The roar of the waterfall drowned out the rhythmic music. His lungs struggled to work, but he took Ada's hand, spun them to face the gathering, and then once everyone had taken their look, he walked them through the mist and into the cramped cave where a single goat stood tethered to a stake.

Outside, no one heard it bleat.

Its fate was sealed.

A flat, empty bowl lay on a stone that had been cut to create an altar. Next to it lay a crystal knife with wolves etched into the blade, and a second bowl filled with milk and bundles of wool.

Jasper pointed to the knife and the empty bowl. "We collect the blood to paint on ourselves. Then we purify with the milk."

The goat bleated.

And bleated.

He hardly heard Ada shuffling up behind him. The screams of bleating victims pierced his ears. One stood out more than the rest—a pixie. A female. A fallen queen, her harem already dispatched.

Jasper's mouth dried. *Can't breathe.* He tried to pull his collar but found he was already naked. He scratched at himself instead, needing to get it off... but unable. *Get it off.*

He shook his head.

He could do this. Almost in slow motion, as though he floated outside of his body, he watched his hand reach for the knife, grasp the hilt, and turn it over in his palm.

"It's just a goat," he mumbled.

"Jasper?" Ada's voice didn't sound right. Not sweet like it used to be, but muffled and unsteady. *Not right.*

"It's just a goat," he repeated. "We hunt them in the wild all the time. It's for the feast. Its sacrifice will feed us, just as the she-wolf hunted for the first shifters before they could hunt for her."

My responsibility.

But the words echoed sharply, causing him to flinch.

Air rasped into his lungs, hot through the mask. His chest heaved. He gripped the knife so tight his knuckles ached.

The goat bleated again, forcing the memory from the Ring into his mind.

"Please..." the black-haired pixie sobbed, her wings nothing but broken, fibrous shells dangling behind her. She raised her hands before her face. The roar of spectators chanted at her plight.

"More!"

"Finish her!"

"Make her pay!"

For what? He'd thought. What had she done?

Why was she here?

"... Plee-he-hease..."

Salty tears ran down her face, creating dirt tracks that somehow fascinated him. It thrilled his wolf more. The tang of metal was everywhere. Blood. On his clawed hands. On his body.

He hesitated.

"What is fun for some, isn't fun for others."

His neck burned like fire, clouding his mind, confusing him.

"Killing is kindness," his mother had said. Or was it "Kindness before killing?"

And then his own voice: "I want to play, too."

He buried his fist deep into the heat of the pixie's chest.

"Jasper!" Ada's voice.

"I'm fine."

"You're not fine. I can feel it. What's wrong?"

"Nothing," he gasped, panting, shutting the valve on his emotions. "I'm fine. We need to... we need to... for the rite."

But it was as though an *elfant* had sat on his chest. He struggled to breathe. He tossed the knife and ripped the skull mask off. Cool air splashed his face and dragged into his lungs. He tried to speak, but his mouth was dirt. His tongue wouldn't work.

Bleating. Pleading.

Darkness crowded his vision. His knee dropped to the rock, lancing white-hot pain up his thigh. He fell to all fours, breathing hard, flaring his eyes wide, trying desperately not to pass out.

Shame. It scorched him.

A cool palm met the searing flesh of his back.

"I can't," he gasped, shaking his head, eyes burning. "I just can't."

The weight between his shoulder blades lifted.

"Don't turn away from me," he begged. "Don't leave."

"It's okay, Jasper," she said, and then she started humming.

Not a falter in her voice. No tremble, no flaw.

Behind him, he *felt* Ada move through the shifting atmosphere. He heard the scraping as she claimed the knife. Calm filtered down their bond, washing over him. Her sweet, ethereal voice captured his attention, giving him a life raft to hold.

The bleating stopped.

In the vacuum of its cries, he felt peace.

He squeezed his eyes shut. *What was wrong with him?*

Scrambling to sit, he rested his back against the stone alter. While he captured his breath, his mate moved swiftly and clinically as she prepared what they needed to complete the rite. She'd removed her mask, and he was glad because he got to see her face. It was filled with kindness as she touched the goat, stroking it, singing to it, and ensuring it didn't suffer well after the last light left its eyes.

The crushing weight of his failure landed on his shoulders. His gaze skated away but landed on the fallen horned wolf's skull.

All he could see was that Well-damned Ring and its gladiator pit. That damned city, Cornucopia, and its inability to follow any laws. He'd thought it had been so fun. So full of life and free from responsibility, but ten years in that Ring, and he'd seen the dark side of abandonment and indulgence. Without a guiding hand to rule them, the people of the city weren't free. They'd become as corrupt as the humans that came before them.

It had to change.

Bleating.

His heart hammered. His vision blurred. Not real. His fingers clenched on the dirt floor, grounding him. *This is real.*

Ada brought the full bowl over and knelt before him to place it on the floor beside them.

"It's not your responsibility." He grimaced. "I should have done it. And, instead, I let you tarnish yourself."

She touched him on the jaw and brought his gaze to hers. A sad smile flitted over her lips before it was lost to him again. A swell in his chest urged him to chase her smile, to find where the sadness came from, because it was deep. She owned her own tragic history. He'd heard some of it when she'd confided in him while he was in wolf form.

"Unfortunately," she said, "this isn't the first time I've had to do something like that."

He searched her eyes for the truth hidden beneath the liquid brown. "Are you broken too?"

She gulped in a deep breath before lifting her glimmering eyes to the cave ceiling. Her change in posture was a physical thing. He saw her take ownership of her features until she forced the tears away.

"The first time I learned to kill an animal without making it suffer, I was eleven. And I'd only learned how to do it the right way because I'd failed at first—epically—" She cut off, eyes glistening and turning red around the rims. That she'd felt the same sort of pain as him, it cut him straight down the middle. It pierced between his ribs in a way he'd never felt before. All he knew was that her heartache was his. He took her hand. Their gazes clashed, and she inched toward him, urgency driving her voice to a higher pitch.

"I knew I had to eat," she said, eyes unfocused. "I would have died if I didn't. But I hadn't been prepared for what happened after, for what I had to do to that animal so I could live." Her sadness turned to anger. "And I shouldn't have had to. In my time, you didn't need to hunt your own food. You could go down to the corner store and buy whatever you needed. My mother should have taken care of me. I know that now. It was incomprehensible. I should have reported her to the authorities, but I was a coward. Sometimes I wonder if I'd never met Harold or Laurel, would I have stayed on that mountain my entire life?"

"Tell me about your friends."

Ada sat down on her haunches. A wistful smile brightened her face. "Laurel and I met while she was on a fishing trip with her family. I was maybe fourteen at the time but had taken over Harold's hut after he'd died. Already, I hadn't seen my mother in years. To this day, I have no idea what happened to her." She shrugged. "I don't really care, to be honest. I only care what her selfishness robbed me of. But Laurel... yeah, she knew something wasn't right with my situation. She coaxed me back to her place, fed me proper city food, and gave me clothes. But it was more than that. It was a lifeline back to humanity."

Ada wiped her nose with the back of her hand and swallowed.

"Anyway, we should probably do the next part of this, right?"

Jasper tore his gaze from her face and looked at the bowl of blood. Embarrassment washed through him. He should have been the one to prepare it, not Ada. It was his job.

Another nightmare to add to his failings.

"What do we do?" she asked.

He lifted her with him as he positioned himself on his knees, facing her. Then he dipped his fingers into the warm blood and swiped them across her forehead, leaving a streak of red. He guided her fingers to do the same to him.

Her intimate touch was a balm on his soul. He pushed into her hand. Contrary to his fear, she didn't flinch. She cupped his face and allowed him to stare into her eyes. In their depths, he saw salvation. Every cell in his body wanted to drink her up, to rub himself over her and cover her with his scent. All he wanted to do was kiss her. And he hated himself for it. Now that his memories were returning, he knew she was too good for him.

"Now we cleanse ourselves," he rasped. "With the wool dipped in milk."

She got to her feet and collected the milk, coming back and meeting him on her knees. She grasped a floating ball of wool and squeezed it out.

"What does this symbolize?" she asked.

"The blood represents how the humans came to the she-wolf, full of rage, unnecessary violence, and greed. The milk we use to purify the blood. It represents new life. The shift into fae."

"So I clean off the blood," she confirmed reverently.

He nodded with an uncharacteristic bashfulness heating his neck. His ears twitched. "And this might sound stupid, but we... um... laugh as we are cleansed."

She snorted. "Okay. Weird, but okay."

"Laughter purifies the soul."

Her expression sobered. "It does. Inside and out. Okay, here we go."

Jasper studied her as she wrung out the soaked wool and was so beguiled by her face that he forgot to laugh until she prompted him. But she wasn't laughing either, so when she lifted the wet wool to his head, he dodged. She frowned and shifted her aim to swipe at his face again. He dodged the other way, a slow curve lifting his lips.

"Stop it," she murmured breathlessly, but the smile was already forming on her face.

He bit his lip to hold his own. "I promise I'll be a good boy."

This made her smile broaden. "Maybe I'll reward you with a treat."

"Don't joke about that unless you mean it."

A buzzing of unsaid intent passed between them, and then she lifted the soaked wool to his head. He allowed her to clean some off, but on the next turn, dodged. They both burst out laughing. He continued to goad her and joke until she cleaned the last off his face.

"My turn, I guess," she mumbled, eyes still dancing from their laughter.

When she dunked her bloodstained wool into the milk, Jasper's fingers covered hers briefly. A spark jolted between them, and she withdrew her hand from the bowl. He went to clean her forehead, but she dodged, grinning at him with mischief. So he flicked milk at her face.

She squealed, laughing. He fell in love with the light igniting her eyes, illuminating all the dark places in his heart. The melody of her sweet honey voice warmed his blood.

"You're beautiful," he murmured, hand lowering after cleaning her face.

A blush stained her freckled cheeks.

Pink milk trickled from her temple, slid along her jaw, and pooled at her dimpled chin, ready to drop. He brushed it away with his thumb, then found his fingers refused to leave the velvet touch of her skin. They slid along her jaw and collected in the hair behind her ear, burying deep.

His gaze snagged on her tongue as it darted out to moisten her bottom lip.

Her lips parted.

They inched closer, their mingled breaths caressing each other's face.

"Give me this," he whispered, and then softly bit the air before her mouth, baring his teeth with painful longing. "Just one more."

From the way she struggled to catch her breath, and the low simmer of lust down their bond, he knew they were close. *Almost.*

Music burst into life outside the cave. The drums and the flute grew in crescendo.

He cursed softly. He would shatter those drums and shove the flutes—

Her hand flattened against his chest, derailing his thoughts.

And just like that, the beauty tamed the wolf. His mind shuttered. His body sang. Ada's brows puckered as she looked at him and swallowed.

The loud percussion of drums vibrated the cave walls. Or was it his heart?

"That's our cue," she whispered, sadness entering her tone... or had he imagined that too?

She stood, bringing him with her until they both straightened, eyes locked.

Someone shouted outside... possibly Clara trying to wrap things up.

Disappointment rocked through him with such violence, he shocked himself. He knew, in that moment, he would do anything to protect his time with her. When next they were alone, nothing would get in his way of claiming her kiss.

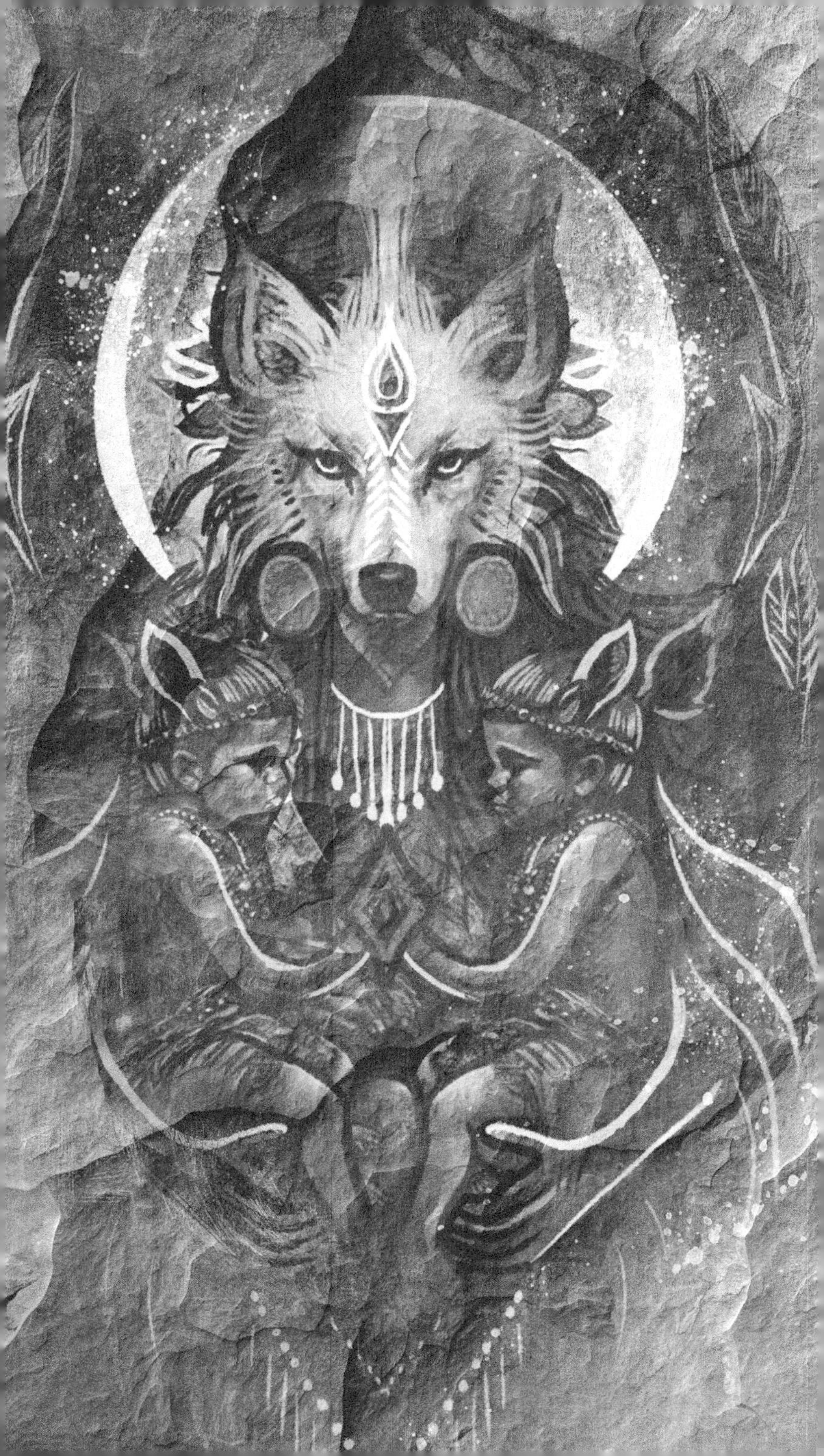

CHAPTER
FOURTEEN

Ada let Jasper guide her out of the cave. The moment they emerged through the waterfall's mist, a deafening roar vibrated through the grotto. The crowd cheered and howled. Bashfulness froze her limbs. Jasper's grip on her hand flinched, tightening almost painfully.

He still shuttered his emotions from her. But she knew enough that his reaction inside the cave was caused by tragic memories. Perhaps the cheering crowd reminded him of something he'd rather forget.

When he'd fallen to his knees in the cave, she'd wanted to take his head in her hands and use her gift to remove his pain. She wasn't even sure if such a thing was possible for mental pain, but wanted to try. Regardless, it wasn't her choice to make. He needed to ask for help at some point, or else he wouldn't heal.

Are you broken too?

When he'd said those words and searched for a connection within her eyes, she hadn't the courage to tell him she was born broken, but had pieced herself back together, thanks to her friends. She now realized this was part of the reason she held him at arm's length. When her mother didn't care enough to keep her alive, Ada had been a child, angry and scared of the world. She knew how hard it had been to glue herself together when she didn't even know what whole looked like. She *would not* be broken again, and that's exactly what she would be if she fell for him, and then if he left or betrayed her.

So she'd done the next best thing she could think of—she'd completed the rite for him. It hadn't bothered her as much as she thought it might. The realization settled in her gut with an uncomfortable feeling.

Destiny.

She'd resented her upbringing in the old world to the point of bitterness, but how could she argue with that one pivotal moment where everything she'd learned about survival screamed in her face—*this is why*. It was as though she'd been training for this time, for a life here where sometimes you had to hunt for food, where creature comforts weren't the same, where sometimes you were so lonely you hurt.

Jasper picked his way through the crowd, leading her by the hand. Someone had taken the goat. She expected to soon see it on the roasting spit.

She knew it was normal, nothing to freak out over, but a silence had entered her mind in the cave. Something had shifted inside her. She'd given up a part of her past and embraced the fae culture as her own. And Jasper?

He may not have revealed what tortured him, but he'd allowed her to see him vulnerable. He'd shared that part of himself, and he'd allowed her to care for him. It was so unlike the exterior he projected to the rest of the world. She felt closer to him in a way she wasn't yet ready to comprehend.

Everyone wanted to touch them—the lucky Luperci—as they paraded through the gathering. But what started out as something almost reverent, ended in hands plucking, grasping, and invading her personal space. Single, male and female fae smothered Jasper. Ada almost lost her grip on his hand. But it wasn't just him they wanted, it was her. Females touched Ada's belly, tugging at the fabric of her dress, praying for fertility and the gift of new life. She thought this event was supposed to be serene, but it turned frenzied and feral, and when someone's fingers caught on her shoulder strap, almost pulling it off, she panicked.

She couldn't breathe.

Were they being like this because she was human, or was it the thrall of the festival?

For a mad minute, she panicked that there would always be a divide between them. Would they ever accept her as one of their own?

Jasper was there in a heartbeat, pushing fae back with a snarl of elongated teeth that made her knees tremble. Fae ears flattened, and they dipped their chins in submission, bowing as they backed away.

"Enough," he snapped to those still trying to touch him. Then, upon seeing the fear he'd just caused, he paused and seemed to catch himself. With a visible effort, he pulled his snarling lips into an easy grin before adding, "It's time to feast."

Cheers whooped. The air became less stifling as the crowd thinned, and a path to the banquet table cleared. There was nothing behind the table except a few feet of grass before the rocky shore dipped down into the pool. Above, tree branches leaned over the setting, dangling tinkling wind chimes and glowing lanterns swaying in the gentle breeze. The music started up again. An abundance of food and drink spread over the entire table length. Glasses filled with liquids of all sorts of colors made Ada's tastebuds water.

In the middle of the long table were two mosaicked thrones. Curved, wooden goat horns crowned the chairs. Or maybe they were actually goat horns... or some other creature she'd not seen before. Next to the thrones, and around the table, were smaller, less gaudy chairs filled with important fae from around the village. Clara, Moon and his mate, Halona. Sun sat opposite the thrones. As Ada's attention shifted to the chairs beside him, she noticed fae not from the village.

Clara had mentioned emissaries from other towns. The Satyrs were there, as were the Oak Men. Next to them were two pointy-eared fae dressed in luxurious silk clothing. Next, another two males with fur-tipped, pointed ears sat on either side of a Viking-type lady with a long silver braid trailing down her back. She glared at Jasper as though she knew him.

But he only had eyes for Ada.

"Are you okay?" he asked softly.

She nodded. "It just got a bit personal with all that touching. Anyone would think they actually wanted a piece of me."

A shiver ran down her spine as her doubt about being human crept in.

"It's because you're astonishing. They worship you."

Ada gave him a weak smile and untucked her hair from behind her ears so they weren't on display.

"Don't hide yourself. This world isn't going to change if we don't ask it." He brazenly tucked the hair behind her ears. "I would never let anyone hurt you," he promised.

And this time, it didn't feel empty. It didn't feel like something a man said just to get in a lady's pants. It was heartfelt. A rush of gratitude heated her blood, and she touched her fingers to her lips and pushed her hand down and out.

Amusement sparkled in his eyes. He brought her fingers to his lips, murmuring against them, "Are you ready for the first feast?"

"First?"

Roguishness replaced his fleeting humor, and she felt a little dip in her stomach.

Uh-oh.

She did *not* need to feel like that right now. Certainly not for him. But even as her heart tried to slam up walls, she knew she was in trouble. He made her forget her senses. His smile was more dangerous than his teeth, and if she wasn't careful, she would walk willingly toward both, happily allowing herself to be devoured body and soul.

"Come on," he said. "The fun part is just beginning."

Placing her hand in the crook of his arm, he was all the confidence she needed. It made her feel honored to have glimpsed his vulnerable side in the cave, and she fell even deeper in thrall with him.

He strode them straight to the banquet table and opened his mouth, presumably to make the introductions, but the Viking-like woman slammed down her glass and stood swiftly. Her two companions joined her.

"You have some nerve, D'arn Jasper," she said, glaring at him. "My brother and nephew are besides themselves with worry. They've been hunting all over Elphyne since you disappeared from the Twelve's house."

He frowned and cocked his head. "Kyra?"

"I'll have you know, it's now High Lady Kyra Night-stalk, Alpha of Crescent Hollow." She scoffed. "I mean, they said you'd lost your memories, but I didn't believe them.

Now look at you, indulging as normal, forgetting about those who care about you. Don't ask me why they bother."

His fingers tightened around Ada's hand, and she gave him a soft squeeze of solidarity. This was *good*. More of his past was catching up with him. Only people who cared got angry like this.

The thought hit her with a jolt.

Who was this alpha who commanded respect? Why did she care for Jasper? Who were they to each other?

"Do you remember me?" Kyra asked. "Or Rush? Thorne?"

This time, recognition passed over his features but was shortly stamped out by confusion.

"I remember enough," he answered curtly.

Ada bit her lip. It was on the tip of her tongue to come to his defense, but she wasn't sure if she should reveal how far the curse marks had eroded his mind. As it turned out, she didn't need to.

Clara shifted back her chair and joined Ada and Jasper. She smiled tightly and pointed at the guests as she said their names.

"You know the Crescent Hollow representatives, and of course the Spring Court King Tian and his Queen Oleana."

"Elves," Jasper murmured to her.

They were the couple in fine silks. Were these the ones Clara had mentioned would be able to train her better?

"The Delphinian Oak Men, Lord Brand and Larch. And then the High Lord Aubrette and his son Lord Win."

The last two were directed at the satyrs. Ada raised her brows. Queens, Kings, Lords and Ladies. She truly was in another time and place.

"The pleasure is mine." Jasper regally bowed his head, then faced his aunt and lowered his voice. "I didn't know this Lupercalia would have so many foreign dignitaries as guests, Aunty."

"Well, if you weren't cloistered in your room for the past week, perhaps you'd know things are different this year."

"The breeding law is abolished."

Clara raised her brow. "That and the Darkfoot pack is proud to have one of our own, not only Well-blessed, but the High King's official heir, as the Luperci."

He narrowed his eyes. "But are you proud?"

She returned his sly stare. "The Darkfoot pack has a long memory." She forced a smile on her face and raised her voice. "Please take your seats, the meals are about to be served."

Ada wasn't sure what had passed between them, but it prompted a flash of pain in Jasper's eyes, and a nod of acknowledgment.

They took their seats on the thrones. To Ada, it was just some fun for the night, but Jasper blended with the regality as though he was destined for the spotlight. The affable grin plastered on his face looked so genuine, for a moment, Ada forgot his pain in the cave.

It unsettled her how quickly he could shift his facade.

The moment the thought entered her mind, she wondered which facade was the real Jasper. The fun one, or the serious one. Maybe neither. Maybe the one he'd been in the cave was it... *Are you broken like me?*

Servers came around to the table, placing entrees on all plates and filling glass goblets with some sort of fizzing beverage that smelled like sour apples. The pan flutes picked up again. A few beats behind, the maracas shook reluctantly. Ada would bet Lake was desperate to either join in with everyone or go home.

When guests sat at their sporadic table settings, the musicians stood down from their steps. Two gangly youths, both of them with pointed ears, and small stag horns growing out of their heads. Next to them, Lake's face was exactly how she imagined—bored and over it.

She caught his eye, waved and smiled. He perked up immediately and shook his maracas with extra fervor.

With the magical atmosphere, wistful music, and fantastical creatures, Ada truly felt as though she'd wandered into a fairytale book.

"So," Sun picked up a piece of meat from his plate, popped it into his mouth, and then looked at Jasper. "I'm going to say what everyone is thinking."

"Of course you are," Moon said drolly. "Maybe finish your mouthful first."

A chagrined glance at his brother, and then Sun leveled his stare at Jasper. "Are you going to tell your Guardian brethren about the raids?"

The small conversation hushed at the table. Jasper tensed, and then carefully took a sip of his drink before placing it back down. "You have been collecting something forbidden at the highest level. Chances are, they already know. Unless you can give a valid reason why, then it's the Prime's call what happens next."

Moon lost hold of his fork. "Are you telling me you have no loyalty to our pack, after all we've done to protect you this past week?"

"You, protect *me*?" Jasper's incredulous words burst out of a smirking mouth. "Correct me if I'm wrong, but I believe it was I who protected your town, and my mate who healed it."

The two shifters glared at each other, their ears twitching back.

"For Crimson's sake," Halona said, throwing her napkin down and then glaring at her mate. "Just tell him who made you do it. I won't have us go down for that royal floater."

Gasps chorused around the table.

Moon's nostrils flared, and his gaze darted between the table guests as though he was searching for signs of danger, but none came. There was something odd that Ada couldn't quite figure out, and then she realized Halona had referred to the floater as royal. Calling someone a floater was reference to them being spit out from the ceremonial lake. Could she have meant King Mithras? If so, that was treason.

And no one complained.

Sun and Moon glanced at their mother, who'd already paused her conversation with the King and Queen of the Spring Court. It seemed everyone at the table waited for the answer. Clara gave her sons a curt nod of approval.

Moon met Jasper's eyes. "It was your father."

The mood darkened. The air chilled. Jasper's gaze darkened in a way Ada had never seen before.

"If there is something you're trying to say, Cousin, then say it."

"Fine," Moon said and looked him directly in the eye. "The Order arrested the King's human advisor, then you—the King's heir—"

"He doesn't intend for me to wear the Glass Crown."

"If you'll let me finish," Moon ground out with a glare. "You disappear, and then you turn up with a human on your arm—"

"Well-blessed human," Jasper cut in, again.

"Doesn't matter." Moon slammed his palm on the table. "You can see how we might be cautious that you are colluding with them."

"You want to know whose side I'm on?" Jasper asked.

"I want to know if you are a Mithras, or a Darkfoot."

"I've never been a Mithras."

"Could have fooled us."

No one responded. Halona's previous comment was treasonous enough, but from what Ada gathered, everyone at the table wasn't happy with the current political climate. Nervously, she tried to assess their body language, but no one revealed a thing except the occasional uncomfortable shift in their seats.

Jasper chugged his drink down, planting the empty glass on the table with a clunk. "I'm on my own side. Always have been."

But the moment he said the words, a wash of shame trickled through their bond.

"Have you no pride?" Sun snarled. "We are your kin."

"He's not cared in centuries. Why start now," Moon added.

Ada noted Clara made no move to intercept.

"Be careful what you say, Cousin." Jasper's knuckles whitened around the glass.

Moon leaned forward. "I'm only stating the truth."

"I put my life on the line to save your village."

"But you just said, you're only in it for yourself."

Jasper clamped his lips shut, and it infuriated Ada because she knew he wasn't this selfish person he claimed to be. Why risk his life to protect the town? Why kill the wolpertinger for her instead of simply running into the woods? Why participate in this ceremony to which he had no obligation? She'd only known him a short while, but from what she'd seen, he'd do anything to protect his loved ones. Maybe no one had protected him. So she spoke up.

"His father tried to assassinate him only days ago. How can he be colluding with someone who wants to kill him?"

Sun blinked at Jasper. "But he legitimized you."

Kyra laughed harshly. "He's been trying to kill Jasper since the moment he knew he was born. You thought the assassination attempts would just stop because he suddenly named Jasper as successor? Rush and Thorne said he'd been kidnapped, tortured, and cursed into obedience. Why would Mithras do that if he had Jasper's loyalty? Why would the Guardians raid the Summer Court, arrest the King's advisor—human advisor, mind you—and then rescue the cursed prince?"

King Tian rubbed his beardless chin. "The High King has certainly been keeping secrets."

"That's an understatement," Kyra mumbled into her cup.

Tian cleared his throat. "That leads us to the reason we've come. During the celebration where the High King announced you as his heir, there were... interesting conversations among the congregation."

Ada sat down with an icky feeling crawling up her spine. She knew enough about conflict to understand when shady deals were being made, and from the stolen glances between the party at the table, there was something they wanted Jasper involved with. And she wasn't going to like it.

Queen Oleander ran her finger around the rim of her glass, then pursed her lips, agitated. "The increase in human slaves around Elphyne has always been something we never understood. The elves are not vicious, or gratuitously cruel. We devote ourselves to education and forwarding our race. But he gifts us with human artisan slaves—glamoured and spelled to perform and dance until their fingers and toes bleed."

The Satyr, High Lord Aubrette, leaned forward and projected his voice down the table. "He has petitioned our banner to follow him into the Unseelie Kingdom and claim vengeance against their monsters invading our lands. What do you say to that, Guardian? Or are you Prince?"

The more and more these people spoke, the more Ada felt Jasper's anxiety churn through their link. His control over blocking his emotions had long since evaporated.

Kyra spoke, leaning forward. "Two years ago, Mithras turned a blind eye to Lord Thaddeus's collusion with the enemy. Now we hear he's asking fae to hoard metal, only for a human raiding party to conveniently turn up. It's clear to me he has grand plans that go against the interests of Elphyne and the integrity of the Well. Surely as a Guardian, if not a prince, you have an opinion about that."

"Why don't you ask the Prime?" Jasper responded. "The leader of the Order would have more to say."

"Deflecting again?"

"It's not deflection. It's simply that I don't know. I was... indisposed... for much of the past decade," he conceded. "I'm only just learning now of what has come to pass."

The satyr slammed his fist on the table. "Much has come to pass. We are not happy with the direction Elphyne is headed. The Seelie High King talks about war with the

Unseelie High Queen. He wants war, and she's brushing it off as nothing but a nuisance."

"Well, she does command the Wild Hunt," Kyra drawled.

The satyr glared at her. "Whether or not she commands the Wild Hunt makes no difference. What matters is that our High King wants to start a war with our own kind to be used as fodder while the real enemy is ignored while they pilfer dangerous resources from our land. And that's only the easily accessed metal, the parts scavenged above the land. If this human leader manages to get a stronghold, he can invade and claim our lands to mine for resources as he sees fit. The Well will die—*fae* will die—and the barren wasteland will expand."

"It will never come to that," Jasper growled, his jaw clenching, his eyes smoldering.

"And how can you be so sure?"

"Because I won't let it."

His words hung heavily in the music laden space that followed. With each passing second, the atmosphere thickened with a foreboding sense of duty. They all knew what had to be done, but no one wanted to make the first move.

Clara stood slowly and looked each of the guests at the table in the eye. "I will say it, if none of you will." Her eyes settled last on Jasper. "Word is Mithras made you his heir only to kill you and claim vengeance on the Unseelie High Queen. You skirt around the truth, but we all know what happened. Some of us were there when he unveiled you to the Court. And we see the remnants of the curse around your neck. He kidnapped and tortured you in the Ring. Yet, you somehow emerged from it all, stronger than before and with a further blessing from the Well." She jerked her chin toward Ada. "We don't need someone on the throne who is complicit in the rape and pillage of our land. We need someone who knows exactly what the Well needs to flourish. We need a Darkfoot. And a Guardian." She picked up her glass goblet and raised it into the air. "To the new Seelie High King Reed—"

"Stop!" Jasper slammed his fist on the table and lurched to his feet.

The table shook with the impact. All eyes were on him, watching.

"A Guardian has no claim to the throne..." He frowned, catching the falsity of his own words, and then mumbled to himself, as though just realizing it, "But I *am* the heir, *and* a Guardian."

Clara's voice turned softer. "Your mother's prophecy is coming true. It may have taken hundreds of years, but you're the last surviving heir of King Mithras's line to exist. There is no one else who can claim the Glass Crown but you. You have to admit, your re-emergence has come at the right time to breathe new life into the land."

No answer.

"What do you say, Jasper?"

Each Lord and Lady at the table raised their voices and started arguing over each other. They all agreed with Clara, but couldn't meet on a plan of action. Conversation became chaotic and heated, to the point Ada thought one of them would reach over the table and strangle the other.

Through it all, they'd forgotten that they had asked Jasper for his opinion. He scratched his neck, eyes darting over the place until his gaze leveled on Ada and brightened.

He stood and clinked his spoon against his glass to get their attention.

"Enough with the arguing. We're not here for that." He grinned charismatically at them and called over a server before saying. "The pack is waiting patiently for their Lupercalia matching rite. It's time to give it to them. Tonight is a celebration to honor the Well. It is a time for strangers to come together and, for one night, forget the trappings of their stations and breathe new life into the pack. Let us have fun and worry about politics tomorrow."

It was clear most of the table wanted to keep talking, but Sun took his glass, tinkled his porcelain spoon against it, and then raised his voice to be heard over the music and revelers.

"Here, here. It's time for the matching ceremony." Sun's half-mast eyes landed on Ada. "And then the hunt."

King Tian stood swiftly. Ada tensed, thinking he would start another argument, but his cheeks flushed adorably and smiled at his wife. "My wife and I have brought a gift from Delphinium to honor the rite. Enough servings of divilixir for all matching rite participants."

Cheers rang out. Fae clapped loudly. Someone whistled.

Must be a good drink, Ada thought as servers burst into action. Trays with small glasses of blue and yellow liquid emerged and were distributed among the tables.

Prim arrived at their side, holding her tray. Next to shot glasses were the same masquerade masks a woman had peddled from her market cart when they'd first arrived at the village. Designed and painted to resemble a wolf, the half-face masks had glass beads dangling from a thin red cord at the ears. Some were unadorned.

Prim placed two glasses before each of them—one blue and one yellow. She dropped a beaded mask before Ada, and an unadorned mask before Jasper. Then she picked up her glass of yellow and held it in the air. With her gaze locked on Jasper, she said, "Here's to purging impurities." She downed it in one gulp. "And then to getting even dirtier."

Sun roared out laughing. Even Moon cracked a smile. Kyra whooped along with her partners. Jasper shot it back with a tiny smile, so did a few others around the table.

"Your turn, Ada," Prim prompted, eyes on the full glass at Ada's fingers.

"What is it?" she asked.

"Everyone taking part in the rite must drink it."

She sniffed the liquid. It smelled like honeyed nectar. Everyone else drank it, so she shot it back, wincing at the burn down her throat. The blue glass remained. *Aw, fuck it.*

Jasper was right. It was time to have some fun. Then, before she lost her nerve, she did the same with the blue shot and slammed it down with a grin splashed on her face.

Prim raised her brows, impressed, and nudged Ada's shoulder with her finger. "You're going to get real dirty then, huh?"

Ada snort-laughed, hand covering her mouth in a hiccup. "I don't know what that means."

She couldn't stop smiling. Her blood was fizzing. It was like her body was taking her down a path her mind couldn't travel.

"You'll find out soon enough," Prim said, and then shot her blue drink back, giving Jasper a wink.

What was that? But Ada had no time to ponder Prim's flirt, Sun drank his, and then slammed the empty glass on the table, shaking the foundations. "Bottoms up."

More laughter erupted.

A pleasant heat built in Ada's blood, firing through her system, and beating out the cool night air. She wiggled and couldn't help smiling at Jasper, but found him sitting still with his fingers around the glass of blue liquid. For some reason, he wasn't caught in the avalanche of revelry, and that small part of Ada that hadn't caught up, tried to pump the brakes. Something was wrong.

"I thought this sort of thing was your scene," she joked. "You're not drinking?"

A smoldering look ghosted his features. Confusion

flitted over his expression, but he just shook his head and shifted the glass away.

Sun laughed and patted the table. Ada couldn't help thinking she was missing something.

"What's the joke?" she asked.

Prim smiled sweetly at her, a blush already tinting her cheeks. "Sweetling, I thought you knew. The yellow is to purge our impurities, but the blue will keep us virile and amorous for hours to come." She leaned close and whispered, "It's what makes the hunt a little more fun."

Oh my dear Lord.

CHAPTER
FIFTEEN

The night was going to end in disaster, Jasper thought, as he watched Ada wade fully clothed into the sacred Lupercalia pool, her gown trailing behind her like a mermaid's tail. With every step, the bioluminescent silt stirred, coming alive. Unlike every other female submerging, Ada was clothed in cream. They wore red. But she didn't need the difference to stand out. The water made her gown cling to her skin, revealing every inch and perfect curve, stealing his breath, making his heart stutter.

When she'd walked in, he couldn't tear his eyes away. Then she submerged up to her shoulders, blond hair trailing on the surface like strings of gold mixing with the red ribbon of fate clutched in her fingers. But the true test of his resolve was when she emerged, inch by inch, on the other side. Water sluiced down her body to reveal the shape of her rear curves plastered to the translucent dress. He clenched his fists and then adjusted the damned mask on his face. At least this one allowed him to breathe. He would rip it off the moment he caught her.

The very idea of sinking his teeth into her caused his inner wolf to pace restlessly, ready for the hunt to begin.

Crimson only knew how his body would be reacting if he'd actually taken the divilixir.

Sun sidled up to him. Like most other hunters, he'd used the bioluminescent silt to paint stripes and patterns down his bare torso to mimic being Well-blessed. With his painted torso and dark hair and similar mask, Sun appeared remarkably similar to him. The only distinction was that Jasper's markings shone brighter than his cousin's. His were real.

"Still think she's yours?" Sun taunted.

A growl rumbled in the base of Jasper's throat, but he swallowed it down as he watched Ada's red ribbon trail behind her, churning in the water, sinking beneath the depths. With every step the females had made to cross the pool, blue bloomed to life and colored the water, making it impossible to see through. There was no way he'd be able to find out which ribbon belonged to her. His choice would be by random touch, just like everyone else's.

Anyone could match with Ada. Even Sun. Even... he shot a sideways glance to the other males eagerly bouncing on their toes, splashing on the shore. Each and every one had their hands on their pants, ready to strip. He wasn't sure whether they would shift for the advantage of using their wolf's nose in the hunt, or whether they simply wanted nothing impeding them for when they caught their match. But their hands didn't leave their pants. Maybe it was the divilixir amping up their hormones.

Didn't matter.

He would find Ada first. The Well would match them. He had faith.

And if it didn't... well, he pitied the poor soul who got in his way of claiming her. He would prove to her they were destined for each other. And they would forget about the politics being shoved down his throat.

He wanted none of it.

A wolf howled in the distance. Night birds took to the sky from branches. The drums beat faster behind them, and the spectators cheered.

All females had now emerged on the other side, dripping with water and smeared with bioluminescent blue. There had to be at least twenty, or so, but Jasper's eyes were only for Ada as she glanced coyly at him from over her shoulder, eyes bright through the slits of her mask.

His heart leapt into his throat at the impact of her beauty. Their Well-blessed marking twinkled up her arm. Wavy blond hair cascaded down her shoulders, shielding her wet chest from indecency. One end of the red ribbon was wrapped around her fist. The long length floated in the water before her, and then dipped beneath the depths, waiting for him.

He imagined he could already scent her unique arousal on the wind.

No longer was his inner wolf satisfied to pace. It hurled itself against the cages of his body, begging him to start the chase, unwilling to accept defeat.

Claim her. Mark her. Mine.

She had no idea what was coming for her.

After tonight, everything would change.

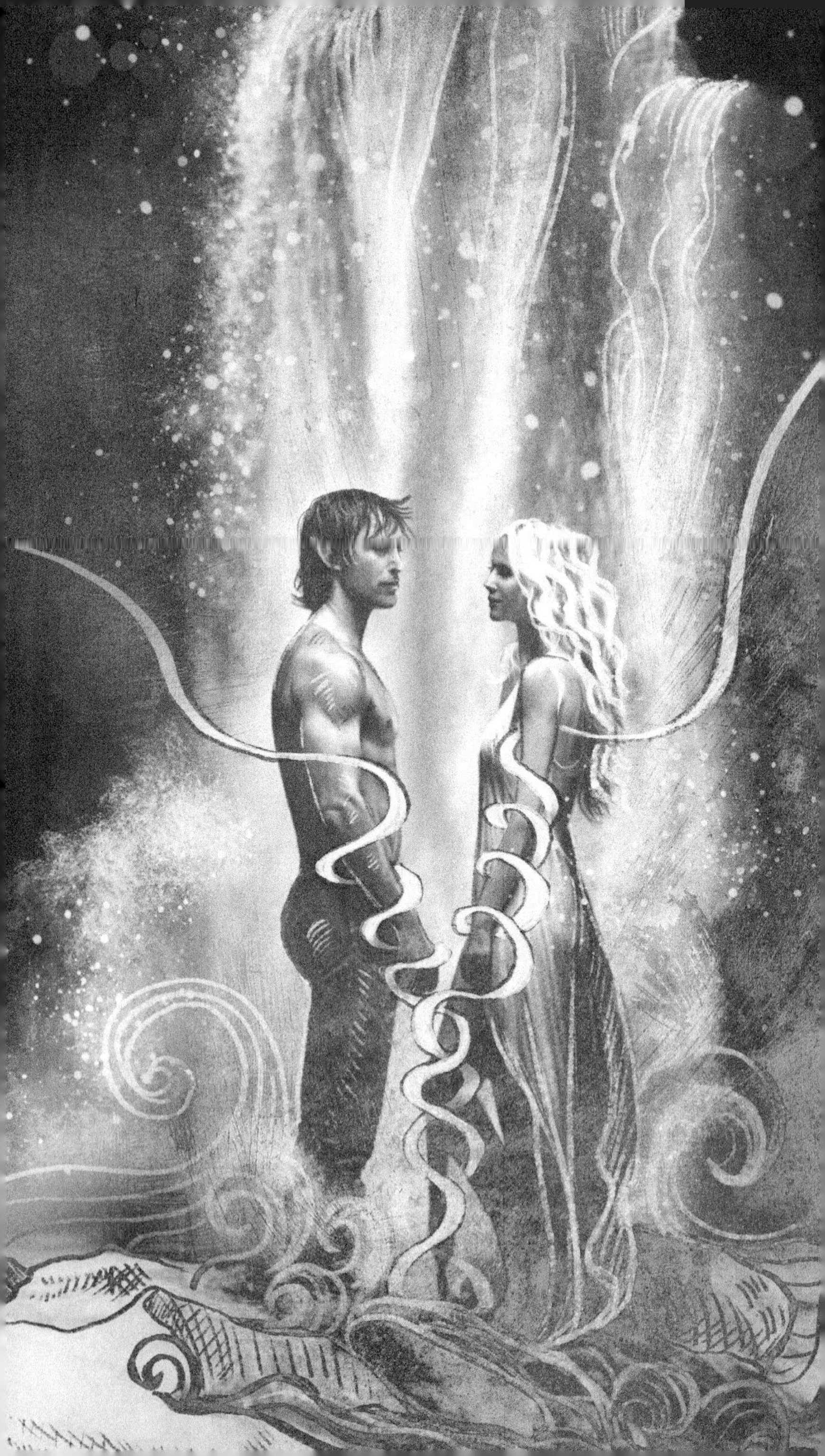

CHAPTER
SIXTEEN

Ada's brief dip in the water had been a balm against her feverish skin, too tight for her body, and already begging for the kind of relief only touch could bring. She shouldn't have drunk that blue liquid, but as she locked eyes with Jasper across the pool churning from the cascades, she found she didn't care.

The liquid had loosened something inside her, freed her from the constraints of propriety. Her limbs were jelly. Her body tingled. Butterflies crashed in her stomach. With each passing moment, a pleasant build of heaviness grew between her legs, and if she wasn't surrounded by the watchful eyes of the gathering, she would have pressed her thighs together to dispel the sensation. Heat flushed her cheeks, and she stifled a moan, grateful for the mask hiding most of her expression. Anticipation was an unknown visitor in the air, come to tease and entice her out of her usual self-imposed safe zone.

This is insane.

What am I doing?

She wasn't the only one on her side feeling a little turned on. The red-dressed females tried not to show their eagerness, but beneath their masks, their pupils were blown and their cheeks ruddy. Their hands clutched and flexed at their dresses or twirled about their ribbons. One or two even touched their breasts, squeezing. Feet danced from side to side, ready to... to what?

A delightful fuzziness swam in Ada's head.

What happens next?

She must have said the words aloud because the masked blond beside her turned with a smile and answered.

"Each of the hunters will pick a ribbon from the pool to see which maiden they've matched with, and then..." She wiggled and squirmed. "Then the hunt is on."

Ada recognized her voice. Her hair had been pulled back into a low ponytail. "Prim?"

She put her finger to her lips. "Shh. We're all nameless for tonight. I mean"—she giggled—"except for you two Luperci. Everyone knows who you are from your clothes, but we pretend, for one night, that we are nameless."

"Right," she laughed. "What happens at Lupercalia stays at Lupercalia."

Approved anonymity for everyone else... so this was like an organized one-night-stand. The moment the thought hit, she blushed from head to toe. Never in her life had she done something so wild and reckless, and she found she didn't care. She was too loose, too excited, too *hot*. She'd been in this world for a week and there had to come a time where she let go of the past and embraced her future. From what she'd learned about the humans of today, she did not align with their beliefs. Which meant she had to fully embrace this culture, these rules, and these traditions.

Or go back to living alone on a mountain.

That was the old Ada. The broken one Jasper had glimpsed. The one before she met Clarke and Laurel. Her heart twinged at the thought of her beloved friends. Sisters, more like it. They would be sad if Ada went back to her isolation. So, embracing these new customs had to be the path to her new future. Perhaps that was with Jasper.

Only one doubt niggled in her mind. She turned back to Prim with a frown. "What happens if someone gets... you know, knocked up?"

"Knocked up?" Prim giggled. "You mean with child?"

Ada nodded, to which Prim laughed further. "Oh, silly. Lupercalia is a fertility rite. That's the entire point!"

Shock bounced around in Ada's skull. She wasn't *that* willing to explore. *Oh my God.* Panic. *I'm not ready for that!*

Moon's words came back to her. No one will force her

to do anything she didn't want. But as the heat of the elixir sparked in her pulse, igniting her blood, she wondered if she'd be powerless to stop herself.

And she wasn't the only one who would have impulse control. The male shifters on the other side of the pool paced and prowled along the shore, eyes skittering between the maidens and the red ribbons they would soon pull out of the water.

Her throat dried.

Naked male chests gleamed under the moonlight. They kept their identities hidden with similar half-wolf mask as the maidens. They all wore red loose pants, just like the females wore red dresses. But even without the change in clothing color, Ada could distinguish Jasper from the feel of him echoing down their bond, the scars on his torso, the glowing marks down his arm, and, of course, the tantalizing glimpse of dark hair trailing down from his lower abdomen to dip beneath his pants.

She'd recognize those abs anywhere.

Gosh. She patted her cheeks. What did that say about her?

Clara stepped onto some rocks by the waterfall so the gathered crowd could view her better. With her arms raised, she called for hush until the excitement dulled, and all eyes landed on her. Only the sound of the cascading water could be heard. That, and Ada's heart smashing against her ribcage.

Ada met Jasper's eyes through his mask. He watched her intently. A bolt of lust speared down their bond. Her hand fluttered to her throat, and a slow, wicked grin stretched his perfect lips. He'd done that on purpose. The bastard knew exactly how to control their bond.

Fuck. She was in trouble.

"Lupercalia is a time-honored tradition of the Darkfoot Pack, and indeed, many shifter packs around Elphyne. It is the celebration of the birth of our race. It is how we honor the Well. And for the first time in centuries, thanks to the appointment of our very own Darkfoot Prince, the unsanctioned breeding law has been abolished. We're finally celebrating Lupercalia the right way again—with a matching ceremony that won't end in execution."

A boisterous cheer rang out.

Unsanctioned breeding? Execution? Centuries? The words bounced around Ada's head. She couldn't imagine living in a world where you were terrified to get pregnant for fear of execution. The enthusiasm of this Lupercalia was completely understandable.

"We're honored to have these two Luperci participate in the hunt this year," Clara shouted. "As tradition dictates, because your identity is compromised, and you are the honored guests, you may choose your ribbon first."

She gestured for Jasper to enter the pool, but he just stood back and folded his arms with a smirk that hid a wealth of mysteries glinting in his eyes.

He shook his head, and then boomed back, "I'll go last."

Shocked murmurs rippled over the gathering. Some fae shot up from their tables, sloshing their drinks in their haste. Some dashed closer to the pool, eager expressions lighting up their faces.

Ada stared at Jasper.

His lips stretched wider, and then he added in a loud, arrogant voice, "My mate needs to be convinced that we are destined to be together, because it is the Well's will."

Oohs and *Ahhs* of agreement coursed around. Ada caught glimpses of fae nodding and smiling in understanding—*the poor ignorant human doesn't believe in the power of the Well.*

It riled Ada to no end. Maybe that was why the next words blustered out of her mouth. "I will enjoy proving you wrong!"

Wolf whistles and loud whoops of excitement. Ada couldn't help smiling as she caught Jasper's wide-eyed stare. Her words weren't all instinctive reaction. There was some truth to it. She supposed, even with all she'd learned about her connection to this mystical force that gave her power, there was still so much unknown. Faith seemed incredible. Unless she saw it with her own eyes, she would take their words with a grain of salt. The arrogant shifter honestly thought he stood a chance of claiming her ribbon, after all the other hunters had their chance.

The pool still churned from the maidens' recent

journey across the water and the cascading waterfall. Blue silt mixed murkily so the red ribbons were hidden and tangled. There was no way Jasper could pick hers out on purpose when he couldn't even see where to put his hand.

That was the whole point, she supposed.

Her heart skipped a beat as the humor dropped from his expression and his eyes narrowed with a secret message—*You're going to pay for your doubt.*

Another shiver of heat pulsed through her. Immediately, the hard line of Jasper's mouth tipped up, as though he'd felt everything she'd projected. Or had scented it.

She said to Prim through the side of her mouth, "There's no magic matching spell in the water, or anything, is there? I mean, he can't cheat and *make* us match, right?"

"Isn't that what you want?"

"Maybe, but I won't make it easy on him."

A beat of silence stretched for longer than necessary. Ada glanced at her new friend, but found a ruthless glimmer in Prim's expression as she stared back. It was the flicker of something dark, and then it was gone, almost like Ada had imagined it like a cloud crossing the moon.

"Nope," Prim replied, her gaze swinging back to Jasper with a smile. "It's just plain, simple water."

Ada's pulse skittered with nerves. She bit her lip and turned back to Jasper as he stood calmly at the end of the line, still watching her.

"Hunters, find your maiden's ribbon!" Clara shouted, throwing her hands into the air.

Whoops, whistles, and drums beat loudly as the hunters launched into the water, pushing each other out of the way in a frenzy. As they submerged to waist length, they thrust their hands into the blue-silt churning liquid and fished beneath the surface until each emerged gripping the end of a maiden's red ribbon. Ada tried to ascertain if hers had been plucked, but it was impossible to sense. No extra tension on her ribbon had been pulled. The lengths were too long, and the cascading water had already shifted it.

Then, before they pulled the ribbon taut to meet their match, the hunters stood waiting. There was one last hunter remaining casually on the shore.

Jasper tossed Ada a cocky smirk and then sauntered into the water, continuing to submerge until the surface hit his muscular thighs. Without removing his smoldering gaze from Ada, he dipped his hand and fished around. How he found the remaining loose ribbon was beyond her, but he did. His smile broadened, and he straightened, slowly lifting his end into the air.

It was red. It was a ribbon. It could belong to anyone.

Ada's heart kicked against her chest.

"Maidens, hunters, gather your ribbons and meet your match."

One by one, each gathered their ribbons, tightening the

length until it pulled taut. The maidens gathered and entered the pool, the hunters did the same. Stretches of red lines lifted out of the water, dripping. Some had criss-crossed on the journey over, some matched straight ahead, but with the tension between them, pairings were irrefutable. To avoid confusion, both parties gathered their ribbons, drawing themselves into the middle of the pool and toward their match, their hunters... or their prey. Ada held her breath as she drew closer, silently begging for none of them to be Jasper, and at the same time, for all of them to be him.

Her ribbon had entangled the worst. It curled and entwined in a mess that reminded her of wool in a knitter's bowl. She ducked beneath other ribbons and waded around people until she could take the anticipation no more. She stopped. Her lungs heaved, lifting her chest until her peaked nipples rasped against her wet dress.

Can't watch. She shut her eyes.

Water sloshed as someone drew close, tugging on her ribbon, levering themselves to her. And then... a butterfly touch on the top of her hand.

Her eyes flew open.

There he was—the same wry curve of his lips, the same amber eyes and blue marks twinkling behind his mask. He tilted his head. The water was waist high for Ada, but only hit his thighs. Splashes from passersby had left trickles of blue silt residue and glittering water running in rivulets down the dips and valleys of his musculature, sharpened by the light of the moon. It was impossible not to be mesmerized.

"What did I tell you?" Jasper rumbled, a hint of amusement in his voice.

"I'm yours," she breathed.

His eyes crinkled as he brought her ribbon-entwined fist to his mouth.

"And I'm yours," he said, lips moving against her knuckles.

"Hunters," Clara shouted. "Scent your maidens."

Held captive in Jasper's stare, Ada froze as he trailed the tip of his nose from her wrist up to her arm until he grazed along her sensitized shoulder. A moan escaped her lips as he reached the intimate spot beneath her ear. One simple, raspy lick of his tongue and heat rushed between her legs. He nuzzled into her hair, murmuring softly for her ears only, "Just so you know, I don't need to do this. Your scent is engraved on my heart. I'll find you wherever you run."

She licked her lips. Damn her, but she was ready for this. He nudged in closer, bringing their bodies together. "I'll even give you a sporting chance and not shift."

"How magnanimous of you." Her palm landed on his chest, and smoothed over the ridged scars, finding pleasure in the slippery and velvety tactile sensation. God, she already couldn't stop touching him. This elixir, it heightened every sense.

A peek over her shoulder showed other couples getting

to know each other with barely restrained interactions. Fingers in hair, noses on skin, eyes full of restrained anticipation.

Jasper smiled against her shoulder. "It's for completely selfish reasons. I want this to last."

The nearby haunting howl of a wolf caused woodland sprites to take to the sky, creating a swirl of lights twinkling like drunken falling stars. It was magical, and it connected with that nature-loving part of Ada's soul. Yes... she could belong here.

Jasper unwound the ribbon from Ada's hand until he held it all, and then he stepped back with an impish look.

Clara spoke as the hunters tied their maiden's ribbons around their biceps.

"Maidens, your first and only warning—don't stray too far from the path, for there are lust-filled creatures in the woods, just waiting in the wings. We aren't the only fae inspired by Spring. It is wolpertinger mating season. Beware.

"Hunters, don't delay in finding your maidens, and may the grace of the Well color your way, blessing the Darkfoot pack's seed as plentiful for the body, as it is for the coming harvest."

Another wolf howled, this time closer. Slowly, wolves emerged from between the gathered spectators around the pool. Then another joined in, and another, until the chorus was deafening. Maidens fled the pool, turning and wading out as quickly as they could. Surprised, Ada looked to

Jasper expectantly. He leaned forward, bared his teeth in a grin and growled, "*Run.*"

Jolting with adrenaline, Ada waded as fast as she could out of the pool and in the direction the other maidens fled. It was the side opposite the dinner party and tables. There was nothing beyond but rocks, dirt paths, and tall trees reaching toward the twinkling night sky. Glowing sprites lazily danced above and darted off in all sorts of directions, like mini fireworks, perhaps to provide the maidens some guidance.

On the shore, Ada hiked up her sodden dress, then glanced over her shoulder, locked eyes with Jasper, and kissed the air in a brazen tease. The line of his jaw tightened beneath his mask, and she knew she was poking the beast, but fuck it. She was having fun. For the first time in... goodness, she couldn't remember. She may as well go all in. God knew her body was up for it.

Taking two steps at a time, she picked her way across the rocks and then ran full pelt down a hilly dirt path twining through the trees. She ran, her heart on fire, her lungs burning, until she reached a fork in the path only fifty feet away and stopped. Three paths. The red fluttering of a maiden's dress went down the left, trodden footsteps down the middle, and the dark right had smooth sand.

More howling pierced the night air. Ada's eyes widened, and she looked over her shoulder. Surely that was the signal for the hunters.

"Already?" she gasped.

Shit!

"Come with me!" Prim emerged from the shadows and took her hand. "I know a secret hiding spot."

With no time to waste, Ada allowed herself to be dragged down the third, less trodden path, and then they bolted. Wind whipped at their hair, laughter bubbled on their tongues. Ada was having such thrilling fun, and her body buzzed with too many distracting sensations, that she failed to comprehend why Prim had taken her hand in the first place. Surely this matching ceremony was a one-on-one thing with their matched partners. So why was Prim helping her?

Further down the path they ran, their feet getting dirty, their faces gathering dust. The sound of running water grew louder.

"In here," Prim panted as they came to a boulder. She rounded it and tugged Ada along with such urgency, her arm almost yanked from its socket.

Suddenly, Ada wasn't having fun. Every step and bounce cut into her bare feet as she slipped on hard rocks and burning sand. Every breath was sharp and hard to draw. Her throat closed. She tugged back her arm, but Prim kept them running.

"Where are we going, Prim?"

"Just a little further."

They burst out from the trees and onto the bank of a narrow river twinkling under the starlight. Ada snatched her hand back and doubled over to catch her breath. She yanked her mask off and threw it on the ground.

"What the hell is going on?" she gasped between breaths.

Prim bent down to pick up the mask and then straightened with a cold look in her eyes.

"It's harder to catch our scent after we cross the water," she explained, then gave a sudden grin. It didn't reach her eyes.

Warning bells went off in Ada's head.

"I'm good waiting here."

"We shouldn't wait, Ada. We should make them work for it. I thought you said you didn't want to make it easy on him."

Ada glanced at the river. It wasn't too wide. It looked easy to cross, but Clara had warned them not to stray too far from the path, and Ada had already faced one wolpertinger during mating season. She wasn't prepared to face another. Especially not on a night that was supposed to be fun. She told Prim this, but a shadow flashed before Ada's face. She raised her hands instinctively, but failed to protect herself.

Something knocked the side of her head. She staggered.

That's weird; Prim's fist dangled oddly at her side with a rock in her hand.

"Why do you have—" Ada's words cut off at the sight of blood on Prim's rock.

Confused, her fingers went to her head and came back sticky with blood. Groggily, Ada registered what had happened too late. With the awareness, pain exploded at the wound site.

Prim swung her rock at Ada's head.

Everything went dark.

CHAPTER
SEVENTEEN

Ada rose from the darkness of her subconscious as someone jostled her body, tugging on her dress. Prim hunched over her but straightened. Blinking, Ada checked around. The moment her head moved, pain sloshed, making her woozy. She grasped her forehead. They were still on the riverbank under the moonlight. Alone.

Wolves howled in the distance and the beat of drums meant they weren't too far from the Lupercal cave. Or was that the pounding of Ada's heart, getting louder and more persistent with each passing second.

Prim had hit her over the head.

Why?

Ada glanced down and discovered something that didn't compute. She was now in the red dress, not the cream. *Prim* wore the cream Luperci dress. Her mask was off, and she was pulling a long, bone pin from her hair, unwinding the length, and fluffing out the long golden strands over her shoulders.

"What have you done, Prim?"

She jolted, only just realizing Ada was awake. With pursed lips, she scowled down.

"*Crimson*, Ada. You shouldn't be awake so soon."

Still muddled, Ada's brain hadn't caught up to what her heart knew to be true. Call her naïve, call her inexperienced, but Ada just never expected her only friend in this town to betray her. Surely there was another explanation. There had to be.

"Why?" she asked again.

Prim's face contorted. "You have no idea what it's like for someone like me, a Lesser Fae. I've been waiting for this chance for centuries. They all act like we're better than the humans, but there is still division between tribes, and division within tribes. It's every fae for themselves. Mana is power. Originally, I had hoped to match with Sun, he is the alpha heir apparent, after all. But then Reed comes back, and he's lusting after someone with the same hair as me. I can smell it on him every time you walk by. And you don't even want him!" Her eyes turned desperate. "Just let me have him. For one night."

"But it won't be one night, will it?"

Prim's lips curved. A glint flashed at her fingers as she moved closer. "Clever girl. Of course it won't be. With the child of the Mithras line growing in my womb, they'll have to take me seriously. I won't let you get in my way."

"And what, you're going to pretend you're me?" Ada laughed. "There's no way he'll—"

Prim launched at Ada, planted her hands on her front and knocked her backward down the slope of the riverbank. Ada tumbled into the slippery mud, crying out as stone daggers poked her body until she splashed to a stop, face first in the muddy silt. She gasped through a pinch in her gut.

"You fucking bitch," she spluttered. Anger bubbled to the surface. Her survival instincts kicked in, and she rolled to the side, using her knee to push herself up.

The pinch in her belly turned into a fiery sting, but she planted one foot in front of the other, glaring at the blond securing Ada's half-face mask on. Prim lifted her chin and swallowed, meeting Ada's hate-filled glare.

"You should have just stayed down, Ada."

She turned and ran away.

⚖

THE MORE ADA moved through the dark woods, the more confused she became. Her belly hurt. Her head hurt. Darkness crowded her vision. Her state of mind caused the effects of the amorous elixir to curdle. Nervous energy pulsed and dragged in her veins. She wanted to puke.

Gulping in deep breaths of cool night air, she used tree

trunks to find her way back to the main path. Stumbling out, she glanced to the right and to the left. Where were they?

Horror visions of Jasper and Prim entwined in hot, naked passion flashed before her eyes.

He would know it wasn't Ada. He would know.

There was their Well-blessed markings. Her scent.

Your scent is engraved on my heart. That's what he'd said. But try as she might, she couldn't fight the rising panic stealing her sense. Prim wasn't stupid. She wouldn't risk everything if she didn't think she stood a chance. She knew if she could get Jasper to lay with her and impregnate her, she'd be safe.

Was it Ada's fault? Had she not acted so standoffish to Jasper, if she'd accepted his claim to be mates in public, would this have happened?

Had he taken the blue elixir?

She couldn't remember.

Were the drums getting further away? Or finishing?

Ada glanced up at the sky but couldn't see the moon. Where was it?

Shuffling to the right. She looked, found nothing, but strained her ears for more.

There—between the branches—a flash of skin. She ducked and winced as the pain in her stomach sliced excruciatingly. Her hand flew to the pain source and hit something hard and wobbly. With a sinking sense of dread, her fingers wrapped around a rod. *Hurts.*

She glanced down with a hitched breath. Prim's bone hairpin protruded from the side of her abdomen. Blood oozed over the red dress, darkening it further. The floor tilted. Her stomach revolted.

And then she did something she *knew* not to do. She pulled it out with a strangled cry. Warm blood gushed from the wound until she slapped her palm over it.

Dumb, dumb girl.

Could she heal herself as she healed others? She tried to call on her gift, but madness muddled her brain. The elixir. The attack. Her heart palpitating. The pain.

Focus.

I can't.

It was not the same as healing someone else. This was her body to search, and it felt too much like her own confusing mind.

Find Jasper.

She staggered onward, feet crunching over leaves and twigs, hand over her side, struggling to keep her eyes open.

There. Another flash of skin in the night. Someone. But as she shuffled closer, the skin became flesh, and the flesh became entwined. Two naked, writhing bodies, lost in the throes of passion, rolling around on a discarded cream, linen dress.

No.

The trees closed in. Ada blinked and flinched away, but forced her blurred, fever-pitched gaze back for a better look. Dark hair. A wall of broad, muscled back, ropy with exertion. Taut ass with feminine legs wrapped around, heels digging in as he thrust into her, grunting with passion. Blond hair on the woman. Eyes behind a wolfish mask that met Ada's stare over his shoulder. Her sleazy, wicked grin of triumph.

Jasper?

How could he? He'd promised. Ada swooned. Bile rose in her mouth. Madness in her mind grew with visions of her past, slamming behind her closed eyes—of her mother's abandonment, of her coming home one time, surprised to see Ada. She'd been almost thirteen. *"Oh, you're here. I forgot about you!"* Her mother's boyfriend laughed.

Ada jammed the heels of her palms to her fevered eyesockets.

She heard her friend telling her there was more to life than hiding away from people. Laurel teaching her to read.

"What's that word say. Spell it out."

"S.I.S.T.E.R. It says sister."

Ada had learned to trust. And Clarke and Laurel had been with Ada to the end. But now, that trust seemed so empty. What did Ada get out of it? She'd opened her heart to a new friendship, and Prim had betrayed her, just as much as Jasper had.

Ada didn't care what the excuse was. Whether the blue elixir had addled their minds, or whether Jasper had lied and couldn't scent Ada so distinctly... or maybe he didn't care at all. It wouldn't be the first time someone had lied to her.

A sudden, overwhelmingly helplessness hit Ada like a tidal wave, causing the floor to shift beneath her feet.

Have to get out of here.

She spun, clutching her middle. She ran as hard as she could; the tears stinging her eyes, the pain in her side burning, until she fell. Crashing down, she hit a log, tumbled and slid to the ground. Heaving breaths turned into big wracking sobs. And every sad thought she'd ever had since awaking in this time culminated in a big, horrid cry.

She'd thought it would be different. She'd hoped people would be different. But they were all the same. Whether now, in this time, or two thousand years ago. They only cared for themselves. Like Prim had said, it was every fae for themselves. God, Ada wanted her sisters. If only she could see them one more time.

CHAPTER
EIGHTEEN

Jasper strolled through the moonlit woods, snapping twigs off branches with a lazy smirk, thinking about how Ada's air-kiss had triggered his hunter instincts. His wolf had snarled for him to start the chase early, no matter the protocol, but when the second round of howls erupted from the sidelines, and the other males dashed off—he'd stopped short and smiled. He knew what awaited for him. And it was the kiss of her plush lips, and the sinking in between her soft thighs.

A shuddering groan of anticipation rippled through him.

He would give her time to come to terms with the idea of their joining. She might be high on divilixir, but he wasn't, and he knew that once she distanced herself from the initial rush, she might think differently. *Crimson*, Jasper thought differently. The old him would have... the old him?

His thoughts stuttered.

The curse marks burned like fire around his neck, blocking his recognition. He frowned, itching with a flush of irritation. The pain of ignorance was fast becoming worse than the pain of his memories. At least if he knew the kind of fae he wasn't, then he could work toward being the kind Ada needed. The kind she'd happily accept as a mate.

Rustling sounds in the leaves stopped him. He'd been so lost in his thoughts, he hadn't noticed he'd walked in on the privacy of a matched couple, tumbling in the leaves beneath a moss-covered tree. The male sensed his approach and shot up with a territorial growl aimed Jasper's way.

Jasper gave him a casual salute and then kept walking, idly plucking another twig from a blackcurrant bush before lifting it to his nose and inhaling deeply. She'd passed this way. Satisfaction bloomed in his chest.

I'm coming, Ada.

Their bond kept them linked. He could *feel* her like a beacon of heat—an extension of himself—echoing silently somewhere to the right.

He tsked slightly as he realized she'd strayed from the path.

"Naughty, Ada," he grumbled to himself.

Hadn't she learned her lesson with the first wolpertinger? Perhaps he should play a game with her, frighten her and pretend to be the very thing they were warned against. He found a few branches shaped like antlers and held onto them, intending to use them as a wolpertinger disguise. This would be fun.

Although, in all seriousness, she needed marking, sooner rather than later. It was the only way he'd feel satisfied other males would avoid her. His teeth ached, elongating, ready for the task. His cock strained hard against his pants and he subtly adjusted himself for comfort.

Multiple scents of arousal clashed across the winds. Hunters had caught their prey. Every cell in his body cried out to catch his.

You have all night. Relax.

He forced the tension to disperse, but the scent of musk kept sending his inner wolf into a frenzy. Fae everywhere were engaged in lustful activities. As it should be on Lupercalia.

A cry caught on the wind. He stopped, tilted his head and pricked his ears.

Was that...?

Ada? No. It couldn't be. He shook his head and continued walking, but was remiss to stop his feet from moving faster. His heart rate picked up speed. He followed the *ping* of their bond connection, ensuring he followed the direction in which the link felt stronger. But the soft whimpers of a sobbing woman sent every hair on the back of his neck standing on edge.

It came from off the path, deeper into the woods, down by the river.

Alarm prickled through him. His first thought was of the mana-warped creatures known to visit the woods. He'd fought them once—*a burn at his neck*. He hissed a curse, hating that he failed to learn whether this wailing was friend or foe. Some of his memories had come back. Some stayed locked behind a gate, and it was impossible to work out how much was missing.

The Well-blessed bond link was weak. It felt further away than the crying female.

Wolpertingers didn't make that sound. Perhaps it was the White Woman? If it was, the Unseelie fae lurked out of her territory. Known to weep and cry for help, the White Woman lured men into her web, glamoured as a beautiful lost maiden, but she was a monster of disgusting bug-like proportions. She ate the heads of her mates, while still mating with them.

A dark memory from the corner of his mind tried to poke through, but his body revolted in horror. He shook his head. Not now. Not another flashback.

"Clarke... Laurel..." More sobs.

Those names sounded familiar. That voice was familiar. He pushed through the trees, urgency spurring him onward.

And then he found her. The sticks fell from his hands. His heart tore from his chest. *Ada*. Injured. On the ground and covered in mud. Not wearing cream as he'd left her, but the red of a maiden.

It was definitely her. The mud-smeared Well-blessed

marks on her arm called to his own. He rushed to her side, fell to his knees and felt his world break apart.

"Love," he said, and took her face. It lolled into his touch, limp, sweaty and weak. "Ada. It's me. What happened?"

She moaned and thrashed her head, squeezing her eyes shut. Sweat covered her pale skin. Why was she so pale? Had she eaten something? Was she—? His gaze snagged on her hands clutching her middle. Blood. Coppery, sweet-bitter blood oozing out of her body. How had he not smelled it?

A snarl ripped out of him when he realized how distracted the hunt had made him. He searched their surroundings for an enemy, but only heard the moans and sounds of lovers beneath the whispering wind. A crow cawed somewhere overhead. The soft trickle of running water filtered in from the nearby river.

He lifted her into his arms and carried her as fast as he could down to the river. The water flowed fresh. It would do.

He gently laid her down on the sloped bank, allowing her legs to dangle into the water, hoping the temperature would rouse her. Under the moonlight, dark blood blended into the water and carried away with the stream, reminding him of the ribbon at the start of the night.

She groaned in protest and tried to swat him away. "No... I want Laurel."

"Is that your mother?" he asked, his heart aching.

"S'not her," she mumbled, scrunching her face drunkenly. Her eyes focused on him as he splashed water onto her wound and tried to pry her fingers away. *Well-damn*, the wound was deep. He covered it with his hand. Betrayal lanced down their bond like hot spice. Her face hardened. She pushed him away.

"Don't you *dare* touch me," she hissed, and then fell back panting, as though the outburst had sapped all her energy.

His heart ripped a little further.

"What's happened, Ada?"

"You..." she ground out. "You were with *her!* I saw you."

"Who?"

"I should never have trusted you. I should never have let my guard down." She tried to scramble away from him. "But I'm a survivor. I don't need you, asshole. You're all the same."

"Who was it, Ada?" He couldn't hide the growl in his voice.

"You know who!" Her voice cracked as she strained to get closer and bared her teeth.

Jasper was too shocked to respond. All the effort in her body released, and she collapsed to the ground. Her head landed hard on the muddy bank. She winced, held her breath, and squeezed her eyes shut.

"I don't need you," she said. "I don't."

"I don't know who you saw, but it wasn't me. I've been

taking my time getting to you. Whoever you saw wasn't me."

He reached for her again, to stanch the blood flow, but she jerked back.

"Ada," he admonished. "Your mind is playing tricks on you."

He dug into his pockets and pulled out the blackcurrants.

"See?" He offered them to her. "Blackcurrants. Not mana berries. I didn't take the divilixir either. I wanted to be clear in the head for this. For you."

A flicker of doubt entered her gaze. It was enough for her to pause. He used the opportunity to push her down gently and then put pressure on her wound. Her eyes rolled, and she visibly forced her awareness back to him.

"Why aren't you healing yourself?" he demanded, exasperated. Her skin was cold. Too much blood had leaked out.

He stilled with a realization that sent fear tracing down his spine. When he was tracking her, the link of their bond had seemed faint. He'd thought it was because she was further away than he'd supposed, but it was something else. Her light was dimming.

Ada was dying.

Panic pierced his lungs like the claws of a foe. *No.* She wasn't dying. He wouldn't allow it. He needed her. He unlocked the hold on his emotions and let her feel it.

Confusion swam across her expression—shock, awe,

and... relief. Her lashes lifted as their gazes met. A tear glistened. It trickled along her lash line and then spilled over her cheek before joining the mud on the bank below.

"You're telling the truth," she mumbled. "It wasn't you. I can *feel* it."

His features hardened, and he pushed all the resolve he could muster into his gaze, hoping she could see and feel the truth of his next words. "I would *never* leave you. Do you understand? I will always find you." Silence. Nothing. Her lids fluttered low. "Ada," he choked, gently shaking her. "You're the reason I'm still breathing. Your voice calls me from the darkest places. I can't... I can't live without you. Now focus! Heal yourself." He took her hands and placed them over her wound, then covered them with his own. "Heal yourself."

"Can't focus," her head thrashed. "I'm too muddled. I tried. Need more training... not good enough."

"I refuse to believe that. You're the only person in Elphyinian history who has removed a curse. And you learned all that through intuition, through compassion. If you can do that, for me—as broken as I am—then you can heal yourself. You're perfect the way you are."

"Flattery..." she mumbled, too tired to finish.

"How do you search for a wound when you heal someone else?"

"I feel it out," she breathed. "Listen for changes... but I can't hear."

"Then use my voice," he said. "Let it guide you as yours

has for me."

"Jasper—"

"You're not dying today, Ada," he decreed. "Now listen to my voice." He slowed down the tempo. "Let it calm you. Let it soothe you. Concentrate. Feel it. Feel our bond. We're the same. We're connected. Start there, then flow back into your body. You got it?"

A frown. A meeting of her delicate brows. And then, a nod.

"I feel you," she whispered, shivering.

Her lips were so blue.

"Keep going. Draw on me. Take my energy."

Her lips parted on a gasp as the first rush of his mana pushed into her. His lids lowered at the rush through their bond. He knew what it was like to take her mana, but this was the other way around. It gushed out of him with staggering force until her fingers heated beneath his touch. The drag on his mana slowed. He panicked, thinking she'd given up, but when he looked down, her skin color had returned.

He lifted trembling fingers from her wound. No more blood flow.

"Ada?"

Her lashes fluttered.

"Love?"

She opened her eyes. Stark need shone in the depths of her clear gaze, no longer clouded by injury. The change in her was remarkable. Her gaze dipped to his rosy lips, and a rush of lust chased him down their bond, winding itself around his senses, coaxing them back to life.

"Ada?"

Gone was the confused, afraid girl.

The woman who slowly climbed to her hands and knees, and then prowled toward him was all confidence, and presumably all healed. Muddy water splashed as she came closer. He washed his hands in the water.

"It worked?" he asked gingerly.

She nodded, a small smile playing on her lips as she climbed on his lap, pushing him back on his hands.

"It worked," she rasped, and then licked his bottom lip before sucking it between her teeth.

He groaned, eyes fluttering, his body turning hard with need. Everything he'd felt before he found her rushed back as though it had never left. Unable to help himself, he pushed forward with his lips, hardening their kiss.

"Ada," he warned. "You almost died."

"Then I didn't." She nipped at his jaw. Licked down his neck. Suckled on his Adam's apple.

He threw his head back to give her access. "You're covered in mud and blood."

"Who cares?"

"This is the divilixir still in your system. It can take hours to work itself out. Take it easy."

"Mm-hm." She didn't care, already grinding against his lap, making his cock swell and strain against his wet pants, demanding Jasper let go of his inhibitions.

But he wouldn't take advantage of her. She meant too much to him. He took her shoulders and gently pushed her back. She resisted, licking the air between them.

"Someone tried to kill you tonight," he growled, hating how weak-willed he sounded. *Crimson*, he wasn't that much of a hedonist, was he? That he couldn't separate sex from... she bit his ear, licking around the lobe, and he forgot. What was he thinking?

"I need you," she groaned. "It's not just the elixir. I need to *feel* you. To know you're here. That you're *mine*."

His brow puckered. When he'd found her, she'd spoken deliriously, accusing him of being with someone else.

She speared fingers into his hair and clenched tight, causing a ripple of pain to spark at the roots. Adrenaline and lust spiked through him, and now he couldn't tell whose was whose. His body hardened with want. His teeth elongated, ready to claim. To mark.

She'd said he was hers.

You're mine.

She'd said it.

It's the elixir, you bastard.

It wasn't him she wanted. It was the Lupercalia spell. Tomorrow this would all be over. But she'd been okay with it at the start, hadn't she? She'd wanted this night. She'd kissed the air in his direction. She'd agreed to this... sort of.

He gripped under her arms and shifted her back until he could meet her feverished gaze.

"I know exactly what I'm doing," she insisted, in a sultry voice that made his cock jolt eagerly.

Damn him to the Well Worms.

"You say that now..." He winced. She'd been so vulnerable before. She'd cried and sobbed. He'd never seen her break a tear in the week he'd known her. He hated to see her so upset, so broken.

She must be a witch, a mind-reader, or a Seer, because her next words came straight out of the dark places he was sure he'd kept locked.

"You want to take care of me?" she asked.

Fuck, yes, he wanted to take care of her. For the rest of their lives. She must have seen it on his face because her features softened. A wave of emotion glistened in her eyes, and then the seductress was back, with smoldering heat.

She put her fingers on her thighs and gathered the dress in an enticingly slow drag to reveal her calves, knees, then thighs, never once unlocking their gazes.

There was something else in that stare, something beyond the sexual challenge. She had been right. She needed him. This went beyond the lust. It was a primal, primitive need for connection and comfort. The same need they'd both danced around since first seeing each other. She kept dragging the dress. Higher and higher the fabric went, revealing skin so smooth his mouth watered for want of its taste. But he couldn't look down. If he did, there would be no holding him back.

"So take care of me," she dared.

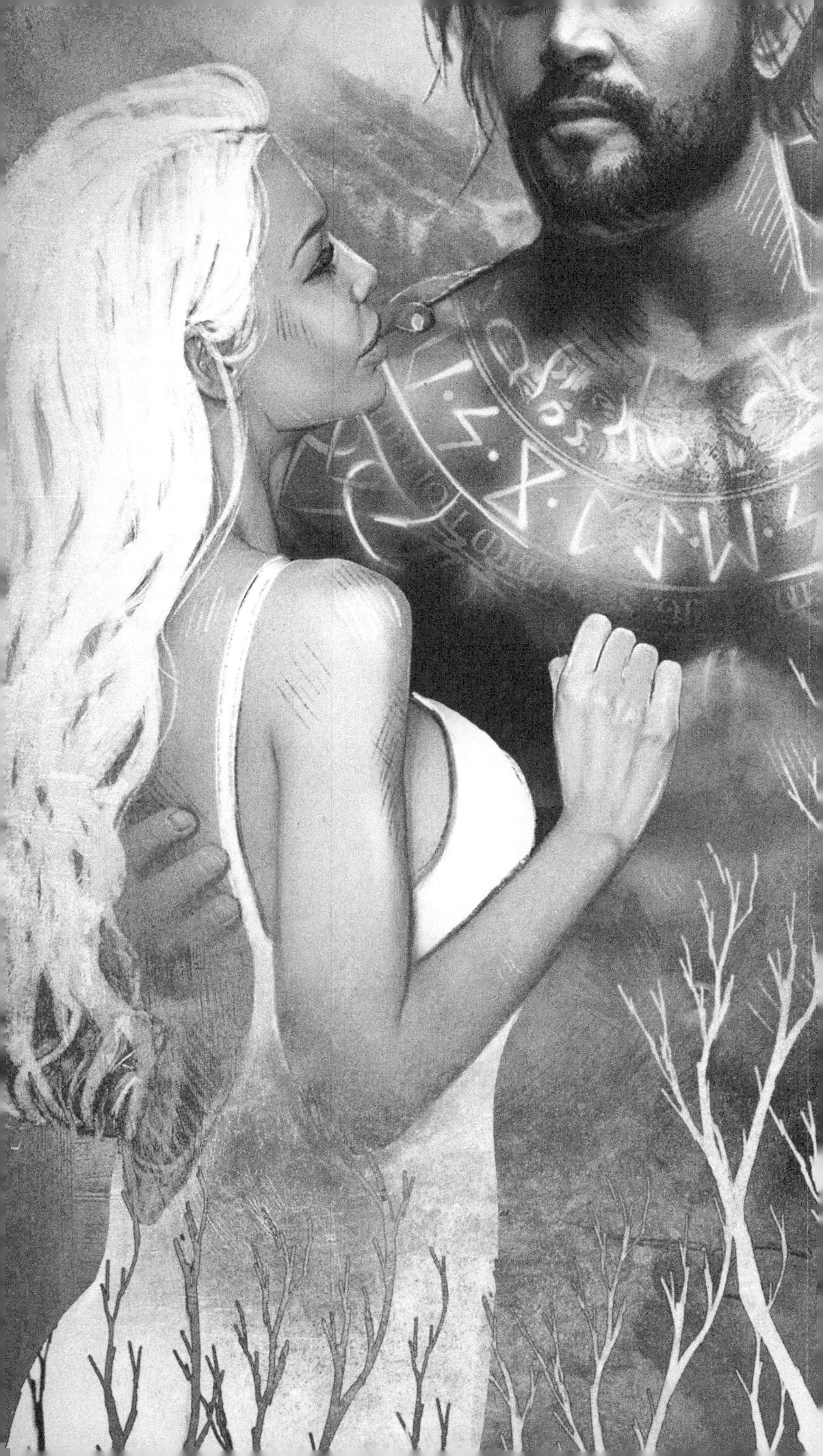

CHAPTER
NINETEEN

Amber eyes flashed gold. That's all Ada saw before Jasper grazed his palms up her thighs, removing the final constraints of her dress. He tested her healed abdomen, probing his fingers over her skin. It set her senses on fire. She moaned and arched into him. He responded with a strangled sound of frustration, and then buried his face between her legs, supping on the sensitive junction between her thighs. She squirmed and writhed, so full of feeling that she feared her skin would float away.

"Jesus," she gasped as he wrenched her panties aside and licked her straight down the middle.

He groaned against her flesh, kissed her inner thigh, and then hooked fingers into her underwear, dragging them off her legs. When he returned, he didn't come up for air. His tongue worked her with ravenous hunger, swirling and probing as though he was made of magic. It felt too divine, too worked up, too intense.

She wriggled back. He growled in disapproval, flattened his hand on her stomach and pinned her down. Then he went back to feasting on her, drawing keening whimpers of bliss, helpless moans, and gasps for air.

There was little Ada could do but thread her fingers into his hair and hold on, submitting to the force of his pleasure until everything inside her wound tight. *Too fast. Too much.* She clutched his hair, threw her head back, arched into him, and shouted her shuddering release.

Panting, trying to pull the stars into focus and figure out what the hell had just happened—she was in pieces—she became aware of the hot-blooded male crawling up her body with heavy-lidded, dark-lashed eyes. He nuzzled into her, rolling his stubbled cheek against her jaw, gently rocking his hips against hers, pushing his hardness to the sensitive flesh between her thighs. If it wasn't for his pants, he'd be inside her, she had no doubt.

"Look what you made me do," he chided, kissing her neck.

His fingers roamed over her front, slipping up her waist, thumbs brushing beneath the pillow of her breasts, coaxing more lazy sensations from her aching body.

"Ada," he murmured against her skin, a note of melancholy. "I wanted to wait until you were better, but you made me *want*." Another growl. He nipped her collarbone, and she gasped. "You make me lose all sense."

Still unable to form words, her weak fingers trailed down his head. "I'm... *Jesus*. Just give me a minute. I'm relearning how to form words."

His chuckle rumbled through him. He stilled with his sharp teeth on her neck. He stayed so silent that Ada thought, perhaps, he was asleep. Which made no sense. He hadn't... finished, had he?

"Jasper?" she whispered. "Are you going to... you know?"

Just give her a minute and she'd be good to go.

He pulled himself up and gave her a lazy, entitled grin. "No, my love. When I claim you, I'm going to mark you, and I want you to be in full control of your senses. You're going to beg me for it. And you're going to remember it with startling clarity. I refuse to do it another way."

Ada's heart stopped. She forgot to breathe. He'd said, *my love*. Was it a figure of speech? Or—?

"Beg for it?" She raised an eyebrow. "Really?"

His lips landed on hers with a guttural groan. All thoughts immediately vacated her mind. She became lost in his salty taste and the torture of his wicked tongue as he probed and drove into her mouth with proprietary intent. Oh, God. He was right. She would beg for it. Why had she waited so long for this?

When he drew back, she chased his lips and tried to claim more. He gave her a self-satisfied smirk that revealed how well he thought he'd taken care of her, and how much more he fantasized about. But then he pushed himself off the riverbank before hauling her into his arms and standing. Feeling rather like a damsel in distress, she clutched him around the neck as he held her.

He smiled down with a barely restrained smolder that promised more wicked things to come. He held her gaze while his thumb grazed her inner thigh and then brushed over the sensitive swell of her intimate flesh, teasing her. She squirmed with a gasp. With her dress bunched and dangling, and no underwear, the cool air traveled straight to her damp core, making her ache deliciously for more.

"Put me down," she insisted, her voice still husky. "Let's finish this."

Playfulness evaporated from his expression, and hard lines returned. "Someone tried to kill you. I'm carrying you."

"I'm seriously fine."

"Still carrying you."

"The entire way back? We're done?" she pouted.

"Yes."

"But I feel great."

"Don't argue," he grunted. "Or I'll swing you over my shoulder and spank you."

She squirmed at the thought, and he chuckled.

"Perhaps you would like that too much."

"Shut up," she grumbled with a smile.

A hearty laugh boomed from him, rumbling through their connection and her heart stopped at the sight. A rush of endorphins crashed through her, simply from watching him smile. He was perfect. Heartbreakingly so.

He swung her around and strode out of the riverbank with a saunter that made her think of the cat who'd caught the mouse. But behind them, back on the river, twinkling blue light caught her eye. For a moment, she thought it was just their arm markings reflected, but this was different. It came from the river. She stilled.

"What's that?" she asked.

Jasper sensed it at the same time. A lethal quiet crept into his posture. Not even the puff of his breath could be heard as he swung back around and they both stared at the blue spot.

Ada knew exactly what it was—the same thing she'd seen in the fountain on the day she'd awoken in this time. Someone was spying on them.

How much had they heard?

With his grip tightening on her, Jasper stepped closer. As the scene inside the blue light came into view, Ada gasped. It was the golden-haired King and his dark, hooded companion. Sitting, watching, and listening.

The King's jaw hardened as his gaze landed on Jasper. A bejeweled hand appeared by his jaw, fidgeting. Something dark and hate-filled flashed in his eyes before he stamped it down beneath a mask of pompous regality.

"That's quite the show you put on, my son." The King smirked as his eyes shifted to Ada. "Or was it your show, Primrose?"

Ada's breath hitched. Jasper tensed to the point of hardness. He pulled her tighter against his front.

"He couldn't see us," he murmured to Ada. "We have to be directly in front of the link."

Like now.

But he'd *heard* them? And he thought her name was Primrose? An icky feeling squirmed through her at the idea of this lewd, evil man listening to their intimate moment. Had this all been a trap? Was this why Prim had hurt Ada?

The King's eyes shifted to Ada, and that icky feeling expanded as he studied her. His gaze shifted to the blue Well-blessed markings of her arm before landing back on her face. "You're not Primrose."

Ada didn't think Jasper's grip could get tighter, but it did. The King's eyes flickered with surprise.

"I must say," he said to Jasper. "You're looking incredibly well for someone who should be dead."

The veiled displeasure in his tone made the hooded companion at his side shift uncomfortably.

"He should be dead," the hooded figure said. "No one survives the ponaturi's bite."

The King's piercing stare settled on Ada again. "Who are you?"

The hooded figure leaned closer. Ada glimpsed a crooked nose and thin lips. "She is not the same female," he confirmed, once again talking to his companion as though he cared little if they were overheard.

Only someone so cocky or drunk with power would believe he was untouchable.

"But she's not just anyone, is she?" The King pointed at Ada's Well-blessed marks, and then Jasper's neck. "Look at his curse marks."

"They're half gone."

King Mithras's lips pursed. "Another impossibility, you assured me."

"I... I don't know what to say."

"It is clear she is one of them—those mana-capable humans from the old world. I want her." Mithras slammed his palm down hard with a slap.

The jolt snapped Jasper out of his daze. He twisted them, hiding Ada from the King's eyes, and then kicked the blue water link, displacing and cutting off the connection. When Ada next looked, the glow was gone. Only the trickling river water remained and the sound of Jasper heaving lungfuls of air as he struggled to catch his breath.

"Hey." She placed her palm over his wildly beating heart. "Are you okay?"

A caged beast stared out of his amber-eyed gaze.

"He knows," Jasper growled, shocked. "He knows."

"That you're alive?"

His gaze clashed with hers. "He knows about *you*. What you mean to me. He'll come for you. It's what he does."

A pained expression crossed his features. Then Ada found herself deposited on the grassy riverbank so fast the wind knocked out of her and she crashed to her knees.

Jasper landed hard beside her and placed her hands on his neck. With a jaw locked tight, he met her gaze.

"Take it all off."

"The curse marks?"

He nodded. "It's time. I need to know everything about him before he comes. I need to know how to stop him. *Now*, Ada."

"Okay, okay." Her mind swirled. Right. Forget about the unwanted thrill still thrumming in her veins from the divilixir. Forget about how he'd just had his mouth between her legs. Forget about how his father had been listening in the entire time. "Right." But... "What if he listens in again?"

Jasper scowled. "He wouldn't dare. Besides, he knows the connection can work two ways. As his blooded kin, I can seek him out. He won't be anywhere near water right now. Do it, Ada."

I can do this.

If she could focus enough while almost dying, then she could do this. With a deep exhale out, she let her breath slide over her tongue, through her lips, and thought of nothing else until the next breath dragged in. She forced herself to be calm and to concentrate on the energy brimming within her. When Jasper had told her to use their connection as an anchor, it had worked. She could sense the difference between that power compared to the sensations in the rest of her body. This was *mana*—the life-force of the Well. This was where her power came from. She reached out to it with her mind's eye. It reacted to her call, like an old friend, a separate entity. Power brimmed inside her, quicker than ever before.

She placed a palm over the ridges of the blue curse marks, slid her mana beneath, and started peeling them from his body. He tensed, the line of his jaw growing tight, but didn't complain.

It hurt, she knew it.

It always hurt him. He tried to hide the fact, even after an hour of stifled agony, but the control on his emotions slipped. His eyes pinched. His lips flattened. And a trickle of torment lanced down their bond.

Ada pulled her fingers away, but he snapped his grip around her wrist. Eyes like granite locked onto her.

The haunting howl of a distant wolf called, springing goosebumps over both Ada's and Jasper's skin. Their gazes flicked to each other. The moon had dropped. Morning birds awoke and tweeted their warning of the coming sun.

"Lupercalia is over," Jasper muttered. "That's all it means."

More howls joined the first.

"Keep going," he growled.

She placed her palm on his Well-blessed bond mark.

"Share it with me," she said. "Let me feel your pain so you're not alone."

Jasper's Adam's apple bobbed as he swallowed. His hand came to her jaw. He pressed his lips to hers, breathing deeply through his nose. When he let go, a wealth of emotion echoed in his gaze. It was her only warning before he gave a curt nod, and the floodgates opened.

A solid wall of pain knocked into her. It took all of Ada's resolve to stop herself from visibly reacting, but the shards of broken glass scraping down her insides were almost too hard to bear. After a few forced breaths, she kissed him briefly on the tip of his nose and continued picking the curse apart.

Long minutes passed by.

The entire process took almost two hours. Sometimes she pulled a piece, and he flinched, his gaze turning inward with gleaned memories unleashing from the dark recess of his mind. Sometimes the pain lessened down their bond. Sometimes he panted like Lake had when wounded and in wolf form. Sometimes the pain morphed into fleeting moments of joy, bringing a tear to her eyes. But one thing remained constant—the further she went, the more memories revealed, and a slow bubbling fury stole over him like an approaching avalanche threatening to crush them whole.

"Last one." She picked off the final blue gelatinous mark. It sloughed away with a surprising lack of resistance.

When it was done, she sat back, unsure what to say.

Jasper became a different man. Before, he'd been loose, almost carefree. But with the rise of his unfolding body, a halo of violence wrapped around his form. He flexed his hands. Muscles in his arms and back rolled and pumped. Veins wreathed in fury.

"Jasper?" she whispered hesitantly.

Dark brows drew together as he studied his hands, turning them over from back to front. Then his gaze ran up his arms, looking at them from all angles. He flexed his hands again. This time, a charge of power crackled in the air. Ada tasted electricity on her tongue, and the hairs on her arm lifted. He thrust an open palm at the river. Water sprung in a geyser straight for the sky. He dropped his hand, and the water followed, falling in a great splash.

Ada jumped back. Her heart leaped into her throat. What the hell had he done... move water?

"He took my tattoos," he mumbled, brow furrowing again. "Cloud's going to be pissed."

"Tattoos?"

"They covered most of my body. Some fae get them to enhance their connection to the Well. Cloud is the Guardian who put them on me. It took him months to craft, and he was very proud of the outcome. Mithras used that *floater* Dark Mage to—" He shook his head, body pulling taut with rage until, finally, he drew his head back and bellowed at the moon, his body shuddering with power. The roar tore through the night, waking the last of the creatures from their slumber. When the last note died on his tongue, he stalked out of the river toward her.

"What did you remember?" Ada asked.

"Everything."

CHAPTER
TWENTY

Jasper paced along the riverbank, still trying to find space in his cramped mind for the memories that had been pushed to the edges for... *Crimson*... how long? He'd been living as a husk, forced to commit despicable acts for the King's sick pleasure for at least a decade. Maybe more.

Images jammed into his mind.

"You get three sets," Jasper said to the young Guardian recruit, and pointed at his uniforms. "You're in charge of laundering them."

Thorne set his simmering glare on Jasper.

"Go away," he snapped.

Laughter roared out of Jasper. The kid had gumption, he'd give him that. His fire will serve him well when he's up against a Manticore with no mana left.

"Go float yourself," Thorne snarled again, fury welling to overtake his despair.

"Been there, done that. Didn't stick. Just like you."

"So what, you think we're the same?"

Now hang on a gosh-darn, faery minute. The boy was yet another of King Mithras's victims—as was he. Jasper's dark brow rose. "We're more alike than you think. One day, you'll get that. Until then, launder your uniform, or don't. I don't really care." The kid scowled, and he looked so much like Jasper's cousin, Moon from his mother's pack. Unlike his brother, Sun, Moon was always so serious. As children, Sun and Jasper had made it their life's mission to unnerve Moon every chance they could. A bolt of compassion hit Jasper. He removed a small package from his pocket and held it out to Thorne. "Here. It's a bit of mana-weed. Just don't smoke it before training. Preceptor in charge won't be happy if you turn up wasted."

Thorne took the package, eyes flaring wide with nervous caution as though Jasper had just handed him the keys to the Winter Court coffers. Jasper knew that smile wouldn't last. The road ahead at the Order was often thankless, brutal, and unforgiving. This was the second from the Nightstalk Pack he'd seen come up the ranks. One, he'd lost. He wouldn't lose this one, too.

"Yeah, I know you're a bit young, kid, but the training will harden you. Smoke it with some friends. We work hard here, but we play hard too." Jasper's eyes twinkled with humor, but his heart sank like lead. "You're among family now, Nightstalk. Get some rest."

Jasper shook his head. Finding his memories was like

coming out of a fog and not knowing he'd been lost. He imagined it would be the way the Crystal City humans felt the first time they left their snowy wasteland and stepped into the lush verdant greenery of Elphyne.

Life was now full of so much more color, both dark and light. His brain hurt. A few hours ago, he'd been a fraction of himself with only a handful of acquaintances. He frowned as faces of friends cascaded in his mind. At least, he'd called them friends once. What would they think of him now?

The Cadre of Twelve—his fellow Guardians. Two of which were wolf-shifters, like him. Rush was alive, not dead as Jasper had feared. Rush's son, Thorne, had rallied the cadre to rescue Jasper from the King's clutches. He remembered it in patches. There had been a ball at the Summer Court. Thorne had also infiltrated the Ring, and was pitted against Jasper.

More fire. More flames. More heat. Jasper's face burned.

"Enough!" someone roared.

A female's grunt of effort, and the flames doused. For a split moment, Jasper felt reprieve, then his skin ached. But... it was a different ache. Clean. He blinked. Blue sky. Dust. A roaring crowd. Blood. A silver-haired shifter scowling down at him.

"Jasper. It's me. Fuck, what have they done to you?"

Pain everywhere. Jasper moaned and forced his eyes to lock onto the male—I know you.

"Rush?" he gasped. "Rush." A whimper. All of Jasper's sins came rushing back. All his failings. "You came. You... I don't

deserve it. I don't deserve to be rescued. Not when I left you... not when—" He'd failed to save Véda.

"Hush, Jasper. It's Thorne. Not Rush."

"No. No. No. I shouldn't have let her die. Véda. She was pregnant. Not her fault. I should have said something." He'd been too afraid to make waves. A coward.

"Jasper!"

"I looked after your son, just like you asked. I kept an eye on him for you." Another moan. But was it enough to replace the kid's mother? His father? A whimper. *"Please don't hate me."*

Jasper struggled to breathe as shame washed over him with the memory.

After everything, Thorne had come for him. No. It wasn't just Thorne... his mate had helped too. His *Wellblessed* human mate. Laurel. Dark-haired, dusky skinned, tall and athletic.

More pieces of the puzzle slammed into place.

Laurel had a red-headed friend named Clarke.

After they rescued Jasper from the King, there was a little girl—Rush's daughter, Jasper realized, startled—*Rush has a daughter!*—who had dragged Jasper upstairs to a room where a beautiful woman had slept. Ada. The girl had told him Ada needed a kiss to wake. She'd called her *Sleeping Pretty*.

Jasper's eyes slid to Ada with surprise. She stood by a tree, a wary eye on him as he paced along the riverbank. Hadn't she called out those names when she was near death? He was sure she'd mentioned the names earlier, too. Clarke and Laurel must be close friends from Ada's time.

It was all slotting together in his mind. It made perfect sense.

Jasper stopped as another thought settled with dread.

Ada would want to know about her friends. But... the more he thought about it, the more he remembered those women had been furious when Jasper took Ada from the house of the Twelve. They'd shouted for him to get away from her. He jammed the heels of his palms into his eyes.

"Sleeping Pretty needs a kiss to wake."

He glanced down at the child, frowned, and then looked back at the sleeping female. His frown deepened. An undeniable urge to go to her swam through him. It was as though something pushed him.

He didn't know how, he didn't know anything, but he knew her.

So he went to her. Her mana called to his like a siren at sea, and like a wave rising to meet the shore, his mana called back. He touched her arm. A spark of heat zipped up his arm. Blue flames engulfed them both, and then he heard a scream.

Behind him.

A redheaded woman.

"Leave her alone!"

Footsteps thudded up the stairs. Down the hall. People he should know came barging into the room, scowling at him as though he'd done wrong. They frowned at his golden-haired female on the bed. The one inexplicably linked to him. They wanted to take her away from him.

She was his. Mine.

Something wild and feral within him growled. His fangs elongated, and a snarl ripped out of his lungs. He picked up Sleeping Pretty, carried her in his arms, and wished himself gone.

He'd portaled himself. That, in itself, was confusing. Usually fae created portals to walk through, not became one themselves. There were a rare few fae races that did. The Sluagh flickered through space. The vampires slid through shadows. But never had a wolf portaled.

And the redhead's anger... it had never made sense. But now he knew why. Ada's friends knew he was to blame for Rush's excommunication from the Order. Even if it was Rush's son who'd come to Jasper's aid, even if Rush was back at the Order, and not cursed—there would be bad blood between them. There had to be.

If Ada's closest friends disapproved of Jasper, what chance did he have of her accepting his mark? What chance did he have of her staying with him? A dark part of him shouted that it was wrong of him to think Ada was his redemption, but he couldn't stop. He latched onto the notion with obsessive, irrational greed.

He wouldn't risk her friends tainting his burgeoning relationship, not when he hadn't marked her yet. The Well-blessed union was too new. Would it be enough to keep her at his side? *Damn the curse.* What had he been thinking, leaving her unmarked? It's what shifters did. They marked their females for protection. He should have done it immediately after the wolpertinger attack, with or without her permission.

Panic bloomed in his chest.

And then she would have hated him.

He simply couldn't risk losing her. She was too important. He hadn't lied when he said she was the reason he breathed.

If her friends told her all the dark, cowardly, horrible—

"Jasper?" she prodded.

He scrubbed his face. "I need time for all this to sink in."

"You're right. I can't imagine how it would feel. We should go back to the inn, and just... you know, chill for a few days. God knows you need the break."

Ada's expression softened as she came to him and searched his eyes. A rush of warm compassion flowed through their bond. He latched onto her, drawing her into his embrace and pressing her against his chest.

He'd startled her into submission. She wrapped her arms around him and then softened against his form.

"So... what now?" she murmured.

I can't lose you.

He plastered a smile on his face and looked down at her. "Now I'm going to take you back to the inn, draw you a bath, and then I'm going to spend the next few days doing as you suggested. But it won't be cold or chilled. The inn is heated."

She blinked for a bit, then laugher burst out. It brightened her face to a beauty that stopped his heart.

She patted his chest. "*Chill* is just something we used to say instead of relax."

He gave a tight-lipped smile.

"My friends would have understood."

He tipped her chin by his finger. "I'm your friend. If you need someone to joke with, it can be me."

She brought her fingers to her lips and then pushed them to his with a sigh. It was a mix of the thank-you sign and a kiss, and the moment her touch landed on him, he knew he was in love with her.

"I miss them, that's all," she murmured.

He cleared his throat and pointed to the woods that led back to the path into town. "How would you like to return? A walk, or portal?"

"Portal?" She blinked.

"Well, not exactly a portal," he frowned, thinking back to how he'd taken Ada from the cadre house and ended up at his old family cottage. He hadn't actually stepped through a portal, he'd *become* the portal. It was the first time he'd ever teleported. But he was over three centuries old. It wasn't unheard of for the Well to gift older fae with new abilities. Did this new skill mean the Well still favored him? Or was it something he'd taken from Ada? Most likely the latter. Why would the Well keep favoring someone like him?

He shut his eyes briefly against the onslaught of blood-filled memories trying to break through. The Well *had* favored him. It made little sense.

"You know what?" he said. "Let's walk back. It's a shame to waste the last of this beautiful night. And if we stumble across a certain blond-haired Lesser Fae, then all the better for a little retribution."

"You don't mean to kill her, do you?" Ada asked.

"You're right. We should probably question her first."

Ada stopped. "She may be a nasty person, but dealing out righteous punishment is a slippery slope. Don't you have a law, or something like the police?"

"Police?" He stared at her. "I am a Guardian. I am above the law."

"But..." A small line appeared between her brows.

He used his fist to make a circular motion against his heart. "I will alert the alpha."

She took his hand, still over his heart. "Are you sure you're okay?"

"Prim stabbed you. I'm not okay." Anger swirled through his body. Maybe he wouldn't leave Primrose to Clara. Maybe he'd pay her a visit the instant Ada fell asleep.

When her grip tightened on his hand, he knew his anger must have rolled onto her, so he quietly reined back his emotions and put a clamp on the bond. It shut off with little effort. He silently marveled at how easy the action had come to him. Damn, he'd felt so impotent under the curse, and hadn't even realized it.

Shame, embarrassment, and inadequacy boiled and bubbled beneath the surface of his restraint. He darted a glance to Ada, checking to see if his hold on the bond had slipped, but she had her head tipped to the sky, astonished at the new day.

Pre-dawn colored the sky in hues of pinks and refracted through the mist curling about the moss-covered woods. The air was fresh, but he wasn't cold. A glance to see if her skin pebbled told him she wasn't cold either. The elixir must be keeping her blood warm.

Woodland sprites flittered over the top branches of gnarled oak trees while songbirds flitted between their usual morning arias and sniping at the sprites getting too close to their nests.

Nature provided the melody for their journey home, and by the time the sound of the Lupercal waterfall announced their proximity, they were both bone tired and ready for sleep.

But even beneath the dull senses of exhaustion, Jasper sensed danger. He tugged on Ada's hand for her to halt.

A coppery taint in the air.

He frowned as an understanding dawned. The howling wolves he'd heard hours ago weren't the signal of the end of Lupercalia. He'd been wrong. Lupercalia usually ran longer. The lovers might be finished, but the celebration and revelers often carried on until the early hours of the next morning. There should be more sounds above the cascading waterfall. His ears pricked, straining.

Nothing.

Even the songbirds had stopped.

He glanced down at Ada. "Something's wrong."

"Another raid?"

His blood turned cold as the King's conversation filtered back to him in fragments. He'd confused Primrose with Ada, meaning Prim was a spy. She was probably the one who'd confirmed the stockpiled metal to Mithras and caused the raid.

When Jasper had cut the communication with Mithras at the river, his father had probably gathered his soldiers and portaled straight here.

That call had ended hours ago.

Jasper's jaw stiffened. He crept toward the waterfall, using his grip on Ada's hand to keep her behind him.

The breaking of glass sent claws springing from his fingertips. Ada's breath hitched. He thought maybe he'd hurt her, but it was only her surprise. He tightened his grip and refused to look into her eyes. With a tug, he kept them moving.

They cleared the trees and crested the path leading to the top of the waterfall where blood splattered down the rocks, blending with the sacred pool, churning the blue water and silt into dark purple. Leaning against an upturned table, picking food from his elongated teeth with a claw, was the King dressed in blood spattered finery. A bejeweled sword hung at his hip, unused and clean.

In the flesh, he was a shock to Jasper's frayed mind. Images and sensations bombarded him: Mithras's voice when he'd killed Jasper's mother; his twisted and perfectly cruel face when he'd watched the Dark Mage paint the crippling curse marks onto his body.

Jasper momentarily blacked out. Just a for a second. But it was long enough for him to delay in shielding Ada from the rest of the scene.

She cried out.

The King glanced up at them, and a slow, sinister smile spread across the disgustingly handsome face that looked too much like Jasper's own, if not for the lighter hair.

Bile burned the back of Jasper's throat.

All around them, littered throughout the grotto, were mutilated bodies of his kin—his old pack—as they lay defiled and discarded. A matched couple's ribbon of fate lay trampled in the mud, all dark with blood. The mask Helona had worn, ripped in two. The maracas and pan-flute from the band. He swallowed, eyes trailing further to find Halona's cold dead hand peeking out from beneath the table, lying in a pool of congealed blood. It had been a massacre. No one had stood a chance in their inebriated and festive state.

A final few manabeeze drifted lazily from bodies before dispersing into the sky.

If Jasper had arrived minutes earlier, he might have saved them.

"About time you joined us," Mithras shouted jovially. His voice echoed against the grotto walls. "I almost sent out a search party."

Us?

The hairs on Jasper's arms lifted as the Dark Mage strode down the stone steps leading from the village. Movement in the trees behind Jasper froze his feet to the ground. Without looking, he scented them. Soldiers everywhere surrounded them.

"Are you ready to talk now?" the King asked.

"There is no talking with you," Jasper replied. "You're insane."

The King shrugged, already bored. "If you won't come willingly, then we'll just curse you again. Or maybe it will be the iron mask."

"And I'll take it off," Ada shouted.

Reckless, brave, and beautiful mate. She attracted the King's attention, and that was a dangerous thing. He squeezed her hand, his heart thumping.

"Is that so, little human healer?" Mithras's gaze raked over her. "My, my. You're even better than the last one, aren't you?"

Every protective instinct of Jasper's flared to life. He tucked Ada beneath his arms and kept her caged at his front.

"Why would I go with you?" Jasper said to steer the

King's attention away from her. "I know exactly what you're planning to do with me."

While he'd been cursed and under the King's influence at the Summer Palace, Jasper had been privy to all of his plans and sick dreams. Mithras was working with the humans, feeding them metal and mana in exchange for scientific knowledge on how to dominate Unseelie High Queen Maebh and her soul eating Sluagh. Mithras's focus had been borderline obsessive. More than once, Jasper had wondered in a haze whether the King was being influenced by the human advisor—Bones was his name. But the advisor had been captured by the Order, and the King was still embroiled with the humans.

His Seelie subjects believed their fearless leader to be the great adventurer who immigrated them from the Winter climate, but Jasper knew the truth. He was just a fae terrified to lose the power he'd amassed. Jasper had long suspected that Mithras had something over Maebh, but there was no proof.

The King pushed off the table and stepped toward the base of the waterfall. He propped his foot on a rock and leveled his stare at Ada.

"You know," he shouted up, studying her more closely. "It's a well-known fact that he's with a different female every other day. He won't be faithful to you."

Ada stiffened.

Jasper bared his teeth, unable to stop the shame

heating his blood. It was true. Just like his father, Jasper had hopped from bed to bed, never settling. Until now.

"Come to me, human. Be my bride," the King offered. "I could use someone with your skills in the family."

"You haven't taken a bride for centuries," Jasper bit out. "You seduce and use every woman you meet before discarding them like chewed up second-hand meat."

Mithras's eyes narrowed at Jasper. "Your mother would know, wouldn't she?"

Anger boiled Jasper's blood, and he wondered if he had enough combined mana with Ada to smite his father where he stood. If only he commanded the elements as well as some of his Guardian brethren.

Jasper's eyes locked onto the water behind the King, bubbling away in the pool and running down the waterfall. He could move the water and drown the King... maybe. If he was fast enough.

The sound of weapons being drawn set Jasper's heart hammering against his ribs, and when the King gave an almost imperceptible nod, Jasper summoned his mana and portaled them away.

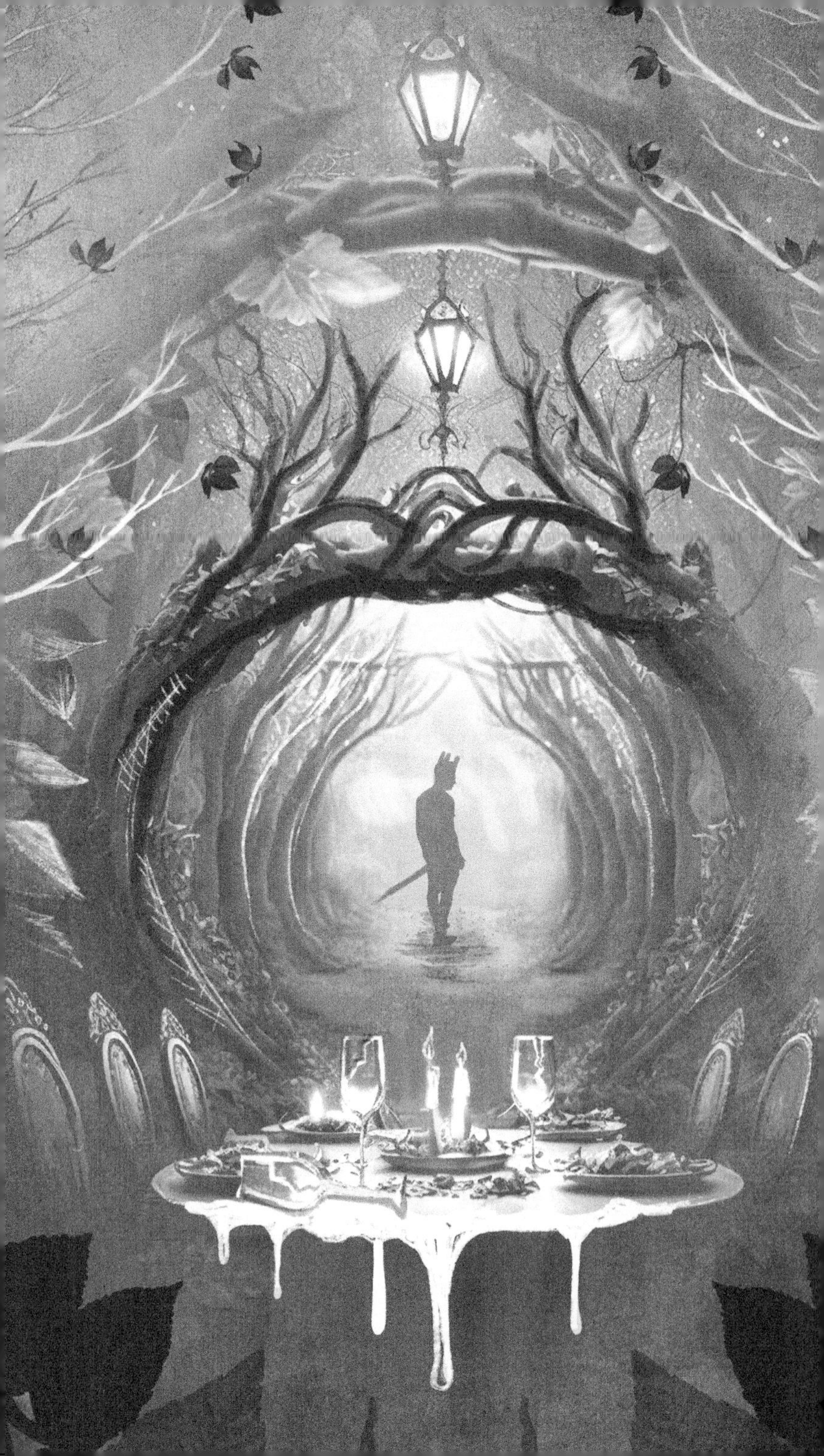

CHAPTER
TWENTY-ONE

Ada felt an incredible shifting of equilibrium. One moment, she was in the bloodstained grotto, the next she was in a high-ceilinged, empty apartment. She dropped to her knees and heaved in air, trying to get the stench of death from her nose.

It wasn't working.

"We're safe. I portaled us here." Jasper crouched beside her and placed a palm on her shoulder. "Are you well?"

She forced herself to nod and swallowed the dry lump in her throat. All she could see was Lake's blood-stained maraca lying on the dirt. "I can't believe the King did that."

This was a whole new level to this world she'd not realized. Tears burned her eyes. Was this the truth of this world—danger from within their own society, and danger without? She thought she was done with that part of her life. She thought upon seeing the green, vibrant life of

Elphyne that the world had changed, but it was just as bad as before.

What was the point?

Without a word, Jasper gathered her into his lap and forced her head down against his beating heart. One big palm landed assuredly on the small of her back, and the other gently stroked her hair. When he spoke, the timbre of his smooth voice enveloped her like a blanket.

"Shh," he said, and only then did she realize tears were streaming from her eyes. "It's going to be okay."

"We should go back," she sobbed, straining against him. "Maybe someone is alive. Maybe I can help them."

"Shh, my love."

"But..."

"No one is alive."

She collapsed and squeezed her eyes shut. "I'm tired, Jasper."

Tired of missing her friends. Tired of having her hopes extinguished. Tired of everything.

"I'll get you cleaned up and then you can sleep."

There was no emotion in his voice, no energy. He was tired too. That was his family, distant as they had been. She felt them rise and walk as he carried her into another room. She wanted to open her eyes, but her strength failed her.

"Where are we?" she asked.

"My apartment in Cornucopia."

She made a non-committal sound and then the next

few minutes were a blur of water, a brief bath, and then finally laying down on a soft mattress.

Sleep stole over her until she awoke with a jolt to the overwhelming mix of sadness and hatred barreling down the bond. She bolted upright in a state of confusion.

Red spattered rock.

Trodden ribbon.

Bloody maraca.

Churning water.

Manabeeze floating into the air.

So much blood mixing with the food and into the elixir glasses. She'd drunk from those glasses, and now they were filled with death.

Chest squeezing tight, she rubbed her eyes. The sheet covering her body had fallen. Her nipples peaked in the cool air. She shivered. Groggily, she lifted the sheet, covering herself.

Ada had slept for most of the day. The moon shone through the window, glancing off the hard lines of Jasper's stern face as he glared outside. His arm braced against the window, fingers curled into a fist. Hair stuck out in all directions, as though he'd obsessively tugged it. Black, buckskin breeches hung from his hips, top button popped at the fly, but he remained shirtless.

The sight of his potent masculinity shot a bolt of appreciation straight through her. She bit down on the sheet, forcing herself to relax at the steady sight of him. No matter what had transpired, she'd always felt safe around him. From the first moment she'd opened her eyes to see his annoyingly gorgeous face, there was a *knowing*... as though she were in the middle of experiencing a memory yet to happen. He felt right.

But from the way his head dipped low, the massacre had affected him as much as it had her.

Holding the sheet around her, she submitted to her instincts and went to him.

"Have you slept?"

A switch flipped and his emotions cut off, silencing their bond. It was the only sign of his awareness of her. Dark circles shadowed his eyes. So she guessed he hadn't slept. He continued to brood, eyes tracking unseen things outside the window.

Had the King found them?

Ada swept her gaze outside and saw nothing but the tops of townhouses. Some appeared in good condition, others were ramshackle and falling apart. None were more than three stories, like the building they were in. Further into the distance, an orange glow emanated from a ground spot, reminding her of a sports stadium at night.

Frustration welled, and she knew he sensed it, because unlike him, she didn't hide her emotions.

"What are you looking at?" she asked, hugging her sheet to her front.

No answer.

Her lips flattened. "Are you going to answer me at some point? Or just hide your words like you do your emotions?"

He flared his nostrils, and then gave up the next words as though they cost him a life. "It's the Ring."

The Ring. Her mind traveled back, thinking, scouring until she came up with an answer. Someone told her it was how Cornucopians solved their differences—a gladiator style battle, sometimes to the death. Had it been Jasper who'd told her? Did he know because he'd been there? Participated?

"Jasper," she said. "At some point we're going to have to talk about things. I know the Darkfoots were your family. What happened was... well it was inconceivable having to witness that." She took a deep breath. How could she handsign an apology if he stared outside. "Will you look at me?"

No.

He stayed as still as a marble statue.

In her mind, all she kept hearing was his wounded plea: *Just leave it in. Let it take me.*

An overwhelming sense of fear swamped her. He had no new visible scars. No new wounds. She couldn't fix him like last time. No curse to pick apart. No poison to drain. The lack of understanding his state of mind drove her to distraction, to the point she found herself checking him over.

She stopped.

What am I doing?

She couldn't keep fighting an uphill battle.

"I can fix your body, Jasper, but you are still broken

inside, and I don't know what to do. You can't mend unless you want to."

His braced fist dragged down the window, and he turned to meet her eyes. Tension cut through the lines of his body, making muscles bulge and strain. Eyes glimmering gold revealed a story more potent than any book or bond. It was that same stare she'd come across when they first met.

Wounded animal.

Caution.

She gathered his fist and pried his fingers open, humming a tune to ease the tension. Nestled inside his palm was a small, heart-shaped, polished amulet made of amber and with a crumpled leather cord looped through the center.

"It was my mother's," he explained, voice rough.

"It's beautiful."

"It's all I have of her, apart from my memories." He turned it over in his fingers, glaring as though it would burn him.

Keep talking. Please.

She tried to quieten her breath, to still her beating heart, so nothing would distract him from speaking.

"I'm afraid that..." He stopped and clenched his fist around the heart.

She covered his hand. "Tell me."

Glimmering eyes met hers. "She died for nothing."

"What do you mean?"

"She died to protect me because she believed I would one day take over my father's reign. I still dream about the day that she put me in the dugout beneath the floorboards and willed me to stay quiet." His voice went so quiet, Ada had to strain to hear it. "I was a coward. I could have at least tried to save her. But instead, I stayed there until her blood dripped down on my face."

Oh, Jasper. Ada's heart clenched. "And then you became a Guardian?"

"My mother matched with Mithras at Lupercalia. He came, they had the festival, and he left. My mother was fine with it. Fae often became with child after Lupercalia and the village helped raise them. She kept the knowledge of her pregnancy from him. She kept me safe for over a decade, and then he found out. Some people think the unsanctioned breeding law was because the Seelie kingdom ran low on food. But it wasn't. Mithras didn't want any child of his to grow and take over his throne. He killed my mother and then hunted me. I became a Guardian so I could stop those like my mother from suffering again," he said. "But I failed at that, too. In three centuries, I've done nothing to make her proud, and now... I—" He shook his head, admonishing himself. "Now it's too late. The entire Darkfoot pack is gone. Because of me."

She thought of the King, of his snide, sick smile. "It's never too late. You can still make a stand against your father. I know you can."

"How? He's beaten me at every turn. I'm just not enough."

"Bullshit," she said. "You survived a ponaturi bite. You killed the wolpertinger—"

"No, you did. He was virtually dead by the time I got to him." He laughed.

"You saved an entire village from the humans—"

"Only to have them murdered."

"—you saved my life!"

Grave eyes settled on her and narrowed. "You *healed* yourself."

"I would never have done it without your help."

She made a frustrated sound. This wasn't the Jasper she'd gotten to know.

"You're such a hypocrite," she murmured, acid coating her tongue. "You *hounded* me, promising that we were meant to be together because some cosmic entity willed it. You didn't give up. Jesus, you made me believe in something bigger than myself. I didn't even realize until now, but the Well—this lifesaving magic—you've dedicated your life to preserving it. I think that's so incredible, I can't even put it into words. But you don't even believe in yourself."

He glared down at her, eyes blazing.

She pushed against his immovable chest. "I believed you. Believed *in* you. After Lupercalia, and the ribbon linked us, I was ready to give you everything." Her voice softened, and she touched his jaw. "Giving up is the only way to fail. It's the only way your mother's sacrifice was for nothing."

Life had been a series of moments Ada thought she'd never survive… until she did. And most of the time, she'd had help. But she'd tried to help Jasper, and there was only so much talking to a brick wall she could take.

He stared at her for so long she thought he'd slipped into a fugue state, but then something flashed luminous in his eyes. He took a step closer.

She went back, her heart already pattering.

He hesitated, eyes wide.

"Don't walk away," he murmured. "Without you, I'm nothing."

Fae couldn't lie.

He truly believed his words, and they cut her like a knife. She deflated.

"Then maybe we shouldn't be together," she declared stupidly… bravely. His hitched breath only spurred her onward. "I don't want that pressure. I can't be walking on eggshells, thinking you hold me up on a pedestal and be afraid to mess up. We have a saying from our time: I'm only human. It means, I'm not perfect. No one is. I'm going to make mistakes. I'm going to fall. But the worth of someone's character is how many times they pick themselves up and try again… do you understand? If you're nothing *without* me, then you're nothing *with* me."

She would always try to fix him. And he would always feel unworthy. He had to pick himself up.

Without her. He had to find out who he was. Without her.

Her words still hung in the air between them, vibrating with tension.

This was it. Her lungs froze as she waited for his response, and when he turned back to the window, she thought she'd lost him. Back muscles flexed as he braced against the glass.

"I won't know what I'm worth unless I submit to the initiation ceremony again," he confessed. "I need to do it for myself."

"The one where two thirds die?" She gaped. "That's not the introspection I was talking about."

"I've done it before, but when Mithras took me, he made me—" He shivered, mouth twisting with a nasty taste. "He made me feel unclean. I need to complete the initiation again."

But he could die. "Has anyone else done it twice?"

He shook his head and faced her. "But I need to know."

She blinked, shocked. "You don't even know if the Well will let you take it a second time. It's too extreme, and it's still waiting for someone else to validate you. What have I been telling you? *You need to believe in yourself.*" She thumped his chest. "And for the record, I believe in you. Even when you couldn't remember your name, I knew you were someone of worth."

The sadness that spilled from his eyes almost felled her. "I've killed children in the Ring, Ada. Children and females. Helpless victims of all fae races. And then I went up to the champion's suite and let them shower me with rewards—sex, elixirs, drugs, indulgence. I wanted to block it all out. And that's only the things I did to others. Things were done to me. Those debasing memories suffocate me so much, I feel like I'm drowning. I've been defiled in the most filthy ways." He put his forehead on the window and stared outside, jaw twitching. "How can you think me worthy?"

Oh, Jasper.

Her heart ached for him. To be held prisoner, to be forced into despicable acts, and then to live as long as he would with the horrible memories. No one should do that alone.

God, she thought she could push him away until he sorted himself out, but she was wrong. Just flirting with the idea of separating hurt too much. She'd thought, maybe, he could learn to love himself if he was on his own. But the truth was, for a moment, she'd let her own fear take over. When he'd said he was nothing without her, it frightened her because, maybe, she felt the same way. And that kind of all consuming love was devasting to lose.

The hard truth was, she was already at the place she feared—the one where she would break without him.

Her eyes brimmed with tears. He'd been cursed, coerced, and abused. Nothing would bring his victims back. Nothing would turn back time. He might always feel unclean. Unable to stop herself, she rushed forward and encircled her arms around him, blubbering her confession against his back, "You're worth it because I'm falling in love with you."

His broad back heaved with a hitched breath. He turned in her arms, eyes wild and disbelieving.

"Shut up," she said before he could speak. "I'm scared, Jasper. I'm scared of how much it will hurt if we're separated, and that's why I said you have to figure this out without me. For a fraction of a second, I thought maybe if we end things now, that I won't get hurt. I still think you need to believe in yourself, but maybe this will help. I'm already in love with you, Jasper. And I won't let you give up. If you're drowning, then I'll pick you up. I'll swim us both to the surface, and if I can't, then I'll drown with you." Tears spilled over. "I won't let you suffer alone."

She rose on her toes and reverently swiped her lips along his. His arms became marble around her while he let her explore his mouth. Her swipe turned into a press, a nibble on the bottom lip, a kiss at the corner. Their breaths mingled and his taste filled her with raw heat. She pulled back.

His molten gaze darted to her mouth.

They stood there, rock solid in each other's arms, panting with stilted breaths.

"Just kiss me," she begged.

His mouth collided with hers. She dropped the sheet and melted with a pained, guttural groan that struck every chord in her body. They kissed, devoured, and tried to touch every inch of each other. His fingers clawed into her hair and pulled her face back, exposing her neck where he licked and sucked and worshiped before coming back to her mouth. When she felt his palm on her breast, grazing over the peak of her nipple, a ragged breath shot out. She shoved her hand down his breeches, eliciting his own hiss of breath.

She smiled against his lips as she found his steely length and stroked.

"Bed," he grunted with a gasp.

"Mm."

Strong hands lifted her by the rear. She wrapped her legs around his hips and ground against his hard length until they both gasped at the sensation. Jasper all but flew across the floor until his knees hit the bed and they fell. Together. Always together, she knew that now. He rolled on top and pressed her into the mattress, holding her still until she squirmed beneath his intense stare. In the way only a lover could, his gaze roved over her body, setting her senses on fire.

Oh, what I'm going to do to you, his eyes seemed to say as they landed on her intimate body parts—her neck, her breasts, her stomach, below...

Something clicked inside Ada.

She wanted to be the one looking at him like he was her world because staring up at him like this, swathed in moonlight, he was some kind of divine perfection and she wanted to take her fill. She reared forward and pushed him down. He landed back with a huff. Displaced air gusted and blew into her face and hair.

"You're so fucking mine," he growled possessively, eyes heating, taking her hips and settling her over him.

"I think we already had this conversation." Her eyes fluttered as he drove his rock-hard erection into her softness. She whimpered, "I won't be marked. But..." He found her most sensitive spot and rubbed. She moaned, slapping her hands on his chest, hardly able to form words, hardly able to hold herself up.

"But what?" he demanded.

"But—*ooh, yes.*"

His dark brow arched as he studied her face, gauging how he hit the right spots from her expression. She was too damned strung out to even care. And then his lips found her breast, drawing her nipple into his mouth and rolling deep. He groaned around her flesh, rasping it with his teeth, wrenching another breathy whimper from her lungs.

"I love how you're so responsive," he murmured, continuing his thumb's rhythm between her legs. "You're aching for me."

"Yes," she gasped.

"You want more." Not a question. A demand.

"No."

"What?"

Panting, she pushed him back down, eyes blazing. "My turn. I want to make *you* feel good."

Defiance blazed in his expression and then softened as

a splash of color hit his cheeks. His ears flattened before springing back up. God, she loved that. He might try to hide his feelings down their bond, but he could never change his body language. Her declaration had stupefied her rogue shifter, and that emboldened her.

"I won't hurt you," she teased, a mimic of the first time he'd tried to mate with her after the wolpertinger attack.

More blood rushed to his cheeks as he grappled internally with something. Choice made, his lids lowered to half-mast. He took her hands and placed them on the buttons of his breeches. The first button was already popped. Holding his gaze, she popped the rest. Every time one came loose, he gave a short groan of anticipation and she sucked in a breath. Goosebumps erupted across his lower abdomen, darkly dusted with hair. She'd licked her lips raw by the time she cleared his pants and revealed his thick erection.

"Ada." His hand landed hesitantly on the back of her neck.

"Mm?" She raked her nails through the trail of coarse hair, causing his hips to buck involuntarily.

"Be... gentle."

Their gazes clashed, and fragility flickered back. That wounded animal.

I've been defiled in the most filthy ways.

Had he been...? She couldn't finish the thought. All that she knew was that he wanted this. Whatever pain he'd experienced, he wanted this to replace it. The thought of giving him pleasure consumed her. She touched her lips to the broad crown of his cock and butterfly kissed down the length, right along the vein.

"Shit. Not that gentle," he bit out and thrust into her, fingers catching in her hair.

But she kept herself slow and light. A feather-light lick. A little stroke. A swirling suck.

"Ada."

She tugged the breeches all the way off, and climbed on top of him, aligning her lips again with his hard, thick length. Looking up at him from beneath her lashes, satisfaction surged. She could give him a wonderful memory. They both wanted this. They needed something to wipe away the bad. Her lips parted wide. She took him inside her mouth and worked his tip with her tongue before sucking him deep. Again and again, she bobbed on him, savoring his taste.

But when she glanced up, a frown marred his brow as he concentrated on the ceiling. So she started humming, like she did around injured animals. She scraped her fingers through the coarse hair at his lower abdomen, trailed them below, fondled his testicles, and then stroked his length. She did everything she could to make him feel at peace... well, close to it.

Skin stretched taut across his stomach. Veins rippled. Abs bunched and twitched. His breath turned ragged and when she hummed a last time, he yanked her off. Suddenly, she was on the bottom and he was above, hands braced on either side of her head, panting. Smoldering eyes blinked as if he was also surprised with the swift change in position.

He was beautiful. A face she'd only ever seen crafted by an artist—mischievous devil and honorable angel at the same time. And he was flush with the passion he felt for her. The notion sparked a moan and a squirm that triggered another round of kissing so hungry, she found it hard to breathe. He was there. In her mouth. With his tongue. His teeth. Salty taste. Deft fingers trailed down her front, between her legs, testing her readiness. A swipe through her slick center.

A groan into her mouth, and his pupils expanded. "You're..."

She nodded.

"I'm going to..."

She nodded again.

He fit himself between her legs and thrust inside. Her back bowed. She gasped at the sensation of him stretching her inner walls. They fit. Just one swift move and they fit.

"You okay?" he rasped.

Another nod.

"Good. Ready?"

She smiled. "Am I ever."

Savoring thrusts began the rhythm of their dance. It was a slow, sensation-filled torment that quickly turned fast, deep, and relentless. Soon he drove into her hard, sparking her pleasure, lighting the fuse. There was nothing she could do but hold on. It was mad, sweaty, crazy lovemaking that made Ada feel alive. It was a heart pulling, vision blurring, lose your hearing, sort of orgasm that hit them both hard at the same time.

Many things had been left unsaid, but when Jasper drifted to sleep, still in her arms, she felt at peace for the first time in a long time... maybe since before... maybe forever.

And maybe that terrified her.

CHAPTER
TWENTY-TWO

Making love with Ada had shaken loose the final, dark memories from Jasper's mind. He slept restlessly. Fitfully. And full of dreams that were too visceral to be fake.

"I'm going to enjoy this," Mithras sniggered, lifting his candle to illuminate Jasper's broken and swollen face.

Jasper wrenched his wrists, metal manacles biting into him. "Fuck you."

An empty laugh. "No. Not me, son."

"The metal won't hold me for long," he warned.

"Yeah, yeah. Guardian. Special. Blah blah. But I don't need long, or rather, she doesn't need long."

Scraping. Skittering. A shadow moved in the corner as a creature came into the light. Long, black hair coated her face, sharp with insect-like bone structure.

Already, his mind shut down. This wasn't the first time he'd been tortured. And it wouldn't be the last.

"I want to hear his screams from the throne room," the King said, walking away.

The definitive sound of the dungeon door closing cast the room into darkness.

Something tugged on his pants, dragging them from his hips.

Her kiss was cold, tasting like earth.

Jasper's eyes opened. Sweat itched his head, slicked his torso, and pooled beneath him on the bed.

"You okay?"

Sweet voice. Not hissing.

He turned. Blond hair. Not black.

Ada.

Her eyes were puffy with sleep. Her lips, still swollen from his kisses. He slid his fingers along her jaw and into her hair, then brought those lips to his so her taste would obliterate the earth from his memory.

She submitted with an agreeable sound, rolling back to let him climb on top of her. He found his way kissing down her body until his lips landed between her legs, to the sweetest taste of all. She was like some kind of drug. He lapped at her with addiction, hungrily tasting it all. He brought her to climax with his mouth, and then was inside her again, his new favorite place to be. He took her with slow and steady strokes, this time making it last, reveling in how each lazy, sweaty thrust made her cheeks flush and her eyes flutter.

When they were spent, and she lay pliant in his arms, he knew he couldn't pretend his life didn't exist forever. She'd been right. He had to make a stand. If he didn't, the nightmares would never end.

Snow tickled Jasper's face as he stood on the frozen shore of the Aconite Sea. The glacial waters rolled all the way to the other side, where an obsidian castle nestled between foggy mountains. Storm clouds gathered, darkening the sky. The vampires would be out early if the sun stayed hidden, and he wanted Ada well within the safety of the Queen's protection by that time.

Humans were tasty. Well-blessed humans, possibly tastier still. Ada would smell like catnip to any vampire scenting her. One of the vampires in the cadre of Twelve had once lost himself to bloodlust around humans, glutting himself on their blood and accidentally killing all. Vampires were dangerous. Not to mention the other Unseelie crawling about the wilderness.

"Is that it?" Ada asked, shielding her eyes from the glare.

"That's it," he muttered. "The Winter Palace."

With black spires dusted in snow, the castle reached high into the air and provided multiple landing points for the many winged fae among the Unseelie. The black stone foundation stood out starkly against the white. Blood red vines crawling over the facade only increased the foreboding image. Along the mountain behind the castle, dark houses from the neighboring city pushed smoke into the air from their chimneys. While it looked less crowded than Helianthus City, Aconite City was half within the mountain itself and shielded from view.

Hundreds of thousands of fae lived here.

Jasper counted on his Guardian status to give him a reprieve from immediate attack. If they chose to recognize his link to the Seelie King first, then Ada and he might be thrown straight into the dungeons.

Both of them had dressed warmly in clothes he'd found inside the Cornucopia apartment closet. None of the clothes were bought by him, which meant other Guardians had visited his place over the past ten years. Most likely Thorne, since he was the only one keyed to the blood-warded lock on the front door. A pang of guilt hit him when he remembered who'd saved him from Mithras, but Thorne and Rush would have to wait. He needed to try this first. He refused to go back to the Order empty handed, and while Ada had taken back her comment about them needing to separate until he could pick himself up, she'd still said it. And it played on his mind. She'd helped chase away his demons last night, but she was right. He had to make a stand.

Fuck Mithras.

"You're very subdued this morning," she noted.

"It's nothing."

"It's not... what happened between us last night, is it?"

"No," he said, a little too quickly. Whether she referenced their lovemaking, or the fact she still resisted his mark, he wasn't sure. But he wouldn't have her second guessing their relationship. "It's just... some dark memories stirred last night."

Concerned eyes studied him. "You were dreaming and kicking about."

He hand-signed an apology, to which she stopped with her hand before he could finish. "Never be sorry for that."

Something cracked inside his chest. He lowered his lips to hers, claiming her mouth in a passionate kiss, only pulling back because she was too cold. Also, he wasn't comfortable being near water. That was how the King had been spying on him. That type of communication could only occur between blooded kin, and Jasper had given him too much already. It was time to go on the offensive.

"Why didn't you portal us straight there?" Ada asked, tugging her fur-lined cape around her body. The icy air had turned her nose and human ears pink.

He adjusted her hood over her head, tucking her blond hair inside. When he caught her frown, he explained, "The Seelie might be more forgiving with your human status. But the Unseelie will bite first, ask questions later. Malevolence is at their core, and if they don't use you for food, they'll do their best to manipulate you for entertainment.

The bleeding feet and finger human artisans the Spring Court Queen spoke of are nothing compared to what they do to humans here. If I portal us into their castle, it would cause surprise. I prefer not to kill anyone before I speak with the High Queen."

"Right."

He summoned his mana to cast a glamour over her ears, just in case. Air shimmered, and it suddenly appeared as though her ears were pointed. Although Maebh would most likely see through the child's trick, it didn't hurt to be safe.

"We landed here first out of courtesy," he elaborated on his answer to her earlier question. "To give them warning that I approach."

She scowled over the sea. "It's quite the warning. I can barely see the castle."

"They know we're here." He gave a pointed look to the crows watching from the skeletal branches of trees scattered before the mountain behind them. A crow cawed impudently and took to the sky, flapping like mad to battle the arctic winds across the water. His brethren, or sisters, followed swiftly, leaving only a handful behind to keep watch.

"We'll give them some time to fly across," he said. "Then I'll take us over."

It had crossed his mind to leave Ada behind within the secure Cornucopia apartment, but there had been too many signs that Thorne had been by. And he wasn't ready to reveal that truth to Ada yet. He needed her to believe he was strong. Someone who picked himself up. He needed a reason her friends had been wrong to shout at him.

At the very thought of them causing a divide between Ada and him, panic tightened across his chest like a writhing, thorn riddled vine. Every instinct in his body urged him to run the other way from that eventuality. Ada was his.

"I suppose while we're waiting, you can tell me about them."

He blanched, thinking she meant her friends, but then realized her eyes were on the trees behind them.

"The crow-shifters?" he asked.

"All of them. The Seelie versus the Unseelie. Back at the, um, Lupercalia rite, they talked of a brewing war."

"Mithras has been making it look like the Unseelie are sending monsters into Seelie land, and vice versa. He knows the Order will stay out of fae politics if it has nothing to do with a danger to the integrity to the Well."

"And Seelie and Unseelie used to be one nation?"

"For the beginning, after the Age of Man was over, there were no rulers. Fae were just trying to survive. If there had to be a ruler, it might have been Jackson Crimson, the founder of the Order. He discovered the link between the Well, our mana, and its resistance of metals and plastics. He led us all, but... he disappeared. The Prime took over the Order, and then Maebh took over ruling the fae. Eventually, the humans had enough of their wasteland and tried to take back control of Elphyne, but the Order, Maebh, and Mithras banded together to beat them back. Even though it was Maebh's Sluagh—"

"What are they?"

"Soul eating fae."

She shivered. "Right. Continue."

"Maebh's Sluagh and their Wild Hunt turned the tide against the humans. But somehow Mithras gained a lot of support among the fae, enough to rally backing for the split of the nation when she clearly had the power to deny him. There hasn't been a fae strong enough to match Maebh's powers in millennia. But since Mithras split and formed the Seelie, she's left everyone south of the border untouched."

"And this is the woman you're asking for help?"

"Yes." He paused. "But I can't ask for help. I just need to tell her about Mithras's plans to use me to incite a war."

"Why can't you just ask for help?"

"In this world, a crown or the title of alpha, is won by battle and blood in two ways. One, because I'm his blooded kin. Two, because I'll pry the glass crown from his bloody hands after I defeat him. If I have assistance, no one will respect me. The crown will be contested."

She chewed her lip. "I get that. Doesn't mean I like the idea of you putting yourself in danger, though."

"This is how I pick myself up, my love. This is how I glue my broken pieces back together." A small, haunted smile lifted his lips. He gathered her closer to him. "Are you worried about me, little human?"

She snorted. "I've seen you rip a heart from someone's chest. I'm not worried about you winning a battle." She frowned, letting herself fall into him. "But I am worried about the toll it will take."

He squeezed her arm and then kissed the top of her head. "It's time to go."

With a dizzying rush, they portaled through space and simply appeared at the base of the castle, their boots crunching in the snow upon landing.

"Oh my God. This is incredible," Ada breathed, shielding her eyes against the glare so she could look upon the enormous black walls.

He tried to see it from her point of view. "Your buildings were not like this?"

"Oh, ours were bigger... but not so finely detailed. It's just different, I guess."

He grunted.

What seemed like a simple stone structure from across the sea, came alive with black-coated soldiers on the ground and dark-winged fae on the turrets, their bows stretched taut with arrows nocked and aimed. The drawbridge creaked open, lowering to provide a walkway from the gatehouse and over a moat that was home to some very nasty Unseelie fae. A dark fae waltzed across the walkway, his black snow-dusted mantle billowing behind. Red lining provided a splash of color, just enough to remind them of blood, danger, and their fate if they opposed the Queen.

The guard stopped before Jasper and narrowed his eyes at Ada. Icicles tinkled in his beard. With the snow dusting his shoulders, it was clear he'd recently arrived from some time spent outdoors.

A long, jagged scar deformed one side of his craggy face. When fae appeared aged, it was usually because their mana had been forced out in such a way that it was irreplaceable. They were effectively cut from the Well, just like humans. This guard had either been tortured, or displeased the Queen... or both.

"What business do you have here, Guardian?" he asked.

"I seek an audience with the High Queen," Jasper replied.

The guard arched his dark brow. "She's busy. Go back to the Order."

Jasper pursed his lips. "It's vital I speak with her. Tell her the safety of her nation is at risk."

The guard sucked his teeth, clearly not convinced, but he knew better than to dismiss a claim of national danger from a Guardian. "You can wait in the guest suites until you are called."

Jasper forced his expression to deadpan. Guest suites meant they would be locked behind doors and seen to whenever it pleased Maebh. It could be today, it could be a week, or even a month from now. He supposed at least it wasn't the dungeon.

Jasper gave a flat smile. "Lead the way."

He took Ada's cold hand, thinking at least they'd be out of the elements. The temperature didn't bother him, but she shivered beneath her cape. They might have a long wait ahead, but he knew how to warm her up. It was the one thing he looked forward to.

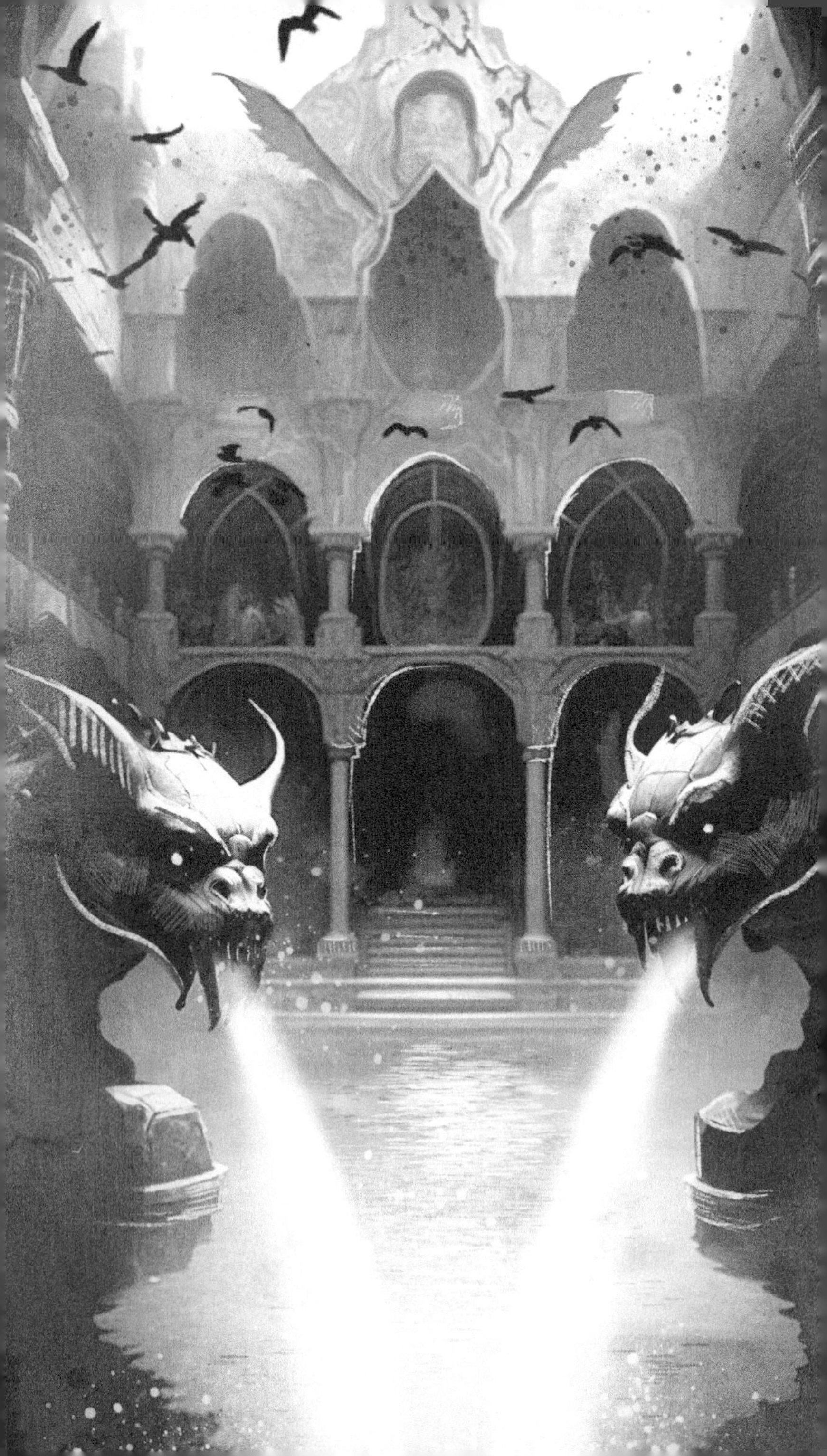

CHAPTER
TWENTY-THREE

Ada gaped the entire walk through the castle to the guest suites. Obsidian walls with glistening marbled veins surrounded them on all sides. Red decadent carpet softened their steps through the halls. After crossing the foyer, they went outside through a sunken courtyard where a crystal clear, bottomless pool sparkled. Surrounding the pool, gargoyle statues sat on a balcony and spurted water from their mouths, adding to the peaceful atmosphere which went against everything Jasper had told her about the Unseelie.

It surprised Ada the pool wasn't frozen like half the sea outside. It could be a hot spring, like the one at the Lupercal cave. If it was a source of power, it made sense a settlement was built around it.

The guard took them beyond the courtyard and up four flights of stairs to an arched, double door with two guards standing outside. Like the guard who'd greeted them, these wore black uniforms. Long coats, black breeches, and mantlets covering their shoulders. Their ears were pointed but had no fur on the tips. Ada darted a glance to Jasper to see if he would explain, but his scowling gaze was fixed on them as though he expected an attack. Probably better to ask when they had some privacy. Clara had said that it could be deemed impolite to ask someone about their race, as it was back in Ada's time. She had to remember to learn when to display her curiosity, and when to hide it.

"You may stay here until the Queen calls you," the gatehouse guard said. The icicles on his beard tinkled to the ground. "Pull the bell rope if you require sustenance."

Jasper gave a curt nod, and when the doors opened, they went inside.

"These are the *guest* suites?" Ada asked, unable to hide the awe in her voice.

The chambers were vast, featured two queen beds, and an opulent parlor with brocade cushioned settees. There were two fireplaces in the rooms, crackling with low heat. The black and red decor included a gothic stained-glass window in the parlor, refracting eery red and shadow into the room. She glimpsed a fractured view of the sea beyond the rose design on the window.

Ada startled when the doors closed behind them with a thud. The guard was gone.

"We're prisoners," Jasper explained, lashes lowering in vexation.

"Oh." She turned around. "At least the digs are nice."

Sighing, he tossed his cape onto a bed and then strode toward the parlor. The hard lines of his cleanly shaven jaw twitched.

She understood his frustration. Standing up to his father had left tiny lines carved between his brows. But something had shifted last night, both good and bad. He finally understood his troubles wouldn't disappear if he ignored them. He could stop Mithras from causing a war, and by aligning with the Queen and going public about his opposition to his father's plans, Jasper was also saving his own life. As Ada understood it, one reason the King had tried to kill Jasper was because he wanted to blame the Unseelie Queen and trigger the war. So if they took that excuse off the table, it had to make Mithras stop, right?

Of course, there were all the other reasons the King wanted Jasper dead.

"So, how long do you think we have to wait?" she asked.

"Could be hours. Could be days."

"I know it wasn't easy for you to come here," she said, meeting him at the window. "This first step in standing up to your father is the hardest, but you've done it. We're here. I'm proud of you."

"It will be done after I speak with Maebh," he grimaced. "Rather, it will be the beginning of the end."

"What will you say to her?"

He glanced warily at the door and lowered his voice.

"We must be careful what we say in the castle, and in much of the city. The walls have ears."

"Literally?" She wouldn't be surprised with all the strange things she'd learned since awaking in this time.

"Could be the fire-sprites minding the hearths, or a fae actually within the walls, or advanced fae hearing. We only know that the Queen hears everything, eventually."

She made a zipping motion on her lips. "Got it." When he didn't elaborate, she asked, "You say 'we' a lot. Do you mean your friends at the Order? The ones who rescued you?"

It was another topic he'd failed to talk about, and it made little sense to her. These were his people. They'd risked life and limb to save him, yet he didn't want to go back and ask them for help.

He gave a curt nod but said nothing else. She ran her hand down his arm, fingers rasping over the wool of his sweater.

"I'm here if you want to talk."

Vibrant eyes met hers, and she had to stifle a gasp. Even knowing him as intimately as she did, when he looked at her, her heart stopped from the impact. When he smiled, she was dead.

A line appeared between his brows, and he dipped his chin.

"You'll find out about them soon enough," he muttered, cupping her jaw. "And when you do, promise not to hate me."

"Jasper," she admonished. "I could never."

His hand dropped from her jaw. "I'll cast a privacy ward about us, just in case they're listening."

"You can do that?"

He nodded and began to move about the room, placing his palm at certain points on the wall. It didn't look like he did much, but Ada felt a tingle of something in the air. When he was done, he came back to her.

"That should do it."

"Can you teach me how to do that?"

His eyes crinkled. "What will you give me if I do?"

She laughed. "Always wanting a reward. I'm sure I can find a treat around here somewhere for you."

Heated eyes lowered to her lips.

A few moments of silence passed while they stared at each other. She exhaled slowly and undid the ties on her cape, twirling to survey the room, knowing full well he watched her. Anticipation buzzed in her veins.

"Well," she said, biting her lip, praying he walked closer behind her. "What shall we do to pass the time?"

Two hands landed on her waist and she almost groaned. He kissed behind her ear. She squirmed down to her legs, shivering into him.

"I have a few ideas," he rumbled, then nipped her earlobe playfully before his teeth landed on her neck and grazed. He exerted the tiniest bit of pressure, just enough to let her know his intentions, but then drew back. "Like I said, when I mark you, Ada, you'll beg me for it."

She scoffed. "I don't beg."

He spun her to face him. "You'll want it so bad that you'll take my teeth and put them on your neck."

"Oh, really?" Who was she kidding? She probably would. She smirked, untying her blouse buttons and walked backward. When the buttons opened, the middle gaped, revealing her complete and utter lack of underwear.

He virtually simmered at the sight of her naked breasts, and then tore at his clothes—lifting his sweater and shirt in one smooth motion, unbuttoning his breeches, and then storming her until she fell back against the bed with a giggle.

ON THE THIRD day of their captivity, Ada sat in the parlor on the settee with Jasper sitting on the floor between her legs, facing the stained glass window. He toyed with the amber heart that had belonged to his mother. Her hands were in his hair, braiding little lengths as he told her stories about his life and about Elphyne and the Well.

"A source of power is where you can replenish your mana stores faster than usual," he said, leaning back into her touch until she scratched behind his ears and he all but purred.

With a smile, she ran her fingers through his hair and sectioned out another piece before splitting the hair into three and twining. "Like what?"

"Usually they're heated lakes, or bodies of water. Like the Lupercalia pool."

"And the one down stairs, right? That was a source of power?"

He nodded. "If any fae run low in mana, they can sit in the water for a few minutes and be restored."

"Cool."

"Otherwise it could take up to a few days to replenish the store from nature."

Ada paused, crinkling her nose. "I've not needed to."

He craned his neck and gave her a heart-rending smile. "That's because you're special."

"You're just saying that to get in my pants." She swatted him.

"Is it working?"

She snorted, and turned his face back to face the front. "When doesn't it work?"

He tried to twist back around but she stopped him with a tug of the hair.

"Ow," he simpered.

"You're ruining my style."

He frowned, still looking back at her. "And you're sure this is a style many males from your time wear?"

"Sure," she mumbled, biting back a smile. "Now, tell me some more stories. What about your friends at the Order?"

He settled back to face the front with a barely

contained huff. "I don't know what they'd think of me now," he confessed. "But it's not good."

Ada's fingers stilled on his head. "They're your friends. They rescued you."

His broad, sweater covered shoulders shrugged. "They don't know the depraved things I did while with the King."

Neither did Ada. Not really. She held her breath, waiting for more. When his words came, they spilled out of him.

"Thorne was the angriest kid I'd ever seen come into the Order, and it was the first time I really saw how my behavior had affected someone else. He was angry because of me. I'd failed to step in and help his mother from being executed. I'd failed to stop his father from being cursed. Then I did nothing to help him as a child until he came to the Order." Jasper tensed. "Thorne only entered the ceremonial lake because his Uncle Thaddeus had forced him. Thaddeus was a cruel man, and I knew it. I could have done something... but..." He exhaled. "Sometimes I freeze."

"I get that," she murmured, and stroked his hair gently, unraveling the braids. "I get scared too. It's why I said those stupid things to you the other day. I thought I was protecting myself. Obviously, I was wrong."

He turned on his knees and slotted himself between her legs, placing a palm on each knee. His hair stood on end, making him more adorable than before.

"Ada," he said, eyes turning solemn. "There's something I've been meaning to tell you, but... I don't want you to think differently of me."

Pain and hurt flashed over his expression. She placed her palm on his cheek.

"Nothing you could say would make me think differently about you."

"You say that now."

"So don't," she said. "If you're not ready, tell me another time. It doesn't matter to me."

"What does matter to you?"

"Your happiness."

His brows quirked up and a playful expression crossed his features. "So if I were to tell you, this made me happy" —his hands slid up her thighs, thumbs angling inside until they hit her apex with a firm, tingling press—"then it would matter to you?"

She squirmed back as heat pooled at his touch.

"Yes," she breathed.

"And this?" He brushed his thumbs over the seam in her pants, creating friction against her sensitive junction.

She bit her lip, nodding, unable to stop her hips from rocking against him. God, she was a wanton addict around him. Since they'd been locked up, it was all they could do. Eat, sleep, talk, and make love.

"And this?" He took her hips and dragged her closer to the edge of the settee—closer to him. He placed his mouth between her thighs and bit through the fabric, making a tiny growling sound as pleasure sparked and fired in her groin.

"Jasper," she gasped, as he gave up the pretense of his game and opened the buttons on her pants. "What about the wards?" Had he set any today? She couldn't remember.

"They're fine," he said, and tugged her pants and underwear down her legs. He tossed them to the side and then pushed her knees wide until she was on display for him.

"And the window?"

They were right near the window. Anyone could see through.

"We're up too high," he grumbled and slid a finger deep into her slick center.

"But... *oh, God.*" She rocked against him, chasing his touch every time he withdrew.

"This is all you need to worry about," he rasped, drugged eyes drinking in the sight of his actions. "This makes me very happy."

Seeing how he watched made Ada even hotter. Curls of heat bloomed low in her belly. Her head tipped back and she submitted to Jasper's insatiable wants.

"Ride my fingers, Ada," he demanded. "Show me how much you want this."

Unable to stop herself, she rocked against him just as he plunged into the heat of her. When he added a second finger, her pulse rabbited. She squirmed and fisted his hair, lifting his gaze to hers.

"Tell me what you want, my love," he muttered.

God... when he called her that. "You."

"Where?"

She rocked her hips. "Here."

A slow, wicked smile curved his lips.

"This makes me very happy," he said, and then replaced his fingers with his mouth.

His tongue did magical things. He sucked, licked, nipped and swirled until Ada's body broke into a million blissful pieces. And yet, he continued to feast on her until the last of her throes died, and she needed a different kind of completion.

She tugged him by the hair, dragged him up and then kissed him. He groaned into her mouth, deepening the kiss.

"Ada," he murmured.

That's all he said. She thought maybe he'd mention marking her again, but he didn't. She would have said yes. The moment hung suspended between them. She saw the hesitation in his eyes, and his words from earlier came back to haunt her.

There's something I've been meaning to tell you...

Before she could let the doubt take purchase, Jasper growled low in his throat, his expression turned intense, and he flipped her onto her stomach, maneuvering her with ease to suit himself. He kicked her legs apart so one fell off the settee, and one stayed on. Then he lifted her hips, angling her rear and positioned his cock at her swollen, sensitive entrance before driving in to the hilt and lying on top of her, savoring their connection.

He gave a shuddering groan that rumbled down her spine and tingled all the inside places of her body.

"This," he murmured into her ear, hot breath against her neck. "This right here, Ada."

She could only nod with a whimper and bite her hand. The sensation of him surrounding her, filling her, was almost too much.

He lowered his lips to her ear and whispered, "This feels like home."

⚖

Some time later, they lay naked and sweaty on the settee. Jasper was on bottom and Ada on top, her head in the crook of his arm with the two of them entwined. Making each other happy had taken all of her energy, and the ability to snooze was all that remained.

Jasper's hand trailed idly down the length of her long hair, starting at her head and running down her back. It was so soothing, she'd nodded off on more than one occasion. She might have napped, but he hadn't. She knew something played on his mind.

"What are you thinking about?" she murmured and ran her hand over his chest.

He inhaled, hesitated, and then spoke. "Nothing."

For a moment, she considered leaving it, but wanted to

know some things herself. "Is it about your father? And how we're going to take him down?"

His grip tightened in her hair. "It was actually about the Ring."

"Oh."

He went back to stroking. "I hate it. It needs to go."

"But..."

"But even if I did become king, it's not in my jurisdiction. Cornucopia is independent. Any change I make as king will be a sign of aggression against the Unseelie people. I'd need her cooperation."

Silence ticked by. Ada's lashes drifted with every stroke of Jasper's hand. Her mind traveled to other things... things that both frightened her and settled in her with a sense of purpose.

"Jasper?"

"Mm-hm?"

"When you become king—"

"If—"

"When!"

He grumbled.

She continued, "Let's just pretend for a minute you will be."

She felt his smile against her head as he kissed the top. "Fine. When."

"What will happen to me?"

"You'll be by my side. As Queen."

A frown tightened her brow. "But I'm human."

"And blessed by the Well."

"It still took the Darkfoot pack a while to get used to me."

"No it didn't. They fell in love with you by Lupercalia. If you can do that to a pack that was ravaged by humans, then you can do it to the general Seelie people. Besides," he said. "We don't even know if that's going to happen. We still need to speak with Maebh."

"I know."

"Let's not get ahead of ourselves. If it were up to me, I'd let someone else take the throne."

"Is there anyone else?"

He paused. "Not really. Not if we don't want Maebh taking the power back."

"And that's not good?"

He shook his head. "She's changed since the first time she controlled all of Elphyne. She's darker, secretive, and merciless. Perhaps even mad. She is very old."

"I'm so looking forward to meeting her," Ada said drolly.

"I can handle her."

Ada sat back and looked him in the eyes. "Just so you know, you're going to be magnificent in whatever future you choose."

His smile crinkled his eyes and Ada went all gooey inside. And then he said something that melted Ada into a puddle.

"As long as you're in it, I believe you."

CHAPTER
TWENTY-FOUR

They waited eight days before the Queen called them. *Eight days*. Jasper could have portaled them both out, but they agreed that doing so would mean giving up. They were better than that, so they used the time to get to know one another, both between the sheets and out of them.

The more Ada learned about him, the more she fell in love.

He was a hero. He battled monsters. He stepped in front of danger daily because it was the right thing to do. He was also funny and fun. In some stories, he told of the shenanigans he would get up to with his cadre. They sounded like an interesting lot, and she looked forward to meeting them.

But then he'd been taken. Things had changed. He still refused to talk much about what happened while he'd been under the King's influence but, like she'd told him already, she could wait. As long as he was happy, she was too. She didn't need to know everything. Everyone was entitled to their secrets. Back in Vegas, when she'd finally attended the local high school, none of them knew the depths of her childhood isolation. None of them knew the only reason she could attend was because Harold and Laurel had taught her how to read.

Jasper also trained Ada more in the nuances of accessing her gift. She couldn't light a flame, but she could shift water with her power—only enough to move the faucet flow and the bathwater around in circles. Thinking of that moment brought another smile to Ada's face.

That bath had been a very happy one for both of them.

And it wasn't all about Ada making Jasper happy. He made her happy in countless of ways. On the bed... by the fireplace... back at the window.

There was a limit, though. After eight days, even her lessons grew tiring. She could heal any ache from her body, but she needed more training. The fact became evident when Jasper struggled to explain what certain elements of mana meant. Apparently, there were fire, earth, air and water, but also chaos and spirit. Each felt differently, and he wasn't proficient in all of them.

To know what spells she could cast, she needed to know her elemental affinities, and that could only be isolated at the Order of the Well. Hopefully, they would get there soon.

Jasper snoozed in an armchair by the parlor fire, and she was in the middle of the very important task of counting the corners in the gothic, arched ceiling when the knock came at the door.

Jasper's ears perked and he sat up. Their eyes met briefly before Ada scrambled off the bed and ran a palm down her front. Because of the long duration of their stay, they'd been given clothing along with food three times a day. She now wore leather pants and a simple black sweater with feathered shoulder cuffs. Her hair draped about her shoulders, concealing her ears.

Jasper was also decked in top to toe form-fitting black —leather breeches and a thin black sweater showing all his God-given talents. It seemed the Queen enjoyed her guests wearing the colors of her brand. Ada wasn't complaining.

"Enter," Jasper rumbled and joined her at the bedside.

She wasn't sure if he'd spoken loud enough to be heard, but the door opened.

The dark guard from the gatehouse strode in. They'd since learned from the servants that he was a vampire named Gastnor. Jasper had warned Ada more than once to be wary around him.

Today he wore clothing more suited to indoors—black pants and a sweater. *Well, what do you know?* Black, black, black.

He motioned for them to follow but said nothing as they walked the long thin hallways.

"If this queen isn't wearing black, I swear I'll pay you whatever you want."

Jasper's lips quirked. Ada smiled back, happy to see the strain lift from his posture, if only for a moment.

"Never make a wager with a fae, Ada," he drawled, clearly amused. "You won't like the outcome."

She snorted and waggled her brows. "You know I'll *wager* with you anytime. Just ask."

This time, a humored huff burst out of him, and by the time they arrived at the throne room, he'd draped his arm casually around her shoulders. "Ada, Ada," he chided with a twinkle in his eye.

"What?" she smiled, looking up at him.

He lowered his lips to her ear. "You're perfect for me."

She molded to him. He kissed the top of her head and then guided her through the enormous arched doorway.

Inside, she was grateful for Jasper's steady touch because she shrank beneath the attention of a room full of gawping fae.

The throne room was an enormous obsidian chamber. The sickly sweet scent of vanilla and rose permeated the air. Red banners dangled from the ceiling between a criss-cross sculpture of bones, antlers, and driftwood that reached from cornice to cornice. Up on a dais, before a stained-glass window depicting violent, deviant scenes involving fae, blood, and animals, sat the Queen on a throne made of black bone. Or maybe it was obsidian, carved to look like bone.

The Queen herself was a striking woman with big dark eyes and pouting purple lips. Long afro hair carried an antler crown crested with rubies. It reminded Ada of the thorns Jesus wore on the cross, the red rubies like blood. Her dark dress wasn't saintly. It clung to her voluptuous form until it flared at the knees and trailed down the steps of the dais where two goblin-like creatures simpered and preened against the lengths. Collars linked them to a stake wedged into the steps.

As they walked down the aisle, Ada couldn't help shivering under the weight of the watchful eyes of the members of the Court. Some fae appeared human, some weren't. Antlers on heads. Antennas. Wings. Faces that weren't human moved with unblinking eyes and slashes for mouths. Underbites with fangs. A few faces were deathly pale, and Ada could have sworn she glimpsed the outline of a skull when looking at one. It was only a flicker beneath his hauntingly beautiful face, as though someone had shone a torch over translucent skin, but then when the light switched off, the skull was gone.

When her gaze landed on two short, thickset old men with long prominent teeth, a shiver skated down her spine. Red berets sat atop their scraggly hair. Skinny, taloned fingers clicked at their thighs, and large red eyes tracked her as she walked by. Their hats were glossy, as though dipped in actual blood, and when she caught the sight of a few flies swarming about, she knew it to be true. Gross.

Jasper squeezed her shoulder as they came to a standstill at the foot of the dais. Gastnor continued up the steps and stood to the Queen's right. On her left stood a stocky man in a dark robe, his face shadowed by the cowl. He clutched a round glass globe.

"High Queen Maebh," Jasper said, and inclined his head.

"Bow, Guardian," she demanded. Her deep voice oozed confidence.

Ada swiftly curtsey-bowed, wishing that she'd at least asked Jasper about the proper protocol. Jasper deepened the incline of his head, but went no lower. She tapped her black-stained fingertips on the throne, long pointed nails ticking.

"I see the ego of your new station has already consumed you," she remarked drolly. "A Guardian *and* a prince. My how times are changing."

Jasper met her gaze.

"Speak." She gestured, barely lifting her finger as though the entire situation bored her.

He glanced around the congregation. "Perhaps we should speak about politics in private."

"This is my court," she drawled. "And these are my trusted advisors. There is nothing I won't tell them."

Ada highly doubted it. This was a power play, anyone could see it. The silence and watchful eyes intended to intimidate, to display the Queen's control of her subjects, and to show she was a woman to fear and respect. And it worked—for Ada.

But Jasper didn't flinch. He arched a regal brow. "Very well. The Seelie High King is plotting against you. He's colluding with humans to frame Unseelie as perpetrators in a rash of attacks. He wants to incite a war, a war which he planned to trigger by killing me and claiming you were responsible."

The Queen stared at him, calculations running behind her shark eyes. Not one person in the room reacted. It was as though they either already knew, didn't care, or were spelled to look statuesque.

Ada was officially spooked.

"I must admit," Maebh said, thrumming her nails. "I was suspicious when word arrived of you portaling into our territory. And curious. They said you've been missing for over a decade, and then the King suddenly announces you're his heir." Her smile failed to reach her eyes. "We've both been around for long enough to know he never intended for you to ascend to his throne. So why come to me? I care little for what happens on Seelie soil."

Jasper scowled. "He's got eyes on your kingdom. He wants to rule all of Elphyne as you once did. The only reason he acknowledged me as his heir is so that he could kill me, blame you, and claim grievance to the Seelie throne."

"If the humans failed to beat my Sluagh and their Wild Hunt, then what makes Mithras think he can?"

"Like I said, he's working with the humans. He's giving

them metal in exchange for weapons that work against the fae."

More silent contemplation from the Queen. Then she made a tedious, limp hand gesture. "I care as much about the Seelie as an *elfant* cares about a mouse."

"You want to know where I was for the past decade?" Jasper growled, taking a step forward. "Mithras forced me to fight in the Ring with an iron mask embedded into my neck. Because the iron was inside my body, it halted my transformation. I got stuck halfway between wolf and fae. They stripped me of my power-enhancing tattoos. They stole my memories. If he can do that to a Guardian thought impervious to metal, what makes you think you can survive what they have in store for you?"

Her eyes flashed. A ripple of power washed about the room like a rogue wind. Ada tried not to shiver for fear the Queen would notice her and do something drastic.

Jasper stepped forward and continued talking.

"During the past one hundred years, since the last war against the humans, their warfare tactics have vastly advanced. They can now inject liquid metal into our bodies and force our mana out. Are you honestly telling me you'd say no to the offer of a metal cage if the Order allowed it? Just one? Or any metal weapon, for that matter. It might halt your use of mana while holding it, but on the flip side, you could kill any magical creature. Imagine the fae you could have under your thumb. Imagine the power you'd amass."

"Are you making me an offer, Guardian? Are you working with the humans too?"

"No," he said. "I want to kill the one who is."

Ada thought it had been silent before, but after Jasper's words dropped, the room was a virtual vacuum. The Queen's rogue wind stopped. Not a feather ruffled on her dress. Not a breath was taken by the goblins at her feet. And her eyes—cold, dark eyes—stared at Jasper so long and hard, Ada thought she was trying to read his mind.

Then the room burst into screeching laughter. Each of the Unseelie fae howled like hyenas until the Queen stopped them with a look, albeit humor-laced.

She raised her black stained fingers and said to Jasper, "Very well. Convince me."

"Convince you?"

"Yes, you want my help to defeat your king, then show me why I should care. He's no threat to me. Unless you can convince me otherwise."

Jasper looked thoughtful. Ada wasn't sure what he'd say. It seemed impossible the Queen would help them with Mithras. They should just leave. But his gaze flicked sideways to Ada, and then back to the Queen.

"How about a wager?" he asked, all smiles and charm.

Maebh's dark brow rose. "I'm listening."

Jasper became the showman once more. He lifted his arms and rotated, staring at the court before settling back on the Queen. "If I beat your best warrior, you will owe me a boon."

A chorus of gasps erupted, including Ada's.

"Very well," Maebh grinned. "But I will have no open ended boon. Name your prize. Use of my Wild Hunt to kill the King? Mana? Metal? What?"

Ada thought it was curious she offered the use of metal, meaning she had some stockpiled somewhere against the Order's mandate.

"After I kill the King, I want the Ring disbanded in Cornucopia."

"That is neutral territory," Maebh said. "Even if you become the Seelie High King, neither of us have the right to disband the Ring."

"Which is why I'm asking for your cooperation. If both of us provide a united front, then Cornucopia will have to fall in line."

"And if the Ring is gone, how do you expect Cornucopian law to work? Will you provide the resources for a guard?"

"I expect you and I to come up with a solution beneficial to everyone."

She pondered his suggestion and then nodded. "Agreed, although, I am surprised you don't simply ask for assistance to dispatch your king."

"I won't need help for that." Jasper walked up to her, held out his hand and said, "A bargain must be struck."

She clasped his hand and studied him. "If you beat my finest warrior, or if I forfeit the match, then I, High Queen Maebh, agree to parlay with you, D'arn Jasper, regarding abolishing the Ring in Cornucopia until a mutually beneficial solution can be arranged."

Jasper repeated her words but added the time limit of four seasons, much to Maebh's chagrin, but she agreed. A spark erupted between their palms, and the bargain was struck.

"Now," the Queen said, rising to her feet with a slow smile. "Who shall you battle? The vampire leader of my personal guard, Gastnor? Or perhaps one of my redcap warriors... oh, no. Of course, you said my best warrior. How silly of me."

She flicked her fingers in the air. A ghostly wind fluttered through the room. The screams of unseen prisoners screeched in Ada's ears, distant dogs barked, and then quite suddenly, a man appeared before Jasper.

Tall, pale, and hauntingly beautiful, he was almost gothic in appearance with his long dark cape—no, *wings*, they were wings—draped down from his shoulders. They shuddered and fluttered as fast as a dragonfly's. Fast enough to make Ada want to rub her eyes. He stepped closer to Jasper and Ada gasped, her heart leaping into her throat. He hadn't stepped. But he'd moved. It was like frames of the film were missing and he'd skipped ahead in the space at spooky irregular intervals.

The Queen smiled. "One of my Sluagh will be your opponent."

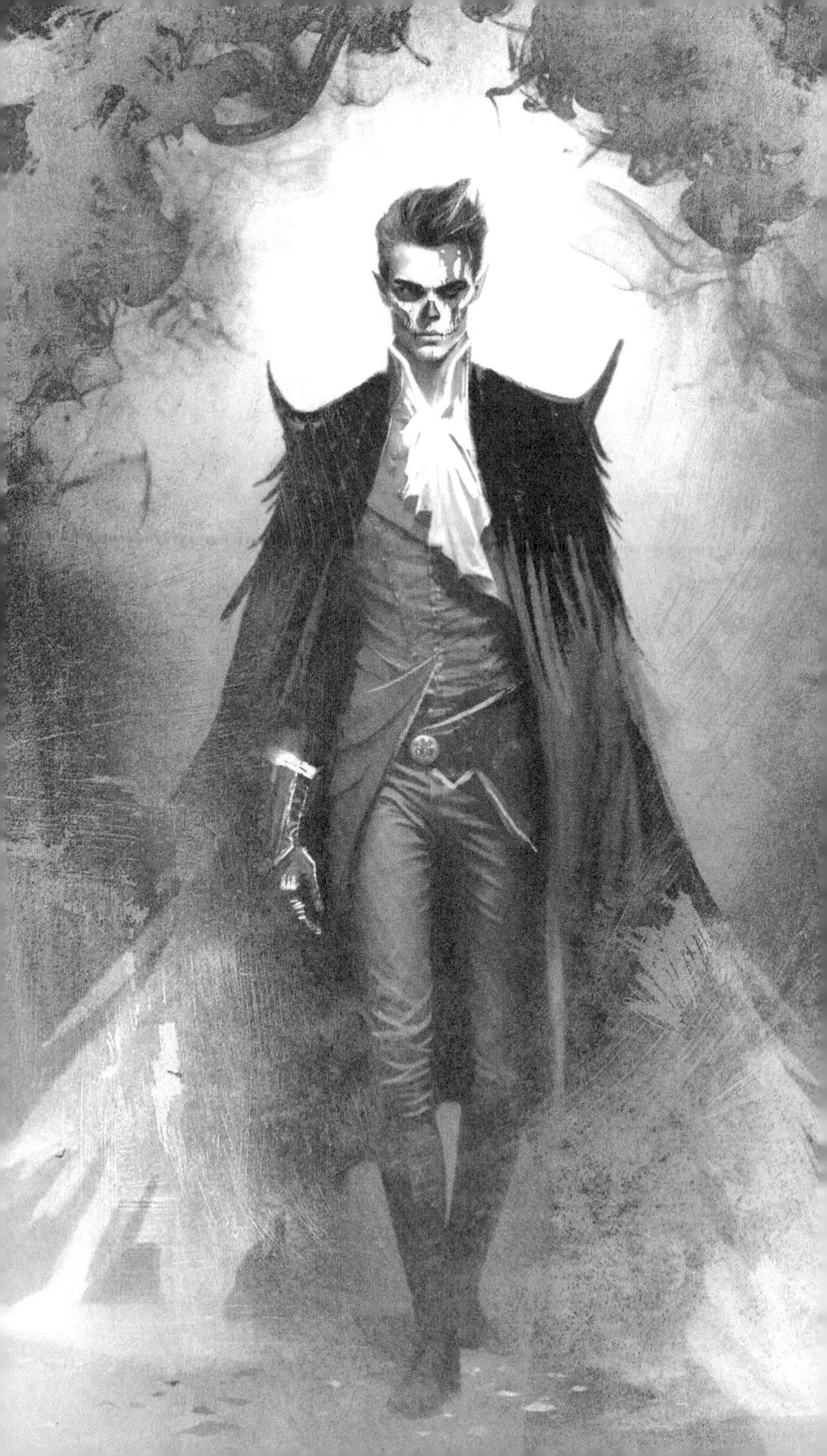

CHAPTER
TWENTY-FIVE

Jasper had hoped Maebh would choose a Sluagh, but hid his triumph. He would have been happy with any fae, to be honest. As long as it wasn't her. All he needed was for her to forfeit, and for that to happen, he needed to trick her just as she was trying to trick him.

The key to defeating the Sluagh was separating its soul from its body in the daylight.

"I thought you were smarter than this, Guardian," the Queen drawled. "Then again, your father captured you and forced you to battle in the Ring for years."

Sniggers tittered around the Court. No one thought he'd win.

"Jasper?" Ada whispered, her eyes wide.

He kept his expression amused and dropped the block on his emotions. For this to succeed, he would need her calm. He jogged over and whispered in her ear, "It's easier to give her some entertainment to get what I want."

He made sure she sensed he wasn't concerned. Her jaw clenched and she nodded. "Give 'em hell, honey."

He winked, loving how confident she was of him.

Perfect for me.

Ada shuffled to the side. He pulled her back to him, remembering something.

"I might have to borrow your mana," he murmured. "Is this okay?"

"Take whatever you need."

Her words hit him harder than he'd been prepared for. They'd spent the past eight days loving each other, yet, in truth, he'd taken more than she should give without giving back himself. He knew her friends were somewhere in Elphyne. On more than one occasion he had an opening to tell her. But every time he opened his mouth, nothing came out. He'd frozen. The thought of disappointing her, of her friends poisoning her against him, was the new source of his nightmares. It was irrational, but still something he couldn't let go of.

Which was why he had to find a way to tell her, or this would all backfire.

He strode back to the empty space before the throne and rolled his shoulders. "You want to do this here?"

"Here, outside—" Maebh shrugged. "Either place, you will still die. And I will enjoy supping on your human mate."

Jasper's eyes narrowed. His humor dropped. Things just got personal. Fine. He would make this end as swiftly as possible.

Making a show of it, he held out his palm and distended a claw from a fingertip. He used the point to scratch bloody symbols into his left palm and then summoned his steel weapon, Ghostmaker. It probably still sat in his room at the Order. When the spell found it, the sword would portal to him. He stared at the Queen while he waited and kept his back to the Sluagh.

"I sense your doubt, Guardian." The Sluagh's voice whispered into Jasper's mind. *"Turn around and face me."*

Jasper remained stoic. His brazen disregard for his safety baffled the crowd, but the Queen narrowed her eyes. She knew he'd just summoned a weapon.

"Metal won't kill it," she taunted. "You know that."

He gave a half shrug. "But it might slow it down."

"Not enough. You have seconds before your life is forfeit. Do you have any last words, shifter prince?" She sneered the word "prince" and he hated it.

He never thought he'd grow attached to the word, but after the King had massacred the Darkfoot pack, and then Ada's subsequent belief he could make a stand, he'd thought, perhaps, he had a chance at fixing things in the Seelie nation. He had a chance to make his mother proud. Perhaps those dignitaries who'd sat at the Lupercalia feast and had urged him to take the crown were right. Perhaps he owed his kin to protect the innocent—beyond the

Order's prerogative. It was the dream that had driven him to becoming a Guardian in the first place.

Before the hour was over, Maebh would eat her words. She would see him as an equal, and when they finally entered negotiations regarding the Ring, she would come to the table with respect.

"Coward." The Sluagh's words slid into his thoughts. *"She will know the truth. She will despise you. Surrender now and save your dignity."*

Jasper tensed, knowing the Sluagh spoke about Ada. His hands clenched at his sides.

Just a little longer.

"Turn around, Guardian. Face me."

A rumbling in the atmosphere signaled his long broadsword, Ghostmaker, coming through time and space, pulled by the spell he'd carved in blood. He held out his hand, ready to claim it. The instant the hilt hit his palm, he dematerialized.

And appeared behind the Sluagh, bringing Ghostmaker's blade to his neck, ready to slice it open. The Sluagh had sensed him coming. It flickered away. Two skips and it was two feet further away. It gathered its bearings and then flickered to Jasper, but this time, Jasper portaled away. And so their game of cat and mouse began, each of them flickering or portaling across the room, trying to catch the other until eventually, the Sluagh's specter, a skull faced blur of shadow and light, appeared like a ghost within its face. Its perfect, debonair mouth twisted into a snarl, revealing sharp jagged teeth, and then it separated its soul from its body with a gust of air.

Even though he couldn't see it, Jasper had been prepared. He waited until he sensed the spirit coming, and then portaled about the room, leading the specter on a seemingly random chase. He could sense the confusion—from the Sluagh, the Queen, and the spectators. None of them had realized how much mana Jasper had access too. He should be tired by now. Spent. But he was only getting warmed up.

With a final dart about the room, he landed behind the Sluagh's physical body, gripped his arm and portaled away.

They landed on a mountaintop covered in snow. Jasper let go of the snarling and hissing Sluagh. It hated sunlight, more so than the vampires.

"My soul will find me," the Sluagh warned, twisting and lashing out with its clawed fingers. Without its soul, it couldn't speak directly into Jasper's mind. Its wings shuddered, preparing to fly. "No matter where in the world you have taken me, I will reunite with my specter, and then I will find you. And I will feast on your cowardly eternal soul."

Jasper's snarl echoed across the mountain. His blade was against the Sluagh's neck before he could blink. "I should run you through right now and be damned with the consequences."

The Sluagh grinned a shark's tooth grin. "You don't have the courage."

Ghostmaker cut the pale neck, just a sliver. Dark crimson oozed from the shallow wound. The Sluagh's eyes widened.

"Yes," Jasper whispered. "I know the blade will kill you without your soul inside."

"That's a lie."

"Is it?" Jasper returned.

His opponent said nothing because it was true. Without this ghostly presence, the body was virtually Lesser Fae. It was sheer luck no one had discovered this weakness so far.

Jasper shrugged. "I only needed a few minutes with you out of the room."

He portaled himself back to the Queen's throne room, knowing that the Sluagh's specter would already be hurtling through the world, arrowing straight back to its body, expending mana.

The Queen pretended to look bored.

"Please don't tell me you're playing a game of fetch with my Sluagh."

He bared his teeth in a grin for he knew beneath her droll countenance was a female fearing the worst. She knew nothing.

Maebh waved her hand. "You know he will be back, at any moment. And all he needs to replenish his mana is to eat a soul within this room. Perhaps it will be your mate's."

Jasper brandished his sword, twirling it around in his hand as he began a slow, steady walk toward the Queen, making sure to show the blood stain dripping down Ghostmaker.

"I think not," he said.

"Oh, really." Her eyes darted to his blade. "Enlighten me."

"You haven't fulfilled your end of the bargain. The Sluagh wasn't your best warrior. Even if it was, I can keep up a game of fetch all day."

Her expression darkened. She knew he was right, and now she knew he'd not killed the Sluagh like he could have.

"Is your best warrior too afraid to face me?" he taunted. "Is that it?"

Fury flashed in her eyes, and she stood, menace rippling from her in waves.

"You test my patience."

"And you manipulated the bargain."

The crowd sniggered and laughed. It was an Unseelie thing to do. If their queen hadn't tried to rig the contest, they would have been disappointed. But the Queen wasn't as clever as she thought.

He knew one thing gave her power among her people; it was her utter lack of fear over the metal killing strength of the humans. All Jasper needed to do was to prove metal had the power to kill her greatest warrior, and her illusion of power would be shattered. She would lose subjects in droves.

The walls shook as the Sluagh approached, coming in at such a force, it displaced sound and created thunder.

Jasper swung his sword, scrutinizing the bloody blade, thinking aloud, "I wonder what would happen if this long, thick piece of steel was portaled *inside* your strongest warrior."

He arched his brow at Maebh. She knew she would either have to admit that metal did, indeed, kill a Sluagh if done correctly. Or herself. Either way, someone would come out looking weak in front of her Court. And it wouldn't be him.

She stilled. She stared.

And the instant the Sluagh flickered into the room, she held up her hand, halting it.

It seethed in fury, but did as commanded.

"I tire of this game. I forfeit," she yawned, then scowled at the Court. "Begone! All of you."

As they scuttled out of the room, unsure of what had transpired, he smiled at the Queen.

She was her own strongest warrior. She held the greatest capacity for holding mana. By sending the Sluagh to fight in her stead meant the bargain was in breech, and Jasper had won by default. She would either have to stand up and admit she was to fight next, but with his threat lying heavy in the air, she would also be putting herself at risk.

By forfeiting, she could save face and retain the mystery.

What she failed to consider was that, in order to get the sword inside the Queen or the Sluagh, Jasper would have had to portal with it, and it was highly unlikely he would survive himself. He was solid. She was, too. Their cells would battle for supremacy in the space, and... he didn't want to risk it. It was the same thing that happened when a portal was activated and the exit on the other side was solid. Leaf had once created a portal that landed in the middle of a wall. It blew up. But the Queen didn't realize that.

Either way, her ego had been her downfall because if she'd thought long and hard enough, she would have known that to beat him, all she had needed to do was attack Ada.

CHAPTER
TWENTY-SIX

Ada's heart was still in her throat as the throne room emptied, and the Queen stepped down from her dais to meet Jasper. Ada still wasn't sure what had happened. Some kind of other battle went on, a psychological one no one understood except the Queen and Jasper.

When the last of the Unseelie left the room, the doors remained open, and the Queen gestured for someone to come in. Two well-built, silver-haired soldiers came in, dragging a prisoner between them.

Both soldiers wore black leather and had the twinkling blue Guardian tattoo beneath their eye. Great metal weapons were strapped to their backs. One had a sword, the other a battle ax. Scruff covered the long-haired Guardian's square jaw, while the short-haired Guardian was clean shaven. From the way their fur-tipped ears perked, they must be shifters. Both glared at Jasper.

Jasper paled as they dropped the prisoner at the Queen's feet.

"We've been waiting for hours," the long-haired Guardian growled.

"We don't like waiting," added the other and folded his arms.

Maebh's eyes narrowed. "You wait as long as I intend you to wait."

"You didn't tell me you had company," Jasper said to her.

"Surprise." More unsaid animosity passed between the Queen and Jasper, but neither acted on it. Instead, the Queen directed hers toward the prisoner, a wicked gleam entering her gaze. "Perfect timing. I find myself in the mood to dole out some punishment."

"Interrogation," the long-haired Guardian reminded her. "We agreed to lend you our prisoner for interrogation purposes only."

"I don't care," the short-haired Guardian mumbled. "Punish away."

The Queen smiled coyly. "Interrogation, punishment... same thing. My Sluagh is feeling a little cheated after the battle he just had, and I want to give him something to make up for it. Human souls are so very tasty."

"Just get the information."

"Oh, he'll get the information," the Queen said. "He'll

hunt around this little man's mind until he finds what we need."

Ada shifted her focus to the prisoner and almost lost the contents of her stomach. He was a man—*human*—with deep-set eyes, a hook nose, and a very familiar face. But it wasn't possible. Was it?

Her reality began to slide. This prisoner was from her past. Like, deep within her past, from when she lived in Vegas. She *knew* it. Where had she seen him?

The prisoner spat blood onto the floor and lifted his head. When he saw Ada, his eyes widened a fraction before returning passive. And then it hit—he was the mercenary who'd attacked Laurel back in their time. He'd kidnapped her to force Clarke to reveal the nuclear codes. He was the same man who'd worked for the man who inevitably caused the apocalypse—the Void.

What the hell was he doing here? Now?

Panic surged, closing Ada's throat. She couldn't breathe. Could barely think. She tugged on Jasper's arm, trying to speak, but her only sound was a hiss as she tried to form words.

"Ada?"

"He's... he's...." Her jaw opened and closed.

The long-haired Guardian stalked over. "He's a dangerous man, yes, we know."

"No, you don't understand. He's from my time. He's the one who—"

"Works for the Void," rumbled the short-haired Guardian.

"You know?" The blood drained from her face. "How?"

A shuffle behind her. A waft of a scent too familiar to be real.

"I told them, Pretty Kitty."

Ada's shoulders tensed. She knew that voice, that nickname. All heads swiveled to the new arrivals at the door. Two women. One red-headed and one dark-haired. Ada's heart leaped into her throat. Her knees weakened.

The women smiled, tears in their eyes as they walked forward. Ada was too numb to move, too scared she would wake from the dream, but when Clarke turned to Jasper and nodded, everything turned pear-shaped.

He nodded back, jaw tight.

He knew them.

What?

"Clarke. Laurel," he mumbled and then shifted his gaze to the two Guardians. "Rush. Thorne."

A sharp snap tweaked in her chest. She clutched her sweater. How did he know them?

"Jasper?" she whispered. "You... know my friends?"

His eyes widened, but he said nothing.

Clarke and Laurel rushed to her. They all crashed together in one big embrace. Ada couldn't stop the tears bursting out. Her friends. They were here. Alive. They smelled the same. Even after all this time.

"Oh my God," she gasped, clutching onto them. "I

missed you both so much."

Her friends were blubbering too. Tears streaming down their faces, smiling despite the torrent of emotion raging through them all. Ada pulled back and looked at Jasper. He refused to meet her eyes. But down their connection she felt everything... shame, resignation, fear.

"You know them, Jasper. How long... how... how long have you known? From the start?" Her voice cracked as the worst scenarios played in her mind.

He'd lied to her? But she thought that was impossible for a fae. *Fae can't lie.* That's exactly what a liar would say. But she'd just witnessed her lover prove he was a master manipulator. And she had never outright asked him if he knew her friends. So he'd never outright lied. She hadn't thought it was necessary. If he knew her friends were alive, any person who cared for her would have said something.

It all became too much.

"I can't breathe." She started hyperventilating.

"We're here," Laurel said.

"It's okay," Clarke added, running her palm over Ada's back. "We've got you."

"He—"

"I know. He took you about two weeks ago. We tried to find you but couldn't."

"He *took* me?"

Oh, my God. That made it worse. Now Ada couldn't look at him. Who was he? Was his amnesia real? Was the curse real?

The past eight days with him had been groundbreaking for her relationship with him. Had that been fake?

The walls closed in.

"I need air," she gasped. "Have to get out of here."

The Queen's voice rang out above everything.

"I will take her outside," she ordered, and pushed through to get to her.

Icy fingers wrapped around Ada's wrist.

"Come, human. Follow me."

"I don't think so," Jasper growled, his sword already in his hand and pointed at the Queen's throat.

The two Guardians stiffened, their eyes darting between the Queen and Jasper. Maebh rolled her eyes.

"You think I need to squirrel her away to kill her?"

"One never knows with the Unseelie." A quiet desperation brightened his eyes as they narrowed. "And you had mentioned something about supping."

"After the stunt you pulled, in *my* throne room, you owe me a moment with your mate."

"I owe you nothing. And you were the one who pulled a stunt first."

Storm clouds seemed to gather in the room. "Be careful, Guardian prince. You are in *my* home. You came to *me* for help."

Jasper's jaw clenched. The other two Guardians, and even Laurel and Clarke tensed. Ada didn't want another battle. Not now. Not when things were already spirally out of control.

Maebh pursed her lips. "I give you my oath. No harm will come to this woman during this visit to the Winter Palace. Now let me get the poor girl some air."

Reluctantly, and probably because Ada didn't refuse—she was still too numb—Jasper stood to the side.

Clarke and Laurel remained restrained and wary.

"It's fine," Ada said to them. "I just need some air."

The Queen wouldn't harm her.

"We'll be right here," Laurel said.

Ada nodded, then followed the Queen as she glided toward the exit, commanding attention with every step.

Maebh took her to a snow dusted balcony overlooking the frozen sea. The blood vines covering the railing gave off a pleasant vanilla rose scent. An icy wind ruffled Ada's shoulder feathers and cut through the gaps in her sweater. Their breath puffed out in white clouds. She shivered and wrapped her arms around herself.

But she was outside. She could see the ocean, the snow, and the sky. Nature always made Ada feel like her problems weren't so big. How could they be under the face of the world? She felt better. Mildly. She inhaled deep breaths, feeling her wits slowly seep back into her mind with every exhale.

"This is good," she said, lifting her chin to the sea. "This feels better."

"So," the Queen drawled, giving Ada an unassuming once over. "You are human. And you are brimming with mana like the other two. What is your gift?"

And here was the real reason the Queen wanted a quiet word. To snoop. As long as she wasn't thinking about Jasper, it suited Ada fine.

"I can heal," she answered.

"A natural born healer. Interesting. We haven't had one of your kind around for a long time. Lately it's been all tinctures and salves. We could use someone of your skills in the Winter Court. Injecting some of your gift into a royal line would be even better." She tapped her lips. "I fear I have no heirs with which you can become betrothed. Perhaps Gastnor will do."

A sick feeling churned in Ada's gut. Being alone with this woman was dangerous. She had to tread carefully.

Dangerous things come in pretty packages.

The Queen had kept Jasper and Ada locked in a room for over a week, simply because it amused her. Or perhaps she'd been waiting for this opportunity the entire time—waiting until she had the Guardians and Ada's friends in the same place. Waiting to see the fireworks go off. Perhaps the Queen orchestrated it all. It couldn't be a coincidence her friends arrived on the same day—at the same time—Jasper was in the throne room.

"It's nice of you to offer," she added meekly, choosing her words wisely. She forced a smile on her face and then held up her blue marked hand. "But, Jasper is my mate."

The moment she said the words, she doubted them. *Is he?*

Would a mate keep the most precious secret from her?

He'd felt fear under all that shame when her friends had walked in. What was he afraid of?

A wry, dark brow rose as the Queen glanced at Ada's unblemished neck. "He hasn't claimed you. Besides, there is much we can teach you here. For example..." She took Ada's hand and turned it over to stroke her palm. "There are two sides to every gift. Did your Seelie prince tell you that? Or did he omit it, like so many other things?" When she didn't answer, Maebh continued. "What is the opposite of healing, Ada? Answer me that."

"Um... injury, I suppose."

The Queen's slow, wicked smile sent shivers down Ada's spine.

Ada gaped. "Are you telling me, I can make someone hurt just as I make them heal?"

Maebh stroked the back of Ada's hand. "The Well has a dark side, and contrary to what others make you believe, the Well does not punish you for using it. All nature has a destructive side. Without it, there is no life." She raised and clenched her fist. The ice in the air suddenly dissipated. "I can create ice. I can take it away."

Ada stopped rubbing her arms. Maebh had taken the coldness away, and in doing so, created warmth. Ada swiped her hand through the air, marveling at the change in temperature. But that churning feeling in her gut wouldn't leave.

"Why are you telling me this?" she asked. The Queen knew Jasper was a Guardian. The use of the dark side of the

Well is forbidden. "Are you trying to put a wedge between Jasper and me?"

"Oh, Jasper doesn't need any help from me to do that."

"What?"

"Well, he's done a fine job on his own, don't you think? I mean, keeping knowledge of your friends from you. Who would do such a thing?"

Ada scowled at her. How she dealt with Jasper was her own business, and the longer she stayed out here on the balcony, the more she realized this was some sort of sick side game for the Queen. The Queen who had just lost face in front of Jasper.

"You're Unseelie," Ada said. "Manipulation is what you do."

Maebh laughed, tilting her head to the sky. "Well, my dear, it sounds like you have it all figured out then."

Ada made a frustrated sound and stepped toward the balcony railing, resting her palms on the balustrade, and stared out to sea. She scoured the icy water, looking for answers only Jasper could give her. What they shared was real... wasn't it?

But could she ever trust him again?

If he continued to hide his feelings, Ada was afraid of how that mistrust would fester.

The Queen placed her palm on the railing next to Ada, her little finger twitching out to reach Ada's. Ada jolted at the intimate connection, but froze, temporarily stupefied. Was the Queen actively *trying* to invade her personal space? What the fuck? Inches away from shouting for her friends, Ada flinched when the Queen spoke.

"Did he tell you he was Unseelie once... before, when our nations were one?"

Ada shook her head.

"And did he tell you what his father did to me?"

Frustrated, she glared at the Queen. "No."

"Let's just say I have more in common with Jasper's mother than he'll ever know."

"So why aren't you helping him to defeat Mithras? Why the game?"

"For me to align with Jasper, a Seelie, would not only look unfavorably among my own people, but it would signal to the fae who've sided with Mithras that I truly am trying to conquer their land by overthrowing their leader. I'm not ready to deal with that level of scrutiny. Besides, as I mentioned, I care little about them. There are far more interesting things happening north of Cornucopia."

"Thanks for the heart to heart, but I'm ready to rejoin my friends. If it's okay with you."

Black eyes flickered with something alive inside, and Ada had a moment to wonder what kind of fae the Queen was. Just a moment. And then Maebh grinned.

"Of course. Off you go." She shooed her.

"Just... go?" Ada checked the balcony door.

"I'm not holding you prisoner. You may leave Aconite City."

Ada bowed, then hand signed her gratitude.

Maebh watched her with calculating eyes, then inclined her head slightly before turning back to the sea and holding out her hand for a crow to land upon. When the bird settled on her fingers, the Queen whispered gently to it, and kissed its feathered head.

What the fuck?

Ada kept mumbling curses to herself on the walk back to the throne room. *What the fuck? Fuckity fuck fuck.* Her mind was awhirl, and by the time she saw the arched doors of the throne room, she broke into a jog.

Relief hit as she burst through. The only people left in the chamber were her friends, and the three Guardians: Rush, Thorne, and Jasper.

She met Jasper's gaze and felt more of his confusion come down their bond. He stepped toward her, but she couldn't help it. Her instincts slammed up and she went straight for Clarke and Laurel, taking the two into a group hug. Tears burned in her eyes.

"I can't believe it's really you!" she sobbed, feeling safe again.

All three of them became another mess of blubbers, rushed words, and teary hugs.

When Laurel patted her cheeks, a ring twinkled on her finger.

"You're engaged!" Ada squeaked.

"Married, actually." Laurel blushed and darted a glance at Thorne. Ada caught sight of a bite mark that looked suspiciously like a healed over, scarred hickey. She pointed, gaping. "Is that a mating mark? You always said you'd never settle down."

Another blush. Laurel pointed her finger at Clarke. "She's the one who's had a child."

"What?" Ada squeaked. And here she was being so protective of her own neck when her friends were dolling mating marks out like candy.

"Laurel, give her a moment to process," Clarke laughed, but also pulled her long red hair back from her neck, revealing a bite mark. "Rush and I have been together for about three years. Since I woke in this time."

Oh. Okay, three years. So, not like candy then.

"You woke? How did we get here?"

"Frozen." Clarke threw up her hands, as if it had boggled her too. "The most we've guessed is that the nuclear winter froze us, but the Well is waking us. From what I gathered, the temperature dropped so suddenly the day it snowed in Vegas that we were"—she snapped her fingers—"snap frozen like peas!"

"Holy shit."

"It's pretty far-out," Laurel agreed.

"You said the Well is waking us?"

Clarke's eyes turned bleak. "You saw Bones. The Void is in this time too. We think the Void dropped the bombs, purely to create the circumstances so he could freeze and wake in a time where the population was small enough so he could control everything."

All the blood drained from Ada's face. "Where is he

now?"

"In Crystal City, locked behind walls of mana-blocking metal. We know he's planning some sort of takeover, but not when or how."

"And Bones?"

"We handed him over to the Queen's guards. The Guardians can't get enough information out of him, but Maebh has ways of extracting the truth."

I'll bet she does.

Thorne broke from his conversation and shuffled closer with a scowl pointed at Laurel. "You should have let me kill him."

Laurel smiled patiently at him. "Babe, I appreciate you want to protect me, I do, but if we want to get ahead of them, we need the information in his head. The human city is still in the middle of desecrated ground. None of us have power there."

Rush removed a smooth stone from his pocket and said, "I think it's time we portal out of here." When Jasper tentatively put his arm around Ada's shoulder, she stiffened and removed it.

"Good idea," she said, smiling tightly at her friends. "I'll go with you."

"I can take us," Jasper offered to Ada.

"I'd rather go with them." She stepped away from him and took Laurel's hand. "I need some time."

She wasn't ready to deal with his betrayal. She might never be.

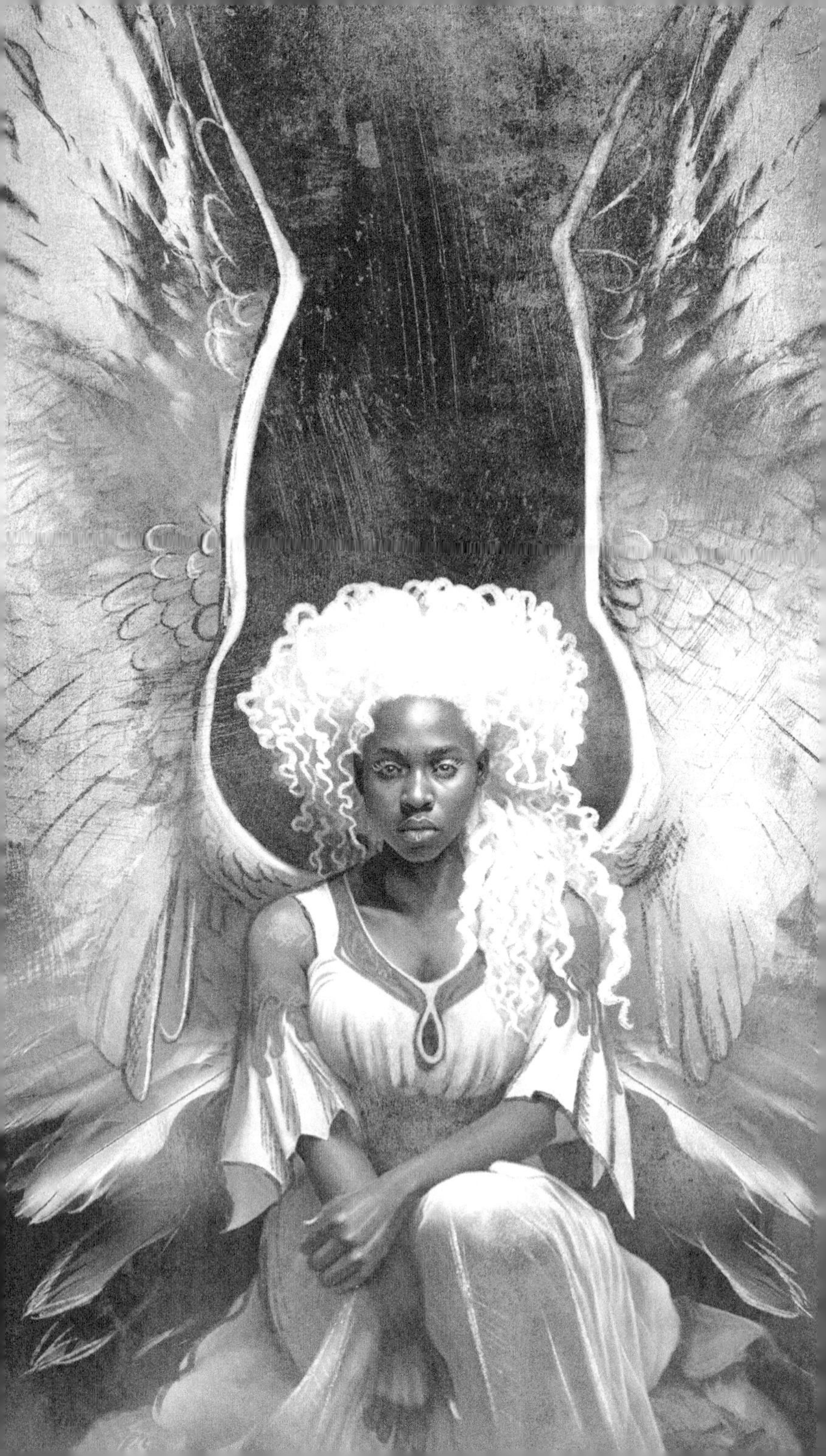

CHAPTER
TWENTY-SEVEN

Alone in his old room at the Order, Jasper stood before the door, looking over the decor as though it were foreign. It had only been ten years since he'd last been there, and in fae terms, that was a drop in the ocean. But the drink tasted like chalk. The air held no warmth. And without Ada, he wasn't sure he would stay.

Would she give him a chance to explain? But what would he say? He'd known exactly what he was doing when he kept the information from her.

The door opened and Thorne walked in.

"Kid," Jasper grunted.

"Haven't been a kid for a long time."

He shrugged. "I know that. It's still fun to call you that. I need my hits where I can take them."

Silence. There were so many things Jasper wanted to say but couldn't. He didn't know where to start.

Thorne pulled out a rolled stick of mana-weed from his pocket and offered it to Jasper, but Jasper declined with a shake of his head.

"You shitting me?" Thorne gaped. "Saying no to mana-weed? You really have changed."

Another half shrug. Ada already avoided him. If he fell back into his old habits, she might... his throat closed up.

"Ten years of torture will do that," he mumbled instead.

"I searched for you," Thorne said, shoving the roll back into his pocket. "The entire time you were missing, I didn't stop. Thought you should know that."

Jasper's gaze clashed with his. "You shouldn't have."

"Why the fuck not?" A scowl twisted Thorne's face so suddenly that Jasper had to laugh.

Still with the same temper. The sudden humor dispelled his tension, and Jasper sighed heavily, rubbing his forehead. He'd thought he'd had a win today, but the look in Ada's eyes when she'd learned he'd kept the truth from her —it cut him straight down the middle. This was the moment he'd feared, and he'd caused it himself.

A knock came at the door, and Rush entered.

Great. Another male Jasper had to apologize to. Another wave of inadequacy.

"I heard through the door," Rush grumbled, shutting the door behind. He glanced at Thorne. "Jasper thinks you should have left him because he believes he failed me."

Thorne's eyes narrowed. He reclined on the bed, putting his hands behind his head. "By not stopping Mithras's soldiers from executing Véda? Wasn't it Thaddeus's fault?"

Jasper rolled his eyes. "Just take my bed. Why not?"

But they took none of his dry humor. Like father, like son. They glared at Jasper.

Rush growled, "I admit I was pissed at you for many years. But you weren't the only one to blame. We all played our parts."

Jasper narrowed his eyes. "What do you mean?"

"He means," Thorne said, "that the Prime used us to get what she wanted."

"She never used me," Jasper replied. "Beyond the usual Guardian duties."

"Oh, yes, she fucking did." Thorne's shoulders bunched. He lit his mana-weed roll and toked, inhaling deep before exhaling.

Rush walked around Jasper's bed to stare out the window, a deep frown on his face.

Jasper asked Thorne, "What do you mean?"

"The Prime played us. She traded you to Mithras so he would keep the sanctioned breeding law active, which ensured my mother would be executed and Rush cursed, which lead to Rush finding Clarke and now the rest of the waking, powered humans before the Void does. They believe if they hadn't, then the Void would have the power to finish what he started and destroy the world. The Prime knew what she was doing the entire time."

"But they kidnapped me years after Rush was cursed."

"That delay was part of the bargain, too. She didn't want anyone figuring out her plan."

Cold, hard fury rattled Jasper's cage. His inner wolf paced about, snarling and growling. Red coated his vision. "She *sold* me to Mithras?"

"And now she wants to put you on the throne," Rush rumbled from the window, still watching something outside.

When Jasper walked over, he saw Clarke chasing after a small silver-haired girl.

The Prime *wanted* him on the throne? "She doesn't get involved with fae politics."

Rush slid his gaze to Jasper's. "We should probably let her explain. She's called a meeting with the Twelve."

"If I see her... I'll..." He flexed his fists to dispel the trembling taking root, and his wolf from surging forward. He wouldn't be able to stop himself from attacking her.

"I tried to kill her, too," Rush confessed. "Almost put Starcleaver through her neck."

"What stopped you?"

"I missed."

They all stared at each other. Then laughed. They laughed out their tension, chuckling whole heartedly over something so stupid. But it felt good to release the pressure.

Rush's eyes turned solemn. "The truth is, I realized that without her, I'd never have met Clarke. And I would never have had Willow. And the Prime may be right... the world may have ended. Still could end."

Jasper still couldn't believe Rush had a daughter, and she was the one who'd led Jasper to Ada. A stone in a pond caused so many ripples.

"And you?" Jasper asked Thorne.

Pity flashed in his eyes before a wistful smile. "I can't argue with the fact I'd never have met Laurel, and now that Ada is here, I believe the dark future the Prime has foreseen will come to pass if we don't work together to stop it."

Jasper rubbed his chest, feeling his heart thud, wishing he could go to Ada.

If you're nothing without me, then you're nothing with me.

He needed to keep picking himself up.

"You say Clarke is a psychic?" Jasper asked.

"Yes," Rush replied.

"What has she seen?"

"She knows the Void wants to take over. She sees fire and destruction in our future. And she knows we have the power to stop it. But, like the Prime said, we need to work with these Well-blessed humans waking from the Old World. We don't like that the Prime was right, but we accept it."

Jasper's gaze flicked to Thorne who clenched his jaw

and gave a curt nod of agreement. Yes, Jasper wanted to throttle the Prime. He wanted to rip her limb from limb. But if two of the most ruthless and honorable Guardians he'd had the fortune of meeting believed the Prime's visions about this Void—the same one instigating raids and murdering innocent villagers—then Jasper couldn't dispute it. The Prime had the entire land to worry about. He was one fae.

Jasper knew if he could go back in time and stop the massacre of the Darkfoot pack, he would. If he'd somehow been granted a vision, then wouldn't he have acted like the Prime had? Wouldn't he have sacrificed the discomfort of one fae for the sake of hundreds? *Crimson*, he'd sacrifice his own discomfort for the sake of one: Ada.

His anger seeped out of him. A ruler couldn't be selfish and worry about one person. A ruler had to think of the many. The Prime was responsible for the fate of the world because without the Well, it died. Jasper may be in denial, he may be a coward at heart, but he would never put his own needs above the innocents.

"Let's go to this meeting," Jasper said and started walking out. He stopped, frowned and turned to his two closest friends. "Thank you. For coming to my aid."

Both of them stared at him solemnly.

"No debt acknowledged," Rush replied.

Thorne nodded the same. "You're family. We don't have debts between us."

THE DREAMS OF BROKEN KINGS

⚖

JASPER FOLLOWED Rush and Thorne up several flights of wide stairs to the council chambers. Water trickled down the stair edges in a cascading stream, ending in a small pool at the base, that in turn, led to culverts winding around the campus. Two crow-shifters flew overhead toward the columned, open plan temple in angel form, shouting down some kind of joke about them being slow.

He flipped his middle finger with a smile. They knew he'd always whined about the wingless Guardians having to walk up the tedious steps when the winged fae could simply fly up.

When they crested the top, Jasper turned and looked over the Order campus grounds. Buildings and training fields stretched for at least a mile on either side. On the surface, nothing seemed to have changed since he'd last been there. He didn't know which was worse, that it was unchanged, or that it had remained so for most of his three-hundred years of service. But the Order wasn't interested in changing the design and architecture, only keeping it the same—just like they wanted to keep Elphyne the same.

Jasper was the longest serving Guardian. There were Mages older than him, the Prime among them, but a warrior? If they didn't lose their life in battle... well, that was it. Most didn't last. He couldn't decide if it was because he'd been a coward, or if he was good at his job.

The library and academy were to the left, and the Guardian barracks to the right. Blue-robed Mages milled about. Leather clad Guardians engaged in battle, honing their skills on the training fields. Metallic clanks from the blacksmith floated across the breeze. It was the only Elphynian smithy sanctioned to craft weapons out of steel.

Coming up the stone steps were Leaf, Aeron, and Forrest. The elves were also unchanged. Leaf was still the leader of the Cadre of Twelve. Aeron still walked with a stiff spine, and Forrest still smelled like the stables. Jasper's nose caught a whiff on the wind with a snuffle.

All so familiar, but so foreign. Still, as Jasper surveyed the unchanged place he called home, and the people he'd called family, he couldn't help thinking that it all looked different. Like he no longer fit in. Like his dreams were bigger than these campus walls.

Jasper turned and went inside the temple, feeling an errant trip of excitement at knowing he'd see the rest of his cadre, some of whom he'd worked with for over a century, maybe two. He'd lost count. When he crossed from the temple into the adjoining council chamber, he almost wished for his sword but pushed the simmering hatred for the Prime down to bearable levels deep in his belly.

With her back to him, the Prime stood between the long, carved marble pillars, staring out to the campus below. Her long white feathered wings draped onto the floor. Water trickled down the columns before running off the fenceless balcony and dripped onto the jagged rock foundation. A slight shift in the Prime's shoulder tension said she knew he'd arrived.

He could walk right up to her and run his claws through her neck. The dark fantasy swirled in his mind for a moment, and then he forced himself to take in the rest of the room. He had to get past her betrayal, even if his feelings were just.

Large human-sized vases were the only decoration. There were no tables, no chairs, just an empty marble floor. Three vampires stood to one side, two crow-shifters on the other.

Jasper nodded at the vampires. They stuck to the shadows and away from the sunny opening, all folding their arms and looking very put out for being called to a meeting during the day. While the vampire Guardians had been conditioned to survive in the sun, they were generally not pleased about it, and preferred night missions. All had shifted their leathery bat-like wings away and wore their Guardian leathers.

Haze nodded his shaved head in greeting. Shade, their unofficial leader, looked suave and slick as he leaned against a vase. He folded his arms and gave Jasper a half-smile. Next to him, Indigo broke out into a crooked grin and came over to slap Jasper on the back.

"Good to see you, wolf."

"You too, bat," Jasper replied dryly.

"Sounds like you've had an adventure or two. I'm jealous."

"Seriously?"

"Sure," he said, raising his brows. "Beats the boring shit we've been doing."

Jasper shot him a wry look. "Keep holding your breath. Maybe there's still time for you to be tortured yet."

Indigo laughed. "That's what I like about you, J. Sense of humor."

The two crow-shifters by the Prime were in angel form, their black feathered wings tucked behind them. They watched curiously, as the crows often did. River's blue black feathers ruffled as he nodded in greeting. Ash did the same. Those two jokers were trickier and craftier than the vamps, but Jasper had gotten used to them. He even liked them. They knew how to party.

One of the Twelve was missing. As if summoned by thought, the air cracked with electricity, sparking a static residue that lifted the hairs on Jasper's arms.

Of course, Cloud would make an entrance. True to form, the heavily tattooed crow-shifter flew down, landing hard on the balcony, finding his footing with the grace of a wildcat. He snapped his wings shut but didn't shift them away. Static ruffled his feathers, an occurrence that seemed to cling to him permanently. He scowled and stalked straight to Jasper, stopping inches away.

"Where the fuck have you been?"

"You missed me?" Jasper kissed the air, his eyes crinkling.

"You wish," Cloud scoffed, his electric blue gaze traveling down to Jasper's neck scars, then to the blue marks on his right hand. When Cloud kept searching Jasper's body with a frown, Jasper realized he'd noted the missing power enhancing oil-slick tattoos. They had both been inked at the same time. Cloud's eyes darted back to Jasper's Well-blessed marks and narrowed.

"So it's true, then," he clipped.

"What?"

"Another one bites the dust." Cloud sucked his teeth and left Jasper with a judgmental glare tossed over his shoulder. "You want enhanced tatts again, come and see me."

"Don't need them anymore." Jasper couldn't help the grin forming on his face. Cloud hadn't changed a bit. Perfect.

"Pussy whipped," Cloud grumbled under his breath as he went to stand next to Shade.

Shade's lips curved. "I think that's precisely the point, Cloud."

Now that the Twelve were all there, the Prime turned around, demanding attention. Her blue dress and white-feathered wings scraped the dust along the ground. Her bare feet were dirty, a fact that always both intrigued and confused Jasper. For a female so rigid and formal, she neglected to care about tidiness and cleanliness. Sometimes he wondered if it was simply an oversight due to her perpetual busyness, but a small part of him—the part that warred with his vitriolic hate—hoped it was the last remnant of the female rumored to have been in a torrid love affair with Jackson Crimson himself. Because if it was, then it gave him a reason not to kill her. It gave another reason why she might be redeemable and not a monster like the ones he used to hunt.

The Prime's solemn gaze settled on Jasper.

Despite his best efforts, he wanted to snarl and snap at her. His wolf wanted revenge. Vengeance. Claws sprung from his fingers. His teeth elongated, ready to bite.

Play time was over.

The Prime fearlessly took in his reaction and crossed the floor to him. Her casual gait incensed him further. Leather creaked around the room as Guardians tensed. No one would be swift enough to stop Jasper's retribution, if it came to that. Then again, she was also powerful, and likely to dodge. If Rush had failed to kill her, then Jasper would struggle. Even if he did succeed, they would take him afterward. Killing the Prime would have dire consequences. Jasper might trust these eleven warriors with his life on a battlefield, but they were all loyal to the Well, first and foremost.

And the Prime was the epitome of the Well's will.

She kneeled before him, pulled her white ringlets to bare a brown, smooth neck, submitting.

Jasper startled and glanced about. Surprise rippled across the room. Shade stepped forward, but the Prime held out her palm, halting him.

"D'arn Jasper," she said, with her head hanging low.

"For the crime of selling you to our enemy, I humbly apologize and accept any punishment, or bargain you wish to inflict on me."

He stared at her for a long time. No one made a sound. He wanted to rage, to rip his teeth into her neck and tear chunks from her body. He wanted her to bleed out. To die, or at least suffer the way he had for the past decade. But that was the thing... it had only been a decade. He'd suffered immeasurably, but he was here, still standing, still alive.

Rush had lost fifty years of his life to her machinations.

"Did you apologize to Rush, too?" he demanded.

She glanced up, eyes narrowing. *Ahh*. Pieces clicked together. This female bowed to no one. She submitted to no one, yet she somehow felt he was different to the others she'd played.

"You didn't," he confirmed. "Nor, I suppose, did you apologize to Thorne."

Leather uniforms creaked, especially from Jasper's two wolf-shifter brethren standing next to him. He knew, without looking up, they were hanging on every word. He'd just pointed out something so obvious that all of them would be searching through their memories, wondering what else they had missed.

Jasper was done being manipulated. It was time he did the scheming.

"I want my bargain rights shifted to Rush," he declared.

The Prime stood swiftly, a crease deepening between her white brows.

There she is. The spitfire, prideful leader.

"You're not concerned with your current situation?" she asked. "You know there is no other way you'll be allowed to leave the Order except for using your bargain."

He smiled. "You're going to allow me to leave, anyway."

Something like respect sparked in her eyes before she clamped her expression down to unreadable. "What makes you so sure?"

"The only reason you apologized was because you want to be on my good side. You know I'll become king. You've Seen it—or someone has. Preceptress Dawn, maybe?"

Rush rumbled, "Keep the boon for yourself, Jasper. It's unnecessary to give it to me. Like I said before, we all have regrets over what's happened."

"It is necessary," Jasper insisted. "It's the least I can do. You have a daughter. I don't. You'll need a favor one day to protect her. Believe me."

"You'll have children of your own," Rush said.

"I'm three hundred. I haven't yet. I may never." His heart clenched at the fear of no future with Ada.

Jasper understood Rush was grateful for meeting his mate, and having his daughter, but Thorne had suffered too. He could give them this. A favor from the most powerful fae in Elphyne would come in handy, especially if dark times were ahead.

"Your family will need it," Jasper insisted, his eyes shifting to Thorne. "Kid, tell him I'm right."

Thorne scowled at Jasper. "You may be right, but it doesn't stop us wanting you to have it."

Jasper didn't deserve their capitulation. He deserved to grovel at their feet for the pain he'd caused them. Yes, the Prime had done everything she could to manipulate the events, but Jasper always had a choice. He could have protected Véda. He could have saved Thorne's mother. Maybe they both saw the agony in his eyes because Rush gave a curt nod, and Jasper exhaled.

Then he squared his shoulders and lifted his chin.

"That's my price," he said.

"Very well," she said. "It is done."

A whisper in the air made them all shiver as the Prime's intention became something bound by the Well. They didn't need to see the boon shifted to Rush; it was simply known. One day, so long as the Prime was alive, Rush could call on the Prime to claim the favor.

"Good," Jasper said. "Now, you didn't call this meeting to prostrate yourself before me, so what is it?"

"Careful, D'arn Jasper," the Prime warned. "You are still a Guardian, so long as that teardrop mark exists beneath your eye. Watch your tone."

Another smile crinkled Jasper's eyes. The Prime's words just proved she couldn't release him from his servitude to the Well. Only death could do that. Even if he had bargained to leave the Order, she would always hold some kind of sway over him.

"So what did your Seer see?" he asked. "How will I ascend to the throne?"

"Contrary to your belief, we have not Seen *how* you ascend, only that a future exists with you wearing the glass crown." She turned her steady gaze to the entire cadre. "And a future where all of you will find a Well-blessed mate."

Eyes flew wide. Some Guardians smiled. Others, like Cloud, scowled.

"The Order will issue new edicts that allow any Well-blessed Guardian to have certain liberties the others do not."

"Such as?" Leaf asked.

"Such as taking a mate and having a family."

"But you've never explicitly forbidden it," he replied.

"Neither have we approved it."

"What if we don't give a shit about being Well-blessed?" Cloud spat.

"Mark my words, D'arn. There is a reason only those in this cadre are being granted this sacred bond. Do you wish to deny a higher purpose?"

His hands clenched, but he said nothing. The Prime continued, "Regardless of which future becomes true, there is a war coming. One like we've never seen. Our best chance at defeating this human monster is to trust in the Well's plan, and to accept the gifts bestowed upon us. Working with humans who understand the world our enemy comes from will be integral in defeating him. We are stronger together."

Aeron stepped forward, also with a scowl on his face. "So you brought us here to tell us about the war we already know is coming?"

"I brought you here because the Seelie High King has committed grave crimes against the Well." Her gaze darkened. "I'm talking about the incidents leading to the massacre of the Darkfoot Pack. Namely, his collusion with the human enemy, and the explicit directions for fae to hoard metal. It cannot be tolerated. It is time for the Order to flex our Well-given rights."

Bitterness lanced Jasper's gut. Of course her retribution wouldn't be for the Darkfoot lives lost, but only for the blasphemy and the metal. But then, this was the very reason Jasper had to step up and take the glass crown for himself. It was *his* responsibility to seek retribution for losing his kin, not the Prime's.

Glances were shared about the room.

The Prime raised her palm before anyone could speak. "We have witness statements from reputable sources explaining how he encouraged them to hoard metal, and to deliberately hide it from the Order. This meeting was called to declare the official warrant for High King Mithras's arrest. He is now a fugitive. All of you are tasked with bringing him in."

Cloud stepped forward, a gleam in his eyes. "Alive or dead?"

"Preferably alive. Being high profile, he will need to stand trial and publicly answer for his crimes." She met them all in the eye. "You will meet resistance from his guard and loyal followers. Be mindful of innocents caught in the way. His life is not worth more than theirs. Dismissed."

One by one, the Guardians nodded and left until it was just Jasper and the Prime.

She leveled her gaze on him, and he wondered how he'd ever thought she'd submitted.

"Well played, D'arn. It seems you've the mind of a king, after all. What shall we call you now? Will you take your Darkfoot name?"

He strode to the freefall edge of the temple and looked over the campus. Wind buffeted his face and brought with it the familiar scent of his home, a home he was about to leave for good. This was the Prime's way of saying he would be free to leave the Order. Free to become king. But would that be as Reed Darkfoot, or Jasper, or as a Mithras descendent? He stifled a shudder. Never a Mithras. Perhaps Darkfoot, but he'd been D'arn Jasper for most of his life.

"Are you certain I'm going to be the Seelie High King?" he asked quietly.

"Nothing is certain, D'arn. You know that."

"Then why did you agree to shifting the bargain to Rush?"

"Because I owe him too, but, unlike with you, I'm not sorry for it. His sacrifice was worth the outcome."

"And mine wasn't?"

"You suffered," she murmured. "Yours is the one that keeps me up at night. You will understand the toll it takes when you ascend to the throne."

"You just said you weren't certain."

"I'm hopeful."

Her words drifted away on the gentle breeze, and in their absence, another realization occurred to him.

"You sent the Twelve after Mithras because you don't think I can take him on my own."

"I didn't say that."

"You didn't have to."

"I'm trying to give you the best chance at succeeding."

"I don't want your help. I don't want anything from you."

"Regardless, the warrant has been issued."

"If I have a hope of taking the glass crown uncontested, I need to do this on my own." He may already have the tentative support of other Seelie factions, but any of them could seek the throne. If he defeated the King himself, Jasper would have a stronger claim.

"Then you'd better be quick."

CHAPTER
TWENTY-EIGHT

Ada sat in the cadre house kitchen, eating a scone with berry jam, catching up with one of her two best friends—sisters—still not believing the turn of events.

"So you got married?" she asked Laurel, who showed her the ring. The jewel was like a tiny snow globe, but with sparkling stars dancing about each other.

"Only days ago. I figure, he gets the mating mark, I get a wedding."

"Days ago? You mean I just missed it?"

"Afraid so."

"Jasper's memories returned a week ago," she fumed. "He knew the entire time who you were to me while we were at the Obsidian Palace. I could have made it to your wedding!"

A high-pitched squeal came from somewhere beyond

the kitchen. In came a silver-haired two-year-old, tearing a path straight for Ada. Her stubby legs moved so fast, she almost tripped over herself. Clarke chased after her, a flustered blush hitting her cheeks.

"Pretty Kitty Pretty Kitty Sleeping Kitty." The little girl's words came at Ada like a machine gun. She launched herself at Ada, climbing up her legs and into her lap. When she was at eye level in Ada's arms, she sighed heavily and made a *phew* sound.

Ada grinned. "Now don't tell me. You must be Willow."

"You want a blanket?" Willow asked, her chubby face screwed up in contemplation. "Last time you were cold."

"Last time?"

Clarke shrugged. "We might not have put enough cover on you when you slept. She sensed you were cold and, yeah. We found a blanket."

"Well, thank you very much Miss Willow."

She gasped, eyes going wide, and then darted a look between her mother and Ada. "You said somefing naughty."

"I suppose saying thank you is naughty to the wrong person, but not to you." The truth was, if Willow had never brought Jasper to Ada when she'd been sleeping, she might never have awoken. She was sure it was the trigger of the Well-blessed union that did it. "You can ask me to do anything now, apparently."

"Mmm." Willow touched her lip. "I want prickleberry jelly!"

"Willow! You've already had one serving today." Clarke made a face at Ada. "It's full of sugar."

"Oh well. I'll just have to find you some more, then." Ada put the ecstatic child down and went to the cupboards. "I don't know what I'm looking for."

"Never mind," Clarke sighed. "I'll get Jocinda to make some more."

"Jocinda?"

"One of the house brownies. You'll meet her soon. A word of wisdom? Never complain to the brownies unless you want to do all the chores yourself."

"Noted."

Ada turned back around and leaned her hips against the counter. Willow had already forgotten the deal and had run back outside again.

"She's beautiful, Clarke," Ada said. "You're very lucky."

Both of her friends sent her eyes full of pity, and she knew exactly what they were thinking. She dashed away tears.

"I don't know what to do," she said. "Am I overreacting? I mean, Jasper knew about you, and he kept it from me. You're family."

"Yeah, well..." Clarke made an awkward face. "That might have a teensy tiny bit to do with me."

"What?" Ada gaped.

"Why am I not surprised?" Laurel raised her brow and pointed her thumb at Clarke before saying to Ada, "She's been awake for three years, and already she's acting as crafty as the fae." When Ada still didn't quite understand, Laurel elaborated. "Her psychic powers have grown astronomically. You thought it was hard to beat her at poker before, now it's impossible."

"Hey," Clarke said. "That's not fair. I was terrible at poker. I cheated."

Laurel poked out her tongue. Clarke grinned, but then met Ada's stare with a loud exhale.

"Okay," she said. "Promise you won't be mad."

"Clarke," she warned. "Spit it out."

"I may have, just a little bit, shouted at Jasper when I caught him in the room with you when you were asleep."

"Why is that so bad? Isn't he some big warrior type?"

"But it frightened him so much, he poofed out of here."

"Poof. Really?" Laurel said sarcastically and then stole the half-eaten scone from Ada's plate and licked the jam.

"Whatever," Clarke replied. "The point is, he got scared. He left. If he thought your best friends hated him, it might have caused some reluctance to come home. Someone who was manipulated and tortured like him would be a little jumpy."

Ada's eyes narrowed at her friend. "Has he spoken with you?"

"No," Clarke said, biting her lip. "In fact... I... well, I've *Seen* some things he went through. So... I guess, I'm asking you to cut him some slack."

Ada pinched the bridge between her eyes. Clarke was

right. Ada loved the guy. She could completely understand why he was reluctant to tell her.

A strange shuffling sound made her drop her hand. Clarke's eyes had turned completely white. She trembled on the spot. Laurel rushed to her side, and tried to hold her body upright, but Clarke's convulsing turned into a full-blown fit.

"What's happening?" Ada asked, taking Clarke's other side and helping her down to the floor.

"She's having a vision," Laurel replied, looking a lot calmer than Ada felt.

"She never used to do this, right?"

"It's something she's picked up in this time. She should be out of it soon."

They stayed with Clarke until the trembling stopped and she started gulping air. Her unfocused gaze darted about until it landed on Ada. Then she grabbed Ada's shirt.

"You need to find Jasper," she gasped, eyes wide with fear.

"What did you see?"

"Mithras, iron, and blood."

⚖

With Clarke and Laurel at her side, Ada rushed through the house of the Twelve, searching upstairs and downstairs for Jasper. When Clarke had awoken from her vision, Ada tried to locate Jasper using their link. As usual, he'd hidden his emotions from her—or he was too far away for them to register. Over the past few weeks, she'd learned that beneath the sense of emotions, she could still feel a connection. It was a little ping of awareness. And right now, that ping felt very far away.

"He's not here," Ada said, after closing Jasper's bedroom door. She hadn't explored it yet but knew the moment she had entered that she felt like an intruder at the same time as feeling like she was home. She needed him here, to explain things, to tell him she forgave him, and to talk about their future.

"They could still be at the meeting with the Prime," Laurel offered. She turned to Clarke. "Did you see any specifics in your vision?"

Clarke shook her head. "Just a lot of blood and water."

"*Jesus.*" Ada thrust her hand into her hair.

"Goddammit. I'd never thought I'd see the day I missed tracking on cell phones," Laurel mumbled.

Downstairs, the front door slammed as someone came home. All three of them jogged through the house to get to the ground floor living room, only to find it was Thorne and Rush returning from the meeting without Jasper.

Blood drained from Ada's face.

Thorne came over to Laurel and curled his hand around the back of her neck. "He gave up an open-ended boon from the Prime so Rush could have it."

"So our family could have it," Rush corrected him. "That includes you, Thorne."

Clarke blinked. "But that's... very valuable."

Still with a flummoxed look on his face, Rush shook his head. "He did it because he still feels guilty for not stepping in when Véda was executed, or when I was cursed and Thorne was orphaned."

Thorne frowned. "Rush tried to tell him it wasn't necessary, but he insisted we would need it for Willow."

Clarke stiffened. "He's not a Seer, is he? He hasn't foretold that it's warranted?"

Ada shook her head. "I don't think so..."

But no one knew for sure.

"Whatever his reasons, we'll have to thank him," Clarke said, fitting herself under Rush's arm. "I mean it."

"He won't accept your thanks," Thorne said. "Trust me."

Ada's heart surged in her chest. Why would he giveaway such an important boon?

Mithras. Blood. Iron.

She had to find him.

"Where is he?" she asked the Guardians.

Thorne shrugged. "He was with the Prime at the temple a moment ago."

"That's just on the other side of campus, right?" she asked, but already felt dread grow because their connection through the Well-blessed bond was not strong, not like it should be if they were within a mile of each other.

"I have to find him," she said, heart thumping.

"I had a vision," Clarke explained gravely to her mate. "I saw Jasper, Mithras, iron, and blood."

"*Well-dammit*," Rush grunted, a calm determination settling over him. "Thorne, you head back to the temple and see if he told the Prime anything about his intentions."

Thorne nodded, gave Laurel a quick kiss on the cheek, and then rushed out the front door.

Laurel turned to Ada. "I'll find Preceptress Dawn. She's the Order's official Seer and might know something Clarke missed. Sometimes pooling resources will help, right?"

"I'll go with you. I speak fluent Seer," Clarke added, then turned to Ada. "You stay here. Jasper might turn up."

When the two of them had left, Ada focused her attention on Rush.

"What happened at the meeting? Anything to upset him?"

A baffled look crossed his face. "It all sounded fine. The Prime apologized for what she did to him, which was astounding but then basically alluded to the fact that she believed Jasper would take the throne."

"That's not so bad." Unless Jasper was getting nervous about it. Maybe he was just taking some time, like he had when his memories first came back. Guilt stabbed her. Maybe she'd been a bit too harsh on him. No, she definitely had. Telling someone to simply pick themselves up after falling wasn't as easy to do. It took time to heal from trauma, and she'd all but tried to force it on him when they'd had that argument in Cornucopia. Damn it. She knew those words would come back to haunt her the moment she'd let them spill out of her angst-ridden mouth.

She could understand why he didn't want to tell her about her friends. He was afraid to lose her. She didn't want to lose him either. The thought of it made her insides cramp.

"Oh," Rush added. "And the Prime declared Mithras a fugitive. All Twelve Guardians are tasked with hunting him down."

Ada frowned. "She's helping Jasper take the throne? Does she not think he can do it on his own?"

"The King has committed crimes against the Well. This is just due course."

"Is it?" Would Jasper see it that way? She knew him, whether or not he admitted it. He put so much pressure on himself. He'd already explained how he believed he should take the crown on his own—to gain the respect of his subjects, and to prove that he could pick himself up. To prove that he was something without her.

So he could be something *with* her.

Ada's throat closed up.

If Jasper construed the Prime's warrant as intentional help... he would believe it an insult to his competence.

"I have to find him," she gasped, eyes wide. "How can I find him? He can portal anywhere."

"Can you feel him through your bond?" Rush asked, folding his arms and frowning in concentration.

"Yes, but it's weak."

"What's he feeling?"

"He hides that from me."

Another frown from Rush. He shook his head.

"Stubborn bastard," he murmured. Then gestured for Ada to follow him. "We'll find a winged Guardian."

All the crows were gone, already eager to hunt down Mithras. The only winged Guardians left were the vampires, and all three were sitting around the dining table next to the living room, playing some sort of card game.

Ada frowned, wondering if they were shifters like the wolves because she couldn't see their wings. And then once she started thinking about their wings, her mind traveled to all sorts of weird places. Like, were they anything like the vampires in storybooks? Could they fry in the sun and die from a stake to the heart? Did they have a soul? A reflection?

"I'm Ada," she said, waving gingerly.

If one deigned to glance at her, she was lucky.

"I need someone to fly Ada around and track Jasper," Rush said.

"Nope." Shade played his card with a slap to the table. It was the only emotion in his countenance. The rest of him was slick, smooth and cut from diamond encrusted marble —hard, yet veined with luxury. Pointed bronze ears twitched under Ada's attention. Soft caramel tipped hair brushed back from his forehead as though he'd ran his fingers through it. She had the sense he studied her as much as she did him, yet it wasn't with his eyes. With a shiver, she turned to the other two vampires.

"Can't," Haze grunted, before she'd had a chance to ask. He scraped his hand over his shaved head, exasperated eyes ping-ponging between the card Shade had just played, and his hand.

"Yeah, I'm kinda busy," Indigo mumbled, eyes glued to his hand. He contemplated with such concentration, Ada thought the boyishly handsome fae might hurt himself. He dropped a card. "Read it and weep, sleep-feeders."

"Fuck me," Haze grumbled.

"You have the shittest poker face, my friend," Indigo snorted. "And now you owe me a feed. I'm hungry. Pay up."

Haze's dark eyes flashed and then rolled in exasperation. "Fine. I'll find a donor."

"I don't mind sharing."

"Fine."

"Guys," Rush growled. "Clarke's had a vision. This is important."

All three vampires lowered their cards and sat back, smoky eyes shifting to study Ada. They had the kind of warm skin, brown hair, and sun-kissed vibe she'd have expected to see on a race that enjoyed living in the sun, not those who hid from it. These vampires weren't the Dracula kind. They were sensual and warm-blooded.

"We've been out in the sun already today," Shade said,

arrogantly arching his eyebrow. "We need our rest for the big hunt tonight."

Haze grunted his agreement. The vampire's hulking, muscular body barely fit on the chair. He stared at Ada a while before asking, "Are you in danger?"

"Not me, Jasper."

Her words had no appeal to him, and he cast his already bored gaze back to his cards.

"Fine," Rush said. "I'll find a kuturi in the stables."

"A kuturi will take too long to prepare. Indi will do it," Shade offered.

"Fine. I'll do it," Indigo said, a dimple flashing in his cheek. He scraped his chair back to stand. "You twisted my fang."

Ada exhaled in relief.

"On one condition," he added, eyes flaring in mischief.

"Not happening, Indi," Rush growled, to which Indigo grinned further and held up his palms.

"I won't go out on an empty stomach."

"What do you mean?" Ada asked. What had she missed?

Rush glared at Indigo. "He wants to feed from you. Jasper would never allow it."

"When a vamp's gotta eat, a vamp's gotta eat," Indigo drawled.

"No—" Rush said.

"I'll do it," Ada burst out.

Rush growled and took Indigo by the scruff of his collar. "I'm warning you. Jasper won't like it."

Haze and Shade stood, menace tightening their posture. The last thing Ada needed was an in-house brawl.

"It's fine, Rush. It's only once, right? I won't be sick or anything, will I?"

"You won't even notice," Indigo smirked. "Not really."

Indigo slapped Rush's hands away with a scowl. "Touch me again, wolf, and sleep with one eye open."

"Come on," Ada said. "The quicker we do this, the quicker we can find Jasper."

Still vibrating fury, Rush folded his arms and glared before snarling a warning, "I'll be watching the entire time. Don't get any ideas."

Rush's animosity would have wilted Ada, but Indigo just smiled and said, "You know we like it when we're watched."

"No, we don't," Shade said as he dealt another hand between himself and Haze. "*You* like it."

Indigo pouted. "Spoil sport."

It was clear where the power balance lay in the trio. Shade didn't even look up, but the other two vamps had fallen in line behind him.

"M'lady." Indigo gestured toward the living room where the curtains were drawn to keep the sunlight out.

What the hell was she doing? Bad vampire movie scenes kept flashing before her eyes. Horror scenarios of throats being torn out and blood gushing. How weak would she feel after this? She'd donated blood a few times when she'd been hard up for cash and had always felt tired. How much would he take?

With her fingers twisting and fretting, she sat down on a couch, eyes darting to Rush who stood by the door, shoulder resting against the jamb, arms folded, eyes like lasers pointed at Indigo as he quietly slotted himself next to her. She couldn't help but feel this was a weirdly intimate moment, despite Rush glaring. Intimate because of the way Indigo shifted himself into the seat, making himself comfortable. And the way he casually flicked lint off the backrest behind Ada. The way his breath changed and grew shallower. She could smell his unique masculine scent.

Indigo brushed fallen hair from her neck with a lover's touch, and leaned in, but she stopped him. Her heart pounded a million miles an hour.

"Not there," she said, feeling unsteady. That place was reserved for Jasper. Rush was right. If Jasper discovered she let someone else bite her where he intended, he would be furious, hurt, and betrayed. The neck was too personal.

Without skipping a beat, Indigo took her wrist and held it to his nose with a graceful touch. He pushed the hem of her sweater sleeve until it gathered along her forearm and then ran the tip of his nose along the flesh, up and down as though tracking a scent... or finding a vein. Unable to help herself, Ada shivered from his feather light touch. Hot breath tickled and goosebumps broke out on her skin. Indigo's dimple appeared in his cheek before he went back to a particular spot on her inner elbow. He licked it a few times with an extremely pointed, and long tongue. Seeing it was a shock to her system. She'd become accustomed to the pointed and arched ears. She'd even become used to the fangs and claws of a wolf-shifter. But seeing that tongue, and the glimpse of razor sharp fangs—so different to Jasper's canines—Ada sensed a dangerous predator about him.

She could barely feel his touch, he was that deft and graceful. At night time, when walking by herself on a street, she wouldn't know if a vampire attacked until it was too late.

The only warning she had was a meeting of the eyes, and then sharp fangs pierced her flesh.

She gasped at the sting, but the pain soon turned into a pleasing tingle, shooting sparks of heat zipping up her arm and then down her spine. Blood welled at the wound, and contrary to her bias, it surprised her to see he didn't suck her blood like they did in the movies. No. He lapped at it lazily, enjoying every oozing drop like it was a fine wine, making little moans of appreciation, shuffling closer.

"Back off, Indi," Rush growled.

"But she tastes so good." He hummed as he lapped, like a child eating their first round of chocolate ice-cream and unable to hide their bliss. "Why does she taste so good?"

Shade and Haze both neglected their game and came over, eyes mesmerized as Indigo laved with his lashes fluttering and eyes full of heat. With every lick of his tongue, the tingles shooting up Ada's arm turned into something more insistent, echoing the throb of her pulse everywhere in her system, especially between her legs. Good God, she was getting aroused. So was Indigo. She could see it in the flush of his cheeks and the sizable bulge straining against his leather breeches.

"Enough," Rush barked, striding over.

But Indigo wouldn't stop. He clutched her wrist tighter.

"Too good," he muttered.

"*Indi.*"

"If I stop now, she won't clot, and it will go to waste."

From the desperate lilt to his voice, Indigo's words sounded like the excuse of an addict.

Rush snarled and put his hand on Indigo's neck, letting his claws elongate until they pressed into the vampire's flesh.

Indigo went very still. The air buzzed with strife. Slowly, he lifted his palms in surrender, but then took one last lick before pulling back with a satiated look on his face, eyelids fluttering to half-mast and dopey. His pink, pointed tongue darted out and traced along his lips, relishing.

"*Bloody Well,*" he cursed. "You taste like..." He made a sound caught between a groan and a shuddering moan. "Fu-*uck* me sideways, Ada, and call it Moonsday. I'm cooked."

His gave a long, drawn out, shuddering exhale as he shifted his hips low on the couch, and rested his head back, eyes fluttering closed, smiling lazily to himself.

"Is he..." Ada clamped her hand on her wrist and healed herself, pleased to see her flesh knit together with ease at her mental directive. She didn't think Indigo had taken that much. The blood didn't gush. It oozed. She felt fine. "Is he drunk?"

Shade stalked closer to inspect Indigo. Shade's perfect bone structure pinched with restraint. He sniffed, his long lashes fluttered as though simply smelling Ada's blood gave him a high. He darted a glance to Haze.

"What do you think?"

Haze already looked scary with his bulk, neck tattoos, and shaved head, but now, as his eyes locked onto Ada with predatory intent, he was positively terrifying. There was hunger in that stare.

"Maybe because she's human."

"Do humans taste better?" she asked nervously. Jasper had mentioned something, but she didn't think it was this good.

"And she's Well-blessed," Shade surmised, ignoring Ada.

"That must be it. Two-thousand-year aged wine."

"You're discussing me like the latest vintage," she snapped. "I'm not—" Not food? Not a drug? Not what? She couldn't come up with the right word that wasn't the truth. A moment ago, the vampires had barely looked at her, probably categorizing her as simply the enemy and food at the same time. Now she could turn one of them into a melted puddle from the simple taste of her blood.

A glance at Indigo, and she knew the vampires wouldn't walk away easily. He still slouched on the couch, making little sighs of pleasure and delight as whatever was in her blood made its way through his system.

Rush's guttural growl tore through the room. "Stay away from her. Stay away from Laurel and Clarke. And especially, stay away from Willow."

"Willow's half-fae," Indigo slurred. "S-she won't taste as good. Don't worry. *Crimson*, I'm not cooked. I'm dead. Fuck. How am I going to fly?"

"You have to," Ada gaped, standing.

He tried to stand, stumbled, and took hold of the couch armrest. "I'm good."

"For fuck's sake, Indi," Rush scowled.

Shade glanced at Haze.

"I'll do it," Haze grunted with a sigh of resignation. "You'll kill yourself. And her."

Haze pushed Indigo on the chest, who then fell back on his ass with a chuckle. "Fine. You take her."

Rush pointed at each of the vampires. "This is your first and final warning. The last thing we need is for all the vamps in Elphyne hearing about this. If a word of this gets out, I'll be coming for you. So will Thorne and Jasper. Understood?"

Something dark and dangerous flitted in Shade's gaze

that morphed him from model to maniac in a blink, and then it was gone. Ada had to suppress a shudder and remind herself that these cadre members weren't normal. They were all dangerous, ruthless warriors. And she was about to go flying about Elphyne with one of them.

"If you think we're the kind of fae who would put our cadre members' females in jeopardy, then you must be getting us confused with your own kind. Vampires don't sell their females out."

A snarl curled Rush's lips. "If you find Jasper, come back and get us."

Haze gestured for Ada to head outside the front exit. "Let's go."

She followed him out.

Haze materialized two leathery, bat-like wings through slits in the back of his Guardian uniform. They snapped out, twice as long as his body was high. Already, he winced at the sun and scowled.

"Let's make it fast."

He closed thickly muscled arms around her and then beat his wings until they became airborne with a whoosh. Ada's stomach dropped to her feet.

She focused on the sense of Jasper down their bond but couldn't pinpoint a location.

"Can you fly around in a circle?" she shouted up at him. "I'll see which direction the link feels strongest."

He gave a curt nod and then flew over the Order until Ada slapped her palm on his forearm.

"That way." She pointed into the forest surrounding the Order campus.

Craning her neck, she caught the frown marring his rugged features.

"What's that way?" she asked.

"The ceremonial lake."

A stone dropped in Ada's stomach. "He mentioned wanting to submit to the initiation trial again."

Haze's wings beat faster, and their speed increased. "Hold on."

It didn't take them long, only about thirty minutes or so. They broke the boundary of the trees and came to an enormous lake stretching for miles. When she saw the shadow of a figure wading into the shallow end of the lake, she knew it was him.

"There!"

Jasper's tanned, muscular back glistened under the sun as he swam toward the center of the lake, gliding through the water with ease.

"Doesn't seem to be anyone else around. He's all yours." Haze put her down on the beach, wincing at the glare of the sun, and then swiftly took off without another word.

Ada ran toward the folded shirt Jasper had left on the sand. She took a few steps into the water and waved, shouting his name. About forty feet away, he turned.

And that's when everything went to shit.

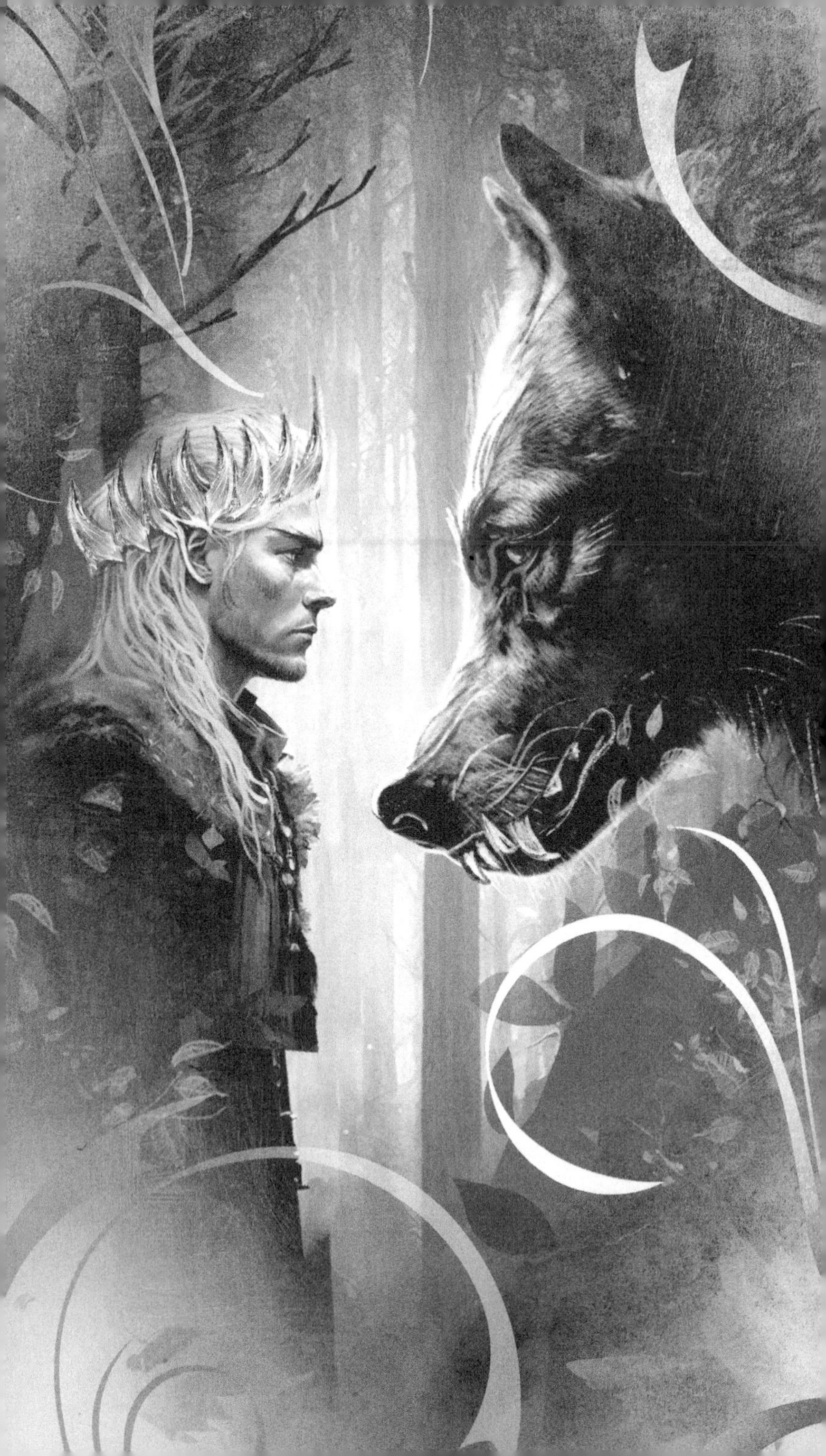

CHAPTER
TWENTY-NINE

Treading water, Jasper's gaze settled on his love. She waved erratically and shouted for him to come back, but he knew if he did, he'd lose his nerve. He'd never face the Well Worms. He'd never know if the past three hundred years had turned him into a coward or if they'd made him stronger.

Mithras knew exactly how to prey on Jasper's weaknesses. Jasper needed this before facing him.

Ada cupped her mouth and shouted. "Come back! I was wrong."

What?

"I should never have said you were nothing without me. It was a dumb figure of speech, that's all." Her voice tightened, becoming high pitched. "I'm nothing without *you*. Please come back. Don't... don't leave me."

He let himself dip beneath the surface, just a fraction,

as he considered her words. She forgave him. Or was she just saying that to get him out? Irrational doubt pervaded his mind. Whatever the reason for Ada's words, they came too late. Something smooth brushed against his leg. And again. He looked down, trying to see through the water, but found only shadow. He'd taken his eyes off her for only a moment, but when he glanced back up, his world collapsed.

Mithras stood behind Ada, his fingers curling around her throat. Coming up beside him was the shriveled Dark Mage, his hunched form carrying something heavy beneath his billowing black cape.

Heart thudding in his chest, Jasper considered his options. Portal there and risk Mithras doing something drastic the instant Jasper disappeared. Or let the worms slithering around his ankles take him down into the dark depths and judge him, hopefully allowing him to return with more power, enough that even without Ada's mana, he could face down Mithras and win. Another worm slithered around Jasper's ankle and tugged. The decision was made for him. He sank beneath the water. The last thing he glimpsed was Ada's tear tracked face.

It was that sight that made him see the truth in his heart. Any decision was better than none. Sitting quietly had left him in that dugout while they slew his mother. Ignoring his identity, hiding out in wolf form at the inn after the first raid, was cowardice. He should have worked to restore his memories sooner. If he had, he wouldn't have been surprised by Mithras's attack on the Darkfoot pack. He might have saved them. And now... slowly sinking down when his heart was still with Ada, he knew inaction would be her death.

He didn't need the Well to imbue him with more power. He just needed to act. So he portaled to the shore, arriving with a splash of displaced water only yards from where Mithras's hands were wrapped around Ada's neck. Not just wrapped, but poised to snap with the slightest provocation. Jasper stilled.

"I'm sorry, I'm sorry, I'm sorry," Ada sobbed, chest heaving, desperate eyes locked onto Jasper.

His beautiful love thought this was her fault. It infuriated him that she blamed herself.

Mithras's hair was straggly. That he even wore his lopsided crown was a sign of how desperate he was to keep it. Panic in his eyes betrayed his true state. It gave Jasper confidence.

"What do you want?" Jasper asked, words slow and enunciated.

"You ruined my life," Mithras snarled, fingers tightening around Ada's neck.

"Tell me what you want," Jasper repeated.

Fire flashed in amber eyes as Mithras studied Jasper. His lips curved into a slithering smile. "All I had dreamed of was to kill you and ensure my reign went uncontested. I had the perfect plan. Name you as heir, kill you, blame Maebh, and incite a war. Simple. But since you went to her and revealed everything, I'm going to have to settle on making you suffer. I want you back in the iron mask. I want everyone to see that I control you."

Did he not know that the Order was after him? Even if he did take Jasper now, he wouldn't get away with the crimes he'd committed. The mad fae had lost touch on reality.

The Dark Mage stepped forward and revealed the package he carried; a newly forged iron mask complete with new bolts to drill into Jasper's neck.

"What did I ever do to you?" Jasper growled, aghast. "That you had to chase me for three hundred years and make my life miserable at every turn. I was no threat to you or your reign as a child, or a Guardian."

"You were a threat from the moment your mother chose to keep you."

Rage simmered in Jasper's blood. He could take out the Mage, but that would alert Mithras who would snap Ada's neck. Jasper could also portal behind Mithras and attack there. But, once again, Mithras was fast. He was powerful. He didn't get to be king by falling there. He clawed his way to the top. A tiny shift in the atmosphere, and Mithras would kill Ada.

There was no other option.

He looked at the mask, reacting with violent nausea. Not again.

But he would do anything for Ada. Anything.

He met his beloved's red-rimmed eyes. Pain aplenty

echoed back at him. She tried to shake her head, but Mithras firmed his grip, choking her. A pouring of love washed down their bond from her.

In slow motion, he saw the end of his life play out. He would pick up the mask. The Mage would bore the bolts into his neck. His mana would be incapacitated, his access to the Well blocked. They might let Ada go. They might not. But the fifty-fifty chance was better than nothing. Maybe she would escape. He hoped.

He swallowed the lump in his throat and picked up the mask. He hesitated before putting it on and locked eyes with the King.

"For the record, I hope you understand that I will get this off eventually, and when I do, your reign will end when I beat you bloody with it. I never wanted the throne, but, Mithras, mark my words, you had better kill me this time, because I'll come for you. And that inevitability is of your own making."

Jasper gritted his teeth and lifted the mask again.

"No!" Ada screamed. Fury surged down their link. Her face contorted. She slapped her palms over Mithras's and... something happened. The air shimmered. Mithras started choking. Tiny black veins squirmed on his face as though his blood had turned to poison. He tried to let go of Ada, but she had a death grip on him. She was doing this to him.

Jasper lowered the mask, stupefied.

The Dark Mage gasped.

With every passing second, the King's fate worsened, and Ada's energy felt grimy. Dirty.

Jasper's breath hitched, realizing what she was doing; accessing the dark side of her gift, mana scraped from the inky side of the Well.

"Stop!" he shouted, holding his hand out. "Stop, Ada, please listen to me."

Her chest heaved in great motions as she sucked in air. Wild brown eyes held his.

"Look at him," Jasper said, pointing to the Mage. "That's what happens when you access the dark side of the Well. You wither. You shrivel."

"Maebh said it was natural," she rasped.

For Crimson's sake, her voice sounded different—slick, oily, deep.

"Ada," he tried again. "Please. Don't do it. You were right, love. We're stronger together. Fuck what we are apart, right? You and me, forever."

She stared.

He nodded and approached her with slow, cautious steps. She lowered her hands. He beckoned her. She took a step—

The iron mask slammed onto his face. He reared back. Strong hands pushed him down. Somewhere, he heard a woman scream. *Ada.* He roared, lashing out, but it was too late. In his tunnel vision focus to get to Ada, he'd missed the Dark Mage approaching from the side. The bolts were now in his neck, burrowing in like an agony filled drill. His link to the Well cut off. He felt no connection to Ada. No mana.

Gone.

Empty.

All because the metal invaded his body. Jasper's hands clutched the mask, and he howled his fury. He'd underestimated the sensation of entrapment, of being locked in a cage again. He swiped to the side where the Mage had been and then charged until his hands landed on something soft and breakable. An arm. Maybe a neck. He couldn't see properly through the iron mask's slits. He squeezed. He dug his fingers in deep until he felt the hot lifeforce running free from the Mage's frail body. He kept squeezing until that body went limp and collapsed. And then he landed on his knees, found the Dark Mage's neck, and squashed it with an irrational need to protect himself. And Ada.

Wrenching himself away, he stumbled around, growling, trying to see through the slits. Flashes of lake, beach, trees. Golden hair. Sniggering smile. Haggard face.

Panting with heated breaths against the iron, Jasper stumbled. The metal tormented him like nothing else. His body screamed for it to be removed. *Take it off! Get it off me!*

Bring back the Well. Bring back life. Love.

Looking up, gasping, he saw Mithras had recovered. He didn't go to his Mage, his faithful companion. He went straight for Ada and, with lightning quick reflexes, he put one hand on the side of Ada's head and another beneath her jaw. He met Jasper's gaze and then snapped her neck.

A sickening wet crunch. Ada's last breath, a *puh* of air. And then her lifeless body fell limp to the sand, tumbling in a dead weight to the side, her blond hair falling across her lax face.

Jasper went stone cold.

No. It can't be. He'd imagined it. He was dreaming.

No!

His every fear had come to life. He'd failed. He lost. *Her*.

Nothing mattered after that. Nothing but the firestorm raging in his blood, beating out the iron sickness. Slowly. Surely. It rumbled into an inferno.

Kill. Revenge. Die.

His mind locked onto those three words and repeated them over and over. With the absence of Ada's lifeforce, breathing compassion into him, accepting him, loving him... gone forever... those three dark words became his anchor.

Kill. Revenge. Die.

He snarled, low and guttural. What's a few more scars? He held his breath, dug his fingers into his flesh where the bolts pierced, and tore them from his flesh. A loud bellow of pain hurtled out of him. *Hurts so bad.* Keep pulling. Get them out. *Kill.*

Murder the fae who'd taken her life.

The mask tore clean off Jasper's face, spraying blood on the white sand. His blood gushed from his neck and he staggered. His connection to the Well hurtled back into him. Mana rose to his will, and he triggered the shift, dragging his entire capacity to pump into the wolf, building him bigger, stronger, more feral. He knew the shift would heal his neck—enough to make a final stand.

The wolf sprang free.

Black, furred paws padded beneath him, so big he'd torn through his clothes. He gave a guttural snarl, teeth snapping.

Mithras stepped backward, stark eyes on Jasper in wolf form. He was so big; he was at Mithras's eye level. One bite, and he was gone.

Options calculated in Mithras's eyes as Jasper prowled closer. He steadied his crown, gaze darting to the dead Mage. Black veins still peppered his face. Ada's attack had weakened him. He was alone, and moments away from becoming wolf food.

Would Mithras shift? *Could* he shift? Or would he run?

Jasper hoped he would flee. He wanted to feel his claws ripping into the coward's back as he chased him down.

Mithras drew a weapon and held it between them. If Jasper was in fae form, he'd have laughed at the *floater* trying to brandish a metal weapon. The Well hadn't chosen him. Hadn't blessed him. All this time Jasper had wondered if he was good enough to be king. He'd wondered why his father hated him so much.

Mithras was jealous.

The King never had the guts to enter the lake.

He never had the worth to be granted the powers of holding metal and plastic and still access the Well.

And the King never had the love of a compassionate woman.

Had.

His heart broke. Ada was gone.

For her, Jasper would do this last thing, rid the world of the coward. He would take him into the lake, feed him to the Well Worms. Let him taste rejection on a metaphysical level. Let him relive the pain he'd caused. Jasper's howl shook the trees, shattering the wilderness, sending winged wildlife fleeing for the sky. When the last note died, he transformed back to fae form, his neck partially healed, fresh scars pulling with an ache.

The wolf couldn't save him from this next task. He had to do it with his hands. The wolf was part of him, not the other way around. Jasper had to make this final stand.

He portaled behind the King, gripped his arms, and then portaled them into the middle of the lake. Even before he let go of Mithras, the worms took hold of him, hungry. They'd been waiting. Mithras tried to take Jasper down with him. He clawed at the surface of the water, scratching Jasper's arms, but Jasper pushed him away with disgust. And the worms took Mithras under.

There was nothing left but a gurgle in the water.

For long seconds, Jasper treaded water, refusing to look back at the shore. He knew what he'd find. Two lifeless bodies. One dark-haired. One blond. One his love. His reason for breathing.

He raised his eyes to the blue sky, painfully aware of what circled beneath. Their recent meal would satisfy them only for a short while. Time was running out.

Wolves howled in the distance. His sluggish heart beat a little faster.

They're coming.

Not the King's men this time. The Guardians. His cadre. His family. Too late.

His mother had bid him to be kind... to be brave. His lover had bid him to accept his faults, to pick himself up. So he'd come to the place where the bravest go. And the cowards died.

Time to end this, once and for all. His bottom lip trembled.

... kind... brave... worth it.

Slimy, thick worms wrapped around Jasper's ankles, and he plummeted.

CHAPTER
THIRTY

Ada's consciousness rose slowly from the deep. A gritty dizziness swam in her head. Apart from that she felt nothing. No pain. No sensation. Nothing. She was a prisoner within her paralyzed body.

Vaguely, sounds came at her from a distance. Someone was fighting. Snarling. Raging.

Mithras had snapped her neck!

It was why she couldn't move. A surge of fear blanked her mind.

Did Jasper know she was alive? She had to heal. Had to tell him. Had to help him. But she couldn't move.

Don't panic. Don't die. *Heal.*

So she shut her eyes, slowed her breathing, her heartbeat, everything. She filtered all her awareness into her body, focusing inward, hunting for the damage.

Mana came to her with a ferocity she'd never known

before. Her gift sprung to life, aggrieved it had been almost cheated of doing all the things she'd wanted to do. She could heal the world if she tried.

Start small.

Start with yourself.

To do so, she had to filter every sound out, especially the howl of grief tearing through the sky. *You're no good to him if you're broken. Heal.*

She thought of everything that hurt, but other hurts sprang to the forefront. Flashes of her childhood. No matter how she tried to push them back, she couldn't. Her mother. Her lack of love. Of how she'd kept Jasper at a distance. All because she was terrified of how much it would hurt to lose him. It was ridiculous. Unfounded. She'd grown out of this.

She wasn't unwanted. She was loved and cherished above all. Jasper loved her so much, he'd become the bravest person she'd ever known. Putting on that iron mask had terrified him, but he did it anyway.

If that wasn't bravery, then what was?

Pick yourself up.

It was time to survive.

Ada focused on the here and the now. She sent her magic scouring through her system, hunting down every last impurity and broken cell it could find, restoring it with life, making it whole. Tingles prickled her feet. Fire lanced down her legs. Her arms twitched as blood flow restored, as her nervous system came to life. Slowly, surely, she healed herself.

And then she felt it... a flicker of life deep within her womb. So tiny it was almost not there. So new. Her hands flew to her stomach. She was pregnant?

Why wouldn't she be? They'd not used protection. She'd been having sex with Jasper since Lupercalia night—the fertility rite.

They were going to be a family.

She rolled to her side and took a deep, shuddering breath. Tears of triumph and joy burning her eyes. She did it. She had to tell Jasper. Had to... her gaze lifted, searching for him, but only found the cold dead stare of the Dark Mage. Scrambling to her feet, she scoured the beach. Nothing. Where was he?

Her bond. She focused on it, and found something close... where? She rotated, homing in on the direction. A splash in the lake, deep into the middle. Jasper's head bobbed gently as he floated, staring up at the sky. His ears were in the water.

"Jasper!" she rasped.

He shut his eyes, and he sank.

Without thinking, without understanding what the worms would do, Ada ran, launching herself through the shallows. All she knew was that she had to get to him. When she could run no more, she dove and swam, kicking her feet. She pushed herself until she could move no faster. She swam until her arms and lungs burned. She followed the sense of Jasper. He was still there, somewhere in the deep, his energy pulsing at her from the depths.

Too long. This was taking too long.

Arriving where she saw him go down, she heaved in air until her lungs protested, and dove. Jasper had said there were creatures here no one wanted to experience. Only a third of initiates emerged alive. Fear skated along her spine as she stroked through the dark water.

Down their bond she felt his eery, calm acceptance. Jasper's emotions were unblocked, probably because he thought there was no one left to hide them from. He was giving up. The knowledge spurred her onward.

A tiny blue beacon glowed gently below—his Well-blessed markings.

She kicked, stroked, and pushed herself down, urging her emotions to scream for her.

Look up. I'm coming. I won't leave you.

Her own blue marks added to the light. Murky shadows twirled around her, circling. The worms were here, but she couldn't look at them. She refused to acknowledge their existence. No time.

Dark hair floating.

Her heart swelled. She reached down, scraped his hair, but missed. Sensing her, his face lifted. Glimmering amber eyes latched onto her. He should have rejoiced. He should have smiled. But no. His face crumpled. His bottom lip trembled. His brows joined in the middle and lifted. He reached for her.

He thought she was dead. An angel.

Another stroke, and she caught hold of his grip. She tugged, trying to reverse her trajectory, but he was caught. Something had him. Dark shadows darted closer, brushing against her. Her lungs burned. She was running out of air, out of time.

But she wouldn't leave him. Never.

So she stopped struggling. She sank. Down, her body drifted, toes first into his awaiting arms. Into the writhing nest of worms wrapping themselves around his body, slithering up toward his heart. Glimmers of blue cast the hard planes of his face into soft, ghostly light. His melancholic happiness washed into her. She took his face between her palms and planted her lips on his. Bubbles exploded from his mouth as he kissed her back. And then he let go. He drifted. Dark lashes lowered lazily. He was out of air. Giving up.

No.

She refused to accept it.

Long, slithering Well Worms wrapped around her legs, squashing her against Jasper.

She took his mouth and angled it against her neck, silently begging him to mark her. To clamp down and bite. When he did nothing but lay his lips on her skin, a silent scream of impotent rage smashed about her body. It can't end like this! She wouldn't allow it.

She'd survived abandonment as a child.

She'd survived being frozen for thousands of years.

She'd survived a knife to the stomach. A broken neck.

And she'd done all those things, not from someone else's actions, but from hers. And now she had a family to fight for. Her eyes flew open. The worms wiggled up her torso, tightening, trying to squeeze the air from her abused lungs. But she knew what to do. She bit down hard on his neck, claiming him for herself.

The watery graveyard suddenly shifted. It moved. Oxygen burst into her lungs. Water splashed and cascaded. They landed hard on something soft, bouncing and sloshing in displaced water. Gaping like a fish, she breathed, heaving in air. And it came. The sweet, ever loving air surged like fire into her lungs.

Where were they?

Plain ceiling. Check-quilted bed. The cadre house. Jasper's room. Jasper?

He'd portaled them here.

Next to her, wheezing, rolling to his side, manic eyes landing on her. He reached.

She grasped his hand.

"You're alive," he croaked. "How?"

She nodded, still panting. "I healed myself." Her eyes watered. She choked. "Because of you. And me."

Pain fractured his expression. "What do you mean?"

"I don't know if you heard me when I shouted at you from the shore, but you were right. I was wrong. We're not nothing apart. We're stronger together."

They stared at each other, laying side by side on a half-soaked bed, holding hands.

More anguish clogged her throat.

"Jasper," she sobbed. "I'm sorry I was too afraid to let you in. I thought if I did, I wouldn't survive it if you left. But I..."

His voice broke. "You survived."

"Because I can't breathe without you either."

He rolled on top of her. "Ada," he whispered. "You came for me."

"I love you... and..." She took his hands and slid them down to her wet stomach. "And there's something else. Our fertility rite was a little too successful."

His eyes met hers, confused. "What?"

"We're pregnant."

His lashes widened. Shock blanked his features. "What?"

She smiled, biting her lip, letting him take it all in and then turned her head to the side and pulled back her hair, uncovering her neck. Even without seeing his face, she felt the shift in his emotions. He let her feel it all: triumph, relief, a pouring of love.

He made a sound, something caught between a groan and a pained sigh, and then he dug his long teeth into her neck, growling around her skin. It didn't hurt as much as she feared. A prick. A sting. Like fine needles. Without removing his teeth, he ripped her shirt open, tugged her pants over her hips, and only when he needed the arm room did he relinquish his hold on her neck. Tearing the last of her clothes from her body, he reared back and studied her, eyes full of self-satisfied appreciation.

"What do you see?" she asked.

"A mother. A warrior. My queen."

"That queen bit is just weird."

"Get used to it." He lowered his head and laved at the bite. The small throbbing pain swiftly turned into heated desire, spreading through every limb, melting her to the core until she became a breathless, whimpering mess.

He groaned. "You're really mine."

She nodded, arching into him.

"We're going to have a child."

"A prince or a princess."

"Fuck me."

"Okay."

He pulled back, eyes bright and crinkled at the edges. "Are you ready?"

"For what?"

He grinned against her neck. "I'm going to take you rough." He kissed her throat. "I'm going to take you hard." He licked down her front. "And I'm going to cover you with my scent."

She moaned as his tongue trailed across to her breast, laved her nipple, then pulled away. Dark, smoky eyes clashed with hers as he dipped his fingers between her legs and speared into her core. Her back bowed from the sensation. Her hips moved on their own, riding his fingers as he slipped them in and out, around and—*God*. Up. Down. In.

She was a shambles of stimulation. His lips on her breasts. His fingers between her legs. He kissed her stomach reverently. And then he moved, taking himself in hand and positioning right where she needed it.

"I'm claiming you, my love."

He thrust in.

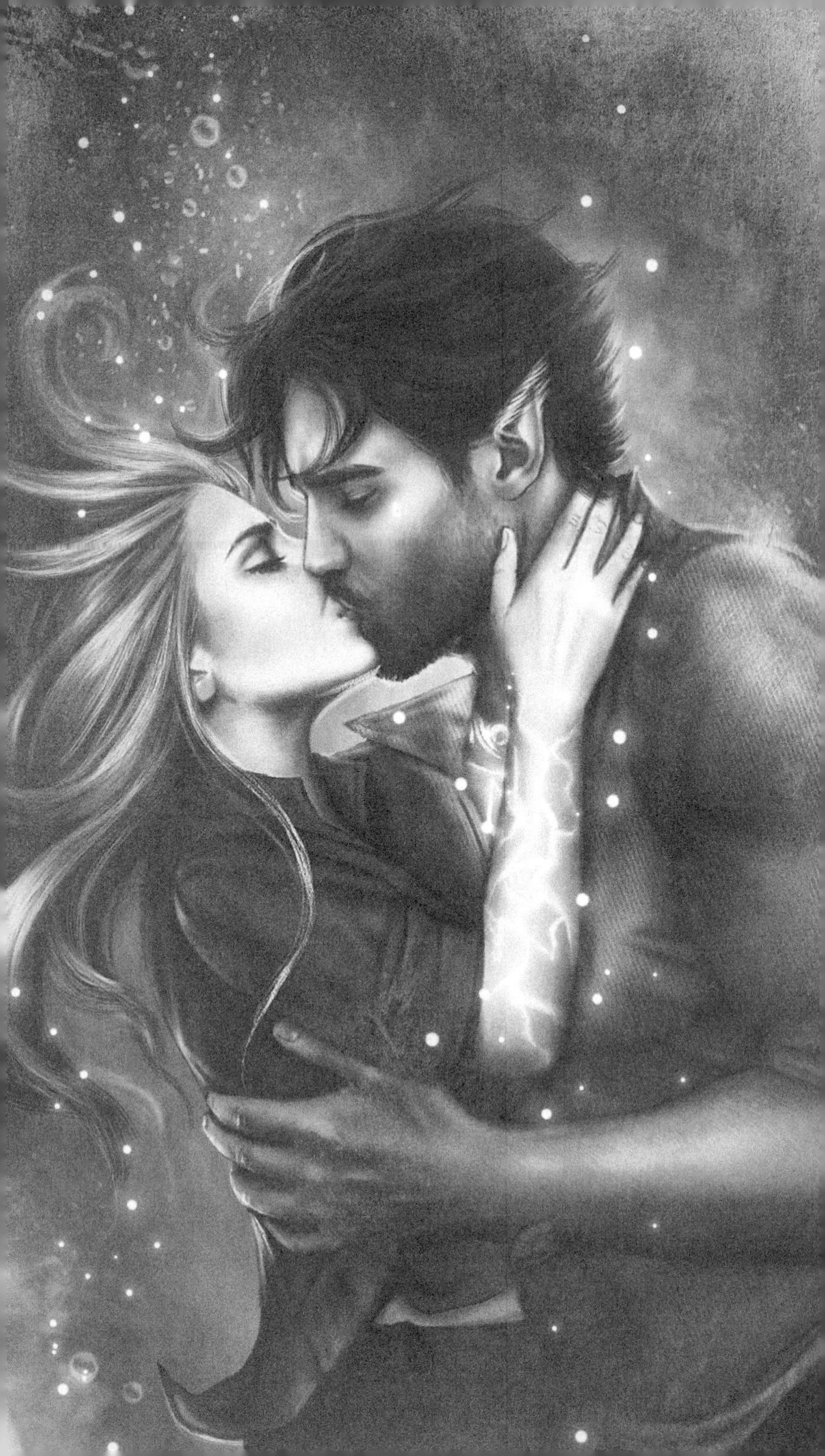

CHAPTER
THIRTY-ONE

Still coming down from the bone demolishing high of Ada's blood, Indigo flew himself to the ceremonial lake. He could see clearly now, but his flight path tipped as though he were in the grip of a hurricane. A storm named Ada.

Human—*Well-blessed* human—tasted like potent, syrupy, pulse tingling bliss. And her blood had satisfied him in a way no other had.

He scrubbed his face, trying to shake the residue of longing from his expression. It had nothing to do with her... but how she tasted. But he'd have to get used to that being his last drop. Ada belonged to Jasper. The entire house heard him mate with her. The walls had shaken. The chandeliers rattled. That's why Indigo had to get out of there.

All he could think of was Jasper biting her neck.

He could smell her arousing blood filtering through the currents of air in the house.

So he came here. To the aftermath of Jasper's recent battle. He'd found out about it from the shifters, and they needed someone to collect the floating, bloated body of the King from the middle of the lake. Haze was halfway back to the Order when he'd heard the forest-shattering wolf's howl. He'd turned back and found Ada diving into the lake, a dead Dark Mage on the sand, and a discarded glass crown. No king.

Shielding his eyes from the sun, Indigo circled the ceremonial lake and located the other Guardians. Rush, Thorne, Leaf and Clarke. Thank Crimson, they were in the shade of a tree. It wasn't that the sun made him sick, it just sapped his energy. And after the hit of blood he'd had, he just wanted to go back to sleep and dream of more. This time with a sexy, naked human of his own.

Arcing back toward the lake, he flew until he spotted the King's body, dove, scooped the disgusting thing up, and took it back to the shore where he dumped it unceremoniously.

"What kind of lunacy happened here?" he asked, landing on the sand. Grains puffed up, stinging his eyes.

Rush narrowed his eyes at Indigo. "Why are you here?"

Indigo snorted. "Why not?"

Clearly he was still wary Indigo would attack the tasty human standing next to him.

"Don't worry, Wolfie. I've can control my bloodlust."

Another snarl, to which Clarke explained to Indigo, "Jasper killed the King. And the Dark Mage. Now we don't know where Jasper or Ada are."

He lifted his pointer finger. "I can answer that."

They all stared at him.

"They're going to Bone Town in Jasper's room."

"Lady present," Thorne warned with a glare.

Clarke waved it off. "I've heard worse. So... they're making up. Excellent."

"They're making up, hard. I could smell it from the living room." Indigo grimaced.

"Ew." Clarke punched him.

He scowled, slapping his hand on the sore spot. The sun made everything sensitive.

Leaf, who'd been inspecting the King's body, walked over. He cast a disapproving glance at Indigo.

"This shouldn't need to be said, but if I catch you sniffing about the humans living in the cadre house, you're out. No warning. You're just out."

"I wasn't sniffing her out on purpose!" He threw up his hands. "Why does everyone think I'll let bloodlust consume me?"

Leaf arched a brow. "You know why."

That shut Indigo up. He ground his teeth and stormed over to the Mage's body. He'd fucked up once, years ago. They never let him forget it. So, he had sensitive tastebuds. So, he sometimes got a little carried away when drinking.

He wasn't the first vampire to kill a meal, and he wouldn't be the last.

The Mage was so shriveled with ink sickness that he must have been sampling mana from the dark side of the Well for years. Between all that viscera and gore, he smelled rotten inside.

Jasper must have been furious to do that much damage.

Footsteps next to him.

"Indigo," Clarke said, stopping.

"Better be careful," he drawled. "I might forget myself and drain you dry."

She scoffed. "You'd never do that."

"How can you be so sure?"

"I know."

Indigo slid his gaze her way and found her watching him studiously.

"What do you want?" he snapped.

Her lip twitched with a mysterious smile he'd come to learn was part of her plotting face. All the Seers had a look that revealed their secret knowledge.

"Nothing," she said, then glanced at the body. "Ew. Can we talk somewhere else?"

"You want to talk?"

"By the trees?"

He went with her, silently rejoicing in the shade, and then raised his brow. "What have you Seen? What insane mission are you about to send me on and does the Prime know about it?"

Her eyes turned to slits. "Can you read minds like the Six? Or are you just intuitive?"

"I'm lucky."

She took a deep breath and glanced over to where Rush, Thorne and Leaf discussed the glass crown.

"When Mithras died, something happened to my visions. They turned... dark. It's as though he was the catalyst for another potential future timeline. All I know is that it's got something to do with Maebh."

Indigo folded his arms. "Why are you telling me?"

"Because I need you to find the next Well-blessed human before the Void or Maebh."

"Me?"

"No one will track and covet her as you will. It has to be you."

His stomach flipped. "Are you saying she's my mate?"

"All I know is that she's already awake in this time. I thought I was the first, but I was wrong. So wrong. There are more, and like the Void, they woke before me. For all we know, she's living in Elphyne, disguised as a fae. She could be anyone."

"How are we supposed to find her?"

She cocked her head. "You've tasted one of us."

She shocked him to silence. Clarke knew exactly what the blood did to Indigo, yet she trusted him to find this human.

"What makes her so important?"

"She was a weapon's maker."

"Like a blacksmith?"

"Much worse. A nuclear physicist."

"I don't understand."

"She knows how to build the bombs that destroyed the old world, and she's out there somewhere. Alone. Hidden. And both Maebh and the Void are already hunting her."

CHAPTER
THIRTY-TWO

A week had passed since Jasper killed Mithras. Or rather, since he'd let the Well Worms take him. He'd spent half the time cloistered in his room with his new mate, ensuring his claim was well and truly staked. The other half, he'd spent at the Summer Palace, talking to the castle staff and soldiers.

Everyone knew about the death of the King. The Prime had made sure of it. They knew it was he who'd taken down Mithras with his own hands, no assistance. Now everyone expected his answer.

He was almost ready to give it but had to do one last thing.

He took Ada's hand and, together, they walked into his mother's old cottage. They went straight toward the soggy beat-up rug in the living room. Jasper bent down and flipped the corner to reveal the loose board. He levered it up, and the one next to it.

Below was a tiny dugout.

"It's so small," he murmured.

"You were only a child, Jasper."

With all that responsibility resting on his little shoulders, he'd felt so much older. A dig around his pocket and he found the heart-shaped amber pendant. He placed it in the dirt and then boarded up the hole. He put his hand on top and closed his eyes.

His mother would be proud of him, of Ada, and of their new family.

"Are you sure you don't want to keep it?" Ada asked.

He shook his head, frowning. "Every time I look at it, I remembered the wrong things. I need to move on, to look to the future."

Touching his fingers to his lips, he then pressed them down on the boards. This all started with his mother. She'd died in this very spot. And he'd finally avenged her.

When he straightened, Ada handed him the glass crown. "Who will you be?"

He turned the crown over in his hands, watching the light twinkle off its shape. Reflections danced about the room.

Clarke had told them about her new visions. Mithras's death had set something loose in the Queen. Darkness crowded everything Clarke foresaw. There were dark times ahead. The Seelie people needed a strong king. They needed someone to make things fun. They needed someone brave.

"I'll be whatever the people need me to be, whatever my family needs me to be."

"But what name will you take?"

He thought about it. Mithras was never in the cards. But he couldn't go back to Reed. He could, however, be both. He could honor his mother and the place he'd spent most of his life. He could honor them.

"Jasper Darkfoot."

Slow clapping came from the darkness. Jasper strained his senses, trying to sniff out the interloper. But what he found made no sense.

"Clara?"

She emerged from the dark hallway, hobbling on a cane. Behind her, more bodies emerged. One of them, the youth Ada had healed. Lake.

Ada ran to Clara and took her in a hug. Then grabbed the boy. "We thought you were all dead."

Clara's eyes watered. "Some of us escaped. But we had to lie low until we were sure. The Prime had learned of our part with the hoarding." Her glimmering gaze shifted to Jasper. "But now a Darkfoot is taking the crown, we're hoping you'll grant us one more favor."

"Clara," he admonished. "I would never let the Order punish you. Mithras manipulated all of you."

Clara's shoulders dropped with relief. "You don't know how it feels to hear that." She wiped her eyes. "It will feel even better when the official announcement is out."

She gave the crown in his hand a pointed look.

As king, Jasper couldn't be a Guardian anymore—technically—and that was harder than he realized to give up. But the teardrop tattoo couldn't be removed. It couldn't even be glamoured away. It was permanent. He hadn't finished facing the Well Worms for the second time, but he didn't need to. He was already everything his mother had hoped. It had just taken a few hundred years to get here. The good, the bad, and the painful—it had all shaped the fae he was today. It was time to stop living up to old dreams and time to make new ones.

He stared at Clara. He stared at Ada. And then he put on the crown.

The End.

(Of the first Fae Guardians Trilogy, Season of the Wolf. Our warm blooded vampires are coming up next in the Season of the Vampire! Click here to read Indigo's story or read on for an excerpt.

EPILOGUE

Pain was his world. Never ending agony filled him from head to toe, bone to blood, flesh to mind. He peeled open his swollen eyes. Dried blood cracked in his lashes. He shook his arms, testing the rope manacles, but he was still securely tied above his head to a wall in the Obsidian Castle dungeon.

What they'd done to him.

What those *things* had done.

Filthy, vile, unnatural *things*.

"Ahh, and so he wakes."

Bones lifted his head.

She was there. The worst one of them all. The Unseelie Queen. Dressed in a revealing dress, a crow sat on her shoulder. She was depraved, wicked, and full of deranged wishes. Next to her was the vile, sickeningly pretty, ghostly creature that had violated Bones's mind. It had raped him metaphysically.

They were all the demons the Void wanted to end.

Bones laughed to himself.

The Void wanted to end them all. They all deserved to die. If they could just find a way to kill the Sluagh, the humans could take back what was rightfully theirs. All of it.

The Queen stepped up to him and placed a long, black nail under his chin. "Oh, my dear human."

"Why haven't you sent me back to the Order?" At least those feral animals were easier to stomach.

"They think you're dead," she laughed. "Whoops."

His stomach dropped. "Why am I still alive?"

"Because when my darling Sluagh ravaged your mind, we found something. A special weapon you humans are building." Her plum lips stretched into a devious smile. "And you're going to tell me all about it, and more importantly, how to make it myself."

NEED TO TALK TO OTHER READERS?

BOOKS ARE OUR LIFE!

Join Lana's Angels Facebook Group for fun chats, giveaways, and exclusive content. https://www.facebook.com/groups/lanasangels

ABOUT THE AUTHOR

OMG! How do you say my name?

Lana (straight forward enough - Lah-nah) **Pecherczyk** (this is where it gets tricky - Pe-her-chick).

I've been called Lana Price-Check, Lana Pera-Chick-ywack, Lana Pressed-Chicken, Lana Pech...*that girl!* You name it, they said it. So if it's so hard to spell, why on earth would I use this name instead of an easy pen name?

To put it simply, it belonged to my mother. And she was my dream champion.

For most of my life, I've been good at one thing – art. The world around me saw my work, and said I should do more of it, so I did.

But, when at the age of eight, I said I wanted to write stories, and even though we were poor, my mother came home with a blank notebook and a pencil saying I should follow my dreams, no matter where they take me for they will make me happy. I wasn't very good at it, but it didn't matter because I had her support and I liked it.

She died when I was thirteen, and left her four daughters orphaned. Suddenly, I had lost my dream champion, I was split from my youngest two sisters and had no one to talk to about the challenge of life.

So, I wrote in secret. I poured my heart out daily to a diary and sometimes imagined that she would listen. At the end of the day, even if she couldn't hear, writing kept that dream alive.

Eventually, after having my own children (two firecrackers in the guise of little boys) and ignoring my inner voice for too long, I decided to lead by example. How could I teach my children to follow their dreams if I wasn't? I became my own dream champion and the rest is history, here I am.

When I'm not writing the next great action-packed romantic novel, or wrangling the rug rats, or rescuing GI

Joe from the jaws of my Kelpie, I fight evil by moonlight, win love by daylight and never run from a real fight.

I live in Australia, but I'm up for a chat anytime online. Come and find me.

Subscribe & Follow
subscribe.lanapecherczyk.com
lp@lanapecherczyk.com

- facebook.com/lanapecherczykauthor
- instagram.com/lana_p_author
- amazon.com/-/e/B00V2TP0HG
- bookbub.com/profile/lana-pecherczyk
- tiktok.com/@lanapauthor
- goodreads.com/lana_p_author

Also by Lana Pecherczyk

The Deadly Seven

(Paranormal/Sci-Fi Romance)

The Deadly Seven Box Set Books 1-3

Sinner

Envy

Greed

Wrath

Sloth

Gluttony

Lust

Pride

Despair

Fae Guardians

(Fantasy/Paranormal Romance)

Season of the Wolf Trilogy

The Longing of Lone Wolves

The Solace of Sharp Claws

Of Kisses & Wishes Novella (free for subscribers)

The Dreams of Broken Kings

Season of the Vampire Trilogy

The Secrets in Shadow and Blood

A Labyrinth of Fangs and Thorns

A Symphony of Savage Hearts

Season of the Elf Trilogy

A Song of Sky and Sacrifice

A Crown of Cruel Lies

Game of Gods

(Romantic Urban Fantasy)

Soul Thing

The Devil Inside

Playing God

Game Over

Game of Gods Box Set

Made in the USA
Coppell, TX
08 February 2025